A Perfect Escape

MADDIE JAMES

Turquoise Morning, LLC
P.O. Box 43958
Louisville, KY 40253-0958

A PERFECT ESCAPE
Copyright © 2013 Maddie James
Digital ISBN: 978-1-62237-211-9
Trade Paperback ISBN: 978-1-62237-252-2

Cover Art Design by Calliope-Designs.com
Copyediting by Turquoise Morning Press

Previously Published, Resplendence Publishing, 2008
Revised/Updated Digital Edition, Turquoise Morning Press: October 2013

Revised Trade Paperback Release, January 2014

For every women who dares to escape.

A Perfect Escape

Megan Thomas is running for her life. From Chicago, from the mob, from her controlling husband. She runs to the only place she ever felt at peace, a North Carolina barrier island she remembers from her childhood. Now she only wants to get lost—lost in someone else's life. A new identity, soothing ocean winds, and a quiet existence are all she needs.

Smyth Parker is running from life. From the business he inherited, from society, from an ex-wife scorned. His only escape is the solitude of uninhabited Portsmouth Island. He doesn't want anything else. And he sure as hell doesn't need a complication named Megan Thomas.

When Megan fears she's been found, she runs again—and straight into Smyth's arms. His isolated island home might finally be her perfect escape. Or is it?

Prologue

The hot-shot assistant district attorney lay face down on the cold slab of concrete. His hands tied tightly behind him caused his shoulders to bow into an unnatural backward arch, even though his body fell slack with fatigue. Bruised and battered, he lay surprisingly conscious, his starched white shirt now limp and soaked with blood. His blood. Thick bubbles of scarlet gurgled from his nose with each labored breath he took. He looked somewhat like a dying fish gasping for air.

What a horrible way to die.

But he hung on a lot longer than she'd expected. Especially for all he'd been through the past hour.

The horror of it all seized her and wouldn't let go. If it weren't for the fact that her own hands were pulled into a vise grip behind her, forcing her into an upright position, she would have bent at the waist and retched all over the floor. The stench of imminent death forced bile into her throat. The shock alone of what was happening—directly in front of her—should have rendered her immobile. She never dreamed Bradford would carry things this far, that he was capable of creating terror of this magnitude.

Without warning, a silver flash arced through the charged atmosphere. She instantly felt, as well as heard, the resounding echo of a single gunshot and simultaneous rip of the bullet. The force sent blood, matter, and tissue flying, spattering her face, clothing.

She was that close. Too close.

An ungodly scream, like the shriek of a wounded animal, rent the air and she realized it came from her own throat. Immediate terror so powerful it nearly rocked her off her feet gripped her and the nausea took over. Her legs went limp and she did what she didn't want to do, vomit down the front of her shirt. Teetering on the edge of consciousness, her head hung, the hands holding her from behind the only thing keeping her from falling onto the floor.

Her own pain brought her quickly back to her senses as someone snatched and yanked a handful of hair at the back of her head, forcing her to look straight ahead.

Into his face. His eyes.

What now?

His evil stare bit back with a sadistic power she never knew he possessed. How often she had seen those eyes look at her so differently. In adoration. In excitement.

In lust.

His power over her, over most women, was his charm. His charismatic demeanor, his enigmatic ability to turn a woman into putty within thirty seconds, their downfall. And she fell into that trap. Probably more deeply than most.

But she'd never seen the veil of evil cast over those eyes before.

Not like this. Not until now.

She'd known his reputation as a shady dealer, not above an illegal act—an egotistical, self-centered, domineering, power-hungry sonofabitch.

But she never expected he was a murderer.

He jerked her hair again, physically moving closer. He brought the pistol up to her chin, the cold, hard snub jabbing into her tender flesh. So vile, so despicable. She found it difficult to keep her gaze pinned to his face, into his eyes. But she needed to. She prayed if she kept the connection he might remember something, anything, that would endear her to him and he wouldn't kill her.

"You see that!" he shouted. "Did you see how I fucking killed that bastard?"

She responded with a quick jerk of her head. He yanked her closer.

"If you ever, ever," he began slowly, his voice menacingly lower, "think about betraying me, you stupid blonde bitch," he thrust his face closer and she could smell his tobacco-stale breath, "I won't hesitate to put a bullet in you. Only I won't be so kind as to put the bullet in your brain. My friend Smith and Wesson here would enjoy having its way with you. I guarantee being ripped apart from the inside out isn't a pretty way to die."

He released her with a forceful push and stepped backward. For the first time in hours she was glad his goons held her upright. "No one fucks with me and lives. You understand?"

She nodded in quick jerks, probably more out of reflex rather than a conscious effort.

An uncanny shiver of relief melted over her. For whatever reason, he needed her around a little longer. She wasn't entirely sure, however, if that was a good thing or bad.

Chapter One

"Just a little bit longer."

Megan Thomas whispered the words, trying to calm herself as she peered through the filmy sheers hanging at the floor-to-ceiling casement window in her living room. She drew in a ragged breath, trying like hell to settle her jittery nerves. The black, late-model sedan sat parked far at the end of their winding drive, to the left of the street lamp's glow. She stood slightly behind the Chippendale chair she'd bought after she and Bradford had married and in front of the exquisitely framed copy of the Picasso they'd found in Spain during their honeymoon.

Once upon a time, all the polish and sophistication of the material possessions in her life meant the world to her.

Funny how little they mattered to her now.

She gripped the top of the upholstered chair back until her fingers hurt.

Relax. Breathe.

Impossible. She couldn't. She dared not allow herself to relax. Not for one second. She'd planned this day for too long. Entirely too long. If she could only make it through the next few minutes, hours, days, she'd have her life back.

Finally have her life back.

Glancing down at her clothing, she knew she looked nothing like herself. So far so good.

She didn't want any semblance of Megan Thomas to follow her out of this house. When she left the front door in a few minutes, she would leave Megan Thomas behind and become Meg again.

Just plain old Meg. Too long in coming. Her main fear now was that Cindy, the girl from the mall, wouldn't keep her word.

She ought to. Megan had given the girl a thousand dollars cash up front and promised her five thousand more if she showed up at eight o'clock this evening. Not to mention the trade they'd made that afternoon—her Jag for the girl's late model Honda. Sure it seemed like a lot of money, but she had a lot of money and she was buying her freedom.

It was no easy feat to accomplish all she had the past two days. Of course she couldn't have done it without Rudy. And Rudy's recent urgings for her to act now, while Bradford was out of town, fit perfectly into the plan. The only hitch being that Cindy didn't get the car until she showed up tonight. And she didn't get the five thousand dollars until she stayed for three whole days and nights in this house. Then she would meet Rudy at the mall for the payoff and the papers to the Jag. Rudy, bless her soul, Meg's only real friend in the world. If it hadn't been for her, she never would have had the courage to escape. And her limited window of opportunity dictated that it all had to come together within the next few minutes. It had to be now, her only chance.

Bradford planned to make his bid into the political arena when he returned from London.

She had to get out now before he charmed his way into the hearts of his constituents with her on his arm. If she didn't leave now, he'd never let her go. He wouldn't stand for a divorce, let alone a scandal.

She couldn't live with him any longer. In fact, she suspected that if she lived with him much longer, he'd surely kill her.

This was her only chance.

She had to admit she felt a little guilty involving the girl, but if Cindy followed her instructions to the letter, she'd be gone before Bradford arrived back home. She'd be fine and much richer. Megan knew if she could lie low until the divorce became final, Bradford couldn't use his conniving manner to persuade her to stay married to him. She was losing herself.

Her soul. Her life.

An engine roared outside her window, jarring her

thoughts. With shaking fingers, Megan inched back the sheers and peered through. The black Honda pulled in the circular drive and skidded to a stop in front of her house. Megan exhaled a long sigh of relief. Cindy, wearing the long black wig Megan bought yesterday afternoon, left the car idling and carried a pizza box to the front door.

The doorbell chimed. Megan took a quick breath, waited for a second, exhaled slowly to calm the jitters in her tummy and then crossed the living room. She opened the door and looked at the girl who was giving her back her life.

"Pizza delivery," Cindy said, winking and then smiling broadly, briskly chewing her gum.

"Oh, yes," Megan replied, trying not to show her nervousness.

"Come on in. I'll get my purse."

The girl stepped in and Megan closed the door. Turning quickly to the girl, she took the pizza out of her hand and laid it on the cherry sideboard. "Hurry," she whispered, "we haven't much time."

Megan pulled off her sweater while Cindy removed the wig and baseball cap. Flinging her blond ponytail aside, the girl took off her own sweatshirt, careful not to remove the T-shirt she wore underneath. They exchanged shirts, each donning the other's over their blue jeans.

Finally, Megan adjusted the shirt around her and then smoothed her hands over her abdomen, rechecking the large envelope taped across her belly. "Did you put the clothes and other things in the trunk?" Megan asked softly.

"Picked them all up at the department store this afternoon. Just like you told me."

Megan nodded. "Good. Let me have your tennis shoes."

Cindy's eyes widened. "My Nike's?"

Megan nodded. "You can buy another pair. And take any of mine you want upstairs." She looked Cindy dead in the eye, astounded as to the likeness they shared even with Cindy being years younger. Megan watched her for weeks, the perfect choice for this little masquerade. From a distance they could pass as twins, the only thing that mattered. "In fact, anything you want as far as clothing you can have. All of it, if you want. Just don't carry them out in boxes. And make sure you do wear my clothes if you go out." She finished tying Cindy's shoes. "But stay in the house as much as possible. Give me the wig."

"Here." Cindy helped to position Megan's blond ponytail under the black fall, then handed her the *Larry's Pizza* cap she wore.

Megan smashed it down over the wig.

"I've left a list of things to do and not to do over there on the hall table by the pizza. Read it and then get rid of the list. The keys are in the Jag in the garage. Don't go out tonight. I mean it. And if you need anything, call Rudy. Rudy only, do you understand? Her number is right there." She pointed to the sideboard. "But only if it is an emergency and be vague. Act like you're me. Your family, your friends, none of them are to ever know about this, understand? It's crucial that you follow my instructions to the letter. Rudy will check on you tomorrow and take care of details about the vehicles. You did bring the title, didn't you?"

Cindy smiled back. "In the glove box. I can't wait to take that Jag out."

"Well, just give it a rest until tomorrow," Megan added impatiently. "And don't use the phones to call anyone you know." She wanted to tell her they were tapped, but thought better of it.

Cindy nodded eagerly. "That's cool. You and your husband playing some kind of kinky game or something?"

Megan looked at her. She'd told Cindy yesterday that part of the deal was that she ask no questions. "Or something." She took one more lingering glance around the beautifully appointed living room and smiled nervously.

Or something.

"Okay, you're on your own. Remember, I'm trusting you." She stared into the girl's eyes momentarily and then laid her hand on the front doorknob. "And Rudy's got the money."

She saw the greed in Cindy's eyes. "Sure."

"Oh." Turning back, Megan reached into the pocket of her blue jeans and pulled out several one dollar bills. Then looking at Cindy, she said, "Do you have any more gum?"

Cindy nodded and reached deep into her front blue jeans pocket. She pulled out a mangled piece of gum. "Here. Last one."

Megan slipped the paper off and popped it in her mouth, then opened the front door. She heard it slam behind her. In her mind, she was shutting out the past. Shutting out the pain.

Skipping down the steps while shifting the bills in her hands as if counting her change and tip, she bounced into the Honda and cracked her gum. Gunning the engine, she shifted into first and peeled down her driveway for what she hoped was the last time.

When she reached the street, her eyes slowly darted right then left. Her gaze lingered only a second on the black sedan and the two silhouettes inside. Then screeching out between the rows of manicured lawns and stately homes, she held her breath. She checked the rearview mirror every block or so for any movement from the sedan, then Megan finally let her shoulders relax. No movement.

Rolling down the window beside her, she simultaneously spat out the gum and cranked up the rock and roll station on the radio as loud as it would go and breathed deeply.

After a few minutes, her hands stopped shaking. She rechecked the package under her shirt. Still intact. She allowed herself to smile.

Her plan worked. So far, so good.

Feeling a sudden surge of freedom, Meg giddily cruised through the prestigious subdivision and out into the heavier traffic of the business district. Opening the door to her new life, slamming it on the old one.

Several miles out of Chicago, she let the black wig

blow out her open window and tumble over the interstate.
She'd done it.
Perfect.

Chapter Two

The cottage sat facing the ocean, nestled in the swale of a dune. It was a Nags Header, built in the early 1930's, sporting sloping rooflines and sweeping porches. One step inside its walls and Meg felt thrust backward in time to an era of balmy breezes, deserted beaches and hot summer days when the screen door slapped hard behind you. The plank floors, ceilings, and walls lent a feeling of old-fashioned charm, along with the push-button light switches and the thick coats of peeling paint on the shutters.

Meg took a deep breath and then exhaled.

She'd made it.

A heated breeze lifted the hair from her shoulders and swirled it about her face. It kissed her cheeks with its salty mist and caressed her body with its warmth. She felt alive. More alive than she'd felt in years.

And safe.

When she'd arrived, she'd run like a child between the dunes for her first glimpse of the magnificent ocean until she'd stopped still and drank in the essence of it all—drank it all in with her eyes, her lungs, and every pore of her being.

She was home.

At last.

Actually, it just felt like home. Her new home. She'd only been here once, at age five years, when her parents were still experimenting with family vacations as a way of saving their marriage. But they soon realized that the Atlantic Ocean and Nags Head didn't solve their problems. They'd divorced not long after. Meg remembered how relaxed and at peace she had felt, even at that tender age, when she could tune out her parents arguing and lose herself in the sand and surf. It was a pleasant memory she'd long harbored.

Even then she'd known escape.

Perhaps it was practice for dealing with Bradford for all those years. Perhaps that's why she was such a master of it now. At least, that's what she hoped.

Closing her eyes, Meg breathed deeply, drawing the ocean air into her lungs. The sea lived in her soul now, the beach hers. All hers and hers alone. Everything in her life was now hers alone. She felt stingy, selfish, but she'd given up so much in her life the past six years. She didn't intend to give up any more.

She didn't care. She'd live her life as she saw fit.

Aloof. Eccentric.

Indifferent.

Any way she wanted. She'd sleep when and if she wanted. Eat when she wanted. Clean her house if she wanted and if she didn't, she wouldn't. If she felt like eating a whole damn chocolate cake, she would. And if she felt like starving herself to lose five pounds she'd do that, too.

She had regained control of her life. *Her* life. Not Bradford's. Hers. If it took until she turned old and blue-haired to prove that point to herself, she would do it. But she didn't think it would take that long. The healing had already begun.

Time.

That was all she needed. Time to heal. And the ocean breezes blowing through her hair.

Turning, Meg smiled at the cottage she'd rented. Though smaller than most of its kind in Nags Head, it suited her perfectly with its two bedrooms, one bath, and kitchen-great room combo. The odd little house sported huge windows gracing the front, a porch that swept the entire width and around one side, and only one door, as if an afterthought. But that was okay, it meant she only had one door to worry about locking each night.

And she called it home, at least temporarily until the rental agency could find her something more permanent and less expensive—probably not beachfront, though. So she intended to enjoy this one for as long as she could. The out-of-town owner didn't usually rent during the early spring, but had consented to let her rent for two months until something else could be found in her price range.

The money she had wouldn't last indefinitely. At some point she'd need to find a job.

But until then, this was home.

Of course, all that was accomplished on the road after she'd left Chicago, stopping at a phone booth in Elizabeth City to make some calls. Cell phone records could be easily traced and the bill always went to Bradford. A rare pay phone was safer. She didn't want to use her credit cards, either, for a pre-paid phone. Cash was the only way she could go.

But that was all said and done. Seven days passed without a sign of Bradford. No indication that anything had gone awry.

No black sedan sat outside her front door.

How good it felt to be rid of the black sedan. Bradford called them her *bodyguards,* but she knew better. They weren't there to protect her. They kept tabs on her comings and goings to make sure she didn't leave. They started following her when she first mentioned to Bradford that she wanted a divorce. His violent reaction told her how difficult it would be to break away. But she had to do it, no matter how long it took or to what depths she had to go. And Rudy, bless her soul, was the only person trusted to get her out of this mess.

Everything seemed all right, now, but that didn't mean she could let down her guard. Not for a long time.

Seven days. One week. Meg let her mind drift for a moment as she turned back toward the ocean to rest her gaze on the rolling horizon. Cindy should have left by now and Bradford should be home from London. No doubt he'd been served the divorce papers. No doubt he'd turned Chicago upside down searching for her. A slow chill traveled up her spine and settled at the base of her skull forcing a shiver. She shuddered to think what he'd do if he ever found her.

But no way could he trace her to here. She'd seen to every detail. Had planned it for too long, all in her mind, the only place Bradford couldn't reach. No one knew where she had gone, not even Rudy. She'd hated lying, even to her best friend, but it was necessary. No way in hell she'd risk being found.

****

Meg reached for the conditioner between the spray of the shower, the hot, stinging droplets tenderly massaging her aching muscles. Late that morning she'd walked up the beach to the pier, had lunch, and then fished in the afternoon. After casting and reeling in the fishing line from the pier for three hours, her arms finally gave out and she headed for home. And now, as she slathered the conditioner into her hair, the shower felt heavenly.

She smiled to herself. Never had she felt so content, so relaxed. With hardly a soul around, each day passed in peaceful bliss. Nothing interrupted her day except the ocean roar, crashing waves, and screech of the sea gulls. The Outer Banks in April felt wonderful, the last week heavenly.

And thankfully, she'd had no contact with anyone west of the North Carolina coastline since she'd arrived.

Her hands slid down over her hair to her shoulders and then fell to her sides. She glanced lower, then brought her right hand up to her thigh. Her bruises were almost gone now. The last ones she'd ever have. They looked like a yellow-green mass high on her inner thigh. As her hand trailed upward to her hip and abdomen she flinched, still a little tender. The bruises there were the same. Yes, she was healing.

Inside and out.

Meg stood for a moment longer in the shower, her head tossed back to catch the cascade of water raining down her hair and back until the hot stinging droplets turned into cool pellets against her skin. Sighing, she twisted the knobs of the shower to the off position, sluiced the water from her face and hair, and stepped out of the shower.

Reaching for the towel on the wooden seat next to the shower stall, she paused for a moment thinking she heard...something? After waiting a moment and hearing nothing more, she shook her head and picked up the towel. She sopped up some of the water from her hair, and then tucked the towel around her body.

"You're just paranoid, Meg," she told herself, smiling.

The bathroom door stood ajar, so she pulled it fully open and stepped into the hallway between the bedrooms. Glancing toward the row of windows twenty feet or so in front of her, savoring the panoramic view of the ocean and beach, Meg caught herself again mesmerized. She smiled and sighed. What a wondrous sight! She knew she couldn't stand there wrapped in a towel for long. Someone would eventually saunter by and glance up at the cottage. But for the moment, the late afternoon sun glinting off the ocean waves held her spellbound.

Then she heard the jiggle of the lock. The door cracked open.

A hard jolt of fear raced through her body, setting her panic at full tilt. *Oh, my God! Bradford?*

Before she could react, a man strode across the floor in front of her, dropped a duffel bag to the carpet, stopped, and turned to stare at her. For a fleeting moment, all she saw were broad shoulders, too-long dark brown hair, and chocolate eyes that widened at the sight of her.

Meg bolted toward the bedroom.

"Hey!" The man's shout followed her.

Just before she slammed the bedroom door shut, he thrust his foot between the door and the jamb, stopping it. She flung her body against it and screamed.

"Sonofabitch!"

Meg hurled herself backward toward the bed. The towel drooped in front. Her arms clamped tight against her sides to keep it in place.

Over six feet of deeply tanned male burst through the door, anger quite apparent on his face, fists clenched into tight balls at his sides.

Meg swallowed hard and scrambled up to the headboard of the bed, tucking the towel around her in all the right places as she tried to flee. Her pulse pounded inside her head, echoing the surf outside her window.

"Who in the hell are you?"

Meg blinked. If Bradford sent this man to find her, then he wouldn't ask her who she was, would he? Relief slowly washed over her. "I might ask you the same question," she squeaked.

His face registered surprise, but he continued to stare. A second later he shook his head and briefly closed his eyes. "Look, I'm tired and I'm not in the mood for a lot of questions. Just tell me who you are and why you're taking a shower in my house."

His house?

This man had not been sent by Bradford, but Meg realized the entire scenario presented quite a different problem.

The owner.

Meg sat up on her knees. "Your house?"

He nodded. "Last time I checked."

"But I've rented it until the end of May."

He glared at her. Meg thought he could probably look a hole right through her. "You what?"

Swallowing, Meg found the courage to state the facts. "I rented this house until the end of May. I've paid in advance. Becky, um, I mean the rental agent, is supposed to find me something else by then. I was told you wouldn't be back until the summer. I'm sure there's some mistake."

He backed toward the door while running his fingers through his hair, then turned back to her. "Becky, huh?"

Meg nodded.

He rubbed his chin. His gaze stayed glued to her while she gathered the towel around her body. Meg rose slightly off the bed.

"I need you out by morning," he stated boldly.

No! She couldn't leave here yet. She loved this little

cottage. It wasn't the best on the beach or the biggest, but...
She gasped and scrambled off the bed. "But I've already
paid. And I..." She found herself only inches from his face,
then uncomfortable, backed up two steps.

He just kept staring, then turned and left.

"Get dressed," he shouted from the hallway. "We've
got some talking to do and I find it extremely difficult to do
it with a woman wearing only a towel."

He walked away, leaving Meg alone in her room.

Damn it all to hell! Smyth Parker headed across the great
room to stare out the window over the beach, trying to
keep his temper in check. Not even the crashing of the
waves into the sand calmed him as they normally would. He
shouldn't have yelled at her, but it's not every day a man
comes home to find a beautiful sea nymph stepping out of
his shower. He didn't need this!

All he wanted was to come home, relax for a week or
two, take care of business, and head back to Portsmouth.
He sure as hell didn't need complications.

Especially attractive complications that came wrapped
in beach towels.

His eyes closed as he listened to the sounds around
him. He massaged his temples.

Migraine. He felt it coming on. With him they were as
predictable as clockwork when he became stressed. And
stressed didn't begin to describe it. He rested his forehead
against the window.

Even through the glass he could feel the ocean's power
and the vibrations of the surf. He longed to be back where
he felt at home with his environment, with himself and
nature. Relaxed. Even the solitude of Nags Head in the off-
season was too much for him.

Just as he opened his eyes, he heard the soft shuffle of
her footsteps behind him. He turned and her wide, green
eyes met him, searching his face. Thankfully, she had
dressed in an oversized beach cover-up and shorts. She
combed her long blonde hair straight back, trailing down to

her shoulders with a few wisps falling over her forehead. And he could tell she'd spent quite a few days in the sun recently. Her skin glowed with an even brown tan tinged with red sunburn. Small brown freckles sprinkled her nose.

Smyth motioned for her to sit and then forced himself to look away. He instinctively knew that when she sat she would cross her legs. And she did. It took a concentrated effort to tear his gaze away from them. Long, thin and brown, smooth and dewy from her shower, nicely rounded calves, bare feet, toenails painted a blaze red.

Damn.

Looking away, he paced back and forth in front of the window, trying to avoid any eye contact with her body. That only lasted for about ten seconds. Then he stopped and let his gaze rest on her as he stood opposite.

Business. Get down to business.

"There's been a mistake."

An understatement. He'd known the minute she'd mentioned Becky's name what had happened. His kid sister had done it again.

She nodded at him and scooted toward the edge of the couch. "I've been thinking. I think I know how—"

"I know what happened," he interrupted. Finally, he let himself sit on the couch angled perpendicular to the one on which she sat. "I'll bet I can spin out the whole story without a hitch. You correct me if I'm wrong." Her eyes dipped in acknowledgment. "You needed a place to stay but for whatever reason there was no place available. You begged and the rental agency said they'd do what they could. Finally, they came up with this cottage. Right?"

She nodded again.

"And the rental agent you worked with…this Becky. Was that her name?"

"Yes."

"Yeah, that's what I thought. She's my sister." He stood. "There was nothing available so my kid sister rented you my house."

She nodded. "Temporarily. Most of the other rentals

are so expensive for long term. But I didn't know she was your sister," she added quickly.

He studied her, watching her eyes. Sea green. They studied him back, clearer now than before. Earlier they were filled with alarm. But why wouldn't they be? He'd scared the hell out of her.

"But it's not that she didn't have anything available. I was being very picky."

"Oh?"

"I wanted beachfront, Nags Head, as close to Jockey's Ridge as I could get. And I was willing to pay for it, even on a temporary basis. And she found it for me."

Smyth perused her for another long moment. "Why so particular?"

He watched her gaze tear away. She stared out the window behind him. A pensive, faraway look came over her. He suddenly felt like an intruder of a different sort.

Finally, she slowly looked back to him.

"It's personal."

Damn.

Not only a beautiful but a woman with problems. Women and baggage, not a good combination. Hell, men and baggage aren't a good combination either.

And he was sure enough carrying around his fair share.

Her gaze pinned him to the couch, her puppy dog eyes widening. His pulse pounded in his temples. Oddly, he felt sorry for her. Why, he wasn't sure, but he felt like he wanted to comfort her.

Neither moved until he spoke.

"So how long are you supposed to be here?"

"About six weeks or so."

"And you've paid in advance."

She nodded, her gaze still connected with his.

Smyth laid his head in his hands, his elbows propped on his knees. He massaged his temples. How in the hell could he throw her out? He ought to take it out of Becky's hide. She knew how he needed to come home occasionally. How could she have invaded his privacy?

When he needed his place, he needed his place. He'd be sure to let Becky know about it the first thing in the morning.

Lifting his head, he watched her again. Sinking further into the couch, she rested against the back, her legs still crossed, one foot hooked behind the calf of the other.

"You can stay," he said abruptly as he rose, "but so am I. Only until Becky finds you something else. And only because I'm too tired to fight about it at the moment." He started across the room and headed for the bathroom. Stopping, he glanced back. "And I'll refund your money, of course. But right now I need a shower, a handful of aspirin, and a good night's sleep. I'd appreciate it if you would be as quiet as possible." He moved toward the bathroom.

He heard her rise behind him, but ignored her. Right now he couldn't think about it, about her. Right now all he wanted to do was fade into oblivion.

****

Meg woke early the next morning before the sun crested the horizon. She'd not heard a sound from the other bedroom. Sleep eluded her for most of the night for reasons she really didn't want to admit. So she'd decided to rise, make a pot of coffee, and take in the morning sunrise from the porch. Perhaps he would also want coffee, particularly if he was fighting a headache.

Dressing quickly in cut-off denim shorts and a T-shirt, Meg brushed her hair back into a ponytail. Since she'd been at the beach, she'd thrown out her makeup, her curling iron and hair spray, as well as her designer clothes. She dressed simply and found she preferred it. Gone was Bradford's china doll.

Tiptoeing through the house, she turned on only the light above the sink in the kitchen so as not to wake him. *Him.* Did he have a name? He certainly hadn't offered one to her yesterday.

But then again, she hadn't offered hers, either. Meg pulled the coffee maker closer and reached into the cabinet for the filter packs. After assembling everything and flipping on the switch, she turned away from the counter and waited, listening to the soothing hiss and gurgles.

Glancing out the windows facing the beach, she saw the crescent of pink just ready to peek above the ocean. Crossing the room, she stepped through the door and out onto the porch.

Rounding the corner to face the ocean, she saw him.

For a brief moment the sight of him in the early morning light took her aback.

He sat at the far corner of the deck, his feet propped on the railing with his eyes glued to nature's morning spectacular. His hands relaxed across his abdomen. Meg stopped abruptly. He turned his gaze slowly to her. For a moment, they simply stared at each other.

Belatedly, Meg found her tongue. "I didn't realize you were out here."

He looked at her for a moment longer. Meg waited for him to speak. Finally, she saw his chest heave as he breathed deeply and exhaled. Then he turned back to face the ocean. "Nothing quite like an ocean sunrise, is there?"

Meg swallowed, then took a few steps forward and leaned against the railing. "No, there isn't." She turned her gaze toward the array of pinks and oranges and grays mingling over the distant horizon. For several moments she simply watched as the sun brought hues and shades of color into the world that one wouldn't know existed had they not witnessed this particular sunrise. The calmness of the morning enveloped her, only the lapping of the waves disturbed the quiet. The bright orb finally lifted itself fully into the sky and the show ended.

Meg sighed. She turned back to him, startled to find him watching her rather than the sunrise. For how long, she didn't know. When their eyes met, she felt an instant longing. A jolt.

Her breath caught in her throat.

How long had he been staring at her?

She broke the connection and quickly turned away, stepping several feet from the railing.

"There's coffee in the kitchen if you want," she offered and turned back into the house.

"Wait."

Meg stopped, not fully turning back to him.

"Would you turn around, please?"

Puzzled, Meg did, looking him fully in the face. He stared at her again. Meg felt a bit uncomfortable. "Do you have a name?" he finally asked.

"Yes," Meg returned after a moment. "Do you?"

He chuckled, then deep laugh lines chiseled their way into his cheeks. Meg was certain she saw a dimple there, but in the pale light she couldn't be sure.

"I'm Smyth Parker."

"Meg...Thompson," she replied, hesitating over the last name.

Smyth rose and stepped across the deck toward her. "Well, Meg Thompson, how about some coffee?"

She nodded and entered the house ahead of him.

Chapter Three

Slim, youthful fingers hesitantly reached out to touch the fine silk of the blouse hanging in the closet. The rough pads of her fingers glided down the soft fabric of the arm until they reached the cuff. As Cindy stood naked inside the huge walk-in closet, she marveled at the clothing, glancing in awe around her. Never in her life had she seen such fine clothing, unless of course, it was at *Lacey's*, that exclusive little shop down on Michigan Avenue where she only dared to look in the window. Never in her life had she dreamed she would be able to buy such things.

But now. Now this was all hers. *Hers!* The silk blouses and slacks. The sequined evening gowns. The tailored woolen blazers and skirts—although they really weren't her style, but she could get used to them—and the lingerie, especially the lacy, sexy stuff. She'd been thinking about changing her style anyway.

She could get used to this. And with the cash, she'd be able to buy lots more. But eventually the money would run out. It would be damned hard getting used to discount stores again. Unless....

A smile lifted one corner of her mouth. She jerked the blouse off the hanger, plunged one arm at a time into the length of the sleeves and relished the feel of the silk against her breasts.

Brusquely, he stepped up behind her, his naked torso rubbing up against hers familiarly, pulling her roughly into him. One hand palmed her breast through the silk, massaging her nipples into firm peaks, the other reached lower, grasping between her legs. She arched her head back against his chest and groaned. His mouth bore down on her shoulder, biting, licking. She gasped as she felt his masculinity throb against her, she shrieked as he bent her forward with a growl and thrust into her, filling her with a type of hot excitement she'd never known before.

Arousing her to a level she'd never dreamed.

Being a rich bitch was all she'd ever thought it was cracked up to be. And she liked it. A lot.

****

Rudy Marshall watched the morning unfold in the house on the hill. Mid-American, upper-class suburbia was all pretty much the same up and down the asphalt, she mused. Tree lined drives bordered large lots, some larger, some smaller than the others. Kitchen lights flickered as households came awake. Busy husbands exited front doors or backed out of garages on their way to work. Wives waved good-bye or hurried small children into expensive sedans or mini-vans to whisk them off to private schools.

At least in most of them.

The house that most interested Rudy, however, sat secluded, a little deeper in the two-acre lot, framed by a number of large maples and pines. The circular drive took up a great deal of the front lawn, a fairly new Mercedes sat before the home. She saw little sign of activity within.

What Rudy suspected several days ago was now a relative certainty. All she needed to do was wait. And she didn't have to wait too long.

As the door opened at the front of the house, Rudy slid a little further into the seat, but not so far she couldn't see. When he stepped outside, she saw him very clearly...and the girl as well.

Bradford Thomas crossed the brick porch. The blonde stood in the open door, smiling.

After opening the passenger side door of the Mercedes, he tossed his brief case inside and closed the door. When he started toward the rear of the car, Cindy joined him. He folded her into his arms and Rudy felt a jolt in her abdomen. When he placed his lips on the girl's, Rudy's teeth clenched. Furious, she watched the girl's hands snake around to grasp his backside and pull him into her. Rudy heard her own breath hiss through her teeth.

She could have been mistaken, but she thought she

heard Bradford moan from across the street.

Unfortunately, she knew Bradford's moan only too well.

Painfully pulling her gaze away from the entangled couple, Rudy heaved in a deep breath. She stared ahead at her fingers wound around the steering wheel, her knuckles white. But the anger within wouldn't allow her to let go.

She couldn't let it go.

He was a disgusting sonofabitch. Thank God Megan had gotten out of there.

With the sound of the engine grinding to life across the street, she forced herself to look again. Bradford in the driver's seat, the car jerked forward. Cindy still on the porch, waved like the perfect little wifey as Bradford wheeled the Mercedes out of the drive.

Rudy didn't care if he saw her, so she didn't duck. She looked straight at him as he exited the drive, almost wanting him to look her in the eyes so he would know. But he didn't and she didn't really care about anything now that she knew the truth. How could she have been such a fool?

Why couldn't she have seen all this time?

Her gaze drifted to the blonde across the street, fully admitting to herself what she already knew—Cindy was the spitting image of Megan and Bradford had replaced his wife quite handily with the decoy Megan had supplied.

How ironic. And how pathetic.

Her heart froze. Frantically, she grasped the rearview mirror and hastily angled it so she could see her own reflection. As she stared into the mirror, she felt her breathing reduce to shallow breaths while a tiny, icy tremor tripped down her spine. Her fingers played over her facial features.

Why had this not occurred to her before? Why could she not see this?

High cheekbones, green eyes, skin that tanned well in the summer, golden blonde hair, small pouty lips—all similar features. Features each of them shared. And body types. She and Megan shared clothing occasionally, their physiques so much the same. And Cindy…when Megan picked her out, they knew she was perfect. Why had she, Rudy, just not put herself in this picture before?

Bradford never cared for her. Bradford obviously had a thing for leggy, green-eyed blondes. And to think she thought he'd cared.

Once.

She'd known it was wrong, from the first time he'd initiated anything between them years ago, but she was sucked in too quickly, too passionately, by his charm. She'd felt guilty.

Damned guilty, and hated deceiving Megan, never telling her what had once occurred between herself and Bradford. But it was so difficult to dredge up the past. She knew that the only way to make it up to her was to help Megan out of her present situation. To get Bradford permanently out of both their lives.

But it seemed she and Megan had handed him Cindy on a silver platter.

And obviously, Cindy had decided to stay.

****

Three hours later Rudy stepped into the outer office of Thomas Industrials' president and CEO, Bradford Thomas. Thomas Industrials owned a string of factories throughout Illinois, Minnesota, Michigan, Ohio, Indiana, and Kentucky which manufactured various nondescript auto parts. The kind of thing that one never thought about being there, but was extremely necessary and important. Like the hinge which attached the windshield wiper to the car or the mechanism that locked the seat belt into place during a sudden stop.

Her heels clicked against the parquet floor as she neared the inner office. She stopped and waited while Bradford's secretary finished with her phone conversation. Nervous, she glanced ahead at the solid oak door with the shiny brass nameplate leading into Bradford's realm.

She tucked her leather case under her arm and looked down as she straightened her suit coat.

She had been summoned.

There were any number of reasons why, so she really had no need to fear this meeting, but she dreaded it with an alarming passion, just as she'd dreaded every meeting she'd had with Bradford of late. But this one would be different. It was the first time she'd met with Bradford since he returned from London. With Megan gone, there was no doubt he'd be loaded for bear.

But as his attorney, and as acting legal counsel for Thomas Industrials, she had no cause to balk at this meeting. She was obligated. And it would look suspiciously awkward should she refuse, cancel, or postpone anything at this point in time.

She'd thought about it at length. When she'd been called early that morning, she'd had no recourse but to get the meeting over as soon as possible.

"He's expecting you, Ms. Marshall."

Startled, Rudy glanced to Bradford's secretary, an older woman who had been with him for some years. Betty punched the intercom to announce her arrival. Bradford answered her in a pleasant, businesslike voice. Rudy had to wonder how much Betty knew, how involved she was.

But looking into the face of the kind-hearted woman with the graying hair, Rudy couldn't begin to believe that the woman knew much. However, she was his personal secretary, and a secretary usually knew more about a man's comings and goings, his business dealings, than his wife did.

In Megan's case, that was probably true. Still, she found it difficult to believe that Betty Price was involved in Bradford's...schemes.

"Thank you, Betty."

"Go right on in, dear."

Rudy stepped forward and placed her fingers around the cold brass doorknob, then pushed open the heavy door. The room was frigid. Bradford always kept the air conditioning at a lower than normal temperature. His reasoning was to keep whomever he'd summoned alert enough to remember what he'd told them, and then make them so uncomfortable they'd take care of business pronto and leave. He was not a man for lengthy business meetings, but a man who believed in cutting to the chase, weeding out the chaff, and getting to the germ of the deal as quickly as possible.

And most times he came out on top. Cream of the crop.

Until recently, Rudy never doubted Bradford's motives or his means to an end. Now, she knew better.

"Sit down, Rudy."

Rudy stiffly crossed the red carpeted room. She barely took in the dark paneling, the heavy brocade draperies, and the obvious lack of natural light. Bradford liked big, bold, dark, brassy, polished, and impressive. It was how he lived his life and the image he projected to the public. Funny how he liked just the opposite in his women. She supposed it was easier to mold them that way.

But she would not be molded.

In a leather wing chair at the left front of Bradford's desk sat Samuel Lockbourne, Bradford's friend, business partner, and vice president of the firm. Bradford motioned for Rudy to sit in the matching chair to her right. He, of course, remained ensconced with a devious smile behind his massive desk of deep mahogany.

Bradford sat back in his chair and continued to smile at her. He waited. Rudy sat up a little straighter and lifted her chin. She refused to exude the intimidation she felt on the inside.

She excelled at putting on a confident façade. She did it routinely in the courtroom as a private attorney. She knew how to build up stout walls of defense around herself even though her insides fluttered like so many butterflies in a glass jar.

"I've called you here for two reasons, Rudy. One is business related, that's why Sam is here. The other is personal. We'll handle business, first."

Rudy dipped her chin. "All right. Something you want

me to look at? A contract to draw up?"

She preferred to cut to the chase, as well.

Bradford leaned forward and shook his head. "No. By business I don't mean Thomas Industrials." He glanced at Sam. Her gaze followed.

"I just assumed, since Sam was here."

"Sam and I have agreed to a new endeavor."

"Another factory to overhaul?"

"No. We're moving into the political arena."

The thought of that both stunned and frightened her, although she couldn't say it entirely surprised her. Bradford had made noises to that end before. Immediately, her throat went dry.

Bradford Thomas had no business in politics, not that every mob-connected businessman wouldn't like to have political connections.

She'd tried to deny it for months, but the signs were all there. And as Bradford lured her closer into the inner workings of Thomas Industrials, her suspicions were confirmed. She believed Bradford had established himself in some type of organized crime network. He never voiced anything concrete and as far as she knew, he suspected she knew nothing.

But she knew more than suspected. When the new young district attorney came sniffing about two weeks ago, Bradford freaked. Obviously someone in the district attorney's office had suspicions, too. And that's why he summoned her here today. She had connections and a working knowledge of the law.

And she knew some things...some things that could incriminate her, too, if she didn't watch her step. So, they wanted to take her in with them. They needed her. And it was going to be damned hard for her to refuse.

Rudy sat closer to the edge of her seat. "I didn't realize you were serious about your political ambitions, Bradford."

"I want you on my team, Rudy. We're going for the state Senate seat."

Rudy tried to swallow, but found it difficult.

"Well, aren't you going to say something?" A crooked grin spread across his face. Rudy could only think that his heart must be just as crooked even though he was such a handsome man—close-cropped sandy hair, flawless skin, perfect teeth, eyes that peered into your soul.

Women will flock to the booths to vote for him, she thought. He had charisma. Just like Jack Kennedy.

"I'm flabbergasted, Bradford. It's just something I never considered. What do you want me to do?"

"I want you to run my campaign."

Rudy felt her eyes widen. "Me? Bradford, I know nothing about doing that sort of thing. I'm too busy. I wouldn't have the foggiest notion of how to go about doing that."

She glanced to Sam Lockbourne who smiled at her, one bent finger resting under his chin. "We need you, Rudy," he said.

Bradford rose and circled the desk, stopping directly in front of her. He sat on the edge, almost giddy with excitement. "I'm not sure the timing for this is right," she told him, thinking of Megan, of her leaving.

"The timing, although not perfect, is fine."

"But—"

Sam rose and slapped Bradford on the back. "She'll come around, old boy. I'll leave the rest to you. I'm going to check on the Tech-Lite deal. I know you'll convince her how important it is for her to be involved." He chuckled and quickly left them alone.

I'm already involved. Up to my ass and then some.

Bradford glared down at her with eyes of steel. "You will do this for me, won't you, Ru?"

He arched a brow and grinned.

There were no choices here. She knew she would. Had to. "I'll think about it."

He grinned. She rose and backed up a few steps, making the distance between them more palatable.

"Now, about Megan." The expression on his face changed immediately to agitation.

Despite the chill in the room, she felt clammy. "Tell me where she is."

"I don't know where Megan is, Bradford. I wish I did."

"No, you probably don't. If you knew, it would be too much. You'd have to tell me and you would betray her trust. I believe you're telling me the truth. Now what are you going to do to help me find her?"

Rudy stood her ground. "Bradford, I have no idea how to do that."

It was a relief to tell the truth. For that she was grateful to Megan.

"Did you know she was leaving?"

"She mentioned something. I tried to talk her out of it."

"Bullshit!" Bradford pounded the desk at his side, then exploded away from it. He paced back and forth toward the draped window. He swirled to meet her gaze. "I don't believe you, Rudy! Megan couldn't have accomplished a disappearing act on her own. She doesn't have the brains for it. But it seems that's exactly what she's done. I've had men working on it ever since I got back. She'd disappeared into goddamned thin air!"

"I don't know why it seems to matter, Bradford. Your bed obviously hasn't been cold lately."

The vile look he threw at her made the skin crawl on the back of her neck. She was on thin ice. She didn't care.

"How warm my bed is does not seem to be any of your concern, Ru. You made your choices long ago."

"That I did. Get her out of there."

"She'll be gone soon enough."

"I would think it wouldn't serve your image well to have another woman occupying your home and your bed with your wife barely gone. Especially if you are running for office."

"No one knows Megan is gone. Besides, Cindy could easily pass for Megan. You know that. It was a good scam, Ru, and it worked. Your idea or Megan's?"

"I told you, I knew nothing."

"Cindy says you were in on it. That you were her contact. That you paid her five thousand dollars."

The stupid little bitch. "Megan paid her five thousand dollars. I simply was a go-between. I only did what Megan asked of me."

"And you had no trouble doing that."

"She wanted a divorce. I don't believe any woman is bound to a man for life if she chooses not to be. This isn't the Dark Ages, Bradford. She has rights. You were denying her hers."

"Rights!" He crowded closer. Rudy drew in a breath and held it, her only defense to stop her entire body from shaking. His eyes penetrated right through her. "Have I no rights here? She is my wife and bound to do what I want. The hell with the law. I'm in the midst of planning a political future. Megan knew that. I need her. A Senator requires either a wife or children. Right now, I don't have either. I've got to get her back."

Rudy snorted. "Maybe if you hadn't beaten her to a pulp, you could have had a child."

Cold fingers reached out and snatched her chin. He drew her face closer to his. "You better watch your fucking mouth."

"Of course, if you need a wife so badly, maybe you could pass off Cindy as Megan. The public probably wouldn't notice a thing."

Her chin felt like it was in a vise.

"Maybe you could disappear and I could pass her off as my attorney."

The message was clear—time for Rudy to back off. After a silent moment, he released her with a snap of his wrist.

"John Walters sent over divorce papers yesterday. I suppose you knew nothing about that, either."

"I suspected. I didn't know she'd contacted anyone." That was a lie. She had convinced John Walters to represent Megan.

"She won't get what she wants."

"All she wants is her freedom."

"She'll never get it." He stepped closer. "If you talk to her, see her, tell her that for me, will you? She'll never be free of me. Not now. Not after what she's done."

"How are you going to handle this, Bradford? I mean, with the public."

"Actually, it's already been handled, right before you got here. Sam and I had a long talk, made some decisions."

"And?"

"And you'll find out soon enough."

Rudy eyed him. What had he done? It wouldn't surprise her, he was capable of anything.

Bradford edged closer. Rudy stood stone still, staring into the perfect Windsor knot of his tie. "Now on to personal business."

She lifted her face to look into his eyes. "I thought we already covered that."

Slowly, Bradford shook his head. His eyes narrowed and a sly grin split his lips. Rudy felt his right hand brush along her thigh through her skirt, his fingers gently nudging between her legs. "It's been a long time, Ru." The words rolled off his tongue like silken honey.

Rudy closed her eyes and stifled the shiver that dared to crawl up her backbone. "We need to keep things professional."

"We need to keep things in perspective."

She looked at him. "Whose perspective?"

"Mine," he growled. "I want to fuck you."

"No."

"You think you can refuse?"

His fingers bit into her left upper arm. His gaze penetrated her eyes. Inch by inch, he bunched her knee-length skirt into his fist until he reached the hem. Without warning, he jerked her closer, holding her steady with his left hand, and with the other he raked the inside of her thigh above her gartered stockings and cupped her between the legs.

Rudy tried to fight her labored breathing, the

sensations gathering where he touched her.

She found it difficult. She didn't want to do this. She didn't. He slipped a finger beneath her panties. His eyes never left hers.

"It's been a long, long time, Ru." He teased her, gently scraped over her tender skin, and then penetrated her with his finger. Rudy vowed she would stand firm. She knew what he was doing…drawing her in, making her his again, forcing her into submission so she would do his bidding. Using her to get his way, to get what he wanted.

And it was sick.

She fought the wave of nausea that hit her stomach.

His finger slid in and out, caressing, then more quickly as his eyes grew wild with excitement. He drew closer to her, his lips raking the skin behind her cheek, under her ear, down her neck.

And she was lost. She knew it from the first touch.

Dammit.

His left arm encircled her, bringing her closer into him. His hot breath rushed over her face. Then he drew back long enough to remove his finger from her and bring it to his lips. She watched as he licked and sucked his wet finger, his eyes daring, rimmed in primal arousal. Then he raked the finger across her lips.

Within seconds, Rudy found herself awkwardly fumbling with the buttons of his shirt and the fastenings of his fly, hating every second of it.

****

The small television recessed in the mahogany entertainment center droned on with the evening news. Bradford Thomas watched with interest as his own face flashed across the screen.

Eyes narrowed, he listened intently. His lips moved as he silently repeated the words he knew had come from his mouth earlier that day. A teaser, something for the public to think about. He'd made no concrete political announcement and he wasn't ready to, yet. He simply set the bait.

And when the news of Megan hit the media, he'd have the sympathetic vote in his back pocket before he'd even announced his candidacy.

Smiling, pleased with himself, he pressed a button on the remote control and the picture faded. He then turned his attention to the man sitting before him.

He drummed his fingers against the sleek desk. Eyes straight ahead, Bradford stared at the man seated in the leather chair. Bradford drew his face into a scowl as he slowly leaned back in his own chair and wove his fingers together. Angling his face first up to the ceiling, contemplating his next move, he then let his gaze drift lower, apprehending the man's attention.

"It is imperative that she be found. I don't want her coming back only to ruin everything."

The man nodded his agreement. Bradford rose and leaned over the desk. "You do understand, though, that I have no desire to see her again." His stare pierced the air between them. "Just find her, so I know she's been found. Then get rid her. Use whatever means you wish. I don't care."

Standing now, the fellow fastened the upper button of his brown jacket, straightened the lapels, and smiled. "I think that can be arranged. Would it displease you if she were...violated before her death?"

Bradford chuckled. Riker was a horny sonofabitch.

"No. In fact it would give me great pleasure to know that someone might get some enjoyment out of her. She's cold as a fucking fish. I sincerely doubt if the experience would be pleasurable for either of you, but give it a try. Hell, have a go 'round for me."

"Yes, sir."

"And see if she's got any money stashed away wherever she's living. The bitch stole over a quarter million dollars from me—and it didn't exactly belong to me. I need that money back."

Bradford watched Riker's eyes gleam. Sex and money went hand in hand with him as well, he deduced. Bradford chuckled inwardly. What else was there?

"I just want her gone. Compensation will be made in the usual manner."

Watching Riker step away from the desk, Bradford breathed deeply, in finality of what he knew he had to do. "Oh, and take care of the other one, too."

Riker lifted his eyebrow. "Sir?"

"The blonde," he returned gruffly. Bradford stabbed the man with his glare. He watched the puzzled look wash over his face, his eyes darted back and forth.

"But they're all blonde."

Bradford's fist crashed down against the rich wood sending a small crystal paper-weight flying. "Idiot! The blonde! The one I've been fucking lately. Get rid of her. She gets on my nerves."

After a chorus of "Yes, sirs," Riker left, and Bradford smiled.

Chapter Four

Smyth shifted the jeep into third gear and pressed the accelerator harder to the floor. He hated crossing this bridge. He hated leaving the islands. When he did, he felt trapped. Hell, he'd been trapped for way too long. Not that he'd actually realized it then, but now...well, it became more apparent each time he met with his ex-wife. Especially now that he finally knew what Crystal was up to.

The Wright Memorial Bridge stretched far in front of him, the only connectors from the Outer Banks to the mainland. As he crested the rise in the center, he glanced at the water rippling across Currituck Sound and the morning sunlight sparkling off the tips of the tiny waves. Then he thought of the sunrise that morning, and Meg.

Like a vision come to life in front of him, her blonde ponytail rippled in the breeze as the pinks of the morning radiated across her face. Her bronzed skin was all a man would want to run his hands over. And her legs. Hell, he saw legs all the time, but he'd never seen legs that made his blood surge quite like that before.

Damn, she was a good-looking woman. He could hardly tear his gaze away from her this morning. But a woman like that he could damn well do without. And would do without because when he finished with Crystal this morning, he'd see Becky first thing and find this Meg somewhere else to stay, even if he had to pay the difference himself. He sure as hell didn't need a woman to complicate things right now. If Crystal got wind of her, she'd run with it like a demon out of a revival.

At a safe distance, Meg followed Smyth Parker's jeep across the bridge. She hadn't wanted him to think she was following him, which she wasn't. After he'd gulped down a cup of coffee, he'd left abruptly. And Meg, having been a bit flustered at the ripples he'd generated in her abdomen on the porch earlier, had needed to get out of the house.

So she got in the car and just drove.

She hadn't meant to follow him, but one had a choice of turning right or left on the main drag through the islands and they had each chosen to turn right. And to get to the mainland, this bridge provided the only choice.

Besides, she did have an errand to run. She might as well do it on the mainland.

She had to call Rudy. Nearly two weeks had passed now and even though she didn't really expect anything to have come from the divorce, her curiosity wanted to know how Bradford had reacted to her leaving. So that's what she'd do, she'd drive inland a bit, and call.

She trusted Rudy, she just didn't want to risk giving up her location. Even if the call could be traced to North Carolina, at least she hadn't given an address. Meg bit her lip and glanced in the rearview mirror. The road branched into four lanes now. Smyth drove on steadily, she slowed her pace a bit, but still kept him in sight. By the time they reached the turn to Elizabeth City, Meg watched as Smyth turned in that direction. She decided to go north. Perhaps as far as Norfolk, Portsmouth News, or Virginia Beach. It wasn't that far and she had nothing else to do that day.

In the end she caught I-64 in Norfolk and drove to Richmond, Virginia. It took a couple of hours, but she needed thinking time. Richmond was a big enough city. If Bradford happened to find out she'd been there, it would take him a while to search the city. On the other hand, it wouldn't take him long to comb Nags Head, North Carolina. It made the drive worthwhile to steer him clear of the islands.

Rudy wouldn't intentionally tell, but Meg knew how tricky Bradford could be. She didn't want to take any chances that Rudy would let something slip, or that he'd tapped her phones to boot. She had to remember Rudy's position as Bradford's attorney, a job Rudy had before befriending Meg. He'd hired her years earlier to work as the corporate attorney for Thomas Industrials. It had only been in the last few years that Rudy and Meg had become intimate friends. So much so she could trust Rudy with anything.

After pulling off the interstate, Meg took a couple of side streets and found herself near the airport, then sought a pay phone. She'd left her cell phone back in Chicago, not trusting that Bradford couldn't get into her account and find out where she was calling from. She found an elusive pay phone outside a small grocery store and made a collect call.

"Where in the hell are you?" were the first words Rudy shouted after accepting the call.

"Obviously not in Santa Fe. I've called every hotel and rental agency in the book. You told me you were renting a house in Santa Fe."

Meg let the line fall silent for a split-second. "Rudy, listen. I'm sorry it has to be this way, but I'm not going to tell you where I am."

"How in the hell am I supposed to keep in touch with you? I've got to know where you are!"

Calmly, Meg returned, "No." She expected this. Hurt feelings. A broken trust. Meg softened her voice. "Rudy, I can't take chances. If you don't know where I am, then you can't accidentally let it slip to Bradford. You are his attorney." She paused for a moment. "And you know how persuasive he can be."

She heard Rudy's sigh on the other end. "You're right."

Meg sensed the coolness in the voice that came through the phone.

"I'm sorry," she finally returned. "I'll make it up to you somehow."

"That's all well and good, honey, but..."

"I'll call once a week."

"What if things get sticky in the meantime?"

"Then you'll have to wait. I gave John Walters power of attorney, Rudy. Thanks for referring me to him. He was very understanding."

"I just didn't think I should be involved, Megan."

"And I didn't want to involve you. John knows what I want and I think he can stand up to Bradford. I don't care if I don't get one red cent from him. I want out. And I want out now."

"I know. And believe me, you're better off. By the way, why didn't you tell me Bradford had plans to go into politics?"

"He told you?"

"He's announcing his candidacy soon. He wants me to run the campaign."

"Even with me gone?"

"Apparently he thinks it won't be a problem."

"I'm surprised. I'd half hoped he wouldn't go on with his plans with me out of the way."

"Bradford doesn't easily change his mind."

Meg knew that. Shaking off the surprising news, she returned, "You won't do it, will you?"

There was a pause. "I have no choice."

"Yes, you do, Rudy. Don't let him drag you in."

"It's too late for me. I'm glad it's not too late for you. Can't you just tell me where you are? Megan, what if there's an emergency or something? Sometimes I just need to talk to you."

Meg fell silent for a minute. She really should trust Rudy, but could she risk it?

"It's only a matter of time, Megan. I'm staring at a phone number on my phone display right now. It won't take me long to figure out the city."

Meg closed her eyes. Sighing, she opened them to stare out across the Richmond airport.

A small craft sailed down the runway and over her head. She grimaced at the sound of the engine. "Okay. You might be doing just that, but I'm sticking to my guns. And I'm hoping you will not betray our trust. In fact, there's nothing to keep me here, Rudy, you know that. I've got enough money to move around for a while. You won't be able to find me. As soon as I know that Bradford is going to really leave me alone, then I'll let you know where I am."

After a moment, she added. "Anyway, it doesn't matter. I'm at an airport and I'm not going to be here long." She hated lying.

A silence filled the air on the line. "You know that a piece of paper isn't going to keep him away from you, Megan. He'll find you eventually. You know Brad, when he's on a mission, he doesn't give up."

Meg knew that only too well. He didn't like to lose. Once hell-bent on a quest, he went after it with all the stops pulled out. If he lost, you didn't approach him for days. He was unbearable to live with. And it only grew worse every year she'd lived with him. Recently, she'd even grown more fearful of him, especially after suspecting that not all of his business dealings were on the level.

"I'll just have to take that risk. I'll run for the rest of my life if I have to."

"Megan, look...there's something else. Bradford knows too much. I feel a little uneasy. He knows about the car. They'll be looking for it."

"How do you know?"

"He made it very clear to me that he has an inside track. In fact, he said he had friends in places who could arrange to have an all-points-bulletin put out on that vehicle. He made it very clear that he would find you, come hell or high water."

Stunned, Meg closed her eyes and let the phone partially slide out of her hand. Catching it against her chest, she let a small, ragged sob escape her throat. Then she shoved the phone back up to her ear. She should have known Bradford wouldn't give up that easily. "How?" she asked weakly.

"The girl."

"Cindy?"

"Yeah."

"Damn."

"That's what I thought."

"What else?"

"I don't know."

There was an extended pause over the phone line. "He's getting a lot of press these days. There are a lot of rumors flying around concerning his political ambitions."

Her brain whirling, Meg searched the area around her. Leave it to Bradford to turn things around to his advantage. What did he have up his sleeve? Her immediate concern, however, was that she had to get back to Nags Head and get rid of the car. A siren sounded loud and long behind her. Paranoia set in and she nervously glanced from side to side searching for the source of the wail. Suddenly, a police cruiser burst from the traffic and zipped across her vision and out of sight. Meg exhaled.

"Sorry, Rudy. I'll call when I can, but I've got to go."

Slamming the receiver back onto the hook, Meg quickly backed away from the phone booth and jumped into her car. After only a moment's hesitation, she twisted the ignition, gunned the engine, and threw the car into reverse.

****

After hours of sporadic driving, of carefully avoiding every state or local police cruiser she happened on along the way, Meg finally pulled into the drive of Smyth's cottage and parked beside his Jeep. Killing the ignition, she sat and faced the house. She sandwiched her car between the cottage she rented and another behind her, shielding the Honda from view of the road. Only the tenants of the nearby cottages could see her car. And an out-of-state car wouldn't cause any kind of alarm, she knew. After all, this was a tourist haven. Even now, in the off-season, it wouldn't be a problem. She'd seen just one other cottage nearby inhabited the past week.

Finally, she decided the car was safe enough where it rested for the night, but she needed to do something about it soon.

Lights from Smyth's house broke through the dark, casting shadows across the dune. As Meg left the vehicle, she walked between the two houses and stepped through the pathway to the beach. She felt safe there, in the dune's shadow. Protected. The ocean, fairly calm, lapped at the shore, the tide high. She stepped closer to the beach's edge and breathed deeply as she watched a slice of yellow glow from the moon reflect off the water.

A cool breeze blew in from the north. She shivered, then wrapped her arms about her.

She'd been driving for hours, thinking. Her brain was so tired of thinking, of planning. Finally, in exhaustion, she sat upon the sand, pulled her knees up to her chest, and rested her forehead on her crossed arms. What would she do?

Somehow, she had to get rid of the car and get another. How? Surely Bradford wouldn't access every police computer in the country, would he? Perhaps it was good Rudy could place her now. Perhaps she'd just have to throw them off the track.

Raising her head, Meg stared out over the ocean. Threading her fingers through her loose hair, she flipped it back over her shoulders confidently. She hated leaving Nags Head. Really hated it, in fact. But, she'd just have to do what she had to do.

Standing, her brain reeling in thought, she turned to head back toward the cottage. A purpose in mind now, she knew she'd spend most of the night working through the details to confuse Bradford.

And she knew by morning, she'd have it.

Smyth watched Meg from the windows from the time he'd heard her car pull up behind the cottage. Watching her there on the beach, he'd studied every defeated movement her body made. After a moment, when she hadn't moved toward the house, he'd stepped closer to the window.

As she sat alone staring into the surf, he couldn't help but wonder about her. She had fallen into his life, for whatever brief moment, and proceeded to turn his gut inside out.

Breathtakingly beautiful, she had a presence about her most men craved. They shared only a brief moment in his living room yesterday, and the encounter on the deck that morning, but she had already woven a spell about him.

He hadn't been able to get her off his mind all morning. And then later in the afternoon after he'd returned from his bout with Crystal, he'd waited for her to come home. Had actually listened for the sound of her car wheels crunching on the sand in the drive. And he hadn't done something like that in years. Didn't want to do it, either. But he had.

She was lonely. Which only made her seem the more vulnerable. And in spite of the rosy skin and bright green eyes and the hair that shone golden in the morning sunrise, the sadness had shown through. A lack of certainty about her. A mystery, of sorts, that made a man want to take her in his arms and protect her.

That was it. For some ungodly reason he wanted to protect her. From what, he didn't know. But there was something there...something in the way those green eyes looked at him that made him want to just hold her.

Her steps echoed across the porch and he stood waiting beside the windows when she stepped inside the door.

"Hi," he said softly.

Meg looked up at him, startled.

"Hi." She glanced at the floor as she took three hesitant steps into the room and then looked up at him again.

"Have you eaten?" Smyth turned away from the windows and proceeded toward the kitchen counter behind him. He lifted a lid from a pan on the stove and leaned over it to sniff.

"I've got chowder and crab cakes. I made plenty. I'd be happy to warm some for you."

Meg stared at him. Her gaze searched his face as if she couldn't believe he actually asked her to eat with him. Had he been that much of an ogre to her yesterday?

"So, what do you say? Are you hungry?"

He watched as Meg shivered slightly, then blinked, as if pulling herself out of a trance, drawing together her resolve. He couldn't help but wonder what secrets this woman kept locked inside.

"Uh, well...I haven't eaten since noon. I guess I am a little hungry."

He pulled out a chair and smiled. "Then sit. It won't take a minute." Moving back to the stove, he turned up the heat beneath the pot of chowder. Then, he transferred two crab cakes to a plate, slid them in the microwave and punched the time into the control pad.

Meg still stood, her fingers wound tightly around the top of the chair in front of her. She wondered if he realized he was whistling. *I shouldn't be here. I need time to think, to put a plan into action.*

She really didn't need to be eating the man's food, either. What had gotten into him anyway? Why was he so damn nice to her all of a sudden?

"Maybe I should just pass on the food."

Watching him, Meg saw the muscles of his back tighten beneath the skin-tight T-shirt. He turned slowly, the microwave buzzer sounded. For what seemed minutes, he stared at her. The smile that lit his face earlier was gone.

"Was it something I said? Or did you get a whiff of my food. Really, I'm not a bad cook." A hint of a grin flashed across his lips.

Letting her shoulders relax, Meg chuckled. She hadn't realized she let herself tense up so and that she'd been holding her breath for a while. Her fingers loosened from the chair. "No, it smells wonderful, really. It's just that I—"

"That you're tired and you don't know me well enough and you're wondering why you ever got hooked up with the likes of me, right?"

The grin was back, a small half-grin that crinkled the edges of his mouth and brought out that small, but well-defined dimple in his chin.

He was teasing her.

Meg huffed out a breath. "I am tired. And I'm hungry, too. I don't know quite what I'm doing here, but if it doesn't bother you, okay, I will eat. Then I'll go to bed and be out of your way."

The chowder bubbled in the background. Smyth glanced back at it, then at her, cocking his head to one side as he studied her. A frown replaced the grin. "You're not in my way."

Meg acted as if she didn't hear him. "I'll be out of here in the morning. Probably be gone several days. Then when I get back, I'll find something else. I'll get Becky on it in the morning. I promise."

Crossing his arms over his chest, Smyth stared at her as he shook his head. "No. I talked to Becky already. I want you to stay."

Surprised, Meg shook her head and stepped away from the table. "I can't. I can't stay here. No. I'll find something."

"Look, I realize this is...awkward, but you don't understand. I'll be gone in a few days and won't be back until August. I've told Becky to let you rent it until then. If you're leaving for a few days now, then we'll probably not spend more than a few hours here together at the most, so it won't be a problem for either of us. Really, I'd like someone to stay here, it might as well be you. You seem to enjoy it so much."

Obviously he could see right through her. She enjoyed this little cottage immensely. "I don't know how I could ever repay you. I mean, I don't know if I can afford the peak season rent for long, but I'd be glad to—"

Smyth waved his hands in the air. "Forget it. Whatever you're paying Becky now will be fine. I'm not concerned about anything more than paying the taxes and upkeep on this place." He turned back to the soup, fished a bowl out of the cupboard above, and ladled it full of the steaming chowder. "I'm really just glad to have someone responsible staying here."

Placing the soup in front of her, he lifted his gaze to hers. "Why don't you sit down now and relax," he said softly. "You look really drug out. Long day?"

Meg pulled out the chair opposite where he stood and finally sat. She hadn't realized until now just how exhausted she was. "You don't know the half of it," she mumbled.

Smyth dipped another bowl of chowder for himself, removed the crab cakes from the microwave and placed them on the table. He studied her and Megan pretended not to notice as he pulled flatware from the drawers and handed some to her. He pulled out his chair and sat down.

For several minutes, they ate in silence.

All Meg could think about was how to get rid of her car. She had no idea about Smyth's thoughts.

After a while, her soup bowl nearly empty and half a crab cake gone, Meg laid her spoon down on the table and lifted her gaze to his. Watching him finish his meal, she couldn't help but wonder if she could trust him. If only there was one person she could trust with her problem. Just one.

"Mind if I ask you a question?"

She watched as his gaze rose to meet hers. Slowly. He swallowed, pushed his bowl back, and nodded. Knowing her face reflected the questions running through her mind, and probably a lot more than that, she decided to plunge ahead. She had his undivided attention.

"About how far away from here do you think a person could drive in one day? About how many miles?"

Smyth tilted his head to the left, keeping their gazes intact. He deliberated for several long seconds. "What direction do you want to go?"

Meg sighed. "I don't know. Not along the coast. Inland. Not north. Probably south and west."

Smyth cupped his chin in his palm, resting his elbow on the table. Still watching, he studied her. Meg knew he was trying to figure her out, but seemed reluctant to ask too many questions. She silently thanked him for that.

"If you drove into the night, you could probably hit Alabama, maybe farther if you kept to the interstate and plugged along at a fairly good clip. You planning to be gone long?"

She shook her head. "No. I want to get back here as soon as possible." She paused for a moment, then decided to ask another question. "Are there any of those truck rental places around here? You know, like a small moving van? I need one."

"How big?"

"Big enough for my car," she blurted out.

His eyes narrowed. Meg could tell he was trying hard not to be surprised. "Your car?"

"Yes."

"You want to tell me what's going on?"

"Not really."

Smyth rose, taking his plate and bowl with him. Placing them on the counter, he plugged the sink, turned on a mixture of hot and cold water, and squirted a little detergent in the stream.

Carefully, he laid the dishes in the sink, returned to the table to get Meg's, and placed them with the others. Watching him, Meg felt confused. She didn't know this man, but yet, she felt compelled to be honest with him—to a certain degree, anyway. But could she trust him? Had Bradford sent him?

No. If that were the case she wouldn't be here right now. Perhaps if she told him just a little.

His back was to her as he washed the dishes. Meg rose from the table and stepped up beside him. Every bit of courage she had in her was balled up just beneath her breastbone forcing her to shiver. When he placed a bowl in the drainer, she picked it up and began drying with a towel from the rack next to the sink. "I need to get rid of my car," she said softly.

His hands slowed in the water, he looked sideways at her. "Why?"

Meg pulled in her lower lip with her teeth and watched

his face. "I don't want to be found."

His hands stopped completely. Turning toward her, he grasped the towel out of her hands and dried his. For a moment, he leaned against the side of the counter, staring into her eyes.

"And the car will give you away?"

"Maybe."

"Are you in trouble?"

"In a way."

"Are you running from the police?"

Meg shook her head. "No," she said. "From someone else. I haven't done anything wrong," she added quickly. "But the police are looking for my car. I haven't stolen it, it's mine. But there's an APB out on it and me. I can't let them find me. I don't want to lead them here. I want to lead the trail far away from here. I just want to sell the car, get a new one, and get on with my life." Her voice nearly pleaded.

Meg's heart pounded against her chest wall. Her breathing came in short shallow breaths.

Why did she tell him all that? She shouldn't have. Her stomach felt jumpy. He must think her some kind of lunatic.

She backed away.

Glancing at the floor, Meg shook her head. She didn't want to look at him. She didn't want him to see the tears near the surface of her eyes. How could she have been so stupid?

"Never mind," she said almost under her breath. "I'll take care of everything." Whirling away from him, she started toward her bedroom...until she felt his fingers grip her upper arm.

Turning back, she looked directly into his face.

"Do you need to sell the car? Do you need money?"

"No," she replied in a squeaky voice, glancing down at his fingers curled around her arm. "No, I don't need money."

He released her and stepped away. Nodding, he

watched her face, questioning.

"That's good. If there's an APB out on it, every dealer in the country will be alerted. There's got to be a better way." He searched her eyes. A momentary confusion hit her. "Get some sleep. We'll talk about it in the morning."

Meg stepped back, then spun and walked quickly down the hall to her bedroom. She left the light off, undressed, slipped into an oversized T-shirt, and slid between the covers of her bed.

She didn't want to think any more about what the day had brought. It was all too confusing—the news about Bradford, the car, and now Smyth Parker.

Could she trust him?

More importantly, could she trust herself around him?

For the first time since he'd interrupted her peaceful existence here, she had allowed herself to admit that Smyth Parker was an intriguing man. An intriguingly handsome, sexy man.

And for the first time since she'd left Chicago, she felt a tremor of fear in her abdomen. This time, however, the fear was not of Bradford and what he might choose to do to her, but a fear of what she might allow herself to feel for a man like Smyth Parker.

If it were at all possible that she could ever feel that way again.

Chapter Five

After nearly two hours of lying in bed staring at the ceiling, Smyth sat up and stared out the window. He'd tried to sleep, but ended up tossing and turning, finally giving in to gaze at the even strips of plank. Every time he closed his eyes, he saw her. When she'd confessed to him about the car, and that someone was looking for her, he'd watched her eyes dart back and forth.

He'd noted the nervous quake of her voice and the long sigh after she'd finally gotten the words out.

She was a nuisance to his life. And she was captivating.

But she also didn't want to be found.

Why?

He didn't know if he would find out the answer to that question any time soon, but dammit, she was worried. And for whatever reason, it worried him. He knew she needed help.

It had only taken him two hours to figure out how.

He pulled on a pair of briefs, jeans, a T-shirt, and sneakers, then shoved his wallet and keys into his pants pockets. Within seconds, he'd slipped inside the door of Meg's room and stood beside her bed, watching her sleep.

Why am I doing this? He had every reason not to. One, he didn't really know her. Two, she was running from something...or someone. And three, if Crystal found out about Meg, she'd take the information and run with it. Not that he had cause to worry about handling Crystal, he had things well in hand there. But it wouldn't help his or Meg's situation at all if she began spreading the word that a beautiful, mysterious blonde was living in his beach house.

And four...he found her just too damn attractive. He didn't need this right now. The timing stunk, but he simply couldn't deny wanting to help her. And he simply couldn't deny it being too soon after his divorce for anything else.

He wasn't ready for a rebound romance. At any other time in his unmarried life, he would have jumped at the chance to get to know Meg Thompson—intimately. But for now, he would have to settle with helping her through this problem with her car. Then in a few days he would be gone. He'd never see her again.

He continued to stare at her. Her sleep softened features made his abdomen clutch in want. He silently swore. It wasn't that long since he and Crystal enjoyed a healthy sex life. Eight months wasn't that long a time. But when he looked at Meg, he suddenly felt seventeen again and wanting it like he'd never wanted it before.

He ran all ten fingers through the long lengths of his hair, then ran his palms over his face. Closing his eyes, he shook his head as if he could erase all that had happened in the past two days. As if it would erase the ache he felt in his groin at that moment.

What in the hell prompted him to enter her bedroom?

Turning toward the door, he'd all but decided to leave her alone, let her work out her own problems, but she whimpered softly in her sleep. He stopped stone still, took a deep breath, and turned to look at her one last time.

She rolled over to face the other side of the bed.

Quietly, Smyth stepped to the bed, positioned one knee on the mattress at her back and touched her shoulder. Oh, hell.

"Meg," he whispered.

She mumbled something softly then tossed her head toward him.

He touched her shoulder again and shook it a little this time. "Meg," he whispered a little louder. "Wake up."

Slowly, her face turned toward his. Within an instant, her eyes fluttered open. Jerking her entire body upright, Meg let out a shriek and scrambled away. Clawing at the sheets, she bolted to the opposite side of the bed, her face frozen in fear, her eyes wide in horror.

"No!" she screamed. "Go away."

She'd awakened too quickly, he thought, and he

frightened her. Berating himself for his stupidity, he called her name softly and stepped around the end of the bed. "It's me, Smyth. I'm sorry I startled you."

Meg backed up against the wall and stared at him with unseeing eyes. Smyth stepped closer, noting how she trembled.

"Please," she whimpered. "Please. No. Not this time."

Smyth stopped. *Not this time?* He realized she was still asleep. Or partially asleep.

Puzzled, he reached out to touch her arm. "Meg. It's Smyth."

She jerked back from his touch. Smyth watched as she cowered against the wall of the small room. Not fully understanding, but with a small niggling feeling of awareness, Smyth stepped to the bedside table and turned on the light. He saw the tears streaming down her face.

He stood frozen for a moment, watching her. Her chest heaved in fright as she gulped in air. Her eyes were wide and then blinked several times as if to clear the haze from them.

Smyth held back waiting for a more appropriate moment to approach her. When at last it seemed she'd finally realized who he was, she brought her hands up to her face, drew in a ragged sob, and slid down the wall to the floor.

Cautiously stepping forward, he crouched beside her and ran a finger along her cheek.

She flinched slightly at his touch and he pulled the finger away.

"Meg," he whispered. "I'm sorry. I didn't mean to startle you. Are you okay?"

She nodded slowly, her hands still covering her face. After a few seconds and another ragged breath she lowered her hands and revealed her drawn face, closed eyes, and wrinkled brow. She sat fully on the floor, her legs stretched out in front of her. Her bunched up T-shirt revealed a pair of white, silk panties. As Smyth crouched there beside her, his eyes focused on her narrow hipbone and the long, puckering scar starting on the right side of her abdomen pointing toward her right hip.

A strong desire to trail a gentle, soothing touch down that scar pulled at him. But he kept his hand away. Dragging his gaze from the ugly scar, he sought her face, a question forming within him. What in the hell had happened to her? He looked at her fully, her face drawn and tilted toward the ceiling, her eyes still closed. Tiny crow's feet radiated from the corner of each eye where she clamped them painfully shut.

Smyth settled beside her, his back propped against the wall. "You want to talk about it?" he questioned softly, not really knowing what he had asked.

Slowly, she opened her eyes. Shaking her head, she stared straight ahead. The tears stopped now. "No," she breathed.

Smyth looked away, then let his head rest against the wall. There was more to this than a simple startled awakening. He knew that. But he decided not to push it.

"What are you doing in my room?"

Her words were hushed and drawn. Smyth dragged his gaze away from the ceiling and looked at her. Eyes swollen, hair disheveled, lower lip quivering, she was still beautiful. He wanted to ask who had hurt her. Wanted to know about that scar. Wanted to haul her up in his arms and comfort her.

He knew, perhaps sensed, that whoever the bastard was he had caused her harm at one time or another. Could that be the reason she didn't want to be found?

"I have a plan," he replied, dismissing any other thoughts or questions until later. "A plan to help you get rid of your car. Do you want to hear it?"

After a moment of searching his face, she meekly answered, "Yes."

****

The night blanketed them in silence as they drove over the bridge and onto the mainland.

Meg stared straight ahead into the darkness, not

wanting to look at him, afraid that if he gave her a sympathetic or questioning look she would lose control. She didn't want his sympathy. Or anyone else's. Never had. She guessed that explained why she'd stayed so long with Bradford.

She'd never sought sympathy from anyone. Therefore no one knew her predicament. Except Rudy.

After Smyth explained his idea, he'd left her alone in the room. She'd dressed quickly, then without another thought, left the cottage with him. Now, after driving the past thirty minutes, an awkward calm surrounded them. Meg couldn't be sure whether it really surrounded them or just her.

She'd told him to drive her car, not trusting her still shaking hands. As he'd rounded the rear bumper, she pretended she didn't notice when he broke out the little light that illuminated the license plate in the back. All at once she wondered just why he would go to such lengths to help her.

Shivering against the night chill, Meg shifted her gaze and stared out the passenger window. She felt grateful that he hadn't asked her anything about the scene in the bedroom and she hadn't offered any explanation, either. She wasn't ready. Didn't really feel like she needed to. She didn't have any type of relationship with this man, her landlord, actually. She would see him for a few days and then he'd leave and she'd never see him again. And come August, she'd probably be ready to find somewhere else to live. As long as it was along the coast.

She'd come to love the ocean too much. Had come to relish the peace that the powerful breakers against the sand gave her. Perhaps she'd go to Maine. She'd always dreamed of New England. Or Nova Scotia, an entirely different country altogether.

Would Bradford ever expect her to leave the country? No. Bradford never expected she'd leave the house. Anxious pinpricks began low in her abdomen and traveled up to her chest.

Bradford. What was he doing now? How close was he to finding her?

She had to keep moving. A new plan, yes. No more than a few months in one place, until Bradford was behind bars, or she truly believed he'd leave her alone. Then just before she left, she'd call Rudy and find out the status of things in Chicago. Then she'd be gone again. It was the only way.

Smyth looked straight ahead. Every once in a while an oncoming car's headlights lit his profile. She leaned her head back against the seat and she watched him in silence. A handsome man with tanned skin and sharp features, he reminded her of summer and water and a carefree lifestyle. Like what she imagined a California surfer would look like.

His rich brown shaggy hair, maybe a little too long, flowed over his head and ears perfectly. She actually couldn't imagine it any other way. Never could she picture him in a short, precision cut hairstyle. Not like any man she'd ever known. His brow ridged across his forehead, dark eyebrows knitted together as if in contemplation. He seemed deep in thought. She wished she knew about what.

Would he think of her? Was he wondering about how he'd gotten himself hooked up with a crazy woman? A woman living in his house? Any other man would have booted her out long ago. But Smyth? For some reason he decided to let her stay. And help her. But why?

Then Smyth turned to look at her and she closed her eyes. Jostling against the seat, her head bounced back and forth as he turned the vehicle. And as she felt the waves of sleep waft over her, she also felt his lingering gaze upon her face.

****

Smyth pulled in the drive and coasted the Honda to the garage door of the house. He killed the engine, then for another moment, sat looking straight ahead. Slowly, he turned toward Meg. Even though she slept silently beside him, curled into a ball on the passenger seat, he was amazingly aware of her. He hesitated waking her, not knowing what she'd do this time. Over the past forty-five minutes, he'd had plenty of time to think about how she'd reacted when he woke her earlier.

He still hadn't figured it out, but he knew she was frightened beyond what most people would have been given the same situation. He couldn't dwell on that. Right now, they had another task to accomplish. One that he suspected might buy her some time—and perhaps, security.

He got out of the car, walked toward the garage, and unlocked it. He threw open the door, the mechanism grinding and squeaking as if it needed a good dose of WD-40. *Too long since he'd been here.* He felt a little guilty. He pulled the string hanging down from a light in the center of the building. A shaft of light bathed the room. Smyth glanced at the older model Mercedes SL parked on the right side of the garage, then let his fingers glide along its side as he walked toward the Honda.

Meg watched him from inside the car. He'd told her a little of his idea. He had a car at a house in Elizabeth City. They would store her Honda there until the heat was off and she could borrow his other car. He failed to mention that his other car was a Mercedes. Just exactly who was Smyth Parker?

Leaving the driver's side door partially open, Smyth sat and glanced over to Meg.

"Hi," she said softly when his eyes met hers.

After a moment, he replied. "Hi."

"Guess I fell asleep."

Smyth nodded. "Yeah. I didn't want to wake you. I didn't want..."

His voice trailed off. He looked out the windshield.

Meg watched his profile. "You didn't know if I'd go ballistic again, huh?"

Turning back toward her, Meg caught his gaze. A hint of a smile played over his lips.

"Well, actually..."

Reaching over, Meg touched his cheek with the tips of

her fingers, smoothing over the stubble growing there. "That was sweet of you," she whispered. At the touch of her fingertips to his skin, she felt frazzled. Why did she do that? Jerking her fingers back and laying her hands in her lap, she sat against the passenger door. "I mean..." she amended nervously, "Thanks. I'm not sure I—"

"It's okay," he interrupted.

His eyes played over her face. Meg watched, wondering how it might feel to kiss him.

Wondering how those firm, thin lips might feel against hers.

She nodded. "Okay." Glancing out of the car toward the garage, she added, "So, are we here?"

Smyth slammed the door shut. "Yes. We're here."

He started the car, put it in gear and allowed it to roll forward into the garage. He killed the engine and they sat in silence. The yellow glow from the light bulb overhead cast shadows around the room.

Smyth turned back to Meg. "Do you mind if we go in the house a minute? I haven't been here for a while. I probably need to check around just to make sure everything is okay."

"Sure." Meg nodded and reached for the car door.

Smyth exited his side of the car and then lowered the garage door. He led Meg through a side door, flipped on the light switch, then continued on through a large laundry room into a hall pantry. Only a few canned goods graced the shelves along with an abundance of cobwebs. Smyth batted one away with his hand as they passed into the kitchen.

"Guess it's been longer than I thought," he remarked as he found another light switch.

Meg followed into a spacious and, she suspected, one time cheerful kitchen that had lost its cheerfulness long ago. An old, oak table sat in the center of the room. Dull white cabinets hung drearily from the walls. Yellow floral wallpaper panels, dingy from neglect, peeled randomly around the room. The ruffled curtains drooped against the windows, having lost their starched stiffness some time back. More cobwebs decorated every nook and cranny and evidence indicated that a family of mice had taken up residence in one of the open kitchen drawers.

Smyth turned to her after throwing his gaze around the room. "I've been away too long. I shouldn't have let it get like this."

"Whose house is this?" Meg questioned.

"Mine."

He turned his back to her and stepped up to an old kitchen cupboard similar to one her Grandma Rose had back in Indiana. It had a porcelain work top, a copper flour bin, and its original porcelain drawer and door pulls. She watched as Smyth opened and closed doors, staring into it as if in memory. Finally, he ran a hand along the dusty wood and turned to her.

"She used to make biscuits here every Sunday morning." He paused, staring just past her.

"She didn't have to. During the rest of the week Ida cooked. But on Sunday, the kitchen was hers. I miss that. I miss her sometimes like crazy."

His gaze dropped to the old oak table. "Grandpa used to sit right there, at the end. When I was a kid I sat next to him. Mom sat across from me, Dad sat at the opposite end. That's when I was really young."

"Where did Becky sit?"

Smyth quickly looked up to meet her gaze. "She didn't. Becky never lived in this house."

"Oh," Meg said softly, averting her gaze. She thought she saw pain in his and it momentarily troubled her.

He paced the room, then stopped at the window looking out over the street. "My mother died when I was four. Cancer. Dad and Grandpa and I lived here for three more years until Dad married Jenna, then we moved out. Becky was born the next year. Grandpa lived here until he died two years ago. He left the house to me. The house in Nags Head, too."

"Oh," Meg repeated. She felt like an intruder. There

was something about this house that haunted him. Perhaps the remembrance of his mother? There were obviously happy times here.

"Where is your father now?"

When he swung around to face her, their gazes connected. "Dead. He and Jenna died in a plane crash over Guatemala a year before Grandpa died. They were on one of those amateur archeological excursions, you know? Anyway, there was an engine malfunction and the plane went down. It was days before they were found."

"So Becky is all the family you have left?"

He paused. "Yes."

"You must be close."

He nodded. "I don't see her as much as I want. My work..."

Meg paused at his hesitance to go on. He clearly didn't want her to know about his work.

She nervously broke the connection between them and crossed the room to an arch between the kitchen and dining room. Smyth passed her, entering the room first, then reached inside for the switch on the wall. A chandelier threw muted prisms of light through its dusty hanging crystals.

"Why don't you live here?" she asked.

His back was to her and she watched as he shrugged his shoulders.

"I did. For a while. I like the ocean. I'm gone too much. Too many memories," he said, sounding evasive.

"What about Becky?"

He turned and smiled at her then. "She's as much a beach bum as I am. When Dad and Jenna died, she got a pretty hefty sum of money from insurance and inheritance. She's got herself a nice little house on the beach in Kill Devil Hills. She knows if she needed it, I'd let her live here. But as of right now, she's content where she is."

"What about you?" Meg watched his face as the smile slowly faded. His eyes grew dark as he searched her face.

"What about me?"

"Content? Where you are?"

"Yes."

"Then why don't you live in the beach house very much? And come to think about it, where do you live when you're not there?"

Smyth stared blankly at her for a moment. "Business," he replied.

Meg knew from the tone of his voice that she shouldn't ask again. In fact, she figured that she'd gotten much too personal throughout the entire conversation. Perhaps she'd better lay off in spite of the urgency in her to know more. She needed to know that her trust in him wasn't misplaced.

Meg stepped away, backed into the kitchen, and then turned away from him. "Oh. Of course."

Feeling his gaze on her back, it took all the effort Meg could gather to not turn and look at him again. She didn't need to know any more about him. She didn't need to know *anything* about him. He was just a man who had dropped into her life for a brief moment. No need to make it anything more than that.

"Let me check the rest of the house. I'll be back in a minute," he said, his voice fading as he started down the hallway.

Several minutes later Smyth returned. Meg quietly followed him back to the garage. He walked Meg to the passenger side of the Mercedes. After opening the garage door, he slid into the driver's seat.

The Mercedes' engine ground to a slow start.

Without a word, he backed the car out, then went to lock the garage. When he returned, he fumbled with one of the keys on his key chain. "Give me your hand," he ordered, his brown eyes locked with hers. Taken aback at the urgency of his voice, Meg hesitantly held out her hand.

He took her hand in his, placed a key in the center of her palm, and curled her fingers around it.

She watched both his hands fold over hers and felt a small tremor start somewhere deep within her. *What is he doing? What does he want from me?* She swallowed a huge lump that suddenly formed in her throat, took a deep breath, and then looked into his eyes.

"It's to the house. In case you ever need it," he whispered, his eyes voicing more than she cared to know, but yet, not telling her enough.

Meg shook her head. "I don't think—"

Reaching up, Smyth placed an index finger on her lips, silencing her. "Sh. Just keep it. You never know."

Chapter Six

According to the clock on her nightstand, it was nearly noon. Meg groaned and turned her face into the pillow. It was the first morning since living in Smyth's house that she'd slept late. Most mornings she rose with the sun, ready to face every minute of her newfound freedom.

But, of course, last night she'd stayed up through the wee hours.

Groaning again, she rolled onto her back, flung her arms to each side, and stared at the ceiling. She remained that way for several minutes, thinking over the situation from the night before. When she couldn't find any rhyme or reason to the events that had occurred since yesterday afternoon, she sighed and got up.

Plodding across the floor, she drew on a robe and proceeded toward the bathroom just outside her door. She paused, listening. No noise or movement emanated from behind Smyth's closed door just across the hall—or in the house for that matter. The bathroom door stood wide open. *Perhaps he's gone for the day. Either that or he's still asleep.*

She took a quick shower, dressed in shorts and a T-shirt with her damp hair loose down her back, and casually headed toward the kitchen.

She spotted Smyth at the kitchen table looking like he'd just gotten out of bed. Hair disheveled, face unshaven, wearing only a pair of swim trunks, he leaned over the table and brought his coffee cup to his lips. His gaze lifted when she entered the room. It took a concentrated effort to keep from staring at him. He looked just too...sexy. Startled at that thought, Meg stopped for a second, then hurriedly stepped to the counter to pour a cup of coffee.

With her back to him, she took the time to gather her senses. Looking at Smyth right now, like he'd just risen from bed, seemed somehow too personal...too involved.

Like they were a married couple getting up after sleeping in on a lazy Saturday morning. Too cozy. Too comfortable.

Hell, Bradford never looked that relaxed in the mornings. She didn't think she'd ever seen him unshaven. She rarely saw him before he showered and dressed, even on weekends, unless he wanted her. Then it didn't matter. Nothing mattered but what he wanted.

As she brought the coffeepot to her cup, she noticed the way her hands shook. *Lack of sleep, Meg, that's all it is.* She gathered her determination and poured her cup half full. *What's wrong with you?* Her eyes closed as she faced the wall.

He makes me nervous. Ever since he touched his finger to my lips last night.

Taking a deep breath, Meg held it for a second, then let it go very slowly, trying to quell her anxiety. That must be it, she was sure. He made her nervous. And the fact that Smyth sat there at the table looking sexy as hell didn't help matters any.

Abruptly, she turned away from the wall and stepped around the table. Without looking at him, she said, "I think I'll have mine on the porch."

"It's hot out there today."

Meg stopped. *It's hot in here.*

"Stay and talk to me."

Resigned, Meg bit her lower lip and turned. Her gaze met his, then she slowly set her coffee cup on the table, and pulled out a chair directly across from him.

Smyth pushed his coffee cup back and crossed his arms on the table edge. "Sleep well?"

Meg shrugged. "Well enough."

"Good."

Silence fell between them. Meg sipped at her coffee, staring at the table. Smyth watched her.

Finally, Meg pushed back her cup and looked at him. "Smyth, about the key..."

"Right. I thought about that last night. I guess I need to write down the address for you.

And if you ever should need to stay there, let Becky

know, too. She can always give you directions again if you can't remember." He turned to a drawer behind him and reached inside for paper and pencil.

"That's not what I mean. I'm going to give it back to you."

Acting as though he didn't hear her, he kept writing on the paper. When he looked up, he slid it across the table. "Here. Keep it. Put it in your purse with the key. Like I said, you never know."

Meg shook her head. She rose and took two steps back, leaving the paper where it was.

"Thank you, but no. I'll go get the key." She turned to leave.

Smyth caught up to her within seconds. He lightly grasped her arm.

"Meg, stop. Let's talk about this."

She turned toward him. "There's nothing to talk about."

"I think there is. I want you to use my house if you need to."

"Why?"

Smyth narrowed his gaze, his face showing disbelief at her question. "Why?"

Facing him fully now, Meg continued, "You know nothing about me. Why are you doing this? Letting me stay here, hiding my car? I don't understand. I could be one of America's Ten Most Wanted for all you know. Why do you trust me?"

He dropped his hand and crossed his arms over his bare chest. He glanced out the windows at the ocean, took a deep breath, and then exhaled slowly. When he turned back toward her, Meg wasn't exactly sure what she was going to hear.

"Actually, Meg, there are several reasons. I trust you're telling me the truth, what little you've told me. Perhaps I shouldn't, but I do. And the reason I do is more because of your actions and what I've observed about you rather than what you've told me. For the simple fact that you're hiding from someone, I want to help you. But last night...last night when I woke you, that was something else."

"You startled me, that's all it was. I was dreaming." Meg stepped back from him, recalling the scene in her bedroom. She suddenly felt cold. She cupped both her elbows into her palms and glanced away from him. Abruptly it all flashed back into her consciousness.

She had been dreaming. And Bradford's angry face, his brutal hands, his threats were there, too. Inwardly, she cringed, trying not to let the tremor force its way out of her body.

"There's more to it than that. That wasn't startled, Meg. That was sheer terror. You were frightened. And I'd venture to say that it wasn't the first time you've awakened to that fear."

"This is ridiculous," she threw back nervously. "I don't know what you're talking about."

Turning, she took three brisk steps toward the hallway.

He followed her, reached out and touched her shoulder.

She whirled. "Don't touch me!"

Immediately, Smyth lowered his hand. Meg had half a notion to spring away from him, run down the hall, and lock her bedroom door. But she didn't. She simply stood and glared at him, folding her arms across her chest.

"Who hurt you, Meg?"

She said nothing, choosing to turn in the opposite direction and stare out the windows at the ocean with her back to him. Her body grew rigid and tense. After a few seconds, she realized he had moved behind her. "His name was...is Bradford," she whispered a moment later.

"Did he hurt you?" he asked softly.

She didn't answer. He edged a little closer.

"Does he have something to do with that scar on your hip? I saw it last night. I didn't mean to, your shirt rode up and it was just there. Did he do that to you? Are there more? What has he done to you?"

Again, she responded with silence. After a moment,

she felt him gently touch her shoulder again. She stifled a tremor, or tried to, but she suspected he noticed. She attempted to stand perfectly still, afraid that if she turned around she would lose control.

Then, he turned her around to face him.

Meg knew she was close to tears. Her eyes felt moist, but for some reason she couldn't cry. She didn't want to think about how she looked, knowing she had screwed her face into a painful expression.

"Meg, talk to me," he whispered.

She shook her head and looked to the floor. "I don't...talk to people...about it."

"Talk to me," he whispered again. "Get it out. For your own good, you've got to get it out."

She shook her head.

"I'm leaving in a couple of days. You don't ever have to see me again. Get it out now. Maybe I can help." He tried to keep his voice low and non-threatening.

"No."

In what looked like defeat, Smyth huffed out a short breath, glanced to the ceiling and then back at her. She could tell he didn't want to force her, but also that he didn't want to let this issue go.

But could she trust him? Could she trust any man again?

Carefully, slowly, he grasped her chin with his fingers. And she let him. She didn't know which of them was more surprised when she let him angle her face up to his.

"If you can't talk, then cry, Meg. Just cry. I'm here."

She wanted to jerk away. She wanted to bolt and run as far away as she could. But he held her in his strong grip and somehow, in that grip, she found her own strength. She knew she couldn't go anywhere.

One small tear fell from the corner of her eye. Smyth reached up and caught it on his fingertip. That one simple gesture was all she needed.

"It's okay, honey. Let it all out. You don't have to tell me anything. Just cry."

Meg squeezed her eyes shut tight and when she did, her tears finally fell. Smyth cupped her face with one hand and pulled her closer with the other. His palms were warm and comforting and suddenly, she wanted to be closer to him. Much closer. As their bodies met, she exhaled with one long tremor and collapsed against him. She melted and the sobs came.

Smyth folded his arms around her and let her cry. He held her and that was all she needed at this moment in time.

Safe. So safe. Inside, she felt ripped apart. Outside, she felt warm and secure. She knew she was crying uncontrollably, clinging to him, clutching, but she didn't care. For once, she didn't care. And for the first time in days, she half admitted how frightened she really felt.

His voice, low and soft, soothed her. His fingers played over her back, easing her tense, aching muscles. His fingertips on her face and raking through her hair relaxed her. And she still cried.

"It's okay, honey," he crooned over and over. "You're safe now. You're safe."

He didn't know anything about her, but he sensed that she needed to feel safe. He made her feel safe.

After a moment, he whispered, "Let's sit." He moved with her toward the couch. "Let's sit here and look out over the ocean and I'll hold you, okay?"

She nodded into his chest.

"You like it here, don't you?"

"Yes," she squeaked, the sobs slowing, her breathing returning to normal.

They sat on the couch facing the ocean and he gathered her into him. He held her there and it seemed so natural, so right. She didn't know why, but it did.

"Yeah...me, too," he whispered into her hair. She wasn't sure, but she thought he might have planted a small kiss on the top of her head.

Meg tucked her legs up under her and wrapped her arms about his waist. Her breathing slowed, the sobs subsided, and she felt so safe...so secure.

"Smyth?" she breathed against him, hesitating to continue. "Bradford is...my husband. I left him, filed for divorce. He doesn't know where I am."

She felt his chin lower to the top of her head. "It's okay, Meg." He tightened his hold on her.

"If he finds me," she continued softly, "he'll kill me."

"No one's going to kill you."

Sitting up, Meg faced him, her gaze penetrating. "You don't understand. He will kill me.

He's told me so a thousand times. If I ever left him, he said he'd hunt me down until he found me." She started to go on, to tell him of her suspicions, of his...involvement, but thought better of it.

Smyth sighed deeply and pulled her closer to him. "Everything's okay, Meg," he said softly against her hair. "Go to sleep if you want. I'm not going to let anything happen to you. You're safe, Meg. I've got you."

"I wanted you to know." Her voice hushed. Meg closed her eyes tight and burrowed into him. Their bodies shifted closer. Within minutes, she and Smyth lay side by side facing each other on the couch, Meg against the back, Smyth's body protecting her. She found herself falling into an exhausted sleep.

Safe, she thought, as she drifted off. So safe...

****

The banging on the front door woke them. Startled, Meg's eyes flew open. Lying side by side and face to face with Smyth, she noticed his eyes were shut tight. She shook him.

"Someone's at the door," she said softly.

The banging started again. "Smyth!" A woman called from the other side.

Meg watched his eyelids flutter. "The door, Smyth. Get up!" She pushed at him, his eyes opened. The door rattled with the banging. Both of them scrambled off the couch.

"What's going on?" Smyth rubbed his hands over his face and raked his fingers through his hair.

"Someone's at the door. A woman."

"What?" He turned toward the door.

"Answer it," Meg returned nervously, pointing to the door.

"Smyth, dammit. Are you in there? I see the Jeep outside!"

The breath whooshed out of Smyth's lungs and he headed for the door. He threw Meg a backward glance. "It's Becky."

Meg felt her shoulders drop. She should have recognized her voice. The door opened and Smyth whisked his sister inside.

"What in the world took you so long?" Becky eyed her brother as she stalked into the room. "You'd think you were in the throes of passion or..."

Meg watched as Becky tossed her gaze about the room, finally resting on her. She stopped abruptly, threw Smyth a wry grin and then glanced back to Meg. Knowing she was probably a mess, eyes swollen, hair in a state of disarray, she figured Becky was drawing her own conclusions as to why her brother had taken his time answering the door.

"Oh! Well, I guess I have interrupted something."

Smyth headed across the room toward the kitchen area. "Don't be a fool, Becky. We had a late night last night. Just got up." He grabbed a bottle of water from the refrigerator, then tipped it to his lips to drink.

Becky sidled Meg another look.

Meg smiled shyly. Several years younger than Smyth, Becky was petite, very tanned, and had the same dark brown hair as his, cut short in a pixie haircut. Slowly, her small, bow lips smiled back at Meg.

"He's right, Becky. I had car trouble last night. We didn't get in until early this morning. We slept late, that's all."

"So is that why Grandpa's Mercedes is parked by the Jeep?" She turned to Smyth.

He nodded. "Yes."

Meg didn't look across the room to him, she knew

instinctively that Smyth turned and was staring at her.

"Oh," Becky repeated. Plopping herself down on the couch, she crossed her legs, rested her arms along the top, threw back her head and closed her eyes. "It's been one helluva day. I've got to talk to the two of you."

Only then did Meg glance at Smyth. She watched as he sat down across from her. Their gazes caught and held.

Becky raised her head and opened her eyes. "Well, I did it. It was hard, but I found you another house, Meg."

Meg swallowed and tried to hold in her anxiety. Finally, she looked at Smyth. It was his call. She didn't want to leave, but it was up to him. His gaze held hers for a moment.

"She's staying here, Becky."

"But you said..."

"I changed my mind, I told you that," he said impatiently. "She's staying here." Smyth never broke the connection between them.

Becky looked from her brother to Meg. She knew Smyth's sister had to be wondering what was going on, but Meg didn't care. *I'm safe here. That's all it is, Becky. I'm safe. He won't let anything happen to me.*

Smyth broke the connection and looked to his sister. "I'm going to be gone in a few days, Becky. After I get my business taken care of in Elizabeth City, I have to get back to Portsmouth.

You know that. She can stay here. I don't need this place. I probably won't be back for months."

He glanced quickly, nervously, back at Meg, and then rose. "She can stay as long as she wants."

"But what about the..."

"My business, Becky," he interrupted loudly, "will be taken care of before I leave here in two days. Two days and I won't be back for a while."

Meg watched him turn and walk briskly toward the back of the house. He was agitated and she didn't know why. He reappeared with a towel. "You ladies stay here and visit. I'm going for a swim," he said brusquely.

Meg noticed that when he left, he didn't look at her.

****

For the longest time Meg watched from the porch. With her legs propped on the railing, she searched the shoreline from north to south, and then let her eyes scan the horizon. She didn't see him anywhere. Since he'd left three hours earlier, Becky not long after that, Meg had the house to herself. Time weighed on her hands. Too much. It allowed her mind to wander. It gave her time to think, worry. And to be disgusted with herself.

Why did she ever think Smyth Parker would be anything more than what reality dictated?

Her landlord, of sorts. And did she consider him to be more? Did a remote possibility exist that there could be more? She didn't know. Confusion ran rampant. Her life held no room for anyone right now. She hadn't even fully rid herself of Bradford. No way could she picture herself with anyone else.

Smyth felt safe. He provided her with a sense of security. That was all. He also made her feel happy. But maybe that feeling was attributed to this place. She'd been happy ever since she'd arrived on the islands. Safe. That was it. He just made her feel safe.

Meg closed her eyes against the current of emotion welling up inside her. There was a lot more to it than that. He made her feel alive...almost sexy. He gave her a reason to feel good about herself.

But she couldn't rely on him to make her feel good, or sexy, or safe, could she? She had to rely on herself. Only. There couldn't be anyone else. She couldn't risk anyone else suffering Bradford's wrath. Couldn't risk giving of herself like that again.

But Smyth wasn't going to be around anyway. He'd all but said that. He'd made it quite clear. He would be gone in two days. Two days. Then she would be alone. Blessedly alone. He didn't want to hang around and make her feel safe anymore. He already regretted what he'd done for her. He couldn't wait to leave. How could she ever expect anything else?

Meg opened her eyes to stare at the blue sky. His departure was imminent. She would be alone. In his house. He would leave and all her security would go with him.

And with that thought, her fear returned.

Rising slowly, she gradually eased the kinks out of her back and legs, ignoring the uneasiness that settled over her. She leaned against the rail to steady herself and watched the breakers pound the deserted shore. A lingering breeze lifted her hair now and again from her shoulders then wistfully left her. Reluctantly, she turned and went inside.

Chapter Seven

The vase crashed against the papered wall. Upon impact, it shattered into thick chunks and tiny slivers of delicate cut glass. Water ran down the intertwined miniature rose and ivy pattern of the textured paper in rivulets as gravity pulled it toward the floor. The huge red roses in the vase fell in a clump on the Oriental rug.

Crystal Parker glared at the man who stood across from her in her dining room, her chest heaving after hurling the vase just past his head.

"Damn him! He's not going to get away with this! I tell you, Matt, if it's the last thing I do, I'll see that Smyth owns up to his responsibilities and gives this baby what's due him. This child is a rightful Parker heir and I intend to see that he has a piece of the Parker pie."

Turning away, she cautiously made her way toward the kitchen door, ignoring the puddle and mess on the floor to her right. Then she turned back to face Matt, just a few feet away. Tall and lean, with long jet black hair and equally black eyes, she knew he watched her every step of the way.

Every time she looked at him she wanted to jump him. It had been that way since the beginning. He had that gaunt, hollow-cheeked look that she loved in a man—almost a cross between rock star and vampire. Vulnerable and easily manipulated, she could get him to do anything for her. And this latest information about Smyth's living arrangements would prove to be very beneficial. Her eyes lowered to his crotch. She knew just how to thank him.

With her hands placed firmly on her hips, she watched his eyes. His gaze traveled down her body, thin except for her abdomen full with child five months along. He gazed hungrily at her.

"You are okay with this, aren't you?" she queried him, narrowing her eyes into tiny slits.

She faced him fully, then brushed one long strand of brunette hair away from her face. "Matt?"

He shook himself. "Yeah, right. Of course, Crystal."

A slow smile traveled across her lips. "Come here," she returned seductively.

She kept the connection with his eyes as he lazily sauntered toward her. When he reached her, he pulled her into him. Crystal threw back her head at the impact and broadened her sly grin.

"We're going to be rich," she whispered as she brought her lips to his ear.

Matt roughly threaded his fingers into her hair and held her face inches from his. One corner of his mouth turned up. His eyes twinkled.

"Yeah," he growled.

Her fingers plunged deep inside the waistband of his jeans. Matt groaned.

Chapter Eight

"Just where in the hell is she?" The sound of her own voice momentarily startled Rudy.

She stared at the opposite wall of her office. "Maybe I should put a P.I. on it." *Or maybe I should just try and find her myself.* Sighing, she closed her eyes and simultaneously rubbed her tired temples.

But she knew leaving Chicago wouldn't solve her problems. In fact, it would probably intensify them. Putting Bradford off had become more difficult. She'd made a mistake, a big mistake, a few days ago when she had let him have her. His continued sexual innuendoes sickened her and she was disgusted with herself. And now he frightened her more than she cared to admit. He knew she and Megan were close and he had every right to believe that she would know where Megan had gone.

Except that Megan lied to her. Megan hadn't done anything she'd told Rudy she would do.

The ease in which Bradford accepted that she didn't know where Meg had chosen to hide was a bit disconcerting in itself. What did he know, or suspect? What else could he do?

The daily papers finally told the tale, running lie after lie concerning Megan's whereabouts. Bradford played the sympathy card again. According to the papers, Megan had been missing for days now, possibly kidnapped. And poor Bradford, playing the grieving husband, appeared devastated.

And interspersed with news concerning the kidnappers' demands—all carefully orchestrated by Bradford and his organization and puzzling the Chicago police department and the FBI to no end—were suggestions of Bradford's political aspirations.

He tossed in all the chips, risking it all in hopes of

garnering support from his future constituents. And he was still using Megan to do it.

Rudy expected any day to learn the news of Megan's reported death. She prayed every night that Bradford hadn't somehow accomplished that feat on his own. Megan hadn't called for quite some time.

There were times Rudy questioned the sanity of seeing through the plan Megan devised.

But in the end, there wasn't a choice. Rudy had to help Megan get out.

Pure and innocent, Rudy knew Megan wouldn't have been able to stand up to Bradford's violence much longer. She also knew Bradford counted on Megan to crack under the pressure and forever be a charm on his arm. He'd needed her as a political pawn, the good to his bad, so people might forget about his tainted past. Megan knew Bradford held her as a sort of hostage in the marriage and Rudy knew that she, herself, was in too deep. But perhaps because she cared so much for Megan as a friend, and because she felt guilty about...things that had happened, she wanted to see Megan get her freedom.

Even at the cost of her own.

Even though, every day of her life from here on out, she would regret her actions and her relationship with Bradford Thomas. But at this point, nothing else could be done. She had to ride the wave until it hit the shore, then hope she could salvage a small ripple to build her life upon again.

There would come a time, she knew, when she'd have to take matters in her own hands and deal with it. And she wasn't looking forward to it.

"Megan," she breathed, "hang in there." For the first time in a long, long time Rudy wanted to cry and the thought terrified her. "Please, please, still be alive."

****

The next morning, Rudy watched the familiar scenario unfold on Sycamore Street. The sickening-sweet scene at Bradford's front door made her want to puke. After he'd left, she waited a full fifteen minutes before leaving her car parked down the street and approaching Bradford's front door. Now, she stared at the girl standing in the doorway of Bradford's house.

"You were supposed to have been out of here a week ago."

"Get out," Cindy spat back. "I did what you and her wanted, now leave me alone."

Cindy reached for the door to slam it shut, but Rudy stepped inside the doorframe, taking the brunt of the slam with her shoulder. She winced, then eased past the partially open door and into the foyer.

"I don't think so, missy," she added sternly. "We've got something else to talk about.

And it has nothing to do with Megan."

"Oh, yeah? What in the hell would you and I have to talk about?"

Rudy paused for a minute, looking the young girl straight in the eyes. She couldn't be a day over twenty, Rudy thought. Bradford should be shot. "You and I have a lot in common, you know that?"

"Like how?" Cindy rolled her eyes. Smacking her lips, her gum popped indifferently.

Rudy huffed. "We both got suckered by Bradford Thomas. He's irresistible, isn't he, dear? Those hands, what he does with his mouth...best lover I ever had." Rudy narrowed her eyes. A slight pounding began in her right temple. She watched Cindy's eyes widen in surprised anger. "In fact, I had him just the other day."

Rudy experienced a second's satisfaction at seeing the hurt that crossed the girl's face.

Maybe if she stung her feelings enough, she'd get out of there. Maybe at least her life wouldn't be screwed up, unlike Megan's or her own. "Oh, surely you didn't think you were the only one."

Rudy tossed her a Saccharin smile.

"I'm the one in his bed, in his house."

"Oh, honey," Rudy laughed, "Bradford doesn't need a

bed or a house, fucking in public places turns him on more than fucking in someplace as boring as a bed. The last time he fucked me, we nearly hung from the goddamned chandelier in his office. And the door was left partially ajar. I think that was Tuesday. Or maybe Wednesday. I'm not sure."

Rudy brought her hand to her chin in thought. "No, Wednesday was when I fucked him while sitting on his lap in the corner booth of a dark, sleazy restaurant up town. Right between the antipasto and the linguini. It was hell getting the marinara out of my linen skirt, but, what the hell, a good fuck is a good fuck, no matter how messy it gets, right?"

The snippet of a woman glared at Rudy. "Get the hell out of my house."

"*Your* house! Gee, now that's really funny. If you think this is your house, honey, then you've really got a lot to learn about Bradford Thomas. Bradford doesn't let his women claim possession to anything, unless it's his dick in their mouths, and only when he wants it, of course."

Cindy screwed her face up in anger and pushed Rudy towards the door. "Get out!"

"Oh, I'm going. Let me give you a little advice though, before I do. Never serve him frozen orange juice." Rudy watched her eyes widen.

She brushed back a lock of hair from Cindy's cheek, revealing the telltale, fading bruise there. Cindy jerked away.

"Too late, huh? Yeah, well, we all learned the hard way. Remember, fresh squeezed, Cindy. He loves fresh squeezed. In fact, he demands it. Nothing but the finest for Bradford Thomas. And don't order his shirt collars too heavily starched. Or forget to shower before you make love or to shave your legs. Not to mention to never look at another man should you ever go out together. Those are all no-no's too, dear."

Rudy turned toward the door, then halted and looked once more into the frightened girl's face. Cindy's expression said she knew exactly what Rudy was talking about. "If you know what's good for you, little girl, you'll turn tail and run the very first chance you get. I mean it.

Just think of it this way, it's good while it lasts, but when Bradford Thomas gets finished with you, he'll toss you aside like so much used tissue. And believe me, there will be somebody younger and prettier and firmer come along one of these days and you'll be out the door." Rudy paused then, and stared the young woman straight in the eyes. "If he doesn't kill you first."

Rudy held the girl's gaze a second longer then flipped the door shut behind her in disgust.

She hoped Cindy was smart enough to get the hell out of there.

****

"If you were going to kill someone, how would you do it?"

Cindy watched as Bradford closed his eyes, his head resting on the pillow, one arm thrown lazily over his forehead. Against his chest, snuggled up into the crook of his arm, she laid her head. He dragged his fingers to her face then threaded them through her golden tresses. They fell to her neck and encircled the thin column. One eyebrow arched in question as he tightened the grip around her flesh.

"Strangling works well..." he replied calmly.

Cindy reached up to her neck and wound her fingers with his, pulling one to her mouth to suck on. "Seriously, Brad. What would you do?"

"A bullet is best," he answered quickly. "Quick and easy. Fast results. Unless they find the gun, there's no way they can pin you to it. And there are plenty of ways to make sure a gun is never found." He shifted his position, then opened his eyes to look at her. "Why? You planning to kill someone?"

Cindy propped her hands on his chest, her chin on top of them and stared into his face.

"No. Just a question."

Holding her gaze for several seconds, Brad inquired,

"How would you do it?"

She waited for a moment, staring just past his head. "If I had a lot of time, I think I'd poison them. Then I'd watch them suffer." She grinned slyly, then brought her gaze back to his.

"But really, I think I'd do what you said. I'd shoot them."

She rolled off of him and rose from the bed. Grabbing a short, silk robe slung over a nearby chair, she put it on and turned back to him.

"Bacon and eggs this morning, love? I've got juice. Fresh squeezed."

Bradford smiled his approval.

****

Rudy's day was extremely long and exhausting. After her encounter with Cindy that morning, she holed herself up in her office until evening, working on a contract for another firm.

It occurred to her that she had put not only herself, but her other clients at risk by associating with Thomas Industrials. As their corporate attorney, if she ended up being dragged down with Bradford and his organized crime syndicate, her other clients might be implicated as well.

It concerned her more than she cared to admit, but she didn't know what to do about it.

Until she could find a way to stop Bradford, she had to keep on even keel, keep doing what she'd always done, and not rock the boat.

There had to be a way to get to Bradford.

In the meantime, she needed to do what she had to do.

At nine-forty-five she stopped working and contemplated whether to step out for a quick sandwich and some coffee, or to go on home and work there. She decided home sounded better.

The day drained her both physically and emotionally. Even though she had work to do, propped up in bed with pillows and a pot of coffee by her side sounded much more enticing.

So she gathered the necessary paperwork and headed for home. Her condo sat at the back of a complex, facing a nicely manicured courtyard. There were nights when she felt very safe sitting on her front step late in the evening drinking a glass of Merlot. Tonight, however, was not one of those nights. She sensed danger as soon as she noticed something wrong with her door lock. An uncanny feeling crept over her when she realized that the lock was shattered. The door swung open easily with barely a touch. From what she could tell, every light in her apartment was on.

She never left the lights on.

Hesitantly, she pushed the door open wide and gasped.

Her apartment looked as if someone had turned it upside down and shook it—furniture overturned, upholstery slashed, books and magazines scattered about, pictures hanging haphazardly from the walls. A few steps inside and a quick glance into her kitchen and bedroom told the same tale. Ransacked.

Bradford. Or his men.

Looking for information about Megan. Had to be.

Abruptly, she raced back and slammed the front door shut. She didn't want to alert anyone who might venture by to see what had happened here.

She had to think.

Her brain raced. As all the plausible scenarios flashed through her mind, she became confused, upset, and angry. What did this mean? What would Bradford do now?

He violated her in so many ways. Her mind. Her body. Her home. What next? Did he intend to kill her, too?

She paced in agitation, kicking at her possessions scattered about the floor. It didn't matter anymore that the crystal ashtray that used to sit on her coffee table was shattered into a thousand pieces. It didn't matter that some of her prized prints were slashed and ragged, hanging from the wall.

It didn't matter anymore that the apartment she had painstakingly decorated, just to suit her, lay in ruins. What mattered now was that she still had her life. And she intended to keep it.

Bradford wanted more than just information about Megan. He had sent her a clear warning. Possessing her body wasn't enough. He intended to possess her soul.

Well, he couldn't have it.

Rudy kicked once more at the rubbish on her floor, vowing not to allow her life to turn into total rubbish as well. She would take her life back and hopefully Megan's, too.

Her eyes focused on the morning newspaper lying at her feet. Megan's face stared back at her. The headline screamed out—*Wife of Industrialist Still Missing, Feared Dead.* She scanned the article. Pain warped through her heart.

God, Megan, don't die on me. I'm going to make everything all right again.

Slowly, she reached for the phone. Thankfully, it hadn't been ripped from the wall. She dialed the number she knew by heart. She'd memorized it weeks ago, after she'd spent an agonizing night contemplating whether or not to dial it.

"Chicago Police? Let me speak with Detective Mack MacDowell."

Chapter Nine

A small light shone beneath the kitchen cabinet. When Smyth arrived back at the cottage later that night, he grimaced at her thoughtfulness. He'd been less than thoughtful when he'd run out on her that afternoon. Quietly opening the door, he closed and locked it, not wishing to wake or disturb Meg. Actually, if the truth be known, he hadn't wanted to confront her, to talk to her.

The only reason he'd stayed away so late.

He knew the moment her worried eyes met his earlier that she'd questioned his sudden brashness, wondering if he'd changed his mind about letting her stay in his house. He knew that after the closeness they'd shared moments before, it was unwarranted. And he knew she was as confused as hell, probably even more than he.

Now, as he lay in his bed staring at the ceiling, he wondered about her. About why he'd let himself get so attached, so concerned. She was obviously a grown woman. One who had somehow managed to escape from a less-than-perfect marriage to find her way here. Why all the concern about her? She had managed so far, hadn't she? She really didn't need him.

The sooner he took care of business, the better. He had no reason to hang around after that. Perhaps the simple look of desperation in her eyes had drawn him to her, made him want to protect her. Perhaps the way she clung to him that afternoon. Or maybe the way she'd felt in his arms, against his body, next to his skin.

Damn! He didn't need this now. Especially now.

He finally fell into an uneasy sleep and rose early the next morning.

He quietly showered and dressed. He had a lot to take care of today—a lot he'd put off facing. But for now, he needed to conclude this thing with Crystal as soon as possible and get on back to Portsmouth.

He risked making coffee, half afraid the aroma would wake Meg. A short time later he heard her leave her bedroom and close the bathroom door behind her. Leaning against the kitchen counter, he sipped his coffee, contemplating whether he should leave before she came to the kitchen. He decided no, he'd avoided her enough the day before. He should see her this morning.

He heard the door handle click. His gaze traveled to the empty hallway.

Meg sniffed the coffee aroma. Still dressed in her robe, she rounded the corner to the great room. To her left stood Smyth, coffee cup in hand, watching as if he expected her. Dressed in slim-fitting khaki trousers, a white golf shirt, and leather loafers, unlike the clothing she had seen him wear, she felt the appeal, the attraction. She'd seen his broad, tanned chest unclothed before, but even now, he still looked magnificent. His narrow waist and slim hips simply defined his sex appeal. He did things to her libido. Megan sucked in a quick breath as she entered the kitchen. Obviously, he dressed to tend to a business matter. He certainly wasn't dressing to please her.

Although it pleased her rather nicely.

"Coffee?" he asked as she headed toward the counter. "I've made plenty."

Meg nodded and reached into a high cabinet to retrieve a mug. "Sure," she returned hesitantly, glancing at him then at the coffee maker. "If you've made enough."

"There's plenty." He brought his cup to his lips. "I didn't sleep that well last night, but I don't think I need the whole pot to get me going this morning."

Meg reached for the pot, his words playing through her mind. He didn't sleep well last night? Funny, she'd tossed and turned herself most of the night. Only after she'd heard him come home did she finally let herself relax enough to get a little sleep. But even that was short-lived.

She'd started awake as soon as he'd turned the shower

on an hour ago.

She turned to him, the coffee cup warming her hands. "So, you didn't sleep well?" she asked casually.

"Not really." He assessed her. "You?"

Meg sighed, then set her cup on the counter. "Actually, no."

"Hmmm." Smyth took one last gulp from his cup, then tossed the rest down the sink. His elbow brushed her forearm as he walked past her, raising goose bumps on her flesh. Meg inadvertently reached over to rub them down as he rinsed out the cup and set it on the counter beside hers. "Must be something in the air."

Right. Like tension so thick you could slice it with a butter knife. *And I'm not sure why.*

Smyth headed toward the couch and picked up a light jacket. After slipping his arms inside and adjusting the collar around his neck, he turned to her. "I'll be gone most of the day. If everything goes the way I expect, I'll probably be heading back to Portsmouth in the morning." He let their gazes mingle for several seconds. "Then the house is yours."

After another pause, he turned toward the door.

Meg watched him prepare to leave. She wanted to tell him the house wouldn't be the same without him. She wanted to tell him not to go...yet.

"Shall I fix us something for supper?" Meg blurted out, not quite sure why, only knowing that she wanted to hold him there a moment longer. If only she could look into his eyes just once more before he left the cottage.

Slowly turning to her, he granted her wish. His eyes perused her face as he contemplated the question.

He shook his head. "No. I don't think so."

"No?" she softly questioned back.

He hesitated. "Why don't I take you out to dinner instead? I mean...I'll be leaving in the morning. I'd like to take you out to dinner."

Meg felt an unfamiliar tingle surge within her

abdomen. Dinner?

Should she?

"All right," she whispered, barely loud enough for her to hear, let alone him.

He grinned, and then reached behind him for the doorknob. "I'll be home around seven."

Meg allowed herself to smile back at him, not allowing her confusion to creep in quite yet. "I'll be ready."

Home. He'll be home around seven.

****

The room gave off as much cold as Crystal Parker herself. Smyth glanced about the attorney's office, taking note of the volumes of shelved legal documents lining the walls, the thick beige carpeting, the bold leather and wood furnishings. Finally his gaze rested across the table at the source of the chilly atmosphere. His ex-wife. Crystal Adams Parker. And as he stared at her, her cold and calculating gaze freezing back at him, he wondered what he'd ever seen in her. Had to wonder why he'd ever married her in the first place. Had to compare her to the woman he'd just left back at his cottage.

He shook off that thought, mainly because there was no comparing Crystal with Meg.

From what he knew already, there was no comparing Meg Thompson with any woman.

Closing his eyes briefly, he finally admitted it to himself. The woman got to him. Bad.

But he wasn't there to think about Meg. He was there to get Crystal Adams Parker out of his life—forever. Then he would leave early in the morning and forget everything. Crystal. Meg.

Everything.

He had to.

In the beginning, he reminded himself, Crystal hadn't been the same woman who sat across the table from him today. At one time she'd been warm, loving, full of life and fun...at least he'd thought so at the time. Now, it didn't seem as clear. Had it all been an act? He was damned near sure of it. An act to get the one thing she craved in life more than anything. Money.

Well, not from him.

Still, how could he be sure that any other woman wouldn't be the same? How could he be sure that Meg Thompson wouldn't throw him for a loop the same way Crystal had? He couldn't.

Crystal's attorney sat to her immediate left. As the door to the office swung open with a soft whoosh, Smyth turned his attention to Martin McGoldrick, his attorney. Martin cast Smyth a glance, then turned to the other lawyer before he sat.

"Aaron," he nodded toward the man while still shuffling papers in front of him. "I think all is in order to proceed."

Smyth liked the way Martin handled things. No nonsense. To the point. Let's get it over with and get out of here before we waste any more time or money. Smyth valued that attitude.

The divorce agreements had gone smoothly enough, but the joint agreement to settle the paternity suit and financial obligations regarding the child were another matter. He and Crystal had both wanted the divorce as quickly as possible. Now the time had come to settle the rest.

Smyth remained adamant that Martin handle things to his satisfaction. And he paid him dearly for it.

Martin cleared his throat. "Let's cut to the chase." He eyed Aaron Turner, then Crystal.

Smyth watched their reactions from across the table. He knew what Martin was about to say.

"Perhaps we can settle this little matter neat and clean and then take it to the judge. As you know, Smyth denies paternity to the child Ms. Parker is carrying. Marital relations had not taken place for at least three months prior to the estimated date of conception."

"But—" Crystal leaned forward. Her attorney laid a hand on her forearm. Reluctantly, she settled back in her seat, eyeing Smyth with a vengeance.

"However," Martin continued, "although it is impossible that he could be the father of the child Ms. Parker is carrying, Smyth is willing to do two things since the child was conceived during the marriage. Until paternity testing can determine the child's parentage, he will pay for all prenatal care, hospital and delivery costs, as well as medical care for the child. Support for the first six months of the child's life will be one thousand dollars a month. Although Mr. Parker denies paternity, he will also set up a trust fund sufficient for the child's college education to be awarded to the child upon his or her completion of high school and acceptance into college."

Martin paused and looked over his glasses to the woman beside him. "And since you were awarded the home you and Mr. Parker bought during your marriage in the divorce decree, as well as other items of monetary value, this is the extent of Mr. Parker's generosity. After the paternity test determines he is not the father of the child you are carrying, the support payments stop. The child is not considered an heir. And there will be no support for you, Ms. Parker. If we can come to an agreement here today, we'll take it to the judge to sign the paperwork. If you do not agree, we will fight to the end, and in the end, we will get what we want."

Smyth watched Crystal's face during the entire time Martin spoke. Her gaze narrowed at him, as if spitting flames. The room became stifling. Her chest heaved as she sucked in breath after shallow breath. And when Martin finished, she turned her red-faced scowl on him.

"It is unacceptable." She slapped one bejeweled hand down on the shiny tabletop.

Aaron Turner curled his fingers around her forearm. "Crystal. Let's talk about this. It's an excellent settlement. Before you go off the deep—"

Crystal stood, jerking her arm from his grasp. "Don't touch me, you imbecile! This isn't what I want and you know it. I want maintenance! I want child support! I want

Smyth Parker's name on my child's birth certificate!" She pounded the table with each demand. "Now you better damn well get me what I want, or I will find someone who will!"

She whirled toward Smyth and Martin. A long, slim finger pierced the air as she pointed across the table to Smyth. "You won't get away with this, you bastard. This child is yours and you know it. I only want what my child deserves, to be the rightful heir to E.J. Parker. This child deserves it and I will see that he gets what's due him! Come hell or high water, one way or another, Smyth Parker, I will get what I want. This child is a Parker heir."

Smyth sat quietly for a moment and glared, his fingers forming a tent as he leaned over the table. He looked at her, angry, desperate, and saw a hateful, spiteful woman. A woman out for her own desires, not the needs of an infant. She wanted nothing for the child. She wanted it all for herself. That's why he'd offered her what he did. The child needed a good start in life, he could give it that. But that ended any obligation. Nothing more.

A picture burst into his mind. The scene five months earlier when he'd arrived at Nags Head from Portsmouth and opened the door to his cottage. The memory jump-started his anger as he pictured Crystal, lying naked on the floor in front of the windows with a dark-headed man pumping the hell out of her, her legs wrapped around him, her fingernails digging into his back, her hair fanned out around her head.

She gasped, panted, and called out that sonofabitch's name.

He guessed maybe he deserved that for spending weeks away from his wife. Maybe it was all his fault. But the fact remained that he had not fathered the child. And the affair had gone on long before he'd left three months earlier. He'd found that out easily enough. It was funny how people talked when you asked.

He rose. "That's the deal, Crystal. Take it or leave it. Time is on my side, not yours. I think I'm being pretty generous as it is." He nodded to Martin, then rounded the table toward the door. He'd had enough.

"Then I'll see you in court, Smyth! I'll see your rotten, slimy carcass in court before this is all over!"

Slowly, with one hand on the doorknob, he bodily turned to face her. "So be it. I haven't a thing to lose, Crystal. Do your damnedest. I'm telling you now, that's the best I'm going to offer. It's the best you're going to get. There's no way in hell I'm claiming your bastard as my legal heir. No way in hell!"

His grandfather hadn't worked his fingers to the bone for half a century to let Crystal Parker squander a portion of it away like so much fodder in the breeze.

Smyth turned, jerked open the door, and slammed it behind him as he left.

Hours later, the sun dipping closer to the horizon in the west, Smyth wearily made his way up the stairs of the porch. Rounding the corner to face the ocean, he stood silently, looking out to sea, mesmerized by the power the ocean emitted. Puzzled by how weak it made him feel at that moment, at how minute and insignificant, he sucked in a cleansing breath and exhaled, slowly.

He needed to get back to Portsmouth. It always made his problems seem so insignificant. He needed that right now.

Dealing with Crystal's demands zapped the very strength out of him.

Then out of the shadows she moved, her hair fluttering in the breeze as she, too, stood spellbound by the vast waters before them. And for eternity, it seemed, he just watched her.

Wishing he could hold her. Just once more. An overwhelming need to be needed washed over him. For once, he wanted to be needed for himself, not for what he could give others.

****

It was nine-fifteen and Meg stood staring at the ocean from the front porch. She'd watched two men and a woman with a pick-up truck and a boat place a huge net out into the ocean for the past thirty minutes. Fascinated, she made a mental note to be up early enough in the morning to see what they'd caught. Then abruptly, she felt a kinship with the fish that would be captured there. Caught in a net herself. She didn't know if she'd ever work her way out.

Why do I continually set myself up for such heartache?

For so long, years actually, there had been no affection, no love. Bradford took from her what he wanted, when he needed it, with no regard to her feelings or wants or needs. Without any regard to her wishes. Why should she ever expect anything different?

Why would she expect to get affection from Smyth? From any man? All she ever wanted was a little tenderness. All she ever got was heartache.

Her chest lifted, then she sighed, a morose, desolate feeling wafting over her. Sometimes she felt like she could simply walk into the ocean, keep walking until the waves covered her and took her under.

Sometimes, she felt like she was drowning emotionally. Why would the physical drowning of her body be any different? Inside, she'd been dying slowly, for the past six years.

Why should she expect Smyth to be her life-line? Could she grasp it if he held it out to her?

Stop it, Meg. This is ridiculous. You've known the man a few days and you're already picking out china. He's nothing to you. And he's leaving in the morning. There's nothing more to it than that. He never indicated anything more. What you've got is nothing more than a juvenile, adolescent crush.

Feeling silly now, dressed in her jade green silk blouse and slim black skirt, she closed her eyes and shook her head. Not really knowing what Smyth meant by dinner, she wasn't sure how to dress, but she figured that a skirt and blouse would fit in just about anywhere. She'd added the pearls and black pumps to dress it up. But she felt overdressed. And embarrassed.

Turning to go change her clothes, she took two steps

to the side of the porch. Within an instant, she sensed him, felt him. She had no idea how long he'd been standing there, watching her.

The wrinkle across his brow was the first thing she noticed. His hair, disheveled and windblown, looked as though he'd run his fingers through it for hours. The corners of his mouth were turned down and his eyes...his eyes were full of pain, worry, longing.

Meg's heart went out to him.

With each breath she took Meg could feel the vibrations surrounding them. She dropped her gaze lower, to his lips and then his throat and found herself raking her tongue over her own lips. Between the two of them, a current pulled and tugged. She wanted to be closer to him. She thought he wanted that too. At last, she dragged her gaze back up to his face. Something passed over his eyes, and she knew he was troubled.

"Are you all right?" she whispered.

"No," he rasped, his eyes searching hers.

"What's wrong?" she asked softly, laying a hand on his forearm.

He lowered his gaze to her lips and sighed. "I want to hold you," he whispered.

Meg's heart thrummed. Slowly, he reached for her, gently pulling her forward, next to his body. When her breasts touched his firm chest, Meg thought she would drown. His arms grasped her tightly and her eyes closed as he nestled her head into the crook of his neck. He groaned and her arms involuntarily wrapped themselves around his back. Holding him.

"I need to hold you," he whispered again. "I need you to hold me."

His fingers threaded into her hair as he clutched her closer. Meg felt his sadness, his pain.

Something was wrong.

For several minutes they stood together. The breeze blew in off the ocean, the night grew cooler. But between them, deep inside, there existed a warmth. Growing. Filling the chasm. Meg felt it. Then immediately wished she hadn't.

Smyth stepped back, breaking the connection. His hands dropped to his sides. Lowering his head, he stared at the wooden porch flooring.

"Rough day?"

He chuckled, then his eyes twinkled and he stared past her for a second. One corner of his mouth drew up. "Yeah, you might say that."

Then his face grew serious, their gaze met again. "Holding you helped, though."

Meg blinked then drew her lower lip in with her teeth. She didn't know how she felt about being his comfort, easing his pain. Finally, she let herself smile back. "Everyone needs a hug now and then," she returned, telling herself that it was just a hug—a friendly hug.

Smiling, Smyth nodded. "I guess so." And then he added while tossing his head sideways. "I'm sorry I'm late. I promised—"

Meg stopped him. "It's okay. We don't have to go anywhere. I was just beginning to get worried."

He searched her face, as if wondering why she would worry about him. "I want to take you to dinner."

"I could fix something here."

"No. You're all dressed up. Let's go." Smyth's gaze drifted over her body, his eyes widening as though the first time he had really looked at her.

Meg shook her head. He looked beat. "Let's do it another time. Really. I'm tired and you look pretty frazzled."

Smyth stared at her a moment longer. For an instant, she thought he intended to insist they go and then he relented. "Tomorrow night. I promise."

"I thought you were leaving tomorrow."

Shrugging, he returned, "I can wait another day."

"Smyth, it's not really necessary. You don't have to take me out to dinner. I don't want you to have to change your plans. You don't have to entertain me."

A sharp look lanced over his face. "I don't want to

entertain you, Meg. I just want to take you out for a quiet dinner. I'm really not up to it tonight, but—"

Meg recognized the strained quality of his voice. Whatever business he'd had today had taken its toll on him.

"Tomorrow night will be fine." She grasped his elbow and turned toward the door. "But right now, let's both get some rest. We can hash the rest of this out later."

Chapter Ten

"My goodness. Look at the fish!"

Coffee mug in hand, Meg slipped her feet into a pair of flip-flops and quickly glanced out the window. The pick-up truck she'd seen the night before was now dragging the net back up the shore. After quietly leaving the house, she walked toward the area where a small crowd gathered.

About half of the net lay on the beach, all sizes and shapes of flopping fish encased in its folds.

Meg cringed. She could almost hear them gasping for air. The truck, driven by the female she'd seen the night before, methodically moved in a perpendicular fashion up and down the width of the beach. When she approached the edge of the water, her partner fastened the net to a huge hook at the front of the truck. She reversed the truck's action, dragging the net and everything in its way onto the beach.

Fascinated, Meg made her way around the crowd and headed for the part of the net still stuck partly in the ocean. Three men picked out the fish they wanted and tossed them into the back of another pick-up. Periodically, they tossed live fish that weren't keepers back into the ocean. Children raced around her, excitedly yelling and pointing at the menagerie.

Upon closer inspection, Meg saw where they pointed. All kinds of things other than fish were caught up in the nets. To her left sat what looked like a decayed horseshoe crab shell. In front of her, a huge mass of jellyfish and many species of undefined fish and sea animals. The children ran past her again as a shout went up from down the beach. Obviously something else interesting had been pulled to shore.

Meg glanced down, then crouched, running her fingertips along the smooth back of a large fish.

"That's a croaker."

Meg drew back her hand and glanced up. Smyth stood silhouetted in the morning sun beside her. She rose and looked into his rested face.

"I thought you were still asleep."

Smyth glanced about him. "I was, but all the commotion out here woke me." He turned to her and smiled. "I needed to get up anyway, but thanks for letting me sleep a little later this morning."

Meg shrugged. "No problem. You looked exhausted last night."

"I was," Smyth agreed.

After a moment's hesitation, he glanced back at the fish. "Looks like they've got a good catch this morning."

Meg followed his gaze. "It sure is a lot of fish. Do they sell them locally?"

Nodding, Smyth stooped down to lift another fish from the net. "To restaurants and markets up and down the coast. I haven't seen them here on this part of the beach for quite a while, though." He tossed the fish back into the net. "Are you up for a walk this morning?"

Studying his face, Meg returned, "Sure. I love morning walks on the beach."

They walked slowly, in silence, in a southerly direction for a few minutes, then Smyth broke the quiet.

"I want to apologize for making you wait last night."

Meg shook her head. "Don't. It's all right. I was tired, anyway. I hope everything is okay, though." She sidled a glance his way.

"It will be. It will just take a little time."

Wondering whether she should delve further, Meg bit her lip. Something was obviously troubling him. He listened to her problems, at least the part she decided to share. Should she offer herself as a sounding board as well?

"Do you want to talk about it?"

Smyth pushed his hands into his pockets and stopped. Looking at her, he held her gaze.

"Thanks, but it's business and I wouldn't want to bore

you."

Meg harbored an uncanny feeling that he hadn't told the entire truth.

She turned and began walking again. "Do you mind if I ask what kind of work you do?" Hopefully a safe enough topic.

Grinning, Smyth looked back to her. "No, I don't mind. When my grandfather died, he left me his tobacco company. We buy tobacco from the farmers and warehouses and sell it again to the companies who produce tobacco products. We've even developed an overseas market. To say the least, E.J. Parker, my grandfather, developed quite a big name for himself, and quite a business in the process."

"E.J. Parker. I've heard of the company."

"I'm not surprised."

"And it's yours?"

"Yes."

"Do you enjoy what you do?"

It took several minutes for Smyth to answer, his face pointed to the sand as they continued toward the pier. "No. Honestly, I don't. That's why I steer clear of the business end of the company as much as I can."

"So why do you keep it?"

He pulled his gaze up to meet hers. "Out of obligation, really. My grandfather and I were very close. I couldn't sell the company. I have a competent slate of executive officers who run things for me. Things are under control. Only from time to time do I need to interfere."

"Like yesterday?"

Meg watched Smyth's face harden for a second and then soften. She felt she might have hit a nerve she shouldn't have touched. "Yes. Like yesterday."

For the second time, Meg felt as though he hadn't been completely honest. But again, his prerogative. She hadn't been totally honest with him about everything, either.

"So tell me about your grandfather." The words were

out of her mouth before she realized it. Perhaps she shouldn't have mentioned his grandfather. Did a safe subject exist? When she risked a glance into Smyth's face, she saw him staring out to the ocean, a faraway glaze over his eyes and a slight smile on his face.

"My grandfather was the greatest person I ever knew."

Meg didn't respond. They stopped under the pier and Smyth sat, leaning his back against a giant wooden support. Meg sat next to him. They both faced the ocean as it rhythmically slapped against the pier.

"My grandfather was my mother's father. When she died, we both were devastated. I was young and couldn't really understand what had happened, I only knew I hurt. Even though he was much older and wiser, his pain was just as deep. We used to sit for hours, it seemed, and he held me while I cried. He shed a few tears right along with me. He never said much, I just knew he was there for me. During those long months after her death, we healed each other and developed a lasting bond.

"It stayed that way until he died. Sometimes even now, I think he's still here, holding onto me, when I feel like crying." He turned to face her. "I miss him terribly. He was the only constant person in my life for years. After Dad married Jenna, and Becky came along, I felt kind of shoved to the side, so I begged to spend time with Grandpa. In reality, looking back, I know Dad and Jenna loved me. Becky adored me. But I was at a bad age, felt very insecure, and didn't see it quite the same way they did." He paused for a minute and took a deep breath.

"At any rate, I spent most of my time here in Nags Head, especially after Grandpa decided to curb his hours at the office. We fished, swam, beach combed—actually we did just about anything we wanted." His head lowered and he stared at the sand in front of their feet. "His heart stopped when we were jogging one morning, just a few yards in front of the house. He hit the sand like a felled tree. I knew he was gone the moment I turned him over."

He turned back to stare at the sea. Meg let the silence

fall between them for a moment.

Finally, she responded, "Your grandfather sounds like a wonderful person."

Smyth nodded.

Meg laid a hand on his forearm. "I know how painful it can be losing someone you love.

Although my parents divorced and I lived with my own grandmother for several years, it hurt when they died. I was in my early teens. My grandmother died a few years back, also. It's not an easy thing to overcome. If you need to talk about it, I'm here."

Smyth reached over and placed his hand on top of hers. His fingertips lightly traced her knuckles and veins— his hand warm, his fingers caressing. He lifted his head and their eyes met.

Inside those eyes Meg saw compassion and caring, as well as hurt and confusion. It took all her effort to keep from gently caressing his face with her own fingertips.

"Thank you," he whispered, the words barely audible. Then he pulled his hand away and Meg sat up straighter. But he still held the connection. "I don't know where you came from, Meg Thompson. You dropped into my life like a lifeline and somehow make me feel everything will turn out all right. Thank you."

Startled at the admission, Meg shook her head. "No. I should be thanking you. You could have tossed me out days ago."

One corner of Smyth's lips rose in a half-smile. His eyes twinkled.

"You're too hard on yourself. I couldn't have tossed you out. You bring a softness and warmth to that old house that hasn't been there for years." Then quickly, he glanced away, as if he'd revealed too much.

He stood and reached out his hand.

Meg glanced up at him. Following a hesitant moment, clasped his hand. After pulling her to her feet, he kept his fingers wound in hers as they retraced their steps back to Smyth's house.

Meg's pulse raced. It felt good holding Smyth's hand. It felt good when he looked into her eyes.

And it felt damned good when he'd held her last night.

Alarm coursed through her. She had no business feeling so damned good where Smyth Parker was concerned.

****

"I'm really glad you thought of this," Meg told Smyth later as they passed through the resort community of Duck. "I'd been thinking of driving up here, but just hadn't done it yet."

"It's a bit different here," he answered. "Most of the area caters to the rich and influential, however, there are a few old-timers around. Personally, I prefer old Nags Head, but to each their own."

Meg smiled and glanced out the passenger window. Yes, she thought she rather preferred old Nags Head herself. Luxurious vacation homes and resort communities graced the northern stretch of the Outer Banks, but there was something warm, inviting, and cozy about the area in which Smyth's house was situated. The northern beaches were nice to visit, but she really didn't think she'd want to live there.

She glanced back at Smyth. "So how much further to Corolla?"

They'd decided in the early afternoon to take a drive to the northern banks. The restaurant he wanted to take her to for dinner that evening was in Duck. On the spur of the moment they'd decided to go early, spend the afternoon sightseeing, and then catch a late dinner. An excited Meg was about to experience her first lighthouse.

"Corolla is literally at the end of the road. It's the town furthest north up the Outer Banks, although there are plans to develop the area north of there. To go any farther though, you'd have to have a four-wheel drive and take the beach. It will probably take us another hour."

"Have you done that? I mean, ridden up the beach?"

"Sure. They are building homes up there now. I've got

friends who like to fish up there. We take a jeep, usually pitch a sleeping bag in the back and spend the night. There's really nothing quite like it."

She pondered that statement. How wonderful to be so free. To do that sounded exhilarating. "Sounds like a lot of fun."

He glanced her way. "It is." He turned back to watch the road, then after a moment, glanced at her again. "Have you ever slept on the beach?"

"Heavens, no."

He smiled. "Then you need to. Want to try it one night?"

Warmth spread from Meg's stomach to her cheeks. Spend the night on the beach? With Smyth? Her mind conjured up some rather unsettling images. Beaches at night were just too damn romantic and she'd been alone on the beach for way too long.

She shook her head. "I—I don't know. I'm not really the outdoors type."

He chuckled. "Ah, c'mon. You only live once, right? What's it gonna hurt?"

Both of us, that's what.

Meg turned away. She didn't want to get into this any further. No way could she and Smyth spend the night together on the beach. He would be leaving in the morning and she was an emotional wreck. Surely he didn't realize what he asked.

"Smyth, look, I—"

"Forget I mentioned it."

Turning to look at him, Meg felt a temporary jolt in her abdomen. Had he sensed her insecurity about what he suggested? The look on his face said that he had.

"Smyth, I didn't mean—"

He smiled and she stopped talking. "I was pushing," he continued. "I didn't mean to put you on the spot. I hope you don't think I was suggesting...I didn't mean to imply anything."

"I know you didn't. It's just—"

"Meg." He slowed the car to a stop. There was no traffic behind them, hadn't been for miles. "I was out of line. Forget it."

Meg dipped her head in a quick nod, then risked a grin. "Forgotten."

"Good. I have a habit of inserting my foot in my mouth."

His gaze held hers for another second, then he glanced in the rearview mirror and stepped on the accelerator. For the next several minutes, they rode in silence.

"When we get to Corolla, there are two things I want you to see," Smyth finally broke the quiet.

He had mentally chastised himself for the past few minutes for suggesting they sleep on the beach. The thing was, well...he had started to feel very comfortable with the woman. And the natural progression said a man should try to test the waters a bit, didn't it? *No, Parker. Not with this woman. Not now. She's vulnerable. You're vulnerable. It's a bad call all around.* He tried to forget it.

He picked up where he had left off. "The first, of course, is the lighthouse. The second, are the horses."

Smyth sidled a glance at Meg's excited face.

"Oh! The horses. I remember reading about them. Will we really see some?"

Relieved that she seemed to have dismissed his earlier mistake, he replied, "If we're lucky. We entered the reserve a while back, but normally you won't see them until we get to Corolla. Generally, they're lounging around in someone's front yard eating their grass."

"And the residents don't mind?"

He shook his head and grinned. "Hell, no. Those mustangs are practically sacred. People want them around the town. However, you have to realize that they're not tame. They're still wild animals. It's just that they are kind of special, you know, the remnants of herds that may go back as far as the Spanish conquistadors or Sir Walter Raleigh. This herd is dwindling, but there is an ever-present movement for preservation. When one dies, everyone mourns. When there's a new foal, it is cause for a celebration."

"That's very cool."

"Yeah, and kind of unique. There's not many areas of the country that can boast of something that special."

They sped by the sign that indicated they'd entered Corolla. Smyth peered out the windshield, over the treetops.

"If you look straight ahead, you should see the lighthouse soon."

Meg sat forward a bit on her seat, searching the tree line. Soon, the lighthouse did appear.

After only a few more minutes of driving, he turned left off the main road onto a narrow, sandy one leading to the historic structure.

The placard outside the red-brick lighthouse said it was built and first lighted in 1875. It also mentioned the 214 steps it took to climb to the top. Meg felt it might take her a hundred years more to make it there. Glad for the landing every twenty-five steps to catch her breath, she tried hard not to show signs of how out of shape she was. Smyth, the rat, seemed to glide up and up without breaking stride. At the top, he looked back at her before reaching the entrance to the outside.

"Are you coming?" he teased.

Meg huffed. "Whose idea was this, anyway?"

"Mine, and you're going to love it when you get up here."

"If I ever make it up there." She pushed herself the last few steps.

Smyth lowered his hand to her and she stretched to reach it. "C'mon up."

Practically pulling her the rest of the way, Meg giggled as they topped the last step and spilled over onto the lookout. Smyth dragged her a couple of steps toward the railing. A stiff breeze immediately hit her in the face.

"Oh, my!" Meg faltered when her gaze fell on the

ground too many feet below. Vertigo suddenly enveloped her senses. He grasped her from behind. At first, she felt his hands on her waist, as if hesitant whether to keep them there or not. Then his chest, warm and strong, crowded up close to her. When his hands snaked around to her abdomen to hold her closer, she surprised herself by leaning back into him.

His warm breath tickled her ear and she relaxed.

"I won't let you fall," he whispered in her ear.

Meg closed her eyes. *You won't? I think I already have.*

****

The Salty Dolphin sat looking over Currituck Sound, just south of Duck. The restaurant was sophisticated but laid back at the same time. As they pulled into the parking lot, Meg wondered if she'd dressed appropriately. But once inside, on Smyth's arm, she felt uncommonly at ease.

Dinner of fresh seafood, a salad, and a glass of wine with the meal, and one for dessert, filled her. They conversed lightly, casually, as if old lovers, Meg thought. He spoke vaguely, bringing up nothing more of his past, clearly avoiding questions of his work. Meg, of course, did the same.

She did not want to spoil the ambiance with thoughts of Bradford and her life in Chicago.

They spoke of only what they knew of their lives together—the brief moment in time they'd shared since Smyth's arrival back in Nags Head.

All the while Meg had to wonder about the Smyth Parker sitting across from her. He seemed at ease with her, too, especially after the day they'd shared together, but somehow out of his element. Or perhaps just uncomfortable. She didn't know which. She just didn't feel that his comfort level had anything to do with her, but had a lot to do with his surroundings. He certainly hadn't seemed uncomfortable this afternoon.

Perhaps he's just not used to dining out. Some men were ill at ease in restaurants, but she dismissed that conclusion as well. He handled himself quite well. Resigning herself to the fact that she wasn't going to be able to put her finger on it, Meg simply relaxed and enjoyed his company. Come morning she wouldn't see him again. Funny how she'd let herself forget that he'd made plans to leave.

Only a few couples remained in the dining room, but the restaurant's bar picked up a few late night revelers. As the surrounding mood changed, Smyth linked his arm with hers and led her out of the restaurant toward a small pier jutting out into the sound from a gazebo.

The moon bathed them in muted light as they silently crossed the weathered wood and entered the privacy of the gazebo. Meg immediately smiled, pulled her arm from his grasp and went to the opposite side of the eight-sided structure. She leaned against the railing for several minutes, closing her eyes to the rhythmic slap of water against the pilings and the faint throbbing of music from the bar. The delicate breeze off the sound washed over her as she became aware of Smyth standing beside her.

Opening her eyes, she bodily turned toward him. "Thank you," she whispered.

"Like it?"

He plunged his hands deep in his trouser pockets. With his shirt collar open and his hair suddenly disheveled, he looked so much more natural now. And much more comfortable. "Yes," she returned softly. "I like it very much."

Smyth's face broke into a grin. Turning back toward the sound, she braced one hand on the post beside her and leaned into it. Lights from the restaurant bounced off the dark waves to her left, twinkling in the reflection. How peaceful. She closed her eyes as he moved closer to her.

Listening, she almost thought she could hear the ocean.

"You know," she told Smyth a moment later, breaking the night's silence, "it's strange.

The sound is so calm, but across that thin ribbon of sand behind us, the ocean rages. I thought a minute ago I could hear it."

"I can understand that," he replied slowly, watching her face. "The same thing is going on inside me."

And me. Startled at both his reply and her thought, Meg looked at him.

"Sh..." his finger found her lips, silencing the question that hadn't yet made it to her tongue. "Listen," he whispered. "You can hear it."

His eyes held hers spellbound for a moment as she listened. His hand dropped to her waist, lingering there, and Meg found herself turning into him.

"Listen," he repeated, as soft as the night breeze.

Meg did, and within seconds, whether her own imagination or the ocean, she heard breakers crashing against the shore. Or something raging inside him? Her?

"Amazing," she whispered, searching his face.

"The land is very narrow here," he explained quietly. "It's not so uncommon in places.

You just have to be very quiet and listen."

Hesitantly, Meg placed a hand on his chest. "And inside here?" she questioned softly. His eyes widened with something she dared not question as her hand lay heavy on his chest. Did she chance going on?

"Is this just a facade? A thin, calm veneer covering some frenzy inside?"

Who are you, Smyth Parker?

It took him several minutes to answer. Minutes spent searching her face, playing over her features. Meg watched him, his hesitation confirming his internal struggle. Did he possess demons as awful as hers?

"Perhaps," he finally answered. "But sometimes I think...looking at you is like looking into a mirror. I see the same things reflected back at me." He broke away and turned toward the sound, leaning into the railing. Meg watched him, her back against the post. A myriad of emotions slid over his face. He knew so much, yet so little. As did she.

After a moment he turned back to face her. "Dance with me?" He held out his hand.

Confused, Meg stared at his open palm. Bradford had been like this, so charming, so romantic.

He'd swept her off her feet and she hadn't landed for six months. But after the wedding...

Could she risk this?

Her heart beat erratically in her chest, her blood thrummed in her veins. After a second's pause, she looked back into his face and took his hand.

"There's no music," she whispered as he pulled her closer.

He chuckled softly. "Oh, yes there is, can't you hear it? Listen."

Again, he placed a finger on her lips. His other arm circled her waist and their bodies met. "Listen," he repeated in a hushed voice. "The music is all around us."

And as though it really were, their bodies swayed to the invisible rhythm. Smyth's finger drew down the side of her face and Meg trembled. He was too close. As his hand slipped to her back, he drew her closer still until her head rested on his shoulder and he dipped his beside hers.

Her eyes closed. She lost herself in the moment, the power of their closeness. She felt their breathing slide in sync as they leaned one way then the other. As one.

All at once, as if the music stopped, they stood still. Sighing, Meg opened her eyes and shifted slightly away from him. Both his hands left her back and went to her face, lifting it to his.

When their eyes met, she saw the desire on his face. As his lips lowered, Meg thought of all the reasons why she shouldn't let him kiss her. And as his lips brushed against hers, sending sweet ecstasy down to her toes, she silently thanked her weak side that she hadn't listened.

Chapter Eleven

Meg heard nothing, but every desirable emotion she'd ever possessed coursed through her body at the gentle pressure Smyth placed on her lips. Suddenly, there was no lapping of water, no muffled music, no ocean roaring on the other side of the island. No fear, no Bradford, no bodyguards watching her every move. Only the two of them suspended. They were the center of the universe.

Smyth's lips increased the tension between them and she flowered and opened to him, letting his tongue penetrate deep into her mouth. Mingling her tongue with his, she drank of the passion and desire they shared. Her chest swelling, Meg reached up to grasp his shoulders to pull him closer, wanting him so much closer.

It was as if someone threw a lighted match into her soul.

His hands moved to her hair, threading his fingers through as he held her to him. She knew she never wanted their lips to part. She whimpered at the gesture and realized she wanted him. Oh, God. She wanted this man like no other. Inside, a tiny voice warned, but she closed the door on it. Never, never had she felt so uninhibited. So relaxed. Panting, breathing in every essence of him, she pulled her lips away, but Smyth grabbed her with a groan and wouldn't let go. He planted small kisses along her lips, her cheeks, moaning her name. Trailing his hands down her neck, her shoulders, he grasped her to him in a never-ending embrace.

His breath hot against her ear, he held her. All he could do was repeat her name in hushed silence. And Meg loved hearing her name on his every breath.

They were alone. Meg heard nothing but the pounding of their pulses.

Smyth knew the millisecond his lips brushed hers that he shouldn't have kissed her. He shouldn't have, but he'd wanted to all evening. And now, knowing how soft, how delectable, how utterly sexy her kisses were, he was glad he hadn't passed up the chance while he'd had it.

In fact, he didn't know how he'd make it through the rest of his life knowing that her lips could bring such pleasure to his.

He felt her deep inside him. She'd touched him. With the simple act of pressing lips to lips, mingling tongue with tongue, her hands on his shoulders pulling him closer, she'd touched him like no other woman had ever dared.

And he'd let her. At a time in his life when it was the one thing he didn't need, he'd let her in—too quickly and too deeply.

And he'd thought *she* was the vulnerable one.

He couldn't let her go. Holding her to him, he breathed against her hair, his brain reeling, knowing there were decisions to be made. Knowing he had to leave in the morning. He wanted her, but she was not the kind of woman he wanted to love one day and leave the next.

He'd lost one woman already like that.

"Meg," he whispered. "I—"

The silence broke around them and Meg stiffened, an awkward awareness enveloping her. At the echo of footsteps coming toward them, they pulled away from each other.

"You bastard!"

The woman's voice, high-pitched and clearly laced with anger, startled them both. Meg jumped back, but Smyth immediately thrust out a protective arm and drew her into him, holding her close.

"Crystal. What the hell are you doing here?" he barked at the other woman.

"What the hell do you care? I want to know who she is!"

Crystal stepped closer and Smyth tightened his grip around Meg. She didn't need to see this, didn't need to encounter Crystal. Not now, not yet. It was all too new. No time to explain.

Damn her! Damn Crystal Adams for making a mess of everything in his life!

"This is none of your business, Crystal. Leave us alone and get out of here." Smyth turned his back to the woman, catching Meg between him and the gazebo railing. He searched her troubled, questioning eyes, then laid a gentle hand on her cheek.

Meg stared blankly back.

Anger flared within him. Immediately, he recognized that this was not the emotion he wanted to feel. He wanted the passion back, the desire. The desire he'd seen in Meg's eyes. Felt in her body. He wanted it back. Why the hell did Crystal have to show up?

Meg's cheek felt so soft. How could he explain? Would she understand?

"I want some answers now, Smyth." The venom bit through the calm air.

Closing his eyes, he braced his hands on Meg's upper arms. Abruptly, he slid them away and turned back to Crystal, shielding Meg. "Go away, Crystal. Anything I have to say to you can be said through our attorneys. Don't make a fool of yourself."

"Fool?" She paced a few steps, her arms flailing. "Fool? You've been making a goddamned fool out of me for the last five months, you bastard. Now you're out canoodling with this blonde, letting her live in your house, drive your grandfather's car. What kind of fool do you take me for?"

Smyth felt Meg's fingers curl around his forearm from behind.

"What is she talking about?" she asked with soft urgency.

"Nothing," he threw over his shoulder. "She's nuts."

"Who is she?" Meg inquired again.

Smyth glanced back at her, eyes wide in skepticism. They'd lost the magic they'd just shared. He feared they might never get it back. "No one." He forced the words through clenched teeth.

"I'm a lot more than no one, honey."

Smyth jerked his head back to Crystal as she drew closer. He wanted to protect Meg from all this. He would have told her, in time. "She's not involved in any of this, Crystal. Leave her alone." He hoped she'd heed the warning his stern gaze threw her way.

Crystal thrust out her right hand past Smyth and toward Meg. "Nice to meet you, dear," she blurted our sarcastically. "My name is Crystal Parker. I'm Smyth's wife."

Anger so urgent, it gurgled forth and out of him before he realized it, caused Smyth to lunge at Crystal. Grasping her by both her upper arms, he forced her away from Meg. Behind him, Meg gasped. Between their encounter that afternoon and now her interrupting his evening with Meg, he had reached his limit. Much more than he could take right now. And he was fast losing it.

"*Ex-wife*. You are not my wife any longer. Now, please leave us alone." He let loose of her and she teetered backward. Immediately he wished he hadn't touched her. She just angered him too damn much.

Crystal steadied herself on the rail behind her. "Not quite, Smyth. It's not over yet," she bit out.

His finger jabbed through the air at her. "I don't want to see you again until we meet in court, do you understand?" he shouted again.

"Yeah, you sonofabitch. I understand perfectly. Little missy over there knows nothing about you, does she, dear? Well, perhaps she needs some information. Perhaps she needs to know what a hard, cold, ruthless bastard you are."

"Shut up, Crystal." Smyth glanced back at Meg. She stood flat against the rail, her hands gripping the top, eyes wide. The fear was back. Her face held the same expression he'd seen that night in her bedroom.

Crystal burst forward again. "I'll not shut up! She deserves to know the truth, Smyth. She deserves to know exactly the type man she's getting caught up with!"

"I mean it, Crystal. Shut up or—"

"Or what?" she screamed. "You gonna shut me up? How you gonna do that, Smyth? Knock the hell out of me? You'd like that, wouldn't you? You'd like to knock me to the ground and kick the life out of our child, wouldn't you? You hate me that much. You hate the child we made together even more. Well, just try, you animal. Just try and hit my baby. Because when you do, I'll take you for every cent your grandfather left you!"

Crystal abruptly turned and headed down the pier toward the shore. Smyth watched her every step. She caught up with a man near the restaurant. When they were at last out of sight, he finally released the breath he'd held for what seemed an eternity with a forceful burst from his lungs. His hands at his side, his fists clenched and unclenched with the additional release of his anger from his body.

He turned back to Meg.

Quick shallow breaths lifted her chest. Her lower lip trembled. Eyes wide, full of fear and misunderstanding, they watched him warily. Drawing in a ragged breath, her body convulsed in a deep tremor.

She was truly frightened of him.

Smyth stepped a half-step toward her. "Meg," he said softly.

"Don't. Don't come near me," she stammered. Her wide eyes grew even wider.

He stopped. Dammit. She didn't need this. Not with her history.

"Meg, Crystal's crazy. Let me explain. I wouldn't have hit her." He reached out to her. "She was putting words in my mouth. I would never do that."

Meg jerked to her right, away from him. "I don't want to know about it. I want to go home."

"I'll take you home, sweetie," Smyth said in a hushed voice. "I'm not going to hurt you. Come here."

She side-stepped him again.

Smyth stepped another half-step closer. "I can't take you home if you won't come close to me."

Meg frantically shook her head.

"I won't hurt you, Meg."

He watched her chest heave, a deep breath whooshed out of her lungs. "But what about her?" She thrust an arm toward the parking lot. "What about her, Smyth? Would you have hit her?"

Smyth saw her confusion, hurt, and anger. He kept his voice calm and non-threatening, hating himself for allowing his anger with Crystal to wreak havoc with his emotions, for allowing him to lose control as he did. "I've never hit any woman, Meg. Believe me. It's a long story. Let's go home and I'll explain it all."

"But what about the baby?" she bit out. Her facial features became animated. Smyth knew she teetered on the edge. "What about the baby, Smyth. Is what she said *true*?"

Watching her face contort in pain, Smyth knew he owed her answers. He just didn't know how to give them to her. Abruptly, she turned away from him, her arms hugging her body.

He watched her profile. It was like she'd withdrawn into herself. The look on her face alarmed him.

"The baby is not mine," he told her. "And I would never hurt a child," he whispered. "Any child. And I would never hit a woman." He laid a soft hand on her shoulder. She jerked away. "Meg," he whispered. "I would never hurt *you*."

She whimpered, dropping her face into her hands.

"Come here. Please."

She lifted her face and moved toward him. Her eyes, dark green in the night, brimmed with tears. She sucked in one breath after another as she let him hold her gaze. At last, she timidly leaned into him and sobbed gently against his chest.

Smyth clasped her to him. Cradling her body against his, he felt their pain mingle, felt her arms clutch and hold him.

"He killed my baby," she whispered softly into his neck, her breath hot against his tear-dampened skin. "He beat me until he killed my baby...pushed me into the corner of a dresser. Hard. I miscarried at five months."

Smyth wanted to kill the bastard and knew if he ever met him he'd be hard-pressed to control his actions.

"Oh, honey, I'm so sorry."

She curled into him like a kitten, pent-up sobs keeping her body tense. All Smyth could do was hold her, console her, until he could get her home and explain the whole ugly mess. Until he could get her home and show her how much he cared, not matter how insane and improbably that sounded. She was getting to him.

****

During the solemn and silent ride back to Nags Head, Meg sat huddled against the passenger side door staring out into the night. The half-hour drive was exactly what she needed to put things into perspective. And, she amended, she assumed that Smyth was doing the same.

His silence said more than his words ever had.

It was hard not to think about the kiss, hard not to relive every tingled nerve ending, every flare of passion he'd dragged up from somewhere deep within her. But she had to forget it.

And she had to keep reminding herself she really didn't know Smyth Parker. Not at all. How did she let herself get into this?

She forced herself to look at him, to watch his profile. The lights from the town illuminated him. His tender actions with her almost said he cared. He was wonderfully handsome. His lips...oh, his lips. How she would like, just once more...

She turned back to stare into the night.

No. She'd seen anger in him tonight. She could never allow herself to get caught up in that again. And what about the ex-wife carrying the child? She didn't know what to make of that.

The tires of the car crunched on sandy gravel and Meg

realized they were at the cottage.

Smyth parked and turned off the engine. For several minutes they sat staring ahead into the night sky. Finally, he turned to her and reached out to gently grasp her hand.

"It's late. There are only a couple of things I want to say to you now, then I want you to sleep on it. We'll talk in the morning."

"You're going back in the morning," she whispered, half afraid for him to leave, half wanting him to. "Aren't you?"

He nodded.

"Oh."

His gaze searched hers out and held tight. "Crystal is my ex-wife, Meg. The papers were filed months ago and the divorce settled. The child she is carrying is not mine. She's fighting for part of my inheritance." He paused, searching her face. "I would never hurt her or the child. I don't believe in dominance. I'm not a violent man. Yes, she angered me, but you have to know that I would never hurt her. But..."

Meg held his stare for a few seconds. She really did feel what she'd witnessed tonight was out of character for Smyth. "But she pushes all the wrong buttons, right?"

Smyth sighed deeply and nodded. "I would never hurt you, Meg. I'm so sorry about what happened to you and your baby. You have to believe that I would never do such a thing to anyone."

She believed him. For whatever reason, she did. But she couldn't take it into her heart and trust him. Even though she wanted him to carry her up the stairs, kick in the door, and make slow, seductive love to her all night long. She wanted it more than anything. But she wouldn't let that happen. Turning, she slipped her hand out of his and opened the car door.

"Good night, Smyth." She didn't even look him in the face. She couldn't. While walking up the steps to the cottage, the thing that kept playing through her mind was that she'd heard it all before. Too much like Bradford's favorite line. *I would never really hurt you, Megan.* No. He would just kill her. And when he found her—if he hadn't already—she would be dead. And he would take out anyone else in his way when he did. No doubt in her mind.

She was glad for what happened tonight, and that he would be leaving in the morning.

Smyth Parker needed to steer as far away from her as he possibly could.

****

Morning came and the first thing Meg heard was Smyth's voice. Slowly, she crept out of bed, glancing at the clock on her nightstand. Seven-thirty-three. As she dressed in jeans and a T-shirt, she realized the conversation she heard was one-sided. She opened the bedroom door a crack and listened to Smyth talking to someone on the phone.

She padded down the hallway toward the great room in her bare feet. Smyth stood with his gaze fixed at the ocean sunrise. He appeared to be drawing power from it. The power he needed to leave her?

He cradled the phone between his shoulder and chin. As he spoke he shuffled the morning paper back and forth. Meg leaned into the wall at the corner of the room and watched, listening to half of the conversation, guessing at the rest.

"I need to leave today, John. No, I know I told you it would be another week, but things have changed. I need to get back."

Smyth shifted the paper, closed it, and then tossed it onto the kitchen table. His hands fell to his hips. Meg watched every motion he made.

"Look. I really don't want to take you away from your family, but you know it will only take an hour at the most. If I didn't need to get back, I wouldn't ask you. There's no one else, John." Smyth paused.

Meg followed his gaze. Three dolphins played not far off the shore. Smiling to herself at the simplicity, she sighed. If only life were so easy.

At her sigh, Smyth turned. Meg caught his gaze but

didn't move a muscle. She simply watched until he finished.

"All right. If you can't make it then, I'll leave right away. I can be there in an hour. Yes.

An hour, no more. I promise. I'll let you get back to your kids."

Smyth replaced the receiver in its cradle, then returned his attention back to Meg. "I'm sorry. I have to leave now."

Nodding, Meg knew what was coming next. "I know."

"We need to talk."

Meg shook her head. "No." He needed to go and she needed him gone. She had a lot of soul searching to do. She suspected he did, also. She continued, "There's nothing to talk about. I understand about your wife, the child. You. The thing is, you don't understand me. It's best you go. There's so much you don't know."

He edged closer as he plunged his hands deep into his pockets. Meg wondered if he did that to keep from reaching out to her. If he did, she was thankful. She would probably melt if he touched her with anything other than his gaze.

"I wish we had more time—"

"We don't," she interrupted. "It's for the best. For both of us. Let's not get into something that will tear us both apart in the end. We need to let it go now." His eyes attempted to penetrate hers. There was so much more that needed to be said, expressed in other ways. "You have to go," she whispered.

For a moment, all she heard was her own breathing. Smyth raked his gaze over her, up and down, finally settling on her face. "I can't give you much of me right now."

"I can't give you any of me," she added, barely speaking.

"The timing is all wrong."

Meg nodded in agreement. "Bad timing."

After a moment, she shifted from the wall, turned away, and walked toward the couch.

He walked silently behind her toward the bedrooms. "I only need to grab my things. I really have to go now."

With her arms crossed over her chest, Meg stared at the ocean and nodded. Knowing he could only see the drop and lift of her head from behind meant he couldn't see the tears that threatened to spill over her lower lids. She could never let him see the pain that pierced her heart.

And the funny thing, if she truly wanted him gone, then why the tears?

She hadn't moved when a moment later she heard him enter the room. On soft steps, he approached behind her, hesitated, then crossed the room and exited the door. It shut with a soft whoosh. Meg allowed a ragged sob to escape her lips as it did.

Had the best thing that ever happened to her just walked out of her life as easily as thistle seeds blowing on a breeze?

She didn't let the thought linger.

Quickly gathering every defense around her that she had ever known, she sucked it all up inside, wiped her hands across her eyes, and headed toward the bathroom. After splashing her face with cold water, she reached for a towel on the rack and told herself repeatedly that she wasn't going to let Smyth's leaving get to her. Wouldn't allow it.

As she lifted her head to dry her face, she stared out the window past the cottage directly behind her. Smyth's Jeep sent tiny sprays of sand in arcs from his rear tires as he sped out the drive. Her gaze followed him to the end where he turned left. Leaving her. Out of her life, forever.

An unexplainable, empty ache filled the cavity where her heart should be. Her gaze slowly drifted back to the drive. Another emotion suddenly gripped her—fear, terror, disbelief. It clutched at her, quickly replacing the ache.

Directly across from the entrance to Smyth's drive sat a very familiar, very black sedan.

Two recognizable men sat inside watching her small cottage.

Chapter Twelve

Meg stood in stunned silence, her feet frozen to the bathroom floor. Clutching the towel in her hands, her fingers grew tight and her blood icy as every muscle in her body tensed. Nearly forgetting to breathe, her brain spun in confusion. Every emotion, every fear plagued her body at that instant and she knew—knew deep down in her soul—that the game was up.

Bradford had found her.

And her only hope, her only security, had just left her all alone.

Deep inside Meg knew she couldn't lean on anyone else. She'd gotten herself this far alone, she could do it again. All she had to do was escape. Somehow. She'd be damned if she'd give up without a fight, for to give up just might mean her life.

Meg tossed the towel to the floor and snatched the curtains shut. Frantic, she ran to the only door in the house and locked it, her fingers shaking. As an added measure, she shoved the love seat against the door, jamming it beneath the doorknob.

Think, Meg.

Racing against time, she pulled the strings attached to each of the shades on the six floor-to-ceiling windows facing the ocean, letting them each drop with a clank. That done, she stopped in the center of the room, allowing her body to catch up with her brain. Nothing more she could do. She secured the door. No one could see in through the windows. Bradford's thugs would be fools to try and break in during the light of day, wouldn't they?

She should be safe until night. All the other windows were high off the ground on the stilted house. Someone would need a ladder to get into those.

Or out, her brain screamed. Oh, God. Who in the hell

built a house with only one door?

When she'd arrived, she didn't think of the drawbacks, only the advantages.

Now what? Curiosity getting the best of her, she headed to the bathroom to see if the car was still there. She slowly pulled back the edge of the curtains. The sedan sat parked in the same place. She could see the outlines of two men in the front seat.

Taking a deep breath, Meg slid to the bathroom floor, hoping she had the day to figure out what to do. Praying they'd only watch her comings and goings for a while and wouldn't strike when she least expected it.

Rudy. Suddenly images of her friend crossed her mind. Too many days had passed since she'd last called her. Should she risk it? Should she call from here? She had to know what Rudy knew. Had she told Bradford?

"What the hell," Meg muttered. "It's not like I'm giving away my hiding place." She needed Rudy's strength right now.

Meg hurried to Smyth's bedroom and picked up the extension. She cradled the receiver to her ear for several seconds as she stared at the numbers, then in resolution, violently punched in Rudy's home number. It was still early, hopefully she'd catch her at home. If not, she'd try the office.

A deep, brisk "Hello?" answered on the other end. Jolted, Meg couldn't speak. Had she dialed the wrong number?

"Hello?" He barked out again.

Puzzled, Meg cleared her throat. "Sorry, I must have a wrong number."

"Who you calling?"

Almost hanging up on the man's brusqueness, Megan tentatively replied, "I'm calling my attorney. Like I said, I've got the wrong number."

"You want Rudy Marshall? Who are you?"

Stunned, Meg paused. "Who are *you*?"

"I asked first."

Meg huffed impatiently into the phone. "Look, I'm not in the habit of giving my name out to strangers. If Rudy is there, tell her it's important. She'll take the call."

"Sorry, lady. I'm kind of busy here. Now you want to tell me who you are or what?"

A little more than aggravated, Meg snapped back her reply. She didn't have time for twenty questions. She was frightened. "Is this Rudy Marshall's home or not? I need to speak to her, now. If I have to, I'll contact the local authorities and see what in the hell is going on there—"

"I am the local authority. How well did you know Miss Marshall?"

Did?

"What are you talking about? She's a good friend, my attorney. Who in the hell are you?"

The other end of the line fell silent.

"Ma'am, I'm afraid I've got bad news." Meg's insides suddenly turned to quivering gelatin. "I'm Chicago police. I'm afraid, well... Ms. Marshall met with an unfortunate accident last night."

"Accident?" Terror ripped through Meg's heart.

"There's been a murder."

Meg felt her eyes close and the very life drain out of her. "Murder?" she repeated in a soft, almost non-existent voice. "Rudy?"

"I'm sorry. It happened sometime during the night. Her cleaning lady found her about an hour ago." After another minute of silence, he continued. "You okay?"

Meg barely heard his last words, the phone slid from her fingers to the floor. A thick cord of fear strangled her, cutting off her oxygen as well as her speech. Suddenly lightheaded and nauseous, she felt as if she was about to pass out.

****

In Chicago, he waited for the phone to click off and the dial tone to sound, but it never did. After another minute of trying to get a response from the woman caller,

127

Mack MacDowell finally replaced the receiver. He stood staring at it for a minute, rubbing his stubbled chin with his hand.

"Everything all right there, Mack?" The question came from his right. He turned his gaze in that direction, watching Ken Moss sift through the contents of a trashed book shelf.

"Yeah." Mack shook his head and glanced again at the bloodstained floor. "I guess so. That was an odd call."

"Why?" Moss lifted his gaze and Mack met it head on.

"I don't know." Distracted, he stared past Ken now, out the window, still shaking his head. "I don't know. I just can't put my finger on it."

Grabbing his jacket, Mack left Rudy Marshall's ransacked apartment.

****

The irritating click of a disconnected line broke through the fuzzy haze surrounding Meg's brain. It was the only thing that brought her out of her fear-filled trance.

Rudy is dead?

With no time to waste, she quickly rose to pick up the phone and replace it in its cradle.

Methodically, without rhyme or reason, she returned to her bedroom and nervously thrust her feet into her tennis shoes. She removed the large manila envelope from between her mattress and box springs, lifted her T-shirt and stuffed it deep into the front of her jeans. The top still stuck up toward her breasts, but she'd just have to deal with that for now. No time to tape it into place.

She tucked her T-shirt into her jeans, added a belt, and then searched for Smyth's backpack.

Hall closet. Her adrenaline pumping, she raced to it. Tossing beach paraphernalia and cleaning supplies to the side, she located the backpack and took it to her room. She stuffed handfuls of underwear, socks, shirts, a bathing suit, personal items, shorts and another pair of jeans in the bag and topped it off with her wallet. The rest she left. Without another thought, she securely fastened the backpack over her shoulders and headed to the bathroom for one last look at her visitors.

Nothing had changed.

Except that Rudy is dead.

Closing her eyes against the ugly scene invading her thoughts, Meg rushed to the kitchen and climbed up onto the counter. Since the kitchen sat on the opposite side of the house from the only door, she knew this window was her only means of escape. The door was not an option, with the nose of the sedan pointed directly toward it. They knew the window was her only feasible way out. They knew that exit from any window meant jumping at least twenty feet.

They just didn't know the desperation pushing her to do it.

Forcing the lower window open, Meg stuck her head out to glance at the back of the house—all clear. As she quickly, but carefully eased her way out, she thought about all those stories of how people survived falls from high places. The only concrete thing she could remember was that they didn't tense their bodies. They tried to remain perfectly relaxed and limber, controlling their fall.

That was what she had to do.

Hanging onto the edge of the windowsill literally by the seat of her pants, her shoulders and head scrunched under the window, she pushed to propel herself toward the dune below—trying to force her body into relaxation.

She fell onto her side with an *oomph*, making a deep impression into the dune. Sand particles filtered around her, in her mouth, and down her shirt. But she didn't suffer any injuries. Thank God for the dune.

Slightly dazed, Meg shook her head, sputtered to spit out a mouthful of sand, and immediately glanced around to see if anyone spotted her. She rubbed at her right shoulder. She might be sore in the morning, but sore beat out dead. Then she froze. She'd not thought about the fact that the house rested on stilts. Luckily, she'd landed on the ground opposite the outside shower, making it difficult to see all the way under the house. If she looked very hard, she could still see the sedan. She just hoped they couldn't see her.

She slowly dug her way out of the dune and crawled toward the beach. When she reached the ocean side of the house that faced away from the street, she glanced around and then stood.

Meg quickly brushed sand from her body and wiped particles from her face.

Without looking back, she raced toward the shoreline. Any evidence of her leaving would be washed away with the morning tide.

She ran north, without a thought to her destination.

Chapter Thirteen

Samuel Lockbourne strode determinedly into Bradford Thomas' office without knocking and slapped the morning paper down on his desk. Bradford looked up in mock surprise.

"Good morning, Sam. Something on your mind?" Bradford attempted a smile at the expression on Sam's face.

"Read the paper yet?"

"No."

"Then read."

"Why?"

"Just read."

After thoroughly inspecting Sam's demeanor, Bradford decided to do as Sam asked. Or demanded, actually. Sam never asked for anything.

Bradford picked up the paper and perused the section Sam laid on top—the city and state news. It didn't take him long to zero in on the small news clip. *Local Attorney Found Dead in Apartment.*

Blinking rapidly, he brought the paper up closer to his face and read the details, willing a momentary fissure of panic out of his chest. What the hell had happened?

According to the paper, Rudy Marshall was discovered in her ransacked apartment early the morning before, cause of death assumed to be strangulation although the M.E. reserved making a definite statement until an autopsy could be completed. The clip briefly stated that Rudy had a private practice, but also dealt on a corporate basis with Thomas Industrials.

"Shit."

Bradford looked up at Sam.

"Did you know about this?"

Bradford shook his head. "I ordered her apartment searched. I thought she might have something there about

Megan, a phone number, address, something. Now that the kidnapping scheme seems to have taken hold, I don't need her stepping back into the picture. I need to find her and have her disposed of as soon as possible. I assumed all had gone as planned."

"What about the other one?"

"Other one?"

"The girl at your house."

Bradford didn't follow.

"Didn't you order them to knock her off?"

"Yes, but...goddammit!" Stunned, Bradford stared straight ahead and peered into Sam Lockbourne's face. "The bastards killed the wrong one."

"Hell, Bradford! We can't afford a slip-up like this. And we needed Rudy. You had her in your hip pocket."

Bradford shot up from his chair and turned to stare out the window. Fuck, how he hated admitting that the thought of Ru being dead ate at him. More so than the thought of Megan leaving him did. Shit! The fucking bastards killed her! He'd counted on having Ru by his side during the campaign. He needed her almost as much as he'd needed Megan. But with Megan gone, he'd thought he could carry on, if he had Ru. The stupid idiots.

He turned to Sam then, trying to hide the look of despair he knew must be on his face. He had to buck up. Get over it. There were things to be dealt with. He waved Sam off. "I'll handle it," he said.

When Sam was gone, Bradford fell into his padded leather chair and contemplated his next move. Surprisingly, even to him, it came to him rather quickly.

****

Later that day, Bradford arranged for a brief and unexpected meeting with Riker. Without warning, he snatched him by his brown suit coat lapels and threw him up against the building in the alley behind the office complex. Rock hard and shaking, Bradford's left fist jabbed an uppercut into Riker's abdomen, forcing a whoosh from his lungs.

It felt good. Real good.

Bradford followed with his body, sandwiching the man between his chest and the brick wall.

"You killed the wrong woman, you bastard," the words bit from snarled lips.

Riker coughed and sputtered, his face red. "But—"

Bradford interrupted, his voice thick and raspy. His fingers traveling up to the man's neck, squeezing. He would get even for the taking of Rudy's life. He would. "Shut up! You killed the wrong one."

"Wrong one?"

"Rudy Marshall. You were only supposed to trash her apartment, not kill her."

Riker's eyes widened in alarm. "I swear, Mr. Thomas. We never touched the broad. She wasn't there."

Bradford eased the pressure on Riker's neck. "You're lying to me."

"I swear. The woman wasn't there."

"Somebody killed her."

"It wasn't me or my men. I would know."

"I hope you're lying." Bradford buried his pistol in the man's gut. "Because I'd hate to kill a man for telling the truth."

"Wait!" he pleaded. "I...I have news."

Giving pause to the man, Bradford eyed him, nose to perspiring nose, then jabbed the gun deeper into his ample belly. "What news?"

"We found her."

Stunned, as if he'd already anticipated the answer to his next question, Bradford glared into the man's face. "Who?"

"Your wife."

Bradford stepped back, releasing the man from his grasp. Riker might just redeem himself yet. Although he would kill him before it all was over anyway. Damn him for taking away Ru.

Slithering down the wall, it took Riker a minute to gather his faculties. Shaking his head, he then straightened his tie and adjusted his suit coat about him.

"Where?" Point blank, Bradford stared at the man, demanding information.

"North Carolina. Some island."

"When?"

"Today."

"And?"

Swallowing, Riker stared at his boss and waited. "They're waiting for instructions, sir. For your go ahead."

Narrowing his eyes, Bradford glared at the man for several seconds longer.

"Kill her."

Inching closer into the man's face, he reemphasized his next point. "Don't fuck it up, either. And don't fuck her. You don't deserve the pleasure. I want her dead by morning. Put whoever is out there on it, tell them to stay until it's done. No one gets paid until I see her body in a big black bag. Do you understand?" He jabbed the man in the chest with his forefinger.

Riker nodded.

"And get it right this time."

"Yes, sir."

Bradford Thomas turned and disappeared into the night. When the time came, he'd rip Riker's hide from his body piece by piece and then feed his carcass to the sewer rats. Fucking imbecile. Goddamned liar. He'd fucked up and killed Rudy.

****

Several hours later when Bradford entered his bedroom, he winced at the noise and the light and the goddamned stench of that cheap bubble bath the girl used. The television was on, a radio blared from the bathroom, and every fucking light in the room had the place lit up like Wrigley Field.

He turned the television off with the remote, then smashed the set back against the wall with his fist. The noise brought Cindy up out of the tub in the adjoining bathroom.

"Brad! What happened? What..."

He glared. She obviously didn't like the look on his face because she shut up. "Get me some goddamned Vodka and orange juice. Now!"

She jumped and wrapped a towel around her body. If he hadn't been so damn agitated with her and that cocksucker Riker, he would have thought the bubbles sliding over her ass as she walked away pretty sexy. But sexy and cute didn't do it at the moment.

He wanted revenge. And he'd get it wherever he could take it.

Cindy returned quickly and handed him the glass of juice and Vodka. He drank it all down at once, held the glass chest high, and looked at her. "Get another one." He shoved the glass toward her. She left again.

By the time she'd returned with the second one, he'd stripped down to nothing. Cindy watched him as he nursed the second drink while he paced the bedroom floor. She waited several minutes before approaching him. She'd learned her lessons well. Almost as good as Megan.

"If you'd like me to run a bath, it might relax you."

"I'm relaxed." He paced to the windows looking out over the street.

"Are we still going out? How about a late dinner?"

"No."

"But Bradford," she whined. "You said that tonight, we would—"

Bradford turned abruptly and faced her. "I don't care what I fucking said. I don't want to go out to dinner!"

Her face screwed up and he hoped she wasn't going to cry. Dammit, he hated it when they cried, it only made him want to hurt them more. Shut them up. But Cindy obviously learned that lesson, too. She turned away and started for the bathroom.

"Where are you going?"

"I'm going to finish my bath."

"No. Come back here."

She didn't stop. "I need to finish my bath."

"You crazy bitch! I said get back here!" He crossed the

room and grabbed her arm.

She turned to face him. "What's wrong with you tonight, Brad? We were going to spend the evening together, you promised me. You said we'd go out on the town. I bought a new dress, a black sexy one like you wanted. I was getting all ready for you. What did I do wrong? What did I do to make you so mad at me? Can I make it up to you?"

If there was one thing he liked about a woman, it was when she groveled. When she knew her place. And Cindy knew how to play that to the hilt. It was her one redeeming quality. Well, maybe she had two.

She was still young and tight.

"My attorney was killed this morning."

Cindy's eyes grew wide. "Oh..."

"She was murdered."

"How...awful." He watched the muscles move in her neck as she swallowed. "How?"

"Strangled, they think. But maybe poisoned."

Every expression on Cindy's face froze. "That's horrible," she squeaked out.

"Yeah. That's what I said."

He kept staring at her and while he did, fragments of a conversation they'd had a while back nagged at him. He narrowed his eyes into tiny slits. "You never met Rudy, did you, Cindy?"

Her face jerked, almost like a tic, and she answered with a meek, "No."

He grinned and chuckled. Lying bitch. "A shame." She reminded him of Rudy when she looked at him like that. "Come here."

She stood still, unmoving, until he reached out and snagged her upper arm, forcing her body next to his. "I want to fuck."

Chapter Fourteen

They'd known they had to be extremely careful and it was imperative that things go according to plan. Bradford and Sam had taken every precaution, had taken every minute detail into consideration in expediting the kidnapping ploy and subsequent reported death of Megan Thomas.

It was dragging on too goddamned long.

Bradford glanced to Sam who nervously paced the office. Sam played his part to the hilt.

The longtime friend, the worried companion, the cool business partner who would be able to calm Bradford in the event of bad news.

Sam ought to have been a fucking actor, Bradford thought.

Bradford sat behind the desk in his crowded office. He glanced warily about the room as he tried to work. Tried to make it seem as if he was working, that business progressed normally, but it was damned difficult. They'd been at this over a week.

Involving the FBI had been risky, but there was no choice in the matter. Once the local police had become involved, and with his profile of a potential political candidate as well as the CEO of a major corporation, there was no doubt they would have to come on board.

They'd anticipated it. He hoped to hell they'd thought of everything. Sam demonstrated a pure stroke of genius when he insisted on sending Cindy on an impromptu trip to New York, carte blanche all the way. Bradford was glad to have her out of his hair for a while. Her greedy little eyes told the story all too well. She liked to fuck as much as the next whore and was fairly good at it considering her age, but she liked money more. And she made out damned good, even if she had to pay for it with a little pain at times.

But then he got what he wanted. He always got what he wanted. And he would get what he wanted this time—Megan dead and the Senate seat. And power.

The two FBI agents lazed about, half dozing, one on the black leather sofa, the other slouched in a chair next to Bradford's desk. The older one, sprawled on the sofa and snoring like a hibernating bear, had balls as big as a hog's. Every time he snorted, his legs fanned back and forth, tightening across his khaki trousers. The other guy had some name like Todd-Fucking-Fag.

Anyone named Todd had to be a fucking fag. The guy's mannerisms and puny voice irritated Bradford immensely.

And then there was the local dick sitting directly across from his desk, eyeing him. He was uncannily quiet so far. Watching. Making him almost frickin' paranoid. Last thing he needed was a nosey detective who wanted to make a point poking around.

He couldn't remember the man's name and made a mental note to find out. He didn't like him. When the time came, he would be mincemeat. But for the moment, Bradford had to concentrate on the task at hand.

The room was a fucking mess. Donut and pizza boxes littered about. Empty foam cups scattered on coffee and end tables too expensive to be insulted with the touch of foam.

Newspapers strewn everywhere. He'd tried to get Betty to clean up, but Hog Balls said to leave it, that he wanted no interference. He just didn't want his fucking nap interrupted.

So Bradford was left to deal with existing in a fucking pigpen. And he'd left a similar scenario at his home.

They all awaited *the call*. When it came, the fag would simultaneously listen in as Bradford tried to keep the guy on the line, listening to the kidnapper's terms, while Hog Balls manned the tape recorder and monitored the device which might be able to trace the call.

The call would come in sometime that afternoon.

Bradford and Sam decided long ago that they would give the FBI just enough time to trace that call with Riker on the other end, at a location just south of the city, ready to deliver the exact message he'd been ordered to give.

Riker, Sam, Bradford, and two men who were to meet their demise later, were the only ones who knew the plan. Bradford ticked off the details in his head. He hadn't forgotten anything, had he? They'd scoured their brains, thought of every possible hitch. The phone taps had been removed from his house, Cindy removed from the picture. He'd given the order to exterminate Megan hours ago and everyone in his inner circle instructed not to call about anything until told otherwise.

Betty was ordered to screen calls as normal.

When Riker made the first fake call, right before Bradford initially contacted the police, he'd used the general line as instructed, the one listed in the phone book rather the private line.

The Feds and everyone else assumed the kidnapper would use that number for his second call.

The ringing of the phone shrilled in his ear. Hog Balls jerked upright on the sofa with a snort, reached for earphones and leaned forward toward the taping device. Todd-Fucking-Fag twisted in the seat to look at Bradford then slowly signaled him to reach for the phone. The agent reached for the extension. And nodded.

The detective rose from his seat and shoved his hands in his pockets. Bradford eyed him.

Simultaneously he and the fag picked up the receivers.

Bradford cleared his throat over the almost non-existent click of the tape recorder.

He heard a muffling in the background, like traffic going by outside. Good. "Bradford Thomas." He lifted his eyes to the detective across the room who now shifted forward to the edge of his seat, then slid his gaze to the agent next to him.

"What about the money?" Riker bit into the phone.

"I've got it. What about Megan?"

"Aw, she's fine, man. Real fine."

"I want to talk to her."

"Impossible. I need the money first."

Bradford looked at Todd and raised his voice. "No. I want to fucking talk to her now!" The FBI team leaned in, shaking their heads. Hog balls whispered, "Don't piss him off."

There was a long pause on the other end. Traffic continued by. Finally, Riker said, "Look man, if you ever want to see her again, you're going to have to cooperate with me. I make the terms here. I'm the one sleeping every night next to your pretty blonde wife. I might give her back, I might not. You know a man gets pretty horny sleeping handcuffed to a pretty, blonde thing like that, night after night."

Damned sonofabitch Riker. Bradford felt his face growing hotter.

Todd knocked softly on the desk, diverting his attention. He mouthed the words, *Keep him talking.*

Bradford shook his head. He knew what to fucking do. Shit, Riker almost had him believing this thing was for real.

"This has been going on for too long. I want to end this thing." That was an understatement. "I want my wife back."

"And you know what I want. Have you got it?"

"Where do I take it?"

"I asked you if you've got it."

"Yeah! Yeah! I've got it! What do you want me to do with it?"

"I haven't decided yet."

"What do you mean you haven't decided?" Bradford stood up behind the desk. He might as well make this good.

"I haven't decided if I want the money worse than I want her."

"You goddamned fucking bastard! What the hell kind of game are you playing?" Out of the corner of his eye he saw Hog Balls wave to Todd. They'd had enough time. Good. Maybe a little longer for good measure.

"I like playing games. This is fun. Isn't it?"

"Tell me how to get Megan back."

Riker paused again, for effect, he supposed. Bradford glanced up. Sam crossed the room and now stood beside the desk. His eyes were clearly sending messages. *Make it good*, they said.

"You've got the mil?"

"I've got it. Some of it's in jewels, but it's worth it."

"No good."

Bradford smashed a hand down on the desk. Todd jumped. "What do you mean, *no good*?"

"I ain't hocking some kidnapped broad's jewels. I want cash. Get it together. I'll call back."

"When?"

The phone clicked off. Bradford registered the hum and pulled the receiver from his ear. His blood pressure was rising. Riker was playing him. Fuckhead.

He heard Todd replace his receiver and sigh, then heard the snap of the recording device as it was turned off. Sam stared into Bradford's eyes. Across the room, the detective rose.

Hog Balls took off his headphones and tossed them on the sofa. "I got a bad feeling about this," he said.

****

Twelve minutes later, two undercover FBI agents dressed in leather and denim and riding Harley Davidson motorcycles sped to the phone booth across the street from the Sunset Motel. They got off their bikes and approached the booth where the receiver end of the phone dangled down inside. One of the men carefully lifted the cord and bent to listen. A disconnected line.

"Dust this for prints," he said to his partner.

He stared up and down street. His narrowed eyes took in the entire scenario—a motel, gas stations, fast food restaurants.

A small flash quickly brought his attention back to the motel. Then almost immediately, he heard the blast and took in the explosion that came from a room directly opposite the phone booth. Both men hit the ground, then cautiously raised their heads to see the windows blown from one of the motel rooms, smoke and fire roiling out. Rooms on either side appeared slightly damaged, as well.

A pick-up truck down the street sped away before either of the men could register that it might be important to follow.

****

Detective Mack MacDowell exited the double glass doors leading out of the building that housed Thomas Industrials. He winced at the afternoon sunlight. He'd been inside all day, in that dark, depressing office. It felt good to get back into fresh air.

The stench inside Thomas' office got to him. And it wasn't the stale coffee, either. The two feds were useless. He'd talked them into letting him stay although he knew they could pull rank on him whenever they wanted. All one of them could do was sleep and the other had all but written Megan Thomas off as a casualty.

Mack did not intend to throw in the towel...not yet.

He was an observer, his only agenda in sitting in with the Federal agents. He wanted to observe Bradford Thomas. He wanted to make him squirm. And when he had everything figured out, he would nail him.

****

Hours later, Bradford Thomas and Samuel Lockbourne crossed the near empty parking garage attached to the building that housed Thomas Industrials. They spoke in hushed voices as they headed for their vehicles.

"We've got to speed this thing up, Sam," Bradford pressed, "I've too many things to worry about without having those two fucking clowns monitoring every move I make. I can hardly go to the goddamned john without one of them trailing me."

"I'm sure it won't take long now."

"And that goddamned detective. MacDowell, I think that's his name. He keeps looking at me like he knows

142

something."

"He's a detective. They all think they know something. Fact is, he don't know shit. He can't. He's just giving you the heebie-jeebies, staring you down like that. That's the way they operate. Don't let the bastard make you uncomfortable. Stare him right back down…right back down."

"I want to kill him."

"Can't. Too risky. Too much else to deal with at the moment. We don't need any cop or detective working on this case to show up dead. Bad idea."

Bradford paused at his car and turned toward Sam. He knew that. But he still wanted to kill him. "So when do we make the next move."

"Heads have already begun to roll."

"Riker?"

"I got a call a few minutes earlier."

"And…"

"Riker kicked the bucket."

"You're sure."

"Positive."

"And the other two?"

Sam cleared his throat and loosened his tie. "They're heading into the city tonight to get their payoff. Damned dumb rednecks. Reminded me of that movie, what was it called? Dumb and Dumber? Where Riker found the motherfuckers, I'll never know. Anyway, they're expecting their reward." He chuckled. "They have no idea they're going to reap that reward with the ultimate sacrifice, though."

Bradford chuckled along with Sam. "So what do we do about Megan?"

Sam shrugged. "Nothing to do. Riker won't call back. The FBI already suspects, I imagine, that the little accident next to the phone booth where the call was made had something to do with the kidnapper. So we wait. After a while, no one hears from Riker or Megan and it's assumed that she's dead in a shallow grave somewhere. Or at the bottom of Lake Michigan. Case closed. You get the sympathy vote and a Senate seat. Que sera sera."

****

Riker chuckled from his hotel room somewhere in Virginia. He thought about Bradford Thomas and all the dirty work he'd done for him over the past few years. He could nail him pretty good, if he wanted. Oh, he'd probably have to do some time, but in the end, it might be worth it. Thomas was in deep shit.

Maybe if he waited for just the right time, just the precise moment, he could use all his knowledge of Bradford Thomas, Samuel Lockbourne, and Thomas Industrials to get him what he wanted.

"You'll be putty in my hands, Thomas," Riker mused, smiling. "You'll be like goddamned kid's play. And for once, I'll get to give the orders. And the first one will be to cough up a few hundred thousand green ones."

He hated to call it blackmail, but there wasn't a better word for it. Yes, that's exactly what it would be called. Blackmail. It had a nice ring to it. And after all these years at Thomas' beck and call, it would be a pleasure being on the other end of mail call.

If Thomas wanted his political future, he might just have to keep ol' Cyrus Riker on the payroll a little longer. Only he intended to up the minimum wage.

Sitting back in his chair, Riker blew a puff of smoke skyward. He flicked the ashes toward the ashtray on the table, but some filtered down on his brown suit coat. He brushed them away. He couldn't contact Thomas right away though, he had to lay low for a while. Damn sonofabitch thought he could double-cross him. He'd seen it coming, though. Outsmarted him.

Had even left a body behind to throw them off the track.

So he had to wait a while. He'd find something to do. Maybe he'd go try and find that blonde wife of his. Nags Head. Had a ritzy ring to it, didn't it? Lucky for them they'd remembered to scan the incoming call list on that lawyer's phone. Narrowed things a bit. His guys were good at what they did after that.

Smiling, Riker reached forward and snubbed out the cigarette in the ashtray. Yeah, that wasn't a bad idea. Find her sweet ass. He'd had his eye on her for a while. Wouldn't mind having a taste of that. Thomas sure as hell didn't treat her right. Maybe he'd show her what making love was all about?

Maybe he'd romance her right to the fucking bank.

Hell, the rich bitch was probably living it up out there, spending all of Thomas' money.

Maybe he ought to get his ass out there before she spent it all.

Yeah, he'd had his eye on her for quite some time.

Chapter Fifteen

Meg punched in the numbers. She hoped she remembered them right.

"Sundance Realty."

"Becky Parker, please."

"Just a minute."

Meg bit her lip as she stared out the small window next to the phone inside the pier bait shop, searching the parking lot and road for any sign of the sedan or its occupants. She was relatively certain no one had followed her. She'd quickly slipped up the stairs at the pier to make the call. Thankfully the owner had let her make a quick local one.

She hoped Becky might be able to help her.

"Becky Parker." The singsong voice lilted over the phone line.

"Becky, it's Meg. I need your help."

"What's wrong?"

"Listen," she whispered into the phone, her hands cupped over the mouthpiece. "I'll explain when you get here. Can you get off work for a few minutes?"

"Sure. Where are you? At Smyth's?"

"No. I'm at the pier north of Nags Head. I don't remember the name. I'm in the bait shop. I'll watch for you. Can you make it soon?"

"Yeah. Is something wrong? Where's Smyth?" Meg heard Becky's puzzlement, but there was no time to explain now. "He left. Please, Becky. I'll explain later. You know where I am?"

"Yes."

"Come quickly."

"I'm on my way."

The phone clicked dead in her ear.

Fifteen long, lonely minutes passed before Meg saw

Becky's Chrysler Sebring glide into the parking lot. Standing at the window, Meg waited for a few seconds to see if anyone had followed her. When it appeared safe, she silently left the window and crossed the room to the wide door. Peeking out, she glanced in the direction of Smyth's house. Again, the beach nearly empty, she saw no one to make her suspicious. She hurried to the end of the pier, and then flew down the steps toward Becky's car. Jerking the door open with both hands, she thrust herself inside, hugged the backpack to her chest, and locked the door.

"Let's get out of here." She didn't look at Becky, but glanced about nervously. Becky obliged, shoved the tiny car into gear and tramped on the accelerator. Meg slumped down in the seat.

Becky headed north out of the parking lot. "Where to?"

Meg threw a glance out the rear window, then looked at Becky. Sighing, she ducked further into the seat. "I don't know. Where's your house?"

"What's going on, Meg?"

"Have you got a couple of days?"

Becky sidled a questioning glance her way. "No. I've only got forty-five minutes. What's with you?"

Resigned, and knowing she had to trust someone, Meg replied, "Take me to your house. I'll explain."

Becky's house sat several miles north of Smyth's on the beach in Kill Devil Hills. A small, flat-top cottage, with an incredible view of the beach, it sat much closer to the road than Smyth's. Becky pulled in the drive next to the house and both women tumbled out of the car.

Quickly unlocking the door, Becky ushered Meg inside, and locked it again. Meg collapsed on the couch. Becky stared at her from the center of her living room floor.

"All right. Now tell me."

Meg knew she couldn't keep any detail from her. After all, just being there put Becky in an awkward place, endangering her. She had to be honest.

Between sighs and excited spurts, it all tumbled out.

Becky stood spellbound, her arms crossed over her chest, her jaw dropping with each sentence Meg spoke. When she finally finished, leaving only a few details untold that she had a hard time saying even to herself, Meg sat quietly as Becky stared at her.

After a moment, Becky shook her head back and forth. "It's always the ones you least expect."

"What?" Meg stared back, puzzled.

"You. Quiet. Beautiful. Looking like somebody's Barbie doll. Never would I have guessed you'd be hooked up with some kind of...espionage."

Meg stood and rolled her eyes. "It's far from espionage, Becky. It's running for my life."

She edged closer to Smyth's sister and reached out to touch her arm. "Look," she added softly, "I don't want to drag you into this. I just need a dropping off place for a few hours. If you don't mind, can I crash here for the afternoon, get my head together, and then figure out a plan? Don't think I'm going to hole up here for the summer or anything. And I don't want to put you into any danger."

Becky's eyes met Meg's. "Stay as long as you want. I'll help in any way I can." She sighed, crossed the room to look out over the ocean, then turned back to face Meg. "You know, Smyth cares for you. He really does. I can tell."

It was the last thing Meg wanted to hear at the moment. "It's impossible, Becky. There's just too much unsettled in both our lives."

"Is that why he went back this morning?"

"He'd planned to all along."

"He wouldn't have gone had he known about this. Did you tell him everything you told me?"

"Some. Please, Becky. Let me deal with Smyth." Like there would ever be that chance.

"Right now, all I'm asking is a few hours to get my head together. Okay?"

Becky stared at her for a moment, then dropped her head with a quick nod. "Okay," she returned softly, glancing at her watch. "I've got to get back to work. I'll be home around five-thirty. You take the day to think about what you want to do and I'll help you. We'll get you out of this mess, Meg. One way or another."

She smiled and Meg couldn't help but smile back. She needed a good friend, one she could trust. She knew she could trust Becky. She just didn't want her to end up like Rudy.

A moment later Becky left. Meg immediately pulled the thick yellow envelope away from her body. Slapping it on the coffee table, Meg plopped to the sofa with a sigh, propped her elbows on her knees and sank her chin into her open palms. She stared at the packet for a moment, then pulled out the stack of bills from inside.

While fanning the money with her fingers, she let a long, cleansing breath escape her lips, forcing it out as if to dispel her anxiety. Two hundred-thousand-dollars-plus in cash would make anyone nervous. Especially when it didn't belong to you.

Abruptly, she shoved the bills back into the envelope and buried it deep inside the backpack. She didn't have to worry about that now. She had other, more pressing matters to be considered.

Meg tried not to think about the thing nagging at her brain. Or the person. Blocking it all—what she'd heard on the phone, what she'd seen across the street—she wandered aimlessly about Becky's house. She consciously checked and rechecked every lock on each window and door and planned two escape routes, if necessary. She fumbled through Becky's music collection, finally selecting a familiar James Taylor disc and slipping it into the player. The slow, sultry voice filled the air around her.

Sliding her hand across the oak entertainment center, Meg crouched to view a lower shelf and assess its contents. Several books, two figurines of mermaids, and a photo album sat behind the glass door. Carefully, she opened the door and slid out the album. Settling into Becky's couch, she drew her legs up underneath her and opened the book to the first page.

Many youthful Beckys, one for every grade of her school years, stared back at her. Becky in pigtails. Becky with no teeth. Becky with big hair in junior high school and a long curly perm in high school.

Meg smiled, reminded of a similar album tucked away in her grandmother's attic in Indiana. Of course it would be dust covered and crackled now, having sat there over the years—no one touching it, no one to care.

Her father, a local college student, had swept her mother off her feet at age eighteen.

They'd married a few months later and lived a happy life together for a while, until her father's indiscretions were no longer tolerated by her mother. Within the span of ten years, Meg had been born, they'd divorced, and both had died. Her grandmother took her in to raise then. It was just her and Grandma Rose against the world. Two of a kind, they used to say.

When Grandma Rose died, some sixteen months after she and Bradford had married, Meg closed up the house and hadn't gone back. In a northern Indiana farm community, there was a lonely, old house just waiting for warmth and children and a woman's touch. She'd always thought that someday she would go back to it. Now, she wasn't so sure. Recalling the memory, Meg looked past the picture album and stared at the floor until her vision blurred.

She'd wanted that for her and Bradford. Children. A loving home. But it wasn't to be. At first, he had been so doting, so romantic. He granted her every wish, and like her mother, she was swept off her feet. She'd found out not long after their marriage that the dreams she cherished had not a chance of survival. Then, she became another possession. One that didn't need wooing any longer, just constant reminders to stay in her place.

Shaking away the thought, she returned to the album. Turning the page, she instantly felt like an observer of private memories. A teenage Smyth hammed the camera shot in front of Becky. One picture showed them splashing each other in the surf. In another, Smyth had buried Becky in the sand, only her head and feet sticking out, Smyth mercilessly tickled her feet.

Smiling, Meg turned the page. More pictures of the two of them. One on vacation, standing in front of a sign at Williamsburg, Virginia. Another with two adults, who Meg guessed were their parents, at Lincoln's feet at the Lincoln Memorial in Washington, D.C. Still another portrayed a more mature Smyth and an older man, fishing poles in hand, leaning over the pier.

Their faces intent, they seemed deep in discussion. Smyth's face show his admiration for the man beside him.

Meg knew the man must be Smyth's grandfather. The corners of her mouth turning down now, she reached out and traced Smyth's profile. The picture couldn't be more than a few years old, she guessed, for he hadn't aged much since it was taken. Time. If only they'd had some time, she would have enjoyed getting to know that man a little better. She could easily have fallen for him. She could easily picture them both in that old farmhouse in Indiana.

Slowly closing the photo album, Meg sank further into the fluffy sofa pillows and faced the ocean. James Taylor continued to croon to her. Eyes closed and head back, she imagined him singing, mellow and melodic, to her. *In my mind I'm going to Carolina....*

Ah, sweet baby James.

Smiling, it reminded her of the same song, miles and months earlier as she lay in her bed in Chicago. It was the catalyst for bringing her here today. She'd listened over and over to James Taylor singing and formed her perfect escape. Now, she knew she couldn't give up. She'd come too far. There was much more at stake than her life. There was principle. There was the fact that a murderer was on the loose. She knew Bradford had killed Rudy.

And with that thought, she knew what she had to do.

Grasping the phone, she hesitated only a second, trying to think if there was any way this call could be traced back to Becky's house. Then deciding that even if it could, it would be the good guys doing the tracing, she punched in the number for long distance information.

The line crackled and the operator asked for the city she wanted.

"Chicago."

"One moment."

After several seconds ticked by another operator took the line.

"May I help you?"

"I need a number for the Chicago Police Department."

"One moment."

One moment. Do they think I have all day? Soon, a computer voice spelled out the number and offered to connect her.

"Chicago Police."

"I need to speak to someone in homicide."

"Anyone in particular?" the bland voice on the other end questioned. She could hear his lips smacking. His name. What was his name? He had said it, hadn't he? "Whoever is working on the Rudy Marshall...murder case?"

"Uh...I dunno. Let's see." Meg heard a hand muffle the mouthpiece, but his voice still filtered through. "Hey, Charley. Who's working that downtown murder this morning? The lady lawyer. Ya know?"

Meg grimaced. Did the man have no tact? Tears stung her eyes, but she choked them back.

"MacDowell," the officer threw back at her. "Ya want I should connect ya?"

"Please." Meg answered quickly and without feeling.

Another moment passed, then a male answered the phone. "Moss, here." Wrong man.

She could tell by his voice, it wasn't him.

"I need Mr. MacDowell," she began.

"Detective," he corrected.

"Okay, okay. Detective MacDowell. I need Detective MacDowell."

"He's not here."

"When will he be back?"

There was a pause on the other end. "Couldn't say."

Gee, you're a lot of help. Should she take a stab at this guy? "Do you know anything about the Rudy Marshall case?"

"Yeah. Why? You know who did it?"

"She is...uh, was...my attorney."

"And?"

"They said she was murdered."

"Yeah."

"Yes. I think I know who did it."

There was another pause on the other end. "What did you say your name was?"

Meg raked her tongue over her lower lip. "I didn't. Look, just listen to me, okay? I'm not going to tell you who I am but I know something. Some things."

"Go on."

Meg could tell by his voice that she had piqued his interest. "I know who did it."

"You know the murderer?"

"Yes. I think so. And also who murdered Allen Crenshaw."

"The assistant D.A?" Again, his interest grew. She could tell the way he questioned her.

"Yes."

He whistled. "Lady. This is a whole other can of worms."

Meg knew that. The Chicago police had been looking for a lead to crack the execution-style murder of the district attorney for weeks now.

"They're connected," she finally said.

"What do you know?"

"Check out Bradford Thomas of Thomas Industrials. Go back and search Rudy's apartment and her office. See if you can find anything that has to do with Thomas Industrials, something you can nail Bradford with. Try to get anything on him you can. He's a dangerous man and probably your murderer."

"Who are you..."

His voice trailed off as Meg let the phone drop to the cradle with a click. After a moment, she buried her head in her hands refusing to give in to the rattling emotions that plagued her. She had to stay strong. For the friend she'd lost that day and for the loss of her own life, trapped in living hell as the wife of a man whose only dream was to someday be Chicago's biggest crime boss.

Chapter Sixteen

"You're early."

Becky tripped in the front door carrying two plastic bags of groceries. "I know. I kept thinking about you and your dilemma all morning, so I decided to take some personal time."

"And go to the grocery store?" Meg took a bag from her and set it on the kitchen counter.

"Sort of." Becky repeated the process with the other bag. "So," she continued, rummaging through one of the bags. "Do you want to go auburn or black?"

A corner of her mouth turned up in amazement. Meg crossed her arms over her chest and stared at Becky. "What?"

One by one Becky shuffled through the items. Lifting two almost identical boxes, one in each hand, she turned toward Meg. "Auburn or black. What do you think? Actually, with your coloring I think either would be fine, but black—there's something exotic about fair-skinned women with ebony hair. Don't you think?"

Meg chuckled. "You want me to dye my hair?"

Becky nodded and thrust the boxes of hair dye toward her. "Uh-huh. Good idea, don't you think?"

Stunned, Meg put them back on the counter. "Actually, I think it's a really bad idea, Becky. I've never once done anything unnatural to my hair. I always thought that was kind of vain."

Placing her hands firmly on her hips, Becky glared at her. "Oh, pooh. Women do it all the time. And if there ever was a time for you, honey, this is it." Crossing the short distance between them, she picked up both boxes again, then linked her arm with Meg's. "You need a temporary disguise. I've thought this out all morning and I've come up with a plan." Grinning at her, she winked. "Besides, I always wanted to do this. I love a good mystery, don't you? I feel like I'm in the middle of a thriller novel."

Meg arched an eyebrow as they walked toward the bathroom. To her, it was more like a horror story. If she had her choice, though, she'd rather be in the middle of a steamy romance novel. This suspense thing was getting a bit old. "A plan?"

Nodding, Becky continued. "Yep. First we alter your appearance—a little hair dye, a snip or two here and there, a change of clothing, makeup, then we go for the big stuff."

Stopping in the bathroom door, Becky laid the items on the vanity top.

"The big stuff?"

"Yeah." She looked at Meg. "I know a place where no one will ever find you."

"Really?" Meg's hope soared as her eyes widened.

"Really. We'll make a go for it this afternoon if you want."

Agreeing, Meg nodded. "We need to move quickly. You're sure no one will find me?"

Becky diverted her gaze to the boxes of dye. "Positive. In fact, I practically guarantee it."

"Where is it?"

Meg watched Becky's lips turn into a smirk and her eyes grow saucer-like. "I'm not going to tell you. Not right now, at least. Let's wait until later."

Puzzled, Meg shrugged her shoulders. "All right. I guess I don't have much of a choice, do I?" She wondered if it was Smyth's house in Elizabeth City. The idea had crossed her mind earlier and she had the key...but she didn't want to involve either of the Parker siblings to any great extent and had ruled that out. If Becky started for Elizabeth City later, she'd just have to tell her no.

Becky shook her head, grinning. "No. You do not have a choice."

"Okay," Meg returned. "Then let's get this show on the road."

"First, the disguise."

Turning toward the bathroom mirror with Becky angled slightly behind her, Meg stared at both their reflections. "Okay. Do your worst."

Becky's face lit up. "You mean it?"

Meg shrugged. "Why not. They will be looking for a blonde. Let's go shorter and black."

"Chin length?" Becky rummaged around in a vanity drawer for a pair of scissors.

Scrutinizing how she would look with short hair, Meg pulled up her blonde locks and turned from side to side. "A blunt cut, all one length, about here, I think." She pointed to about an inch lower than her earlobe. "And yes, black. Might as well go for the total opposite look."

"You can always dye it back later."

"Yes. I suppose. Maybe I'll like it, though."

"Perhaps."

Ninety minutes later Becky stood behind Meg running a blow dryer over her new hair.

Long blonde locks were scattered about the bathroom floor. Meg glanced at the mess the two of them had made, then at herself and the abrupt change in her appearance. She almost didn't recognize herself. She knew it would be hard for Bradford's thugs to recognize her.

Suddenly feeling safer than she had in a long time, Meg smiled. Stepping back from the mirror, she surveyed the results of Becky's handiwork. Not bad, really. And to think, a cut and dye job back in Chicago would have cost big bucks. Here, she got it for free and it looked just as good. But the best part of all—she looked nothing like Bradford Thomas' wife anymore.

"Here. How about makeup?" Becky pushed bottles and tubes around in the vanity drawer.

Meg shook her head slowly, still eyeing the effect of her ebony hair against her skin and eyes. "The old Megan never went out of the house without makeup. I think I'll just stick to the plain Jane look."

Becky brought her gaze up to meet Meg's in the mirror. "Honey, you're anything but a plain Jane. The results are stunning."

"Different. That's for sure." Turning to face her, Meg grasped Becky's hands. "Thanks," she said softly.

After a small grin, Becky said, "No problem." Then clearing the vanity of towels and paraphernalia, she swept the items aside and dumped them appropriately in either the hamper or wastebasket. "I'm starved. Let's eat. I'll make a phone call, then we'll get you on your way."

Appreciative of all Becky's efforts, Meg simply nodded. Within hours, she'd be somebody else again. Meg Thompson would join Megan Thomas in her memory bank of somebody she used to be. She'd already decided that by the time Becky got her to wherever she was taking her, she'd have a new name and a new background to go with her new look. And she'd never, ever look back.

A few minutes later they left Becky's house.

"Do you want to go by Smyth's cottage?"

Startled at the thought, Meg was almost repulsed. Becky turned out of her drive and onto Beach Road.

"No!" Meg gasped. "Why would I want to do that?"

Becky shrugged. "I just thought you might want to drive by, just to see if they're still there."

The thought of an encounter with Bradford's men made her nauseous. Meg shivered. "I guess I would like to know if they're still there.

Nodding, Becky braked for a stoplight. "We'll just drive by like everybody else. No gawking or slowing down. Nothing out of the ordinary. Then we'll just leave."

"All right."

As they neared the cottage, Meg felt her stomach grow queasy. Her right hand clutched at her abdomen.

"I don't know about this," she whispered.

"You'll be fine. Where were they this morning?"

"Just on the other side of the garage near the road, right by Smyth's drive. We'll be on them before we realize it."

Becky drove on, seemingly oblivious to their task. Meg pulled the ball cap Becky shoved at her down firmly over her head. She pushed sunglasses up on her nose. Watching the view pan out in front of her, she tried to quell her jumpy stomach. They were almost there.

"I'm not going to look. I'm just gonna drive. You glance back and see if you see anything." Becky directed her eyes straight ahead.

Meg saw the garage. She felt the car rush on, Becky's foot never left the accelerator.

Coming even with the garage, Meg let her gaze casually drift left. There it was! She looked directly into the windshield of the black sedan waiting to pull out of the driveway.

Jerking back toward the road in front of her, Meg gasped. "Oh, my God. They're leaving." Her heart vaulted. Meg clutched the backpack against her.

Becky's gaze hit the rearview mirror. "They've pulled onto the road behind us."

"Damn! Oh, God, Becky. I'm sorry. I didn't mean to get you..."

"Hush. Let me think. They're not following us. They can't be."

"They are! I know it!"

"Calm down, Meg."

Meg watched Becky glance in the mirror again. "Are they still there?"

"Yes. I'm turning."

Without a blinker, Becky abruptly turned up the next street toward the by-pass. Meg clutched the backpack to her chest and squeezed her eyes shut. "Well...?"

Becky exhaled, then adjusted the mirror behind her. "They turned, too."

Meg thrust her body around to look.

"Turn back around! Don't be obvious. Maybe that was a coincidence!"

Trembling, Meg slumped down in the seat. "Sorry, Becky. It's just—"

"They turned again."

Eyes wide, Meg turned to face Becky. "What?"

"They turned back there. They're heading back toward the cottage."

Without a chance to breathe, Becky slammed her foot on the brake and signaled to turn left.

"What are you doing now?"

"Wait. You'll see."

Becky turned into a row of shops and made a huge U-turn. Turning right out of the parking lot, she headed back up the by-pass. Not far down the road, she turned into a gas station angled slightly across the street from Smyth's cottage. Meg jumped out of the car and paced back and forth, glancing now and again at the cottage. She flipped open her cell phone and her mouth moved. Talking.

Meg watched, her heart pounding. The sedan inched its way up the drive toward the cottage. Finally stopping, both men stepped out of the car. One circled to the left, the other to the right of the house. Meg felt a heavy lump form in her throat. She didn't think she could swallow if she had to. She knew she wasn't breathing. All she could think about was that if she hadn't seen the car when she did this morning, they could be coming after her right now.

Becky opened the door and sat down.

"What do we do now?

"Wait."

"What did you do?"

"Called the police."

Meg stared at Becky. "Are they on their way? What did you tell them?"

"That two men in a black sedan were breaking into my brother's house. That he was away on business and that I saw them when I was passing by. Couldn't be closer to the truth."

"And they're on their way?"

"So they said."

Meg turned back to the scene in front of her. Suddenly, the man who circled the house to the left came running around to the back. He looked to be shouting for the other man. When he caught up with him, he pointed around to the left. The open window.

"Damn," Meg whispered. "He sees the window."

Becky didn't seem to be listening to her, spellbound at the scene unfolding before them.

"They know you're not in there."

"I know."

The men jogged around to the right of the house and up the steps to the porch. Watching, both women gasped as they saw the flash of the pistol as one man shot off the door lock. Meg had to wonder how desperate these men were to get her, if they'd risk exposing themselves in the light of day like that. Quickly, they shouldered through the door. It took three tries to get in past the couch barricading the door. Then they were out of sight.

Both Meg and Becky sat in stunned silence for a moment.

"I could be dead right now."

"But you're not. Remember that. You were smart and escaped."

"I know. Let's get out of here."

"Wait."

Both men burst through the open door. Racing down the steps, they took long strides getting to the car. Within seconds the sedan turned and headed out the driveway, sending sand flying in its wake. The car turned north onto Beach Road. As it drove by, Meg heard the police siren's wail in the background.

"Too late," she whispered, her chin in her hands. "They're too late."

Becky pulled out of the gas station. For the next hour she drove and Meg stared pointlessly out the car window. Telling her they were heading south, Becky then let the conversation die. South was not Elizabeth City, so she didn't have to have that conversation. Where they were going meant nothing to Meg, she knew nothing of the Outer Banks save Nags Head. She just let Becky take her. Wherever she was going had to be better than where she had been. Besides, she had a new life waiting for her…somewhere.

She barely registered the drive through the small, seaside villages of Frisco, Waves, and Salvo, then on further down through Buxton and Hatteras Village. When Becky drove onto the ferry, Meg stirred a little.

During the forty minutes on board the ferry, she and Becky stood near the front of the boat and fed the seagulls crumbs from a stale McDonald's biscuit left in a napkin in Becky's car.

They didn't talk about where they were going. It was the first time in hours she felt she could let her guard down a bit. Of the seven vehicles on the ferry, not one of them was a black sedan or resembled any of Bradford's thugs.

They finally arrived on Ocracoke Island. As they drove toward Ocracoke Village at the southernmost tip of the island, Meg decided the time had come to find out a little more about Becky's plan.

"Do you think you ought to tell me where you're taking me?"

Becky smiled. "I suppose so. We're nearly there. Is there anything we can stop and get before you leave?"

Meg shook her head. "No. I'm fine. Anything I need I can get later."

Becky screwed her lips up tight. Meg noted her nervous glance. Becky shook her head. "I don't think so."

Puzzled, Meg watched her profile. "Why?"

"Where I'm taking you, you can't get anything."

"Nothing?"

"No."

Becky continued. "There are no stores for…miles. It's totally isolated. Not many people. Even the mail doesn't come regularly."

"There are still places like that left?"

"At least one."

"In this country?"

Becky laughed. "In this state."

"Really?" Suddenly, Meg anticipated her new home.

"Yeah. And we're almost there. After you leave this

island it's a short hop, skip and a jump. I'm afraid though, that you'll have to go that leg without me."

Startled, Meg stared at her. "Why?"

Becky exhaled, huffing a small breath up to catch her bangs.

"Because I just can't go that far. It's another thirty-minute ferry hop and I've got to get back. It's almost seven now. By the time I get home it will be pretty late."

Meg turned to stare at the village rushing by her window. "Oh. That's okay. Just tell me what to do."

Becky turned her vehicle and parked looking out over a small harbor and wharf.

"Where are we?" Meg asked.

"Silver Lake. It's the harbor of Ocracoke Village. Been here since Blackbeard." She turned to face Meg. "This is where I stop, Meg, so let me tell you what you need to do from here."

Meg nodded. She turned in her seat and listened.

Becky's brown eyes sparkled at her and Meg had the distinct feeling that she enjoyed what she was doing. She certainly hoped Becky realized she was putting all her trust in her.

"I called ahead for a ferry to take you across to the next island. It will take you about thirty minutes, like I said. When you arrive on the island, it won't be long until dark, so make sure you get where you're going quickly, it will be easy to get lost."

"I'm not sure I'm liking this."

Becky smiled and reached for Meg's hand. "No, really. It's fine. From the dock you need to walk straight inland. There's only one road, so you can't miss it. You have to walk about a half-mile which should take you about ten minutes or so. It will lead you into a small village. Immediately to your left is a white, clapboard church with a tall steeple. Further up the road will be a cluster of houses. Three on the left, two on the right. Keep walking until the road makes a Y. You go to the right. There you will see a general store and another house. That's the one you want."

"The house?" Meg's brows drew up in question. She tried to picture the village in her mind.

"Yes. Knock on the door. I tried to get a message to the people living there, but I couldn't. No phones. Radio must be down. Just tell them I sent you, that you need a place to stay for a while."

Alarmed, Meg shook her head. "But how will they know that I'm not some nut case who might murder them in their sleep?"

"I told you, just tell them I sent you. They're family. Everything will be fine. Tell them I'm coming out on the weekend. That's a few days away, but it won't matter. They'll be good to you and take care of you. Right now, that's what you need. And the best thing of all, Meg, is that there is no way in hell those men can trace you to there."

"You're sure?"

"Positive. Just wait until you get there, you'll see." Becky glanced at her watch. "You need to go. There's the ferry."

Chapter Seventeen

The storm blew in quickly over the Atlantic. Waves sprang forth, beating against the side of the dock in a small fury as Meg stood facing the inlet between the two islands. In front of her and to each side was nothing but water. The island rose out of it behind her. The ferry drifted out of sight, and an unnatural and premature darkness settled around her due to the storm. Salt spray stung her eyes and the wind whipped her hair.

Quickly turning from the ocean, Meg jogged off the dock and onto the narrow sand road leading inland. Under her breath she whispered Becky's instructions. Take the road away from the dock. One half mile. Church on the left. Cluster of houses. Take the right at the Y. House across from the general store.

She repeated the process as she trudged head-on into the island. Somehow, she felt a little safer away from the fury of the ocean winds. It was alarming how quickly a storm could blow up out here.

Above her, thunderclouds raced with the wind, boiling in the evening sky. Meg quickened her steps. With the backpack securely fastened across her back, she looked to the ground, counted every step, and marched on.

By the time she reached the church, she breathed a sigh of relief just at having found the village. But as that notion crossed her mind, a finger of lightning split the sky. Thunder cracked a few seconds later, and within a few seconds more, fat raindrops fell on and about her.

Meg picked up speed. She hated storms.

Running now, water streaking down her face, she raced past the cluster of houses. Dusk rapidly overtook her and she had to squint through the rain and the dark to see the road in front of her. Moving as quickly as she could, she finally came to the Y and bore to the right.

She ran against intermittent flashes of lightning, the howling of the wind through the scrub pines and bushes, the boom of thunder, and increasing rain. She was half-afraid to admit her fear, even to herself.

So, she ran. Searching through the black mist, she looked for a light, something, to indicate houses, buildings, anything that could shelter her. She saw nothing.

Finally, determined not to let her frantic mind take over, she wondered if she should turn back. At least she knew where the other houses and the church were and they could offer shelter.

She stopped in the middle of the road in desperation. Wanting to cry, ordering herself not to, she stood, her arms limp at her sides, and stared straight ahead.

What in the hell have I gotten myself into? In one day I've found out my best friend is dead, escaped from the mob, changed my identity and my hair color, and traipsed through a rainstorm to find shelter in a place where I know no one, and they don't know me. Or even expect me. Am I insane?

In the next instant, the night lit up and a roar crashed all around her. Jumping, Meg glanced about. Illuminated within the electrical storm, she saw it. To her right stood an old, white clapboard house. A porch ran the entire width of it and Meg thought to herself that at the very least, she could get shelter from the storm there.

Running, she let her feet take her in the direction of the house. Lightning flared again just as she neared the steps. Stumbling onto the porch, Meg raced to the front door and pounded on it.

Relief flooded through her.

"Anyone home?" she shouted frantically.

She pounded again. Silence.

"Excuse me? Is anyone here?" She called out as she looked into the dark house through the small windowpanes in the front door. She saw no movement inside.

Stepping away from the door, she let her shoulders drop, refusing to think of the situation as desperate. *Okay, Meg, there's a nice chair over there. At least you're out of the rain.*

Maybe you can get a little sleep. And in the morning, you can figure out what to do.

Resigned, she turned from the door and headed toward the chair. A squeak, then a clank of metal sounded behind her. Meg halted. Within a few seconds, the outside screen door opened a crack. Meg slowly turned, and stepped forward. "I'm sorry to disturb you, but I need some help."

The door opened wider and a man stepped out onto the porch. "Meg?" The hesitant voice sounded all too familiar.

Lightning flashed and Meg clearly saw the man standing on the porch—Smyth Parker.

****

Throughout the remainder of the day after he'd arrived in Portsmouth Village, Smyth saw to his usual tasks. He'd straightened his house, put away the few items from his trip, and then set out to see how the village had fared while he was away.

Walking through the town with a practiced eye, Smyth checked for any maintenance the structures required—a loose board, shingle, or shutter. He rattled locks and peeped in windows.

He liked to keep things intact, even if it wasn't really his job. The maintenance man only came once a month.

With the wind whipping through his hair, Smyth stood at the crest of a dune and surveyed the peaceful island before him. Home. Back to his salvation. The sea always calmed him. As a child growing up close to the coast, he'd begged his parents to take him to his grandfather's cottage nearly every weekend. Remembering those times, he sighed at the simplicity, the relaxation he'd felt even then being close to the water.

It had carried over into his adult life. After the deaths of his parents, then his grandfather, he had sought the solace of the sea as so many others had done before him. And after the difficulty dealing with his marriage to Crystal, he'd embraced it fully. He knew he never should have married her. He'd simply wanted companionship, someone to comfort him, spend his life with. He'd been naive enough to grasp at the first woman who came along and played into his emotions. He'd mistakenly taken what Crystal offered him as commitment.

Stupid.

And now, he couldn't leave the solitude behind, didn't know if he ever could. Portsmouth was his home now, would be for a long time, if he had anything to say about it. It offered him the best of everything. All he needed.

The ocean. The morning sunrises. Solitude.

Shaking his head, he walked back toward the village. There were times when he thought about the mess his life had become and wasn't sure he would ever be content again.

Abruptly, fleeting images of Meg and him together passed through his mind. Just as quickly, he dismissed them. With nothing pressing, he walked back home. The seven houses, church, and general store that made up Portsmouth Village stood sturdy and stark white against the crisp blue morning.

Once there, he took stock of the supplies he needed so he could send the list with Frank Harvey next time he came. He had enough water for the week if he was careful, but mentally chastised himself for not thinking to bring an extra five gallon container with him on the boat.

There were other things on his mind when he left. Damn! He needed to prepare better for a longer stay. He wished he hadn't gotten distracted those last few days.

If Frank could pick up the few things he needed next time he came up from Harker's Island, he'd be set for a while. His needs were few and simple. Time, space, and the ocean breeze was all he ever needed. Even companionship ceased to be a necessity anymore, a good thing since he was the only inhabitant of Portsmouth Village.

Frank, one of the rangers in charge of the Cape Lookout National Seashore, came to visit about twice a month. He'd take the ferry from Harker's Island and drive up to Portsmouth on his ATV with supplies. He was due within the week. Smyth knew if he could radio a message to him this evening, Frank would bring the extra items— *if* he could get the radio up and going. It had been temperamental the last few times he'd used it.

He always looked forward to Frank's visits, but then he was always ready for him to leave again. Other visitors, tourists mostly, some fishermen, were sporadic and he never knew how many or when, but he enjoyed them also. The thing about visitors was that they'd also be gone in a few hours. Once he'd showed them the village, let them wander about visualizing the tiny sea town in its prime, and listened to the history he spouted to them, they were ready to leave.

Portsmouth Village was a novelty, an oddity. The only ghost town on the east coast. A town with no inhabitants. Except for one.

And he liked it that way.

He napped in the afternoon, knowing that spring didn't bring many visitors. Normally, visitors didn't start coming until June, when family vacations started. A few fishermen might venture his way, though most headed for Portsmouth. He really didn't expect to see anyone other than Frank for several weeks. It was too early for the tourist season. And even then, they trickled in, just a few every day. Or every other. Some weeks none at all.

Later, rested and his mind clear of the haze that had fogged it over the past week, he rose to fix himself a quick supper. The back porch offered the most spectacular sunsets, so he'd sat within the screened walls and ate. As the sun set, he watched until the black thunderclouds took over, swallowing the brilliant pinks and oranges, while racing with breakneck speed over the horizon.

He was nearly asleep, the rain pelting the tin roof above him, thunder lulling into a hypnotic dreamland, when he thought he heard pounding on his front door. Starting awake, he jumped to his feet, initial fleeting images of Meg crossing his mind. It was then that he realized he'd been dreaming of her. He'd even thought he'd heard her voice.

What his mind tried to consciously avoid all day, had taken the liberty to entertain in his sleep. Who was he trying to kid, anyway? He cared too much for her. Even after such a short time. He wondered if he could ever escape it.

In his mind's eye he still saw her standing on the porch in Nags Head, her hair blowing soft around her face, her profile pointed to the sea. Her voice, gentle and soothing, wafted toward him on the ocean breeze. The sound of it calmed him and made him ache all at the same time.

Again, he jerked his head toward the front, sure he heard pounding.

Puzzled, knowing it was impossible, Smyth entered the back of the dark house and crossed the two rooms width of it. Must be a loose hinge on the screen door, he thought, and made a mental note to start a list for maintenance. He opened the inside door, but found the screen door latched tightly shut. When he cracked it open, he saw someone silhouetted against the black night. The person turned and he saw the unmistakable profile, but....

And then she spoke.

"Meg?" It couldn't be, could it?

She stepped closer as a shaft of lightning split the sky around them.

Her hair?

"Smyth?" Her voice was small and weak.

Grasping her arm, Smyth hauled her inside the house and shut the door. Beside the door, he flipped the light switch. It took two or three flickers, the generator sometimes as cantankerous as the radio, then the lights came on fully, still only dully lighting the living room. He got a good look at her.

Meg? What the hell?

"Smyth. I didn't know it was you. She told me...I mean, Becky told me...family, but..."

He heard her, but he wasn't listening. All he saw was her hair.

Her hair. Her beautiful blond hair? The dark strands

were plastered around her head from the rain. She looked like a waif, a street urchin waiting for a handout. He reached out and gently grasped a lock of wet ebony silk at her earlobe.

Watching her eyes, he sensed something wrong, very wrong. "What happened to you?" he asked quietly. "How did you get here?"

She shivered and he glanced lower. Her clothing clung to her body, forming to every curve and dip. His backpack rested at her feet. One hand smoothed the tendril of hair back into place.

"I dyed m-my hair. Actually...Becky did." Her teeth chattered as she spoke. It didn't make sense. He picked up the backpack with one hand and with the other grasped her around the waist, pulling her toward the back of the house.

"W-where are w-we going?"

"To get you out of these clothes. You're freezing."

"I know."

He pulled her into the bathroom, dropped the backpack on the floor and began running a tub full of hot water. Turning to her, he placed both hands on her shoulders. "I'll bring you clean towels. Take a bath. Then we'll talk."

Dammit! What the hell happened? He watched her slow nod.

Before he released her, he searched her eyes. "Meg. Are you okay?"

Drawing in a ragged breath, she exhaled slowly and nodded again. "Yes. I think so. N-now."

Worried, he touched his cheek to hers. Leaving her for a moment to get towels, he returned in time to see her turn off the water and sit on the commode to untie her shoes. As she gazed at the floor, he watched a small tremor ripple over her body. Her hands stopped working the knot on her soaked tennis shoes. Crouching down in front of her, his hands stilled hers. For a moment, she continued to look downward, then slowly lifted her face to his.

The trembling lower lip and the silent tears spilling

over her lids were nearly his undoing.

For a moment, they shared the visual embrace, then Smyth untied each of her shoes and removed them from her feet. When he stood to leave her, she glanced up and he saw a hint of a smile cross her lips.

"Thank you," she whispered.

He nodded, then left her to bathe in private.

She undressed, then two minutes later Meg silently eased herself into the hot bath and closed her eyes. The water prickled her skin with warmth. Supporting her head on the back of the tub, she tried to slide into a relaxed calm, but found it hard. The hot water attempted to loosen and lengthen her taut muscles. She stretched each limb to urge the process along a bit. She hugged herself, but the shivering wouldn't stop.

Circling her head to both the right and left helped ease her tired neck muscles. She slid even lower into the water, ducking her head entirely beneath to rinse the wind-driven salt-spray from her hair, then settled comfortably with the water resting under her chin.

With forced calm, she ran her hands over her face to sluice away the excess water, then combed her short hair straight back with shaking fingers. Staring ahead into the pool of swirling water in front of her, her vision blurred and the image slowly materialized as the waters stilled.

Rudy.

The tears came. Starting slowly, they built until flowing down her cheeks, dripping like random raindrops into a bucket.

It was too much.

Too much. Rudy, oh God. Poor Rudy.

The anger hit her then. Why? Why did he have to kill her? It wasn't fair!

Meg slapped the water with her fist sending a large spray into the air, against the wall of the tub, and over the side. Sucking in a frantic breath, she tried unsuccessfully to avoid the gasping sob trying to escape. The angered cry, full of pain, wrenched pitifully from her throat and then continued, one after another. Uncontrollably. She didn't think she could stop. She wasn't sure how much more she could take.

"I'm so...sorry, Rudy," she murmured between sobs, bringing her wet hands to her face, tears mingling with bath water.

She was barely aware of the bathroom door opening and of Smyth's strong hands pulling her body from the bath, rivulets of water falling to the floor. Grasping with both hands he gathered her wet, dripping body into a large beach towel and silently clasped her to him.

"It's all right," he breathed into her ear. "It's all right, Meg."

"No," she choked, shaking her head. "It's not."

Smyth threaded his fingers through her short locks and held her head still to look into her eyes. "What happened?"

"H-he killed Rudy. M-my friend." Her voice broke in raspy sobs. "He killed her."

"Oh, God. No."

As he pulled her tighter against him, Meg felt his strong arms, his warm body, and wanted to melt into him. She wanted to simply let her body flow into his and stay, forever. He cradled her to him for several minutes, holding, caressing, and whispering to her.

Meg shook with every breath, every sob that exited her body. He only held her closer, tighter.

"I-I can't stop trembling."

"I have you," he whispered, his breath fanning her cheek. "I have you."

"It all happened so fast...it seems like so much...I just don't know...I don't know..." Meg knew she was babbling, knew she made no sense. Her arms slipped around his waist and she buried her face into his chest.

Oh, Lord. I can't lose myself in this man. I can't. Her body shook again and he continued to hold her, comfort her.

Smyth drew away, his hands moved to her face and cupped her cheeks in his palms. As he searched her eyes, his fingers played over her features, brushing back the short, black length of her hair, his thumbs gently grazing her lips. Slowly, he shook his head and Meg wondered if he couldn't believe that she was really there, or if he felt the same thing she experienced at the moment. Confused and wanting, all at the same time. Knowing that nothing could come of the two of them together.

"You make me feel so safe," she finally whispered, their gazes connected. "So safe." Her arms moved to wrap around his neck and he lifted her, carrying her out of the bathroom to a small bedroom across the hall. There Smyth set her on the bed and hesitantly stepped away.

Meg tugged the towel closer around her.

He searched her face, suddenly seeming unsure of himself. "I imagine the clothes in your backpack are all wet. I'll find you something to put on." His gaze held hers for a second longer, then he turned to rifle through one of the dresser drawers. After a moment, he tossed a pair of sweat pants and a sweatshirt beside her on the bed. He stood watching her, then turned for the door.

Hesitating there, he glanced back and took half a step forward.

"I need to know what brought you here like this. I want to know everything, Meg."

Her gaze held his for several heartbeats. Her chin dropped in agreement. "I know," she said softly.

Smyth left her to dress. Meg knew the time had arrived for her to be completely honest with somebody. It might as well be him. Maybe then she could be honest with herself.

****

Smyth knew the second he held Meg in his arms that he shouldn't, but it was an involuntary thing he couldn't control. He'd had her out of the tub and into his arms before he'd realized it. Hearing her sobs, he knew he would go to her, and knew the moment he saw her that he wanted her. But then again, he'd known that all along. It was just hell admitting it to himself.

He stood looking out a window facing the porch while

the storm raged outside. He also knew that he shouldn't want her. The storm. It rivaled the one going on inside him at the moment. He'd always been able to escape his problems when he returned to Portsmouth Island.

Even if only temporarily. It never dawned on him until just that moment that he never really escaped them. Instead, he ran from them, avoiding them. Now, one of the problems he'd tried to avoid by leaving Nags Head that morning smacked him dead in the face, invading his sanctuary without warning. And he wasn't quite sure how he should handle it.

Or if he wanted to handle it.

He knew he couldn't escape Meg, or his feelings for her. Six months after his grandfather had died, and he was thrust head-first into the family business, he'd known he couldn't hack it.

Even with his degree in business, he knew he wasn't cut out for the corporate world. At least he had sense enough to admit it. Now the company belonged to him, but he was literally a figurehead having turned over the running of the tobacco business to his grandfather's long-time and trusted friend, Art Thurman.

Art always contacted Smyth with finalized details of projects or concerns or major business moves, but other than that, the business ran quite smoothly without him. Smyth secured enough income from the business each year to keep the houses up and to provide for his needs—his and Crystal's when they were married. But now his needs were few. Shaking his head, he recalled his marriage. Reason number two for needing Portsmouth. Crystal could never understand why there wasn't more money. Why he didn't lavish roses and diamonds on her every day. His biggest mistake was telling her how much his grandfather had been worth when he died. He hadn't realized how Crystal had mentally transferred all that wealth to him.

Granted, Smyth, and E. J. Parker Tobacco were worth millions, but Smyth hadn't necessarily wanted the lifestyle that came with it. He hated parties and crowds, and that was exactly what Crystal loved. It hadn't taken him long to figure it out. Unfortunately, they were married by that time.

Crystal wanted that lifestyle, in fact, he truly believed that was why she'd married him.

They met in just that setting, however, she hadn't known Smyth was out of his element there, rubbing elbows with the elite. He'd made his mistake when he'd let her think that he felt totally at home.

It served his ego well, at that point in his life, to think that he'd made it in the social world. Little did he realize during that brief six months that he wasn't cut out of the same mold as those people. When he finally accepted it, he'd left it all behind without a thought.

Why he'd tried to make himself into someone or something else, he'd never know. He wished to hell he hadn't. He wouldn't be in this mess with Crystal.

Glancing back into the center of the room, he watched Meg cautiously approach him.

Abruptly, every reason why he couldn't get involved with her crashed over him. The mess with Crystal far from over, he'd made a pitiful husband to her. Why would he think he'd ever be any better to anyone else? And he couldn't ask another woman to put up with his lifestyle. Too moody, he needed his solitude and at times he needed—and wanted—no one in his life.

Meg was too beautiful, too gentle, and too vulnerable. And as much as he wanted to take her to his bed right now, he knew he could never do that. It would never happen. No matter what. He couldn't chain her to his life, damning her to his solitude. It was unthinkable. And it wouldn't happen.

Moving closer, his gaze caught hers and held. In his sweatshirt and pants she looked so small. Suddenly all he wanted to do was hold her, take care of her, erase all her problems—bury them along with his and whisk her off to a magical place where they'd always be together and their problems couldn't follow.

He broke the connection and turned toward the couch.

"Let's sit down," he threw over his shoulder. Nervous anticipation of the time they would be spending together in the next few days filled him. How he would avoid her, he didn't know, but avoid her he must. There was no way off the island until the ferry came back from Ocracoke.

With the radio down and no hope of fixing it that night, she would be there for a couple of days at the minimum. Smyth watched Meg sit on the couch and look up to him, her large green eyes searching his face, questioning. After a moment, he sat beside her, deciding to plunge away. He, no they, needed to face this head on.

"Okay," he said quietly, "tell me everything."

Meg lowered her gaze. After taking a deep breath, she glanced back up at him. She worried with the hem of the long sweatshirt, wringing it in her hands. Could she sense his uncertainties?

She sighed nervously.

"What happened after I left, Meg?"

Quickly, she returned. "I saw the black sedan."

"What?" Puzzled, he gazed at her profile, she continued to stare straight ahead for a moment. When she turned to face him, her eyes dry, but full of pain. *God, her life must be hell.*

"In Chicago, the black sedan followed me everywhere. Especially when Bradford was out of town. There were always two men in the front seat. I guess their job was to make sure I didn't go anywhere I shouldn't, or be with someone I shouldn't have been with."

"Did you ever do that?"

Meg shook her head briskly. "Oh, no. Never. I loved Bradford...at first. He was so romantic and kind. I never thought about seeing anyone else. In fact, I devoted my whole life to him. But the day I started noticing the sedan was the day he started changing. I asked him about it once and he made it very clear to me then. I was his possession. He was just making sure I did what I was supposed to do, be faithful and loyal to him. I never gave him reason to suspect otherwise. He just simply felt it necessary."

Smyth tried to embrace the ease at which she obviously accepted the man's behavior as normal. "And you went along with this?"

She shrugged. "I had no choice. It bothered me, but there was nothing I could do about it.

Just like there was nothing I could do about the taps on the phones, the clothes and makeup he made me wear, the way he told me to act around others, the fact that I couldn't have a job, and the way he..." Smyth watched the look on Meg's face turn to one of horror and regret. She shook her head and turned away. He took in the small tremor that rippled across her back.

"The way he what?" he questioned softly. She didn't look back at him. "Meg?"

In a flurry she turned and put distance between them. Her eyes flared with anger and pain. "You know already. I as much as told you. I don't want to go into it again."

"Meg." Smyth reached out to grasp her elbow.

Meg flinched and drew back. "The way he touched me, damn it! The way he talked to me, hit me. The way he used violence to get every damn thing he wanted, whenever he wanted!

The way he took my body, even when I didn't want him to. Is that what you wanted to hear?"

Dumbfounded at her outburst, Smyth stared at her, his hands falling loose at his sides.

Realizing that she'd been through a lot just in the past day, let alone in the past years of her life, he let her anger and hostility slide, dismissing it as only hysterical reaction.

"No," he said softly. "I didn't want to hear that. I don't even want to think of that happening to you, Meg. It tears my heart in two. But you need to face it and get it out of your system. You need to talk about it."

Meg closed her eyes. It seemed every muscle in her body melted as her stature shrank and a ragged sigh escaped her parted lips. "I'm sorry," she mumbled, then turned away. "You didn't deserve that."

Smyth stepped behind her and gently placed his arms

around her shoulders. He prepared for her to tense, but she didn't. Thanking God for that small victory, he drew her closer. "Let's forget about what happened in the past," he whispered. "For now, at least. Someday we'll have to cross that hurdle. But for now, tell me about today."

As he closed his eyes, she leaned backward into him. He cringed as he realized he'd admitted out loud that they might have a future.

Smyth let her rest against his body while he held her. His face dipped close to her neck and he could smell her sweet, fragrant scent. Knowing that he should be pushing her away, he realized he couldn't.

She needed him. And he, right now, needed her.

After a moment, she started speaking, slowly and softly as he held her. "When I saw the car and the two men this morning I knew that somehow Bradford had found me. I panicked. So I decided to call Rudy, my best friend. She was also Bradford's attorney. That's when I found out she was murdered."

"And you think Bradford did it?"

Her hands reached up to clasp his, tightly wound around her waist.

"I know he did."

"Why?"

"Because she helped me get away, was helping me with the divorce. Maybe he thought she would tell him where I was. I don't know. Anyway, she's dead. I know he did it. Or some of his men did."

Alarmed, Smyth turned her in his arms and looked into her face.

"This is really complicated, isn't it?"

Meg huffed. "You can say that again. Are you sure you want to hear all this?"

He nodded and watched one corner of her mouth drift up into a half-smile.

"Are you sure you want to get yourself involved in this? I mean, you could send me back on the next boat and wash your hands of the whole thing. I...I don't really want you and Becky in any more deeply—"

"Let's sit down." He led her back to the couch, keeping her hands tucked inside his, his gaze firmly attached to hers.

"You're here. I want to know everything. Tell me."

Hesitantly, he watched her eyes search his face. "You're sure?" she whispered.

Nodding, he continued, "I don't understand Bradford's motivation in all this, Meg. I mean, besides the fact that he simply wants to keep you under his thumb."

Meg swallowed. "It's simple. Bradford wants into politics. It's been his goal ever since I can remember, but he's been waiting for the right time. Now, I gather, is that time. He needed a prim, proper little wife on his arm and I wanted a divorce. He wasn't about to let that happen."

"A lot of men in politics are divorced. That's not such a stigma these days."

"But marriage helps to promote the family image. Bradford even wanted a child, but after—" Meg turned her head from him and sucked in a deep, painful breath, then hurriedly continued. "I told him no. I couldn't stand raising a child in that environment. Bradford also had several black marks against him.

"Years before Bradford and I married, there were some problems with some of his factories. Union trouble. Some men were killed. Around that same time a woman who worked for him was also killed, raped and strangled, and left in the parking lot of one of his warehouses.

Reportedly she and Bradford had been seeing each other on the sly. She was married, I think.

Bradford, of course, denied everything, but the press bit into the story and chewed on it for a long time. It followed him around for a while. The case was never solved.

"He's been fighting that bad boy image ever since. Some people have forgotten it, some haven't. So I guess he's ready to strike the proper family man image to the public. That's why he needed me. The thing of it was, the public didn't know the half of Bradford's schemes. I didn't either until recently."

"Such as?"

"Drugs, money laundering, gambling, smuggling art, tax evasion...murder. You see, I found out something quite by accident one day. Bradford, my husband, has become involved in organized crime. And he is itching to take his power into the political arena. Bradford Thomas is a dangerous man."

"How could you live with that?"

"I couldn't. That's when I started planning my escape. It took me months, but finally all the right pieces fell together and I pulled it off. Only now, they've found me. Guess I wasn't so good after all."

"How did you get out of my house?"

"I jumped out the kitchen window and ran to the pier. From there I called Becky and she picked me up. We cut and dyed my hair," Meg fluffed her short black locks and rolled her eyes, "...and then she had this brainstorm about sending me to live with relatives. She just didn't tell me it was you. I'm sorry. I know you weren't expecting me."

Smyth shook his head, now more worried than ever. "Don't worry about it. You did the right thing. You're sure they didn't follow you here?"

"Pretty sure. Becky called the police and told them about the sedan and to check your house. We didn't wait around to see what happened, but I'm sure no one followed us here. That drive down Hatteras is desolate. It would be easy to see someone following us."

He nodded in agreement. "What about Becky? Do you think she's safe?"

"I don't know how they could have made the connection."

Her gaze held his for several seconds and she continued. "Look, Smyth. I know you don't want me here. I have to admit, I didn't picture you out here on this island like this. I thought you were off taking care of business somewhere. I won't be in your way and I won't stay forever. Just let me get my bearings straight, then I'll be on my way again."

Smyth stared at her, listening to her last words, a lump forming in his throat and his pulse pounding in his ears. He didn't want her to leave. And all this time he'd been expecting her to be so honest with him, when all he had done was hide the truth from her. Somehow, he knew he had to make it up to her. Somehow he needed her to stay— at least for a while.

"You can't run forever."

"I'll run as long as I have to. Forever is a word I'd just as soon not think about. Sometimes I don't even know if there is such a thing."

Alarmed at the determined tone of voice and the set expression on her face, Smyth knew that if running was her only option, she would continue it for as long as she had to. And it killed him to think of her doing that. That he might never be able to find her. He had to help her, had to see this problem through.

If they were ever to even consider a future together.

Glancing down, he noticed their fingers tightly woven together, resting on his thigh and wondered if he'd ever be able to break through her shell. Suddenly he wanted to, very much.

Chapter Eighteen

"The party's over, sweetheart. Time to go."

Staring at the young girl, Bradford almost wished he could keep her, but knew it was impossible. She provided a necessary diversion while he sifted through his problems with Megan, but she wasn't Megan. And now that Megan was gone and he had a plan, he'd have to keep the image of single, but stable. The playboy image was too risky for someone vying for the state Senate. He had to get rid of her. Now.

She had become a nuisance in the worst way and he wanted her gone. Besides, most of the time she wasn't very good anyway. She had gotten too selfish, too demanding in bed.

Her eyes wide and lower lip trembling, she stared back at him as if all this surprised her.

He chuckled. Dumb blonde broad.

"B-but Brad. I thought..."

Slinging a robe at her, he watched her catch it and clutch it to her nude body. "You thought wrong, honey. It was nice for a while, but now you're history. Get lost." His gaze raked over her body, still moist from the shower. "And dry off, you're dripping on the carpet."

Dismissing her, he turned and walked across the room while unbuttoning his shirt. Whisking it off his body, he tossed it on a nearby chair. He unzipped his pants, dropping them to the floor, briefs following, and moved away from the puddle of clothing.

His thoughts turned to Riker. Damn bastard. If he'd done his job right, Bradford would be rid of her now. He should have seen to Riker's demise earlier, but he'd needed him for one last, little assignment. But at the least, he'd found Megan. Finally some good news.

No one could stand in his way now. Rudy, although

he'd needed her, was gone. In time he would have had to dispose of her anyway. He might as well just get over it. Megan would soon be gone, too. And if the blonde idiot behind him didn't get the hell out of here, he'd see to it that she was gone by sun-up as well. All necessary, he justified to himself. It had to be done for his career—for the future of the organization.

Standing at the bedroom window, he pulled back the sheers with one finger. Night. He liked the night. Anything could and would happen then. People made mistakes in the night. Big mistakes. Ones easily hidden in the shadows and mist. The night played havoc with the eyes.

Bradford chuckled.

He felt her hand on his shoulder.

With one brisk swish, his fist exploded into the air and he backhanded her across the face. Cindy flew backward against the bed with a shriek, falling to the floor.

"Bitch!" He followed her in one huge stride and bent over her cowering body. "I told you to get lost!" he shouted. "You have a death wish or something?"

"No," she whimpered, sobbing. "I...I'm leaving."

Grasping her upper arms, Bradford lifted her bodily, harshly, and tossed her across the bed. Feeling himself harden, a thrill raced through him.

He jerked her robe open.

Cindy cried out. "No, Bradford. I said I'll go. I'll go," she sobbed, trying to kick and push herself backward away from him.

Grasping her shoulders, Bradford straddled her lower body, pinning her to the bed. "You look a lot like her, you know," he snarled, "but you aren't her."

"I know," Cindy said weakly.

"Rudy's dead."

He excited in the startled look on her face. "Rudy's fucking dead. Did you do it, Cindy? Hmm? Doesn't matter, sweetheart. Megan will be dead by morning, too. Wanna guess who is next?"

Cindy shrieked and tried to struggle against him, but

she couldn't. He found it funny, but her wriggling only made him that much more aroused. That and the fact she was truly scared out of her wits. He guessed the thought of dying did that to a person. For him, it only heightened his sexual hunger.

His breathing labored with a combination of exertion and sexual anticipation. Violence made him hard, made him want to dominate, to force women into submission, to make women cower at the sight of his maleness. It was better that way.

Always. Incredible. Like a drug.

****

The hanging light over the table near the window provided the only illumination in the cramped hotel room. It reflected an orange glow from the tacky, burnt sienna bedspread, casting an eerie haze about the room. Jack Cooper sat on one of the mussed beds and stared across the room at Mel Daniels, wondering what in the hell they should do now.

The woman had given them the slip. He made a tent with his fingers and shook his head, knowing that he and Mel had screwed up royally.

"What are we gonna do, Daniels?" His gruff voice broke the silence.

Mel Daniels leaned back in the brown upholstered chair and flicked cigarette ashes at the ashtray on the table. He poked the cigarette back in his mouth, clasped his hands behind his head and squinted at Jack through the smoke drifting around his head and swirling into the light.

"We still do the job. Just a little setback. Ain't no dumb, blonde broad who got away from me yet. This bimbo ain't that smart."

"But how?" Cooper rose and paced three times back and forth across the room. "Seems to be pretty smart to me."

Daniels' eyes narrowed. "I got ways."

Cooper picked up a motel brochure, flipped through it, then slammed it against the wall.

"Yeah! Well you must know something I don't, 'cause I don't see how in the hell we're gonna catch up with her now. I think we need to call Riker."

"No!" Daniels sat up. "Riker warned us not to come back until the job was done. That's what I intend to do. Don't you worry, we'll find her."

"Like I said, you must know something I don't. It's like she disappeared into thin air."

Daniels grinned. "There are ways. Besides, if Thomas says to find her, I find her. And remember, we don't get paid until we do. I ain't going back empty handed. Getting paid is one thing, getting axed is another."

Dropping his hands to his knees, Daniels leaned forward in the chair. His gaze penetrated Cooper's. "Naw. We ain't calling Riker and we ain't going back until we get her. Understand?

Ain't nothin' gonna stop me now. That blonde bimbo is mine. Come hell or high water. I don't care which. She's mine."

Jack stared at his partner for a second. "So what do we do next?"

"Next? We move. Now. It's dark, so we go back to the house and see if anybody's home. If not, we search for anything, anything that might tell us something. Then in the morning, we check out the owner of the house, his relatives, the neighbors, whatever it takes." His grin broadened. "Then we find her."

Chapter Nineteen

Meg woke late to one of those mornings after the previous night's storm, bright sunshine, everything washed clean, and the air smelling like earthworms. She went to bed the night before exhausted and wanting only to lose herself in sleep. Now, showered and dressed, she thought her new hairstyle odd as she looked at her reflection in the bathroom mirror, then made her way down the hall to the living room in search of Smyth.

But he was nowhere to be found.

After a few minutes, she scrounged around in the kitchen and made herself a cup of instant coffee using bottled water she found in the cabinet. She took it to the front porch to wait for him. At least that's what she assumed. She hoped he planned to come back. Certainly he wouldn't have left her to fend for herself.

No. He wouldn't do that.

A calm like she hadn't felt in ages washed over her as she sat in the wooden porch chair, her feet propped on the railing, and sipped her coffee. All around her she realized a sort of serenity—a feeling of contentment somehow foreign to her. In fact, she wasn't sure she'd ever felt that way before. Until now.

No city sounds, engines grinding, horns honking, no sirens, people talking, radios blaring.

She heard no boats, no kids playing on the beach. Nothing. For the first time in her life Meg believed she'd experienced the true sound of silence and it felt wonderful. And cleansing. She'd like to spend about half a lifetime here, she noted.

Sighing, she sank deeper into the chair. Maybe her whole lifetime. If only that were possible.

Closing her eyes, she leaned her head back against the chair and reveled in the simple peace that existed around her. For a moment, she absorbed it. But suddenly, as if blasted at her with a bullhorn, the silence broke.

Nature shrilled at her with a pure, unadulterated resonance. Gulls shrieked in the distance.

Small birds fluttered and chirped in the dwarfed trees and bushes on the other side of the porch.

The surf pounded the shore just out of her sight. She had never before thought of silence as deafening.

A breeze played with her hair, swirling it softly around her forehead. The warmth of the morning gently wrapped about her. Her thoughts drifted to the previous night's conversation with Smyth. Throughout the night, his comforting words came back to her, time and again, caressingly invading the blank recesses of her dreamless sleep.

As always of late, she realized that more than just her surroundings had something to do with her feelings of security. It was Smyth. She couldn't deny it.

He meant more to her than a refuge in a storm. And she was pretty sure he felt the same about her. But the thought of that tore at her heart because she knew how very difficult it would be to cross the hurdles they both had to make a go of it. It was just too confusing.

The birds stopped chirping.

Snapping her eyes open at the footsteps walking determinedly up the porch steps, Meg sat up in her chair as Smyth slowly topped the last step to the porch.

"Good morning."

His voice, smooth as fine leather, sent instant shivers down Meg's spine.

"Hi."

"I see you're up."

Meg wavered, then smiled. A small thrill zinged through her at the sight of him, irritating her to no end. Why in the hell couldn't she tamp down her emotions?

"Yes," she answered as calmly as possible. "It took me a while, though. I helped myself to coffee. Hope you don't mind." She awkwardly lifted the cup. "Want some? I can go back in and—"

Waving his hand, Smyth stepped closer. "No, thanks. I had some earlier." He glanced hesitantly around, then back to Meg. "Want to take a walk? I'll show you the place. It's a beautiful morning."

Meg stood and set the cup on the porch railing, stretching as she did. Feeling a bit of awkward tension between them, she was glad it looked as though Smyth had decided not to bring the previous day's adventure into the morning's conversation. "Sure. I need to work the kinks out."

"Rough night?" he questioned as they left the porch and headed toward the road.

Meg glanced at him from the side. "Not really. I was so tired and mentally drained I think I fell unconscious the moment my head hit the pillow."

Smyth kept his gaze at his feet as they walked toward the general store. Meg also noticed his hands were shoved deep in his pants pockets, keeping them safely away from her. "Well, I'm glad at least one of us slept," he muttered softly.

"You didn't sleep?"

A look of alarm crossed his face as he jerked his head back to her.

"No," he answered. "I didn't."

When Smyth didn't elaborate further, Meg glanced away from him and studied her surroundings. She really didn't want to contemplate the meaning of that last statement. Did it show his concern about her being here? Did he think she brought trouble to the island? Did he want her to leave?

"So," she paused, plunging her fingers into her own shorts pockets while they meandered along the sand-dirt road. "Tell me about Portsmouth Village. What exactly is it you do here? I mean, I have to admit, this isn't exactly what I pictured you doing."

Smyth glanced at her cautiously. "Just what exactly did you picture?"

Shrugging her shoulders, Meg went on, "Oh, I don't know. You spoke of business. And you said your grandfather left you his company. You're gone all the time. I just assumed..."

"You assumed I was some jet-setting CEO in a suit, right?"

Angling her gaze toward him, Meg grinned. "Well, it was kind of the image I had in my mind, I guess. I don't know why, it just seemed..." she shook her head, staring. "No, now that I think about it, your hair is too long, you wear the wrong clothes."

Smyth stared at her with a blank expression. He started to speak, his stare biting. Meg wondered what she'd said wrong.

Finally, he spoke, "So I guess you're disappointed?"

Stopping her steps, Meg crossed her arms over her chest and looked him straight in the eyes. "Disappointed? Why?"

"That I'm not the businessman you assumed."

Meg's lips curled into a thin grin. She wondered what made him so doubtful this morning. "No. Actually, I'm kind of relieved. I don't care if I ever see another business suit as long as I live."

Watching Smyth's facial features relax, Meg sensed a release of some sort of built-up tension. "Although I'm still rather curious about what it is you do here." She glanced around her, then back to Smyth's face. "Come to think of it, I haven't seen another person since I arrived."

She started walking again and Smyth matched her steps. "Of course I did kind of arrive on the sly in the dark of the night," she added.

"That's because we're the only people on the island."

Meg stopped. "We're what?"

His gaze penetrated hers. "We're the only two people on the island," he repeated, every facial feature fixed.

"But—" Meg glanced about her. They'd passed the general store and were nearing the fork in the road. To her left she could see the corner of one of the houses in the cluster down the way. She knew the church stood beyond. Her gaze landed back on Smyth's face. "But why the general store, the church, the houses...where are all the people who live here?"

"Lived," he corrected. "Gone. They all moved away years ago."

Confused, Meg let her gaze dart about her again. "And you live here?"

"Part of the time."

"Why?"

Finally grinning, Smyth took Meg's hand, pulling her down the road again. "It's National Seashore, Meg. Maintained by the federal government park rangers. I'm a volunteer caretaker of the village."

Meg still didn't totally understand and her face must have shown it. Why on earth would someone volunteer to be the only living sole in an uninhabited town?

"Come on. Let me show you something, then you'll understand."

Smyth cut off the beaten path, leading her between two white clapboard frame houses. If no one lived here, then why were the houses so well kept? Soon they were out of the dwarfed trees and walking through calf-high sea oats that tickled her legs. Her hand still in Smyth's, he tugged her along as the dune inclined slightly.

Within seconds, they passed through a cut in the dune. Meg found herself instantly spellbound by the massive morning-kissed, sun-glistened waters of the Atlantic.

Again, silence and simplicity rang true within her. Meg felt her chest swell as she took in a deep breath, then fall in a thorough, cleansing exhalation.

"Wow," she whispered, not taking her gaze from the sight before her.

"Yeah." Smyth wove his fingers tighter with hers. "That's the reason I'm here. I'm addicted to it."

For several minutes, Meg simply absorbed the sight.

"You know," she began after a while, feeling the ocean's mystique, "there is so much energy out there. It's incredible, perpetual energy. Constantly pounding the shore. Wearing it down, bit by bit."

She felt Smyth's gaze turn to her, but didn't look at him. "I can feel it, can't you?

Standing here, like this? I can feel that energy ripple up over the shore, my body waiting to absorb it." Breathless, she finally turned to him. "Do you know what I mean?" she whispered.

Nodding, Smyth agreed. "I know exactly what you mean." His gaze penetrated hers.

"I've always felt stronger here. Maybe you will, too."

Meg felt every muscle in her abdomen tighten as she held his gaze. Lingering for a moment, she finally turned back to face the ocean, their clasped hands their only body contact. "I already do," she replied softly. "It's strange. I'm a lot like this island. For years the ocean has beat away at its shoreline, grain by grain swept out to sea, scattered throughout its depths. Bit by bit, taking it apart and rearranging it, making it into something else, forming it into the shape of its own liking.

"And me. That's what has been happening to me all these years. Bradford has been chipping away at my facade, my personality, my being—trying to make me into something I'm not, wanting to form me into an image of the ideal woman, his porcelain china doll, fragile and needy."

Turning now, with the mist of tears stinging her eyes, she faced Smyth. "But he didn't, did he?"

Shaking his head, Smyth grasped her other hand, turning her to fully face him. "No," he whispered. "He didn't. He won't."

Meg glanced at the ocean once more, then slowly let her gaze drift back to Smyth's face.

"I am like this island. The ocean may change its shoreline, may alter its appearance, but it can't touch its heart and soul. It's still there and still strong. Probably stronger, surviving whatever punishment the ocean dishes out."

Her gaze darted back and forth over his face. "I want to be like that. I want to be stronger after all this is through. I don't want Bradford Thomas to have one iota of my being. I don't want him to have my heart and soul. I'd rather be scattered to the winds than for him to possess anything of me."

Smyth brought his hand up to cup her cheek. "You are strong. You couldn't have come this far if you weren't. You will make it."

A rush of desire swept through her as his fingertips gently scraped her cheek. "I don't know, it could be a hard road."

"You don't have to travel it alone."

The implication of his words frightened her. Meg shook her head and exhaled deep, looking to the ground between them. "I don't know...I don't know."

Smyth tucked a finger under her chin, forcing her gaze to his face.

"You don't have to do it alone. Do you understand me?"

Meg understood. He was offering himself. All of a sudden she realized why he hadn't slept well the night before. Obviously he wrestled with her presence as much as she had. Maybe he just didn't know how to handle it.

"I don't want to drag you into this. This is my problem."

"I can make it my problem." His brown eyes seemed darker as he spoke to her.

Half wanting him to take all her problems away, half wanting to run from him, Meg heaved a sigh and grasped his hand, pulling it down to her side. "We both have too many problems, Smyth. I don't want to complicate your life."

Just before he broke away from her, Meg saw irritation flash over his face. Stalking away, his back to her, she watched the muscles flex over his broad shoulders while he combed his fingers through his hair. Abruptly, he turned back to her.

"Why won't you accept any help from me?"

The sudden anger in his face alarmed her. She answered him quickly. "It's not your problem."

"What if I want to make it my problem?"

"You can't."

"Why?"

"I won't let you."

"Won't let me, or you don't want me to? There's a difference. Am I not good enough for you? Perhaps you'd rather have a man in a suit after all."

Angered now, Meg thrust her hands in the air. "*Let* you, Smyth. That's what I said, that's what I meant. Who you are? And the fact that you don't wear a suit doesn't even enter into this. I think that's your problem, not mine. Obviously that ex-wife of yours did a number on you or something. I don't care what you wear or what you do for a living. I simply am not going to drag you into this. I can do it on my own."

"Can you?" he returned sarcastically.

Meg felt the breeze off the ocean warm her, or perhaps it was her blood pressure rising.

Suddenly, she grew tired of playing games, with Smyth or anyone else. Stepping closer to him, she stared straight into his fuming eyes and wondered if hers reflected that same anger. Her pulse pounding, her heart swelling, she knew it was now or never. She had to lay it all out on the line.

And she had to be honest with him. It was the only way.

"Look," she huffed out. "I'm so tired of making up excuses and alibis. I don't know who I am anymore. I don't want you killed. I couldn't live with that. If Bradford ever does catch up with me, there is no doubt in my mind that he would kill both of us. I can't knowingly put you in that position. We've already risked too much.

"If I let you help me get out of this situation, then that means I'm going to get close to you. I don't know if I can handle that right yet. It's too soon. I've just come out of one hellish nightmare and right now every single one of my emotions is laid bare for the world to trample on. I don't know you well enough to lay myself open to that, even though I'm severely tempted."

Meg forced out a deep breath and went on, slightly unnerved at the flare in his eyes at her last statement. She had to get it over with.

"And the more I'm around you," she continued softly, "the more I feel I'm falling for you and I'm afraid you've got problems of your own to deal with. I don't know how well I could handle falling in love with you and then have you turn around and leave me."

Knowing she'd revealed a whole lot more than she really wanted, Meg felt like running, but her feet were frozen to the spot. She shook her head and looked away.

"How do you know I would leave you?" he returned blandly.

Tossing her gaze right back at him, she immediately felt the hurt in his voice. "No," she returned on a whispered breath, "you probably wouldn't. I would end up leaving you and breaking both our hearts."

His expression unmoving, Smyth clutched at her hands and pulled her closer. "It's too confusing right now. We need to figure out where we're both coming from. We need time."

Meg nodded. "Confusing isn't the word for it. Right now, I'm not even sure I should be here. I'm so mixed up. I don't know what's happened to Rudy. I've been worried about Becky ever since you mentioned the possibility of them finding her. I don't know if Bradford's thugs tailed me here. And I don't have any inkling of what's going on in your head. So I really think that the best thing you and I can do is stay away from each other until the next boat comes, or whatever, so I can get off this island and away from you because I honestly don't know what will happen if I don't. It scares the hell out of me."

Meg huffed out a quick breath and looked toward the village, tears aching to spill from her eyes. Not meaning to bare her soul so completely, she wished she could take back about half of what she'd said.

First, she felt his warm hands snaking up her arms, raising the goose flesh on her skin.

When his fingertips grazed her shoulders, she shivered and vowed she wouldn't look at him, but as his palm smoothed over her neck and under her jawbone, she was drawn to him like a magnet.

Turning to look into his face, she felt all self-control wash out of her as her gut tightened and then seemed to melt into molten liquid. His eyes, deep brown and filled with desire, searched her face. His gaze finally rested on her lips. A craving to be close to him swept over her in an instant, making her suddenly alert to every molecule of testosterone oozing from his body.

Meg's pulse pounded in her ears and every defense she thought she possessed had cut out underneath her like a dangerous ocean riptide.

"I'm scared, too," he whispered as she watched the slow movement of his lips. "I'm afraid the best thing that ever happened to me is going to fade away before I have a chance to make it work."

Tears slipped over Meg's lower lids and slid down her cheek. Her lips trembled as she started to speak. "I...I can't be the best thing that ever happened to you. Things are so uncertain.

There may be no future."

"There's today."

Her eyes met his and suddenly it all made sense. He was right. All they really had was today. As one hand slipped around her back, pulling her closer, the fingers of his other threaded into the hair at her nape. Meg closed her eyes and waited for his lips to capture hers.

She didn't have to wait long.

Chapter Twenty

The warmth of Smyth's lips on Meg's radiated throughout her being. Pressing against him, she felt every hard plane and angle of his body. She ached for him. Ached to be physically closer to him. Ached to feel his flesh in her palms.

As his arms closed around her, the kiss deepened. Smyth's tongue thrust between her lips to rim her teeth and then parry with her tongue. While he explored the recesses of her mouth, passion surged from deep within her. Her hands moved to his shoulders and neck, fingers threaded in the long length of his hair.

She devoured him or he devoured her, she wasn't sure which. At length, Smyth broke free of her lips with a gasp, then immediately tipped back her head to expose her neck, raining kisses down to her collarbone and back up again.

Panting, Meg heard herself groan and whisper his name, then tipped her face up to meet his gaze.

Inches apart, he stared into her eyes. One hand brushed back the fine baby hairs from her face. His gentle and desire-filled gaze made her melt against him.

"We need to talk," he whispered as he held her close to him. His mouth left a trail of feather-soft kisses across the base of her neck.

Meg physically experienced his passion for her against her belly, but more than that, she felt it in her heart and soul. Knew it from the look in his eyes. Sensed it in his voice. The fire ate at her from within.

"I know," her voice barely more than a whisper on the ocean's breeze.

"Tell me what you're thinking," he breathed against her sensitive skin.

"I can't...think."

His teeth caught her lower lip. "Do you want me to

stop?"

Meg closed her eyes and let him assuage with his lips and teeth every sensual nerve ending on her face. She clutched him closer to her and took all he had to give.

"No...Yes," she finally murmured against his cheek while his tongue raked across her earlobe.

"Hmmm, you sure?" he asked.

She nodded against him, knowing full well she didn't want him to stop. She didn't know if she ever would. But she had to stop him.

"We...have to talk," she gasped.

Slowly, Smyth pulled his face away from her neck, but kept the embrace intact. His eyes kept constant contact with hers, never breaking the connection. "We're moving fast, I know.

Meg, I've never felt like this before. I can't tell you how much I want you."

Wanting to believe him, knowing how much she wanted him, Meg felt her chest swell and the tears sting the backs of her eyelids. "I know, I—"

"...but we do have to talk," he interrupted.

Nodding, Meg agreed.

"We need to slow down."

She nodded again, tracing her index finger over the dimple in his chin. "Yes."

Bringing his hands up, Smyth gently cradled her face in his hands and smiled at her. "We have plenty of time."

Sighing, and feeling the tears spill over her lids, Meg felt the elation she'd savored just seconds before vanish as her face fell into a frown and fear pierced her heart.

Time was the one thing she didn't have.

****

Foamy fingers of water swirled around their feet as Smyth silently led Meg along the water's edge. For several minutes they walked hand in hand down the beach, their shoes left high on the dune behind them, bare feet warmed by the sand. In his heart Smyth knew he cared for Meg more than he'd ever cared for another woman. He could easily fall in love with her, if given half a chance. Hell, he probably already loved her.

That's why he knew he had to tell her everything. She'd confessed all her problems to him, he had to reciprocate. It all had to be out in the open before they could get past today. He had to know that after all this other garbage was finished, there would be a future for the two of them.

A future with Meg. Suddenly, he wanted it desperately.

Strands of his hair flew back into place with the breeze as Smyth lifted his head to look at her. He felt the salt spray on his face and Meg's small, soft hand lying loose in his. The ocean continued its never-ending drone in his ear. Finally, avoiding the confession no longer, he stopped walking and turned to face Meg.

To his left lay a large piece of driftwood, part of an old pier splintered by a long ago storm, now washed ashore and lodged deep in the sand.

"Let's sit here." He motioned to the wood and studied her face.

Meg nodded and walked the few steps, then sat. With her green eyes turned up to him, he followed, knowing she watched his every movement.

Finally he took a breath and began.

"You know nothing about me."

Meg nodded slowly. "Yes," she whispered. "I guess I don't, really." Staring into his eyes, she shook her head. "That's not entirely right. I know quite a bit about you, Smyth."

His name on her breath sent his insides on fire. He ached to hear her call out his name in passion as he covered her body with his. Now, he couldn't dwell on that. Now, they had to come to an understanding.

"How could you know much about me?"

"I know you're troubled. Your ex-wife is the source. I know your parents and grandfather died in the past few years and that Becky is your only family left. Somehow, this place enters into the picture as pretty important to you, from what I can gather. Those are the obvious things."

He watched her face, her small lips moving with each word, her eyes widening and narrowing as she spoke, her nostrils flaring slightly with each breath. "And what are the not so obvious things?" he asked before he'd even thought.

It took her a minute, but she answered as her gaze played over his face. "You are a sensitive man," she whispered. "You love nature. I don't think you're cut out for the fast lane or the corporate world. You don't like crowds. And I think your family was very important to you, especially your grandfather. I don't know what went wrong between you and your ex-wife, but I have a feeling you shouldn't have married her in the first place." She stopped and Smyth felt his face redden. "Oh, and at some point you took a family vacation to Williamsburg and Washington, D.C," she added quickly.

Watching the amused expression that crossed her face, Smyth couldn't help but be surprised at that last statement.

"How did you know that?"

"Becky." He answered her simultaneously.

"Actually," Meg went on, "I peeked at her photo album while she was out yesterday afternoon. It was very insightful."

"Oh, really?"

"Yes, it was."

He watched her for a long time as she turned to stare out over the ocean. The startling effects of the short ebony hair shown against her lightly tanned skin as he watched the breeze blow the locks away from her face. Though he preferred the long blonde tresses of before, Meg was a beautiful woman at any rate. And he sat spellbound watching her, wanting her, wondering how long he would have with her.

He also wondered how much he really knew about her, how much she had left out about her marriage. He wondered, as his smile quickly faded into a frown, how much pain the bastard had caused her before she escaped his clutches.

She turned to him rather quickly and he tried to smile again, wanting to erase all her pain.

Desperately wanting the two of them to resolve their conflicts so they could get on with their lives.

"I want to tell you about Crystal."

Meg nodded blankly and Smyth found himself telling her the whole story, not the condensed version, but the entire story. He told her about inheriting the tobacco empire after his grandfather's death, about how he reveled for a few short months in the glory of being a multimillionaire, and how Crystal had wormed her way into his life in a heartbeat. He told her how it took him months to realize that all the things he was doing after his grandfather's death were just to avoid the pain. That it took him too long to come to his senses.

"I was a terrible husband." He stopped and searched Meg's face, gazing deep into the ocean-green depths of her eyes.

"Why do you say that?" she whispered back.

"Because I was." He tore his gaze away. Drawing one leg up to place his foot flat on the wood, he rested his elbow on his knee, his chin against his upraised fist. "I knew from the beginning that I shouldn't have married her. Oh, at first I thought married life was great. We'd lie around in bed most of the time reading or eating or drinking champagne. We played up the rich life to the hilt. But after about a month I got antsy. I was tired of lying around, so I started making myself more useful around the office.

"A few more months went by and I realized I wasn't cut out for the corporate life, either.

I made the necessary arrangements with my grandfather's long-time friend and associate to oversee the tobacco business and I took off for Portsmouth. I visited here often growing up and loved the solitude of this place. Finally, I volunteered with the Park Service and began spending time here. Months at a time."

"You loved it that much that you would desert your

wife?"

Feeling his breath catch in his throat at her statement, he knew how terrible it sounded.

But it was the truth and she had to know. "By then I knew I didn't love Crystal, but I was running from my problems. I knew a divorce would be sticky so I just avoided the whole damn issue. Mistake number one."

Meg didn't bat an eye. "What was mistake number two?"

Feeling his chest tighten, Smyth held the connection between them.

"The second mistake was letting it all go until Crystal got pregnant."

"But you're not the father of her child?"

"No."

"Are you sure?"

He hesitated only a second. "Damn sure. I hadn't been home for months when she turned up pregnant. And the fact that I caught her in the act with another man only clinched the deal."

Meg's eyes widened only slightly. "That must have been hard for you."

Shaking his head, Smyth continued. "No, actually it wasn't. I knew I didn't love her and I suspected she wasn't staying at home waiting around for me to show up every three months or so. Frankly, I didn't care. I just wish she hadn't gotten pregnant before I decided to finally file for divorce."

"That's a problem?"

"That's a big problem." Smyth raked the fingers of his right hand through his hair in a gesture of agitation and sighed deeply as he glanced back out over the ocean. "I should have realized it sooner, but if Crystal and I divorced, I knew she certainly would be entitled to some sort of settlement, but if there was a child involved, there would be..."

"Your inheritance," Meg interrupted. "I see."

Slowly, Smyth drew his gaze away from the ocean to

look at Meg.

"But I want you to understand, if the child were mine, I would give him or her everything I had. It's just that the child isn't mine and I don't like being conned."

"I understand that, Smyth. Perfectly."

"I'm not trying to weasel out of any of my obligations. My grandfather worked hard to build his business, I can't let her tear it apart."

"Is it sticky?"

"Very."

"Are you fighting it?"

"Tooth and nail."

"And it still helps to escape here and forget your problems for a while?"

Smyth watched the urgency in Meg's face, as if she were suddenly seeking answers to questions he wasn't sure he could give. "I come here every chance I get."

"Do you forget?"

"For a while."

"Do you think it will help me forget?"

Smyth paused a moment before answering. Finally, after watching her moisten her lips with her tongue, he answered. "It's the only place in the world where your troubles can't follow you. It will help you forget."

"Good," she replied on a whispered breath.

"Then do you want to stay?"

She nodded. "For a while. I need to forget...for a while."

"Will you allow me to help you with this problem?"

After a brief pause, Meg returned, "I can't answer that question right now."

Smyth reached to grasp her hand. "Okay. All you really need to do right now is forget. The rest will work itself out in time."

Meg perused his face for several long seconds. "You've really hit on your own piece of paradise here, haven't you?"

Feeling his gaze play over her face gave Meg a quick and deep sensation of longing to feel her chest pressed up against his. How she envied him, at this point, the opportunity to get away from everything that bothered him. To forget. But was he really forgetting?

Smyth finally shook his head from side to side, very slowly. His gaze never left hers.

"Perhaps it seems like paradise," he whispered, "the thing is, paradise often comes with a price. I just hope the cost is not too high."

"The cost?"

"Yeah," he acknowledged with a quick nod of his head. "The cost of trying to appear ignorant, or of trying to fool yourself into believing that you can avoid your problems for the rest of your life by hiding out on this island. I know it's wrong, but it's too late for me. I'm addicted.

But you can't put yourself in that position, you know that, Meg? You can run for a while, but sooner or later it's going to smack you dead in the face."

Meg felt a jolt of fear slice through her abdomen at his words. Why was he saying this?

"What do you mean?" she asked determinedly, trying not to act shocked.

"I'm simply saying that I avoided my problems for too long and I'm going to pay for it in the end. I just wonder if there is a way to solve your problem before it gets out of hand. I don't want you to make the same mistakes I did."

Meg stared into his eyes. "It's already way out of hand. And I realize it's inevitable that I will be found. I just want to experience a little bit of paradise while I can. Do you have a problem with that?"

Slowly, Smyth shook his head. "No," he answered softly, gathering her into his arms. "I don't. I just think that we both need to be realistic—paradise usually doesn't last forever."

Chapter Twenty-One

Sleep didn't come as easily the second night on the island and Meg found herself counting everything from sheep to the stars out her window, but it didn't help. Images of Smyth's kisses kept coming to mind and for the first time in quite a while, she ached to make love with a man. And she desperately wanted that man to be Smyth. She'd thought sex was dead to her long ago, but Smyth made her body zing with anticipation every time he drew near to her.

She suspected it would probably take only a little coaxing from her for it to happen and she was sure he felt the same. Life, at the moment, remained too uncertain for each of them. And she didn't want to let herself, or Smyth, in for more hurt than necessary. He was right. Paradise didn't last forever.

No, she couldn't make love with Smyth. Not even knowing that she desperately wanted to more than anything. But until she knew that Bradford would leave her totally alone, until she faced that problem head on, she didn't think she could ever be free to truly love again.

Restless, she turned over and pulled the covers up to her chin, trying to will her body into relaxation. Fantasizing about making love with Smyth finally accomplished what she had not been able to do—imagining his hands caressing, his mouth invading, his body languidly covering hers, their erotic coming together, and the sated clasp of their bodies as they both fell into an exhausted sleep.

Finally, Meg slept.

****

Smyth woke in a disoriented state of trying to figure out where in the hell he was, why his dreams had been interrupted, and what caused the blasting sound in his ear. Finally recognizing the noise as a scream, he tore from his bed, raced down the hall toward Meg's room, and barreled through the door to find her screaming in her sleep.

Meg buried her face in her hands as she sat rigidly in her bed, tears streaming through her fingers. As she gulped in air, agonized cries exited her throat. Smyth sank beside her on the bed in the dark room and immediately said her name while folding his arms around her.

At first Meg resisted, jerking from him, but Smyth calmly repeated her name and caressed her arms until he could feel an involuntary relaxation coming over her. A cold sweat enveloped her body, her T-shirt damp with perspiration, but he held her to him, trying to warm and comfort her at the same time.

"Meg," he cooed. "Honey, it's me, Smyth. You're dreaming. You're having a nightmare." He pulled her closer and she hesitantly let herself lie against his chest. Repeated unwitting jerks of her body allowed her to sink into the folds of his arms. Smyth exhaled and clasped his arms tighter around her and lowered his face into her sweet-smelling hair.

"I have you, honey. Everything is all right. You're okay."

Her arms snaked around his waist and gripped like an iron vise. She turned her trembling body fully into him. Smyth held and rocked her, stroking her back, cooing words of comfort.

Knowing he could do nothing else at the moment, that she desperately needed to exorcise any demons she could, when she could. And all the while he wished he could take away the pain.

The uncertainty. The hell her life had been. If only he could change places with her and let her enjoy her life so he could love her and keep her with him forever.

Finally, Meg's sobs quieted, but she clung to him just as tightly and wouldn't move her face a fraction from his chest. He could feel her hot breath against his chest and he felt himself grow hard. He wanted her. Wanted to love away her pain. But it wouldn't happen. Not tonight.

The one thing he knew he couldn't do was leave her. He wouldn't.

"Better?" he whispered against her cheek.

He felt her nod against him, her silence telling him more than her words ever would.

"I'm not leaving you," he told her.

She only gripped him tighter and he knew she didn't want him to leave.

Managing to put only enough space between them to reposition their bodies on the bed, Smyth pulled the blankets around them both, gathered Meg into his arms and rested her head against his chest as they lay down.

He felt the dampness of her tears as he held her, worrying about her, feeling her small body next to his, absorbing her pain. He knew for the first time in his life what it felt like to fall totally in love with a woman.

****

Meg woke early the next morning. Her first thoughts centered on how real her fantasy of making love with Smyth seemed. In the next instant, she remembered the nightmare.

Simultaneously, she felt his heavy arms wrapped around her. For several minutes she kept her eyes closed, not wanting to risk moving a muscle, fearing she would break the magic spell.

Smyth felt so warm and so good against her. She loved being wrapped in the secure cocoon of him. She relished the feel of his chest against her cheek and the warm waft of his breath over her forehead. She didn't want it to end. Ever.

Involuntarily, she squirmed closer into Smyth and his arms drew tighter around her. She heard and felt his heavy sigh as one hand reached up to gently thread his fingers though the hair at the back of her neck. Something went haywire inside of her, like the grand finale of fireworks on the Fourth of July, and then settled heavily, deep in her pelvis. And she wanted so much, desperately, to reach up, press her mouth onto his, and let him bury himself in her.

And before she realized it, her eyes grew misty with the sting of tears because she knew she couldn't let that happen.

She was falling hopelessly in love with Smyth Parker.

A deep sigh escaped her lips.

"Meg?" The whisper came hesitant and low against the top of her head. "Are you awake?"

After a moment, she nodded. "Yes."

Shifting, Smyth slid down where he could look at her, their faces across from each other on the pillow. Meg watched his eyes as they searched hers. He still held her very close.

Oh, please, Meg begged. Don't let him kiss me, I won't be able to stop myself.

"How did you sleep?"

Meg swallowed a huge lump in her throat, her mouth incredibly dry. "Better...after you got here," she admitted.

"Good. You want to talk about it?" His voice was still as soft and caressing as the night ocean breeze.

Bits of the nightmare flashed before her at that instant and she tensed. "Not...right now.

Maybe later."

"All right."

Smyth stared into her face a moment longer and she knew he would let her set the pace—not only about last night, but everything else as well. Every molecule of her being was so aware and attuned to him that she could barely stay put.

"Thanks for coming in here. For staying."

Smyth moved closer, his right hand reaching forward to touch her cheek. Meg's eyes closed at the touch. "I couldn't have left you," he whispered. "Not even if you ordered me away."

Her eyes opened and she held his gaze for an instant. "I needed you."

He brushed his thumb over her lips and she trembled at the touch. She watched his gaze drop to where his thumb lingered and before she realized it, he'd reached forward and captured her in a soft, fondling kiss. Meg closed her eyes and her heart trilled as she savored the feel of his lips on hers. The fireworks begged to explode within her and she knew it would take just one caress of his fingers in the right place on her body and she would be lost. His hand cupped her face, pulling her closer as he nibbled and tasted. Then he broke away, leaving her breathless.

"I need you more than you know," he softly returned. After a pause, he glanced away, then flicked the covers up around her, tucking her safely in, and looked back into her eyes.

"Sleep. You've had a restless night. I'll fix us something to eat."

He left her and Meg suddenly felt so alone.

****

Harsh realities become more evident in the light of day and as Meg entered the kitchen later that morning, she realized the reality of spending the night in Smyth Parker's arms.

It was damn difficult to keep her hands off the man.

Standing in his kitchen, wearing only a pair of shorts and flip-flops while flipping eggs with a spatula, Smyth's broad, tanned chest was too inviting. She wanted to touch him, to slide her hands over that wide chest, but she sucked in a quick breath and stopped dead in the center of the kitchen. She wanted to walk straight into his arms, like lovers would do after a night of lovemaking. It felt so natural. Except for one problem.

They weren't lovers and they weren't going to be. Something twisted in her gut. God, how awful that sounded...and felt.

He turned and caught her watching him. A broad, welcoming smile stretched across his face.

"Hi. I thought you might sleep late but I heard the shower so I fixed breakfast. Hungry?"

Cautiously, Meg stepped farther into the room. "Um...you might say."

Smyth gestured with the spatula. "There's juice in the

refrigerator and coffee on the counter. Choose your poison."

His casual banter made it a whole lot easier for her to relax, but she still had to keep her guard up. He was just too irresistible for her own good.

Meg sidled past him and poured herself a cup of coffee, feeling she needed something harder than juice to calm her jittery nerves. She carried her coffee cup to the kitchen table and sat down.

Smyth dished two fried eggs onto plates followed by several crisp slices of bacon and four expertly triangled wedges of buttered toast. He juggled the two plates in one hand, his mug of coffee in the other and joined her at the table.

"There. That should do us for a while. Eat up. It's going to be a long hike to the shelling beach this morning."

Meg's eyes met his from across the table. She half expected questions about her nightmare, not this about-face.

"Shelling beach?"

Smyth ate a bite of his breakfast, then glanced up at her. "There's a great beach about a mile from here. We'll have to walk a little ways through salt flats, but it's worth it when you get there. Best shells around. The sand is clean. Absolutely no competition. Most of the visitors don't want to walk that far through ankle-deep water. Actually, it's really not that bad. The water is warm and when you get there, you'll never want to leave."

An uneasy silence settled between them and Meg found herself staring at her two fried eggs, a sudden heaviness lying over her chest.

"I never want to leave already."

The words were out of her mouth before she could stop them. Alarm coursed through her abdomen and spiked up to her heart. Feeling her cheeks flame, Meg dropped her gaze to her lap.

Stupid! Why in the world was she leading Smyth on like this?

Meg took a sip from her coffee mug, then set it down with trembling hands. She looked up to find Smyth's gaze fixed on her. The desire in his eyes, the warmth he emitted, almost more than she could bear. He cared for her and it killed her inside.

"Smyth..." she began softly and squirmed in her seat.

"I don't want you to go back."

Not a fraction of an inch of his face moved. Meg heaved in breath after breath and felt a little dizzy. He didn't want her to go back?

"I have to. Sometime."

"Stay with me here. No one will ever find you."

Meg looked at him. It was as though his soul poured out of his pleading eyes.

"We can't be sure of that."

"I won't let anything happen to you."

"Smyth," she began again, her lips parched and her throat dry. She wanted to say yes, take care of me, let me stay with you forever. But she knew it was impossible. "There's so much you don't know."

His demeanor didn't falter. "Then tell me. Tell me everything, Meg. Tell me what frightened you so last night."

Meg's fingers curled around the fork by her plate. *What frightened me? You, for one! And that damn nightmare!* Huffing out a quick breath, Meg glanced to her right, gripped the fork and jammed it quickly against the table. Abruptly standing, she paced across the floor to the kitchen window, crossed her quivering arms tightly over her breasts, and tried to fight the swirling emotion playing with her equilibrium.

Her gaze fixed on the scrub pines out the window, she began softly.

"I'm afraid of so many things I have no idea where to begin." Smyth's chair squeaked on the old linoleum. She felt him behind her and her eyes closed. He felt so warm against her back.

Her protector. But he couldn't protect her from Bradford. No one could.

His arms embraced her and she melted against him.

"Tell me about the nightmare," he whispered.

Her eyes fluttered open and she continued to stare out the window. Sighing, she suddenly wanted the poison out of her system. She wanted him to understand.

"I dreamed about the assistant district attorney."

After a moment's hesitation, Smyth questioned her. "I don't follow you."

She shook her head. "No. I've told you everything else. Only two people know about this. Me and—"

"Rudy?"

Nodding, Meg let her hands slip over Smyth's arms and she held tight as the tremors started again. The dizzying sensation of a few moments earlier returned. The words tumbled out.

"A few months ago I told Bradford I wanted a divorce. He was furious, of course, and told me it would never happen. He told me about his plans to go into politics and that he needed me by his side to do that. He threatened me, telling me if I pursued a divorce, he would kill me. He assured me he'd done it before and he had many ways of making it look like an accident. He made it damn clear I had no choices where our marriage was concerned. He also told me that if I didn't think he would, to make sure and read the morning paper."

"What was in the paper?"

"Some new hot-shot district attorney who was on Bradford's tail had been murdered, execution style. The police found neither motive nor killer."

Smyth felt Meg's fingertips dig into his arms. She trembled and he knew what she was about to say. "Bradford killed him." He said the words for her.

She nodded and he heard the ragged sigh as her head dropped in defeat. "The D.A. had some sort of vendetta against him, I gathered. That day Rudy came to see me. She told me that whatever I had to do, I had to get out of the marriage. And then she told me about the assistant D.A. and confirmed my thoughts."

"How did she know?"

"I'm not totally certain, but I think she has some sort of inside track into most of Bradford's business dealings— legal or otherwise. I really don't want to know."

"Damn..."

"If that is true, and if she knows for sure that he killed the man, Bradford probably threatened her life as well."

Smyth tightened his grip around her and lowered his face to her cheek. "What did you do then?"

"I did a lot of thinking. I knew I had to figure out a way to escape."

She dropped her arms and Smyth released her. After carefully turning her to him, he searched her face. Running his hands up and down her arms, he pulled her closer. "Is that when you ran?"

Slowly, Meg shook her head. "No. I ran months later. I formulated a plan, thought about it for weeks. All I needed was a lucky break. And I got it. Bradford was leaving for several days in London. He was in a hurry, and then something abruptly came up that he had to deal with before the flight, which in turn made him agitated. He paced the bedroom, looking for something he'd lost, then someone came to the front door. That's when he made the mistake and left his briefcase upstairs with me. Unlocked. I'd never seen his briefcase unlocked in all our married years.

"It was risky, but I opened it and rifled through the contents. I didn't know what I was looking for, anything, I guess. I found a small, maroon, leather-bound book. Leafing though it I found phone numbers and addresses, but for some reason, one stood out more than the others. It was by Rudy's name, but it wasn't Rudy's phone number. I quickly jotted the numbers down on a scrap of paper, crammed it deep between the mattress and box springs, then stuffed the book back into his case and shut it. I'll never forget those numbers."

"And then he came back?"

"Fortunately, he flew back into the room and left in such a hurry he didn't give me or his briefcase another thought. I was so shaky, I waited until late into the night to even contemplate what I might have stumbled onto. When I did think about it, I played with different arrangements of the numbers until it finally hit me. His safe. I just hoped it was the safe he had at home.

"So I tried it. And it opened. I waited, half expecting alarms to go off, but there were none. I didn't know what I was looking for, I just looked. When I pulled the contents out of the safe, I knew I had little time to waste. The only thing in there was a large envelope full of money. I took it, called Rudy to tell her I wanted to take her out to breakfast the next morning, and then we set the plan into action. A few days later I pulled out of my driveway in a used Honda I'd traded my Jaguar for and I've never looked back. Until now."

Smyth looked at her, as if contemplating all she'd told him. "Meg, have you told any of this to the police?"

"Yes. The other day, after I found out Rudy was dead. I called and talked to a detective in Chicago. But I don't know what will come of it, or if they believed me."

"Do you think you should go back and talk to them in person? You've got some pretty alarming evidence."

"I really don't have anything, Smyth. All I've got is hearsay."

"But Rudy's dead. I'd think that's enough to warrant an investigation into Bradford. And if they could get him behind bars, then you would be free to get your divorce and be on with your life."

Meg shook her head. "I don't think it works that easily. Bradford would find a way. He wouldn't stay behind bars for long. I don't think what I have is enough."

"It's a start."

It was the urgency in Smyth's voice that frightened Meg, then the shivers of fright that tripped down her spine and curled back again to settle just under her breastbone that added to her fear. Didn't he understand? She had thought about all that. "No," she returned bluntly, pulling away to put space between them. "It's useless. I can't do it.

I'm not sure I would be believed"

"We'll do it together. I'll go with you."

Suddenly, the thought of him going back to Chicago with her frightened her more than the thought of facing Bradford alone. Images of her nightmare flashed before her eyes. "No."

Meg broke free and stepped out of his grasp. Frantically, she spun again and faced him.

She knew he was right. She had evidence, but not enough. And he wouldn't be going with her.

"No, Smyth. We're not going back."

"I'll go with you. You need me. Let's get this thing over with so we can have a life together."

"I needed you last night. I don't need you to go to Chicago with me. It's too risky."

"Dammit!" Smyth jerked away and paced the floor beside her, raking fingers through his already tousled hair. "Listen to me, Meg. I don't have to remind you how dangerous the man is.

He wants you dead. You're going to be running from him for the rest of your life. Do you understand me? What do we have, you and me, if we can't get this thing settled and get him behind bars? We have nothing, Meg. We have nothing!"

Meg stared at him. "Putting Bradford behind bars would be like putting one snake in a bottle. There are others out there who would just as easily kill me, and you, because Bradford ordered it done. He's that powerful, Smyth."

Desperation washed over her. It took a valiant effort to hold back the tears. She didn't like him being upset with her, but she knew no other way at the moment. Knowing she was pushing him away didn't help matters either, but she couldn't, wouldn't, allow him to even think about going to Chicago. The thought of him tangling with Bradford or his men frightened her to no end.

"I'll not let you put yourself in jeopardy for my sake."

"Then what about our sake, Meg? What the hell do we

have here? I want to do it for us, so we have something to look forward to together. Don't you understand that I love you? That I want to do it for us?"

His words washed over her in a torrent. Emotion from anger to fear to elation ripped through her. And the only way she knew how to react was to ignore all of it, except that tears found it hard to ignore any emotion.

"Don't you realize?" she shouted back, fists clenched at her sides, tears spilling over.

"Don't you realize what will happen?" Meg abruptly turned from him and started toward the door to the back porch. She had to get out of there. She felt icy cold and claustrophobic.

And she needed to clear her head. *He loves me?*

Abruptly, she turned back, the pain of that realization stung deep. "My nightmare last night had everything to do with us, Smyth. But the man getting his brains blown away wasn't the assistant D.A. That man was you, Smyth. You! And Bradford pulled the trigger." She was sobbing now and didn't really care. "And all I could do was stand helplessly by and watch." She drew in a ragged breath, jerked open the screen door, then faced him.

"I don't wish to have that image playing through my mind for the rest of my life. Because if you go back with me, Bradford will kill you just for the sheer joy of making me watch you take your last dying breath." She sobbed and reached for the door handle. "And I love you too much to let that happen."

Meg gasped at the horror of what she'd said as she exited the porch and tripped down the steps into Smyth's back yard. For the time being, she needed to be alone.

All alone.

Chapter Twenty-Two

Deep in the night, the shadows hid the gun quavering in her hand. One hand poked an errant string of blonde hair back over an ear. Shaking so, she clasped the gun with the other hand, needing both on the butt of the pistol to steady it. She pointed it at the sleeping figure beneath the blankets.

Without thought or malice, she took a deep breath. Finally, her hands calmed. Once, twice she fired the gun, the bullets slammed into his inert body. Blood spurted in a wide arc after the second hit and she squealed as some of it splattered on her clothing. Damn, she'd have to change.

His body jerked at the first hit, but after the second, which hit him square in the back of the head, he didn't move. For good measure, she fired off three more shots in rapid succession, not really caring where they punctured his body. She lowered her weapon.

Shaking uncontrollably, she let the gun slip from her fingers to drop on the carpeted floor and could only stare at the dead man in the bed.

Finally.

Finally the bastard was dead.

It was difficult to describe the feelings that wafted up inside her. Anger that he forced her to do this. Joy that he was finally gone.

Satisfaction. Relief.

Hastily, she gathered her wits about her, picked up the gun and crossed the room. She rifled through the closet and pulled out another shirt and a pair of blue jeans. Avoiding getting blood on the new things, she quickly changed, tossed the soiled clothing into the back of the closet, and quietly slipped out of the house.

****

Smyth let Meg have her solitude for the rest of the day.

She'd made it quite clear when he'd run after her that she wanted to be alone. He told her this was the place for it and left her, realizing that so many times he had done the same thing. She was safe, there was no reason to be concerned. For him, the island could cure just about any ill one could conjure. Perhaps it would be the same for her.

She'd come back to the house in the early evening and with lowered eyes mumbled a greeting as she passed him waiting on the porch. He listened as she fixed a sandwich in the kitchen, then called softly to him moments later that she was going to bed. He let her go and didn't interfere.

He'd needed the day to himself to think. And all day long his thoughts came up with two conclusions. He loved Meg. And one way or another, he had to free her of her demons. With or without her consent.

He stared toward her bedroom, wondering what conclusions she'd reached today.

Meg felt anxious about falling asleep. Darkness was usually a comfort, but not tonight.

She didn't want to suffer through another rendition of the nightmare. Her sleep-deprived mind left her exhausted and heavy with the thoughts of her afternoon. As she'd walked, staring at the sparkling sea, she thought of Smyth. As she sat and dug deep holes into the sandy shore that washed away with each receding wave, she'd contemplated what to do about their situation.

What to do about Bradford. Her life.

She'd always wondered if she could kill Bradford, but the answer always came up the same. She didn't have the guts. She was a spineless jellyfish when it came to Bradford. Not that she could have killed, even at her best, although she'd wished him dead over and over again.

Sometimes she wondered how she'd had the strength to leave him. But she had and that was all that mattered now.

But she had killed him. In her dreams she'd killed him time and time again. She'd poisoned him. She'd hired a hit man. She'd shot him in his sleep. And every fantasy that played through her mind brought her such disgust she could hardly stand herself. For she never in her life thought she'd actually consider killing another human being, but at the same time she'd been desperate. And in so much pain. She'd wanted him to hurt, and hurt badly.

Perhaps that's why the fantasies returned that afternoon, Meg thought as she lay staring into the night. Was she desperate again? Had she found something so precious in Smyth and this place that she would risk everything to kill Bradford and be done with the entire mess?

Panic rushed up inside her and Meg shifted to her side and drew the cool sheets up to her chin. She squeezed her eyes shut and forced out tiny tears, but held back the sobs. Desperate wasn't the only word for how she felt at the moment. Hopeless. That was a better word. The whole damn situation was hopeless.

Chapter Twenty-Three

"Watch out for jellyfish. They sometimes get caught in the salt flats after the tide goes down."

Meg abruptly stopped, planted her feet in ankle deep salt water, and looked at Smyth, her eyes wide. "What do you mean, watch out for jellyfish?"

His boyish grin melted Meg's heart. He looked like a mischievous youngster at that moment. And she felt as though he was leading her into an adventure, of sorts, that she'd probably remember for the rest of her days. His tanned chest and face reflected the sun, which also brought out the golden highlights in his brown hair, creating an irresistible sun god image.

And as he reached out to her, Meg knew he wouldn't lead her into harm. Ever.

"Oh, c'mon," he coaxed, grasping her hand and pulling. "It's not that far, see?" He pointed straight ahead. Meg heard the ocean and saw the shoreline. They would be out of the salt flats soon.

"You've got your beach shoes on, so if you do step on anything, you won't get stung."

Meg glanced down at her feet through the clear water and lifted one foot into the air. "Yeah, but these mesh sides offer little protection here, don't you think?"

Smyth tugged her hand. "Come on. I'll watch out. I won't let you step on anything."

Meg drifted forward and Smyth pulled her the rest of the way. They walked hand in hand for a few more feet toward the shore. "And even if you did get stung," Smyth began again as they waded through the water, "we'd just rub a little sand in it, wash it off with salt water, then put some of that anti-sting stuff on it you've got in that bag there."

"In this bag?" Meg lifted the backpack she'd borrowed

from Smyth a few days earlier and removed it off her shoulder.

"Yeah. I packed some first aid stuff in there along with our lunch."

Meg swung the pack back into place. Smyth carried the larger bag, which held a blanket, water, a couple of books and nets for dipping up shells in the shallows. It was early morning and they'd planned to stay the day.

"You pack sunscreen?"

He nodded. "Like I said, shouldn't be afraid of a little jellyfish. A Portuguese Man of War, now that's another matter..."

Meg sidled a little closer to him and gripped his hand tighter. "But they're not around here, are they?"

Smyth stared off toward the ocean. "Well...you never know. Not usually, but—"

Meg playfully whooped him on the shoulder with her backpack.

"Hey, be careful! I don't like my peanut butter and jelly smooshed."

Meg swung the pack into place again. "If you don't shut up about jellyfish and Man of War, then you'll have more to worry about than your peanut butter, mister." Then she grinned and Smyth swept his arms about her and drew her closer to him.

Their bodies touched and Meg sighed. He felt so good pressed against her. She'd awakened that morning to find Smyth preparing for their hike. They'd called a truce and had made one pact before they left. They were to think only of today. Each promised not to bring up anything of the past...for today.

Tension still existed, yes. And both of them walked on tentative ground when it came to their relationship or their future. But for today, their only mission was the walk to the shelling beach.

And now, as she looked up into Smyth's face, an intense expression washed over it. "You know I'm only teasing about the jellyfish. I'd never let anything hurt you," he said.

Meg searched his eyes and felt his words as well as heard them. "I know," she whispered.

Smyth tenderly brushed his lips against hers. Meg found the light touch exquisitely sensual and stimulating. Her arms moved up to his shoulders and she pressed closer into him.

The kiss deepened, Smyth's tongue gently nudging between her parted lips, playfully circling her tongue. Her heart swelled and even though she knew she shouldn't be kissing him, shouldn't be enjoying the kiss so much, she found herself wanting more. And she thought, *think only of today.*

Smyth broke away with a gasp, his hands now placed on her upper arms. "Ah, Meg." He dragged the words out, closing his eyes for a moment as if savoring every second of the kiss. He opened his eyes and looked at her. "Let's get out of the flats."

Meg nodded, keeping the connection with his eyes. Smyth pulled her to his side and each wrapped an arm around the other's waist, sharing their closeness. They walked several more yards until out of the salt flats and on the firm, sandy beach. Smyth led Meg down the beach a bit further, not far from the thundering ocean waves, and dropped his bag to the sand. Meg dropped hers beside his and each simply looked to the other, as if anticipating what came next.

"Uh..." Smyth parked his hands on his hips and looked down the beach. "Want to check out the shells now?"

Meg nodded. Smyth fished a mesh-net bag out of the back pack and two nets. Then grasping her hand, he pulled Meg closer to the shore.

****

Laughing, Meg raced through the wet sand near the shoreline, Smyth close behind. With wind blowing through her hair and sand tickling the soles of her feet, she felt giddy. And happy.

Happier than she'd been in perhaps years. She turned

abruptly and planted her feet. Smyth sailed into her, catching her at her waist and spinning her around. Both laughing now, Meg struggled out of his grasp and started into the sparkling ocean.

Thigh deep in the surf, she turned and watched Smyth, still standing on the beach. Bathed in sunlight, she splashed water over herself and toward Smyth. She smiled suggestively and beckoned to him with both hands.

A sense of vast freedom enveloped her. She was free. *Free!* To do and experience whatever she wanted. There was no one to stop her. No one looking over her shoulder. And no one watching her every move.

Except Smyth. And that was all that counted.

A crashing wave from behind pitched her forward. Still giggling, she righted herself and quickly regained her footing. The wave succeeded in completely wetting her one piece bathing suit. She itched to dive in and let the buoyant saltwater caress her skin.

With one hip hitched out to the side, Meg crooked her index finger and motioned for Smyth to join her.

It was all he needed.

Smyth splashed his way closer. Meg shrieked and turned, diving into a wave rolling up from behind. Smyth did the same, surfacing only seconds after her just a few feet away. He kicked forward, she kicked away backwards, still facing him. Still smiling.

"You can only go so far, Meg," he teased, treading water.

"You can't get me," she flirted back. "There's a big ol' ocean out there."

"We'll see about that." Smyth dived into the water before Meg had time to react and grasped her around the waist, pulling her down with him. She kicked for a second, but the instant his hands molded to her body and they drew closer together, she quieted, settling her hands on his shoulders. Propelling them both upward, Smyth and Meg broke the surface together.

Both gasping, facing each other in the water, Smyth

stared into Meg's now serious face.

The waves pushed at them, forcing them closer to the shore. Smyth felt bottom and stood holding her, the water lapping around their shoulders.

Gingerly, he pushed Meg's hair back out of her face and ran his thumb along her cheekbone and jaw. Her eyes closed and he dropped his scrutiny of her pert, beautiful face to her heaving chest, sparkling with salt-glitter from the ocean. He lifted his gaze into her now open eyes and peered into the depths of her desire.

And he knew they were going to make love.

Pulling her closer, he wanted her to feel how much he needed her. He closed his eyes at the ecstasy he felt when their bodies slid together.

Never had such emotion crossed his soul. Never had he felt for a woman what he was feeling now. More than just a physical thing, it was with dire passion that his love for her had built to a level of utmost prominence. And all he could fathom was that he wanted to love her slowly, gently. To let her know a man's need to possess a woman didn't come with violence, but with tender emotion and desire.

Meg grasped his shoulders and then lifted her body and wrapped both of her luscious legs around his waist. A huge sigh whooshed from him at the pleasure that bordered on excruciating pain at the feel of her against him, at the feel of him throbbing against her. And he didn't know how long he could last, standing there, holding her, without ripping her suit from her body and plunging into her, right here, right now.

But that wasn't the way he intended to do it.

"Meg..." he rasped, tangling his fingers in her hair, pulling her face to his mouth. "Oh, honey. Meg." He trailed his mouth over her face, devoured her lips. His tongue traced a path from her lips down her neck. "I want to make love to you."

She clutched at him, one hand kneading his chest, her palm stretched over his wildly beating heart.

His hands trembled. They raced over her back, down to her buttocks, pulling her closer, urging her body to wrap around him more fully. Meg moaned and squeezed her legs tighter. He thrust against her waiting body. His hands played over her rear, the fingers of his right hand slipping beneath the leg of her bathing suit.

"Smyth..." She whispered his name, her breath hot against his neck.

"It's just the two of us, Meg," he gasped. "Think only of us."

"I can think of nothing else."

A wave burst forth and caught them, propelling them toward the shore. Smyth held her tight, not wanting to risk losing her, not wanting their bodies to apart for one second.

Not wanting to feel the void of that separation.

He lifted and carried her toward the shore, still wrapped around him, her breath hot against his neck, her arms clinging. Tumbling to the blanket he'd laid out earlier, they rolled and melded their bodies, neither wanting to risk parting.

Smyth tucked Meg beneath him, pinning her to the soft bed of sand under the blanket.

Reaching up, she grasped his face in her hands and pulled him to her lips. Her tiny kisses rained over his face as she lovingly and softly caressed him with her lips. He tasted her, tiny droplets of saltwater still clinging to the tender skin of her neck, behind her ear, and then lower over the sweet mounds of her breasts.

He settled against her, and he heard her ragged sigh of pleasure as her legs parted, allowing him to fall into the cradle of her thighs, his arousal snug against her soft mound.

She arched her back at the pleasure she felt where his hard body rocked against her. Her eyes closed. His hands snaked along either side of her neck and smoothed down her chest. His lips, hot and moist, slid toward her collarbone and found the racing pulse in her neck. He licked and she felt her pulse surge lower, just where he surged against her.

"Smyth..." His name escaped her lips on a sigh as a finger lifted one strap of her suit and then another, urgently pulling it down over her shoulders and arms until his hands smoothed it to her waist.

Suddenly, he drew back and Meg opened her eyes to look up at him. A cool ocean breeze blew playfully over her breasts, teasing and taunting them into even harder peaks. Goose bumps sped over her damp flesh. She watched his face as he watched her, his gaze roaming over her breasts, then he looked back into her eyes.

"You're so beautiful," he whispered. Meg's breathing came in small pants. "Meg, what do you want? I'm not sure how long I can..."

His eyes pleaded and Meg could tell how much he cared, how much he wanted her—how unsure of what they shared.

With one finger, she reached up to touch his lips. "Love me," she whispered. "All I want is for you to love me."

With all the emotion she'd ever dared to own, she gave herself to him. Smyth's gentle caresses, his soft kisses held her prisoner to his ardent possession of her body. With her total being she felt compelled to give of herself fully, for even if they shared only this one afternoon, this one fleeting moment of loving each other, it would be enough to last a lifetime.

She knew he would make her whole again.

Smyth lowered himself to suckle first one breast, then the other, his hands kneading and palming her flesh. Meg sank into a silken abyss leaving her with no more room for coherent thought or speculation about what they were doing or how they'd come to be there.

They were simply a man and a woman loving each other. And falling deeper into that chasm of devotion.

Never had physical closeness been so exquisite, so beautiful. Smyth's lips caressed and took her flesh into his mouth, teasing and tantalizing with his tongue. His lower body teased and tantalized her with altogether different sensations.

And then all melded together. Smyth shifted against her and captured her mouth with his.

She tasted the bitter salt on his lips, which only heightened each sensation she felt. Tiny granules of sand trapped between her back and the blanket pricked every nerve into awareness. Smyth's chest hair brushed warm and golden against her sensitive nipples, urging the coil inside her to wind tighter and tighter. His hands were at her waist, pulling and tugging her suit down around her hips. She alternately wanted the fabric separating their bodies gone, but hated each time he pulled away to remove it.

Within seconds, grasping and groping fingers had removed both their suits. Passion stirred and built, every sensation crested, and the tiny bud of her sexuality swelled as Smyth fell against her and urgently slid between her legs. She opened for him and willingly let him in. His controlled yet hesitant thrusts titillated and teased. Unable to stand the tentative movements any longer, she wrapped her legs around him, urging him deeper inside her, straining against him, until the coil buried within her sprung, blessedly providing her with spellbinding relief, and releasing her eons later into a sated calm.

Somewhere in the midst of her passion Meg felt Smyth shudder and tremble as he softly called her name. Their bodies stilled, they embraced and folded into one another, and Smyth drew the blanket around them, making a cocoon of their own little world. Seconds before Meg fell blissfully asleep in his arms, her only coherent thought was that she'd made love, really made love, for the very first time in her life.

*****

The wind ruffled the blanket around them as Smyth watched the sun sink lower in the sky. They needed to start back soon. The hell of it was, he didn't want to move. Ever. He didn't want to risk breaking the spell.

They'd made love. Her panting, sighing and calling his name had been his undoing.

When he'd slid into her velvet softness, her body sheathing his in warmth and gentle squeezing caresses, all thought of loving her slowly and tenderly escaped him. He'd had no control. When she'd wrapped her legs around him and her body exploded in total pleasure, he'd lost everything.

All willpower. All sense of time and place. The passion he'd felt making love with her rivaled only by the raw emotion he'd experience when she'd pressed close against him in her sleep, her soft tears wetting his chest.

Meg snuggled closer into him and he hated waking her. If it were only possible to stay this way, this close, forever. He shifted, sitting up on one elbow. "Meg?" With his forefinger, he stroked her face. "Wake up, honey. We've got to get back."

Groaning, Meg squirmed against him and he had to fight the urges stirring within his groin again. "Meg?"

She pulled back and her eyelids fluttered open.

"Hi," she returned huskily, smiling.

"Hi," he softly answered, smiling back. "You okay?"

She nodded and her eyes searched his face. "I'm wonderful. You?"

"You were beautiful. We were beautiful together." He lowered his face to lightly touch her lips.

Meg kissed him back. "Do we need to leave now?"

Rising up on one elbow, Smyth glanced at the late afternoon sky.

"Regretfully, yes."

"I don't wanna." Meg buried deeper into the blanket. "I want to spend the night on the beach. You and me. Under the stars. Like you said."

Smiling, Smyth remembered their conversation a few nights earlier.

"Meg," he whispered, ducking beneath the blanket himself. He found her face and tipped it up to his, her eyes wide and dark in the shade of the blanket. "I want to take you home. Make love to you in my bed. Sleep all night with you in my arms."

She nodded and tilted her face up to plant a moist kiss on his lips.

"Let's go home," she whispered.

Dusk fell rapidly as they crossed the dunes and headed into the village. Twilight twinkled with an orange glow as the sun raced lower in the western sky over the sound. As they walked arm in arm toward Smyth's house, an incredible peace washed over Meg and she felt contentedly happy.

She could see the radiance in Smyth's eyes when he looked at her and she wondered if he saw the same in hers. Meg knew, without a shadow of a doubt, that she saw love in his face. And she felt it from the deepest recesses of her own heart. For now, she didn't intend to let anything spoil her happiness. Nothing.

She decided early today that there would be no more talk of Bradford and her previous life while she was here with Smyth. She'd found a bit of paradise and wanted to enjoy it while she could.

"Are you hungry?"

Meg grinned. "A little. You?"

"Actually, I'm starved. I was trying to think what we've got at home to fix for dinner.

You know, when I came over this time, I really wasn't thinking about dinners for two. I hope you don't mind, I usually just heat up some soup, fix a sandwich, or something."

Meg linked her arm a little tighter with his. "You know I don't mind. Whatever you've got will be fine. Should we go back and get more food?"

Smyth stopped and looked at her, a puzzled expression on her face.

"Depends on how long you think you're going to stay."

Searching his face, Meg spoke softly. "Depends on how long you want me."

One corner of Smyth's mouth turned up in a devilish grin. "Then I guess I better get the radio working. I may need to call the ferry over sometime next week. We'll be okay until then."

As they sauntered down the sand-gravel road toward his house, he tucked her close into his body. She loved the feel of him next to her. It was all so perfect, his attitude so matter-of-fact as though he wanted her to stay forever. And right now, she didn't think she'd ever want to leave.

What the coming night might bring filled her with anticipation.

A shrill hum sliced unnaturally through the air. Puffs of gravel dust ripped up several feet in front of her. Meg stopped short and turned a questioning look at Smyth. The second one hit, zinging through the air and striking very close to Smyth's right foot. The realization, however confusing, suddenly hit both of them.

"Get down!" Smyth grabbed Meg and threw her toward the side of the road, pushing her under a stand of scrub pines. He covered her body with his. "Don't move!"

Her pulse pounded in her ears. "What's happening?"

Smyth placed a silencing finger on her lips. He didn't want to frighten her, but at the same time she needed to know the truth, as uncanny and as impossible as it all sounded.

"Gunshots."

Panic burst up inside her. She wanted to scream. Her worst nightmares materialized right in front of her. Her voice conveyed her terror. "But you said we were the only people here, the only people on the island," she choked out.

Smyth pulled her further under the trees and waited for night to fall. It was their only chance.

"Obviously, I was wrong."

Chapter Twenty-Four

Night covered their escape while an eerie silence embraced them. No insects sang, no birds called. It even seemed to Meg that the waves ceased. All that existed around her was an indescribable, muffled roar in her head and the memory of the singing zip of the bullets as they bisected the air before them. She felt only Smyth's arms wrapped protectively around her and his warm breath against her neck.

Smyth stealthily moved her through trees and growth, keeping her body close and in the shadows. She sensed his apprehension. The mere fact that their sanctuary had been invaded, however impossible it sounded, startled her more than she cared to admit. And Smyth's nervous, no-nonsense demeanor in the fifteen minutes they'd held silent vigil under the pines disturbed her even more. Smyth was her security. Her rock. Her protector.

She needed his strength as hers rapidly deteriorated. And neither spoke the thoughts drumming through their brains.

"Stay here and stay low," Smyth whispered as they crept up the back porch steps of the darkened house. For now, no more shots.

No noise. No indication from where, or whom, the shots had come.

They had no way of knowing if he'd moved. Still watched. Intended to kill them now, later, or toy with them for a while.

Meg crouched against the wall, her fingers clutching Smyth's hand. His gaze met hers and held, his fingers brushed her cheek. She trembled, more frightened than she'd been in a long time. She shuddered, not wanting to contemplate what they might find in the house.

"Everything will be fine," he whispered just

centimeters from her face. "I won't let it be anything else."

The determined set of his jaw gave Meg temporary strength. He nodded to her that he was leaving, going into the house. And she nodded back, understanding. She squeezed his hand, not wanting to let go.

"I'll be back in a few seconds. If you hear anything—*anything*—out of the ordinary, run. Do you understand me?"

Silently, Meg nodded again.

"Stay in the trees or break into one of the houses. Do what you can, but stay out of open spaces. Stay off the beach. Stay hidden."

He crept to the door. Meg's fingers slipped out of his hand. The last touch lingered on fingertips. "Smyth," she breathed, her voice shaky, barely audible. "I love you." A ragged gasp caught in her throat.

He stopped and glanced back one more time.

"I love you, too," he whispered, his stare intense. Their hushed voices settled around them.

"Take me with you."

"No, stay here."

"I'm going with you." Meg crept closer. "I'm frightened."

Smyth sighed and pulled her next to him, held her tight for an instant. "All right. I just don't want any surprises when I get inside. Everything's been so quiet, he could be anywhere. Stay close, keep next to me."

Meg clutched him and nodded. "I'm like glue. You're going to have to peel me off later."

Cupping her face with both his hands, he drew her closer and briefly touched lips. "I might actually enjoy that if I didn't have to worry about a sniper breathing down my neck." He grinned and for a moment Meg felt safe. "Save that thought?"

Meg managed a grin. "Sure," she whispered.

Smyth's face turned serious as he glanced at the door. Squeezing her hand, he pulled her in that direction. The carefree moment abruptly ended.

Smyth entered the house. Meg followed close behind.

They slipped in the screen door and Smyth immediately latched the hook from the inside. Placing a finger on his lips, he led Meg away from the door and into the corner of the kitchen, motioning for her to crouch down and wait. Without a sound, she understood. He had to make sure the house was okay. Safe.

Then he left her.

Meg heard barely more than the beating of her heart against the night's silence. She closed her eyes and leaned her head back against the wall, silently willing her legs to stop trembling. She sensed rather than heard Smyth searching, room to room, throughout the small house. Thankful the house had only one floor, she didn't know how much longer she could take being away from him.

She heard a creak and her eyes shot open. A shuffle came next, followed by a screech against the wooden floor. Meg's breath caught in her throat. She bit her lip to prevent calling out.

Then another bump followed by a rapid succession of smaller ones. A splat. An umph. Followed by a low string of curses.

A brassy taste flowed through her mouth and Meg realized she'd bitten her lip until it bled. Hugging herself to stop from shaking, the tears slowly ran down her cheeks. Frightened, not knowing whether to come to Smyth's aid, sit still, or run, Meg found she could do nothing.

She sat, paralyzed with fear.

At last she watched a shadow slip into the kitchen. Her teeth chattered as the silhouette made its way across the room. Her breath came in shallow gulps. And she was suddenly cold.

Very cold. The shadow crept toward her and then stopped.

"Meg?" Smyth whispered and crouched down in front of her. "I can hardly see you."

A sigh of relief whooshed from her lungs and she lunged forward.

Smyth's arms immediately embraced her.

"Are you okay?" His nose nuzzled the hair around her ear.

"Scared out of my wits," she tossed back on a whisper. "What happened in there?"

Smyth rubbed his hands up and down her arms. "I bumped into a chair and then hit my head on a shelf on the wall. Books fell. A large one hit my toe. That's all." He pulled back and Meg peered into a face she could barely see. "Come on. The coast is clear, I think, but I want us to get comfortable and stay put. I don't think they'll try to shoot in the night, but you never know. Wait here."

Meg watched as he closed the inner back door and locked it. Coming back, he closed the curtains at the windows, checked the locks, and picked up the backpack he'd left by the door earlier. "Damn." Meg could barely hear the curse but didn't like the tone of his voice.

She moved cautiously across the room, coming up behind him. He stared down at the desk. "What is it?" she asked nervously, one hand resting on his shoulder.

"I don't know why I didn't think of this earlier."

"What?"

"The radio."

A moment of elation swept over Meg and for the first time she had hope they would get out of this situation all right. In the shadows she could see him crouch over the radio, his hands working with the controls.

"Then we're…"

"The back's ripped off and the wires are gone. The controls are smashed. It wasn't working right anyway, and I needed to fix it. But now it's beyond repair until I get new parts."

The air rushed out of Meg's lungs. Fingers of panic raced up to her throat. She couldn't breathe. She felt dizzy. And she knew her nails were digging into Smyth's shoulders. Up until now, there had been no indication that the sniper had been in the house. But now…now they knew differently. Abruptly, Smyth grasped her arm and turned and led her out of the kitchen.

"Come on."

She faltered. "Smyth, what are we going to do?"

He turned and glanced back at her, leveling his gaze on her face. "We wait for Frank.

He's the other park ranger. He went for supplies and should be back later tomorrow or the next day."

She wondered if that was entirely the truth or he was just trying to pacify her. Hadn't he said earlier that afternoon that he'd have to call for supplies next week? "But what if—"

Smyth rapidly shook his head back and forth. "Don't even think about it, Meg. Frank will get through. He's a good man and can sense danger. I don't want to think about him walking into this mess either, but there is no way to warn him. We'll just have to say a prayer that he gets through all right."

Meg looked to the floor and hugged herself. This couldn't be happening, could it?

After Smyth bolted the door and checked the windows in the front of the house, she followed him into his bedroom where he fumbled next to his bed and pulled something from between the mattress and box springs. He dropped a few items into the backpack and then, as an afterthought, grabbed the comforter off his bed.

"If there's anything you need, get it."

Meg studied his face for a moment. "In my bedroom."

He led her there and flashed the light beam low about the room. He checked the windows. With her back to him, she opened the drawer to the bedside table and quickly stuffed the manila envelope inside, along with her wallet. She could replace everything else in time.

There wasn't much left anyway, only a few articles of clothing.

She turned to face Smyth. "All right. I'm ready."

"Then let's go."

"Where?" Meg whispered.

"Somewhere where I can think and you can sleep."

"Where's that?"

"You'll see."

Meg followed Smyth out of the room. In the hallway, above their heads, Smyth pulled on a string descending from the ceiling. Pull down stairs to an attic unfolded in front of them, creaking into the night. Smyth carefully and quietly fixed the bottom hinged section of the ladder in place then turned to Meg.

"You go first. Hurry. I'll have to pull the stairs up after me."

Meg cautiously crept up the ladder-type stairs, looking into the black hole above her.

Smyth ascended after her into the cool, dusty attic. Two-thirds of the way up the ladder, he reached back behind him to unhinge the bottom section and flip it forward, leveraging himself in the opening. He lifted himself up and over the edge into the attic. Reaching as far down as he could to trigger the balance, he jerked and pulled at the screeching stairs, finally maneuvering it up enough that they could catch it and pull the stairs up flush with the ceiling.

Fumbling in his backpack, he produced a coil of rope, tied one end to the unhinged edge of the stair, threw the other over a rafter above his head, and tightly secured that end.

The last thing he did was reach over the side and pull the string up through the tiny hole in the plywood base.

****

Smyth sat with his spine pressed against the back wall, far away from the pull-down stairs, the attic floor hard and cool beneath him. He had thrown the blanket over his shoulders.

Meg's head lay in his lap with the remainder of the blanket wrapped around her. She slept.

Finally. It had taken him an hour of massaging her back and holding her before she could relax enough to sleep. But he couldn't sleep. Didn't really plan to. He had too much to think about.

Not one unusual sound emanated from the island all

night long. Half expecting the sniper to crash through a window or door, he'd kept one ear open for anything and an eye on the rope attached to the stair, anticipating even a tiny jerk. He'd figured this guy would either sit and wait them out, or he would lambaste his way in with one swift swoop. Either way, they were sitting ducks. Why in the hell had he purposely put them in a position where they had no way out?

Of course, one hand rested on his pistol in the backpack all night long. He hadn't told Meg he had it, afraid it would frighten her. He didn't really know how much of a match the 9 millimeter would be for a sniper's rifle. If this guy really wanted them dead, he wouldn't stop at simply shooting them. He could burn the whole damn house down around them and there wouldn't be a soul to stop him.

There had to be another way for him to protect them. A way off the island. And he'd stayed awake the entire night thinking about it.

The sun peeking through the louvered air vents at the far end of the attic announced the rapid approach of dawn. The gulls called out, beginning their daily quest for food. He heard nothing else. It was too late for them to do anything now. Too risky. They'd have to wait.

He had enough water and food in his backpack to keep them throughout the day. By dark he'd have a plan.

He hoped this guy wasn't too impatient.

****

The lone figure stood high on the dune, perched over the uninhabited village like a buzzard waiting for its prey to die. He dragged his right hand to his mouth and pinched the cigarette between thumb and forefinger. Drawing in a final drag off the butt, he then flicked it aside, the red ashes filtering down among sea oats and sand, smoke curling up from his nostrils.

His eyes never left the small village below.

Knowing he had them over a barrel, he grinned, the corners of his mouth curving only slightly at the ends. It was nearly over. They couldn't stay holed up in that cottage forever.

Sooner or later they had to make a move. And when they did, he'd be waiting.

Chapter Twenty-Five

"So how long do we wait?"

"Not much longer."

Smyth shifted from where he sat, tucking the pistol in the waistband of his shorts and covering it with his T-shirt. Meg still didn't know he had it.

"We can't sit here another day. It's stifling up here," he justified, "we're running out of food and water, and the longer we sit, the more vulnerable we become. A few hours after dark, we move."

He watched Meg's eyes, barely visible in the darkening attic as dusk fell around them.

There was alarm there, but also trust. Whatever it took, he knew she was with him. And whatever they encountered, they would do it together. They'd made it through an entire day in the attic, making minimal noise, sleeping, listening. Everything was quiet and eerie. Nerve-wracking. And Smyth knew he couldn't stand it much longer.

Now or never. And he had a plan.

Long ago one of the residents had left a small boat on the sound side of the island. Smyth had used it now and again on calm days for fishing, so he maintained it regularly. A small craft and a bit unreliable. He'd never ventured far from the island with it, but with their present predicament it seemed somehow more trustworthy than leaving themselves to a fate with the gunman.

All they had to do was get to it without alerting the sniper, then set out for the mainland.

Or more than likely, Ocracoke or Portsmouth.

Unfortunately, he had absolutely no idea where the sniper had positioned himself. And the more he thought about it, the angrier he became about holing them up in the attic where he couldn't see out. But he couldn't dwell on that now. They had to move.

And when they did, it had to be done quickly and quietly.

Dusk fell and more hours passed in silence. Neither of them fidgeted nor spoke, resigning themselves to the importance of total quiet. Meg sat only a few feet away from him, too still for too long. Almost as if she'd slipped into a state of shock over the past day. She worried him, but nodded to his questions and made quick replies to brief attempts at conversation. Neither of them spoke the obvious—that Bradford's men had found her. And that the sniper out there probably had orders not to leave until she was dead.

She'd not spoken the words, nor had he, but the knowledge hovered between them like a dense fog.

Then it was time.

Slowly, Smyth rose, stretching the kinks out of his back and legs as he did. He felt her gaze upon him as he gathered their few belongings.

Placing his steps carefully, he walked toward the attic stairs. As if on cue, Meg rose and gingerly picked her way across the attic behind him. When he reached the rope, he stopped and turned, catching Meg's gaze and holding it. For an instant he wished that it all could have been different. That they had met under normal circumstances, with each of them unattached, without all the past baggage. He would have liked that. There might possibly have been a wonderful future for them.

Lifting his hand, he cupped her cheek and watched her eyes close at the gesture. She nuzzled his palm slightly, pressing into his hand. His chest tightened. Suddenly, more than anything, he wanted that future.

They were simply going to have to fight a little harder for it than normal people.

"We're getting out of this," he whispered, inches from her face. He watched the tiny beads of tears squeeze from between her eyelids. "All of it, I promise you."

She nodded and opened her eyes. Tears spilled over

both lower lids. "I believe you, Smyth Parker."

He quickly brushed his lips across hers, and as abruptly, stepped away from her. "Stay close and listen for anything unusual. If you sense or hear anything out of place, squeeze my arm, okay? Don't say anything. Just squeeze my arm."

"I understand."

From that point on, he knew they had to be extremely quiet. The next few minutes would tell the tale.

Smyth untied the rope preventing the stairs from being lowered and the casing immediately shifted downward a few inches. He felt relatively sure the sniper was not in the house. He'd locked all the windows and doors before they came up to the attic. They would have heard something if the sniper had forced entry. But still, he cautiously knelt beside the opening and pushed the stairs down a few more inches where he could risk a glance into the hall.

He saw nothing but the darkened hallway. Rising, he glanced at Meg. Jerking the pistol out from his waistband, he handed it to her. She reached out both hands to grasp it, her face an open question.

"Can you handle a gun?"

"No." She shook her head wildly, shoving it back toward him.

"Yes, you can. I'm going down first, then I'll check out the house. You stay here, don't come down the stairs unless I call for you. If you don't hear me, hide behind something and wait."

"I don't know what to do." Her eyes glanced at the gun held loosely in her hands.

"Just aim and pull the trigger. It's automatic and won't kick much. If I don't come back, stay here. Shoot the bastard when he comes up the stairs."

"But where—"

He avoided the alarm in her eyes. "Meg. It's only if I don't come back. Only if he's in the house. If he's not, I'll come back to get you. I don't want to leave you without something to protect yourself."

"But you should have it," she pleaded.

"No," he shot the words at her in a firm voice. The stunned look on her face said he'd been a little harsh. He hadn't intended to frighten her. He just wanted her to be safe and have some means of protection. He reached out to touch her cheek again.

"I'm coming back. Don't worry. This is just in case."

Her glazed eyes stared back at him. She licked her lips and held the pistol a little tighter.

"Don't be long."

Smyth shook his head. "I won't," he whispered.

Meg watched him leave as she tried to swallow the huge lump in her throat. He pushed the stairs down and they creaked incessantly into the night, screaming out as if in warning of their approach. It sent a terrifying chill up her spine. Had the sound echoed over the entire island?

The bottom stairs flipped forward and after Smyth descended three steps he jumped rather than climb down the last few rungs of the ladder. And Meg was left alone.

She glanced nervously about her, peering into the dark. She stilled her body, listening for any sound, afraid to move. Her eyes adjusted to the darkness. She realized it probably wasn't in her best interest to stand over the open hole leading down into the house. So quietly, avoiding boxes and other paraphernalia, she slipped several feet away and crouched behind a large box.

And waited. The pistol shook in her hands.

It seemed forever before she heard a sound from below. She thought it would have been easier if she did hear something. Noises, any noises, would give her some indication of what was happening to Smyth, but she heard absolutely nothing other than the steady drone of the ocean outside the attic walls.

Taking periodic deep breaths calmed her shaking hands, but her nerves remained alert, on edge, ready to react at a millisecond's notice.

And after what seemed a small eternity, her mind jerked at the telltale creak coming from the bottom of the steps. Her finger curled around the trigger of the pistol, the weapon hard and cold in her hand.

The creak sounded again. Closer. And again.

"Meg?" The whispered voice called out to her.

Meg's pent-up breath pushed out of her lungs. "Smyth?" she called out quietly. It was his voice, wasn't it?

For an instant, Meg froze behind the box. Was her mind playing tricks on her? It was Smyth, wasn't it?

"It's okay, Meg. Come on down." The voice came from the top of the stairs. She heard a clump as a foot hit the attic floor. She trembled and ice-cold blood ran through her veins. Her brain turned fuzzy. Blood pulsed through her arteries, echoing inside her skull. Pounding. Confused. Was that Smyth calling to her?

Was that his voice or the sniper playing a trick on her, coaxing her from her hiding place?

Both hands gripped the pistol as she forced it straight out in front of her. Her palms grew sweaty and damp. Her fingers shook, the gun heavy in her hands. How long could she hold the weapon outstretched in front of her? Suddenly it was hot and stuffy in the attic. Perspiration rolled down the side of her face. The pounding grew louder and louder in her ears, like breakers crashing against the shore.

He called to her again. Calling. A stranger's voice? Should she shoot? *No! It might be Smyth. But what if it's not? What if it's Bradford? The sniper? Oh, my God! I'm losing it. What's happening to me?*

"Meg."

The voice came from right in front of her. Her tears mingled with the perspiration on her damp face. Her hands shook wildly. No way could she aim this damn gun! Or pull the trigger!

She couldn't keep her hands still.

"Meg. I'm turning the flashlight on my face. It's me, Smyth. It's okay. You can come out."

Then suddenly, the beacon of light burst upward in front of her and she saw him. Smyth. Not five feet away.

Oh, God. I could have killed him.

Meg flung the pistol away and leaped from her hiding place.

"Damn you!" Within seconds, she was in his arms, crying, holding him.

For a while he simply held her. Then after a moment he pulled away from her, looking into her face, the flashlight still illuminating the area around them. "Everything's okay, Meg.

Everything's okay."

He caressed her cheek with the back of his fingers.

She pushed him away. "Damn you! I was so frightened. I couldn't tell if it was you or him!" The words tumbled out quickly and she sobbed. "I don't ever want that gun in my hands again!"

"It's okay." He replied calmly. He played the flashlight over the floor, its beam catching the glint of the gun. He retrieved it, switched off the flashlight, and then pushed the gun back into his waistband. "My fault. I shouldn't have given it to you."

"It's not okay," she blurted out, tears trailing down her cheeks. "None of this is okay! I was so frightened. I'm so tired of all this. I'm so tired of spending every waking hour fearful of what's going to happen next. And when I finally think things are working out, something like this damn sniper has to interrupt it all and we end up on the run again. Then I'm pointing a gun at your heart ready to squeeze the trigger!" Her entire body shook with emotional turmoil. Her words poured out attesting to the level of her fear. "Dammit! Don't you understand? I could have killed you!"

Smyth grasped her elbow. "But you didn't. It doesn't matter."

"That's not the point!" Meg pushed him again and Smyth faltered backward, stunned.

"How in the hell could you put me in that position, Smyth? Why in the hell did you give me that stupid gun in the first place?" With her hands balled up into tight fists, she pummeled his chest and cried out. "I can't take this anymore. I don't want to do this anymore! I nearly shot you, dammit! I nearly tore a hole in your chest and all you can do is stand there and say it doesn't matter. Don't you see?" she sobbed. "It matters, Smyth. It matters one helluva lot. I could have killed the only man I've ever loved in my entire life!"

With that, Meg flung herself backward and ran into the shadows. Sobs wracked her throat and tears rained down her face. With the back of one hand, she tried to swipe the wetness from her eyes, but she still tripped blindly into the dark.

Within seconds, she felt Smyth's hands clutch her upper arms and grasp her to him.

"Meg," he whispered softly. "Meg, come here. Stop."

"I've got to get out of here. This attic is making me insane." She struggled against him, wiping at her eyes.

He clasped his arms around her chest and held her to him. She resisted, but knew it was impossible. He held her and after a moment her body melted against him.

"Meg. I know. This whole mess is making me crazy, too. But don't do this. Don't pull away from me. Let me help you." His voice provided a steady calm. "Look, we need to get moving. It's over. You didn't pull the trigger. We can't dwell on that any longer. We have to go. We've got to get off the island. Now."

After a moment, she reluctantly nodded. They stood in the dark for several seconds just holding each other. She knew he was only trying to protect her. They needed each other. Getting angry wouldn't solve anything or make the situation go away. They had to work together to find a way off the island.

Meg relished the feel of Smyth's arms around for her for a few seconds longer. Too quickly, he broke the connection and grasped her hand, then led her toward the attic stairs.

Chapter Twenty-Six

It seemed they walked for hours into the eerie night. With her hand clutching Smyth's right arm, he led the way through scrub pines, sea oats, and brush until they were close to the sound side of the island. Listening for steps behind them, Meg half expected to feel the sting of a bullet in her back before being alerted to the telltale zing of its approach.

She barely breathed the last hour of their trek. They had but one purpose, to make it to the boat. Once there, she felt they would have met a milestone, they would be halfway to freedom.

And after that, well, she didn't even want to think about what would happen. She knew deep in her heart that she couldn't stand living a life like this anymore. She wasn't cut out for the constant running. For the terror of not knowing who, or what, lurked around every corner. Not if she wanted any kind of a life for herself. With or without Smyth.

After this was all over, she had to find some permanent way out of this mess. She'd promised herself as much. She had to get Bradford behind bars so he would leave her alone.

If they ever did get out of this mess.

Smyth stopped suddenly. She let out a small squeal as she plunged into his back. He placed a silencing hand over her mouth, signaling her to be quiet. For what seemed forever, they stood quietly and listened. After a moment, Smyth removed his hand.

They took their time crossing to the sound. It was well into the early morning hours with the sun about to creep over the horizon at their backs. They knew they had to move quickly. The pungent smell of brackish water penetrated Meg's nostrils. They were quite close to the island's edge, almost to the dock where Smyth said they should find the boat.

Smyth's body warmed hers. Edging closer to her, his hands gripped her upper arms, pulling her to him. She felt protected for the moment, but never, not even for a second, did she forget the danger of their situation. And she knew he hadn't forgotten it either. The cold butt of the pistol in the waistband of his shorts stabbed into her belly, reminding her of the seriousness of this whole episode.

She searched his face. Reaching out, he traced her lips with the pad of his fingertips. A shiver ran over her entire body and she burrowed closer into him. His arm wrapped more securely about her.

Oh, God. She needed him. And she never thought she'd need anyone again. *Please*, she silently prayed. *Let this all be done with soon. Let us get out of this alive. Please let us at least attempt a life together. Just a chance, God. That's all I ask.*

She felt Smyth's lips against her ear. "The boat dock isn't far," he whispered softly. "Stay close."

Meg nodded against him and he pulled away. One of his hands trailed down her arm to clasp her hand. He quietly led the way into the dim light of dawn. Meg felt as if she were heading into a tunnel of unknown.

They neared the dock. She stubbed her toe on the edge as Smyth stopped and turned, releasing her hand. The lap of the waves rhythmically rocked the dock beneath her feet. But there was a problem. As far as she could see, no boat.

He moved away from her, his fingers slowly slipping out of her hand as he stepped out over the dock. Suddenly every hair on the back of her neck stood on end. The skin crawled on her back. Eeriness swept over her and she hugged herself.

Smyth played the beam of his flashlight into the water to the left of the dock. The beam searched through the dark abyss for the boat, their only way out. Looking straight ahead, she watched Smyth and tried to decipher the look on his face reflected above the dim light. Then glancing lower, she caught the half-submerged boat spotlighted in the yellow shaft. Her spirits sank to a depth she'd never known.

Without warning, a sweaty palm clasped over her mouth from behind, stifling her attempt at a scream. The intruder hauled her body roughly up against a hard muscle. Cold metal jabbed into her neck. And then she heard the bellow of laughter gurgle from the man who held her.

Frantically meeting Smyth's gaze, she watched his eyes widen in horror as his hand swung the flashlight around, blinding her.

Hopefully blinding the gunman, too.

Meg squeezed her eyes tight and prayed. Then without thinking past the next instant, she swiftly ducked and jabbed her right elbow backward into the man's groin. When she heard his howl, she knew she'd met her mark. She struggled out of his grasp.

Suddenly, a contradictory mixture of silent slow motion and fast forward erupted as Smyth leaped onto her assailant. They rolled off the dock into the sand. Meg couldn't tell where Smyth started and the other man left off. Groans and umphs from the two men struggling on the ground mixed with her own screams.

The flashlight bounced to the sand at her right. She saw glints of metal reflected in the beam as the men rolled on the ground. Ribbons of light from the rising sun reached out to the sound side of the island. She grabbed the flashlight and played the beam over the shadows of the scene hoping to find anything to help defend them.

A large piece of wood, a rock...a gun?

Her breath caught in her throat. There, a few feet away, she spotted the pistol, evidently knocked away in the struggle. The second she reached for it, grabbed it, she heard the sharp crack of a single gunshot behind her. Then silence. Dread gripped her from the inside out.

Afraid to turn around, afraid to know what had happened, she froze. The only movement came from her heaving chest, the breath rasping from her lungs, and the lap of the waves against the dock.

Without warning, the most awful mangled scream

pierced the early morning air.

"Meg!"

Hastily, she twisted her body back to the two men. She dropped the flashlight and gripped the gun with both hands. One man stood rising over the other. Her heart vaulted in fear.

Finally, she heard the groans of the man on the ground.

"Meg?" Smyth's voice was frantic.

Terror welled in her. She pointed the gun at the figure. He stepped closer. It wasn't Smyth.

"Meg. Shoot him."

Meg aimed the gun. The man's hands were empty. Glancing to the ground, she saw the other gun beside Smyth, just out of his reach. And a puddle of blood beside him.

"Oh, my God!" she gasped and backed up.

The man stepped forward. She shoved the gun toward him. "Don't come any closer," she ordered.

"Give me my gun, lady."

"No!" Her hands trembled.

"Give it to me."

"Shoot him, Meg!"

"I swear I will. Don't come any closer."

The gun shook in her hands. Her finger curled over the trigger.

The man stopped and stared at her.

"Smyth, are you all right?"

"I'm hit."

The gunman eased forward again. Meg shouted, "Stop! Stop! I mean it. I'll kill you!"

"You don't want to do that."

"Yes, I do."

"No, you don't."

"I will, you bastard. Stop where you are!"

The man stepped forward again. The gun shook uncontrollably in Meg's clammy hands.

Despite the cool morning, perspiration dripped from

her face and tears ran down her face. She backed up a step. "I'll kill you. Don't come another step."

He took one.

Meg held her breath and squeezed the trigger.

The gun exploded in her hands. The bullet hit the man in the upper left chest near his shoulder, knocking him backward to the ground.

Meg watched his eyes widen at the split-second of the impact. He hadn't believed she would do it. But she did. She'd shot the sonofabitch.

He rolled onto his side in the sand, moaning. Meg kept the gun trained on him and crept closer. She kicked at his right shoulder and pointed the gun directly into his face. He stared back up the barrel, looking directly into her eyes. This time she held the gun steady in her hands and she knew the man realized she meant business.

"If you dare to move from this spot, you mangy SOB, I'll blow your head off. Got it?"

She noted the slight twitch of his head. She moved slowly, the gun still pointed at the man, and backed away toward Smyth. She never took her eyes or the gun off the stranger.

"Meg."

She fell exhausted behind Smyth, tears streaming from her eyes. "Are you all right?" Her gaze fell to his bloody thigh.

"Meg," he whispered again. "It's all right. I'm all right. I think it's just a flesh wound, but I need something to put pressure on it."

She continued to sob as she wriggled out of her shirt, still watching the sniper, her bathing suit on underneath. Smyth carefully tied the shirt around his thigh, then wrapped his arms around her waist and held her tight. Meg kept the gun trained on the man on the ground.

"It's all right," Smyth cooed to her. "And it's almost over."

The groaning grew louder in front of them and Smyth abruptly broke the embrace.

She managed a few words. "Is...is he going to die?"

"I don't think so, unless he loses lots of blood."

The groaning escalated, interspersed with a periodic curse or two.

"God, I can't believe I shot one of Bradford's men."

Smith looked at her. "Meg. I hate to tell you this, but he isn't one of Bradford's men."

She stared back. "What? How do you know?"

"Because I know him."

"What?"

"He's my ex-wife's lover."

Meg sat back on her heels in shock. "Crystal's lover? The father of her child?"

Smyth nodded. "I would assume. I guess by getting rid of me, they wouldn't have to worry about the paternity suit. Damn. I didn't think Crystal would resort to this."

Meg's brain swirled in confusion. All this time she'd thought Bradford's men had tracked her down. Momentarily, when she'd shot the man, she'd felt a sense of relief. Now, the feeling disappeared. And she didn't know if it would ever return. She would spend the rest of her life looking over her shoulder.

A strange whine rent the air as Meg struggled to comprehend what was happening to her and around her. As the noise grew louder, she moved closer to Smyth.

"Thank...God. Frank."

"What?" Meg looked into Smyth's pale face.

An all-terrain vehicle burst through the scrub pines and up the beach. Startled, Meg jerked back.

"It's Frank," Smyth answered.

The ATV ground to a stop not far from them. Frank Harvey jumped off as he surveyed the scene. "Smyth, what the hell? I heard the shots."

"He's hurt," Meg cried out, frantic now that maybe, just maybe, help had arrived.

"So I see." Frank looked from Meg to Smyth and back again.

Smyth tried to get up. "Time to explain later, Frank."

The sniper groaned from across the way. Smyth tossed the man a glance and then back to Frank. "You got a two-way on you?"

Frank reached for the radio at his waist. "Always."

"Good. Call the Coast Guard. Get a boat in here, probably too windy for a chopper. Have medics meet us at Ocracoke. And alert the authorities. This guy tried to kill us."

Smyth fell back into a slump against the sand. Meg could tell that just getting those words out took a lot out of him. And that scared the hell out of her.

****

When they reached Ocracoke Island, both Becky and a helicopter were waiting at the harbor. Meg vaguely remembered Becky saying she would come on Friday. Meg had lost all track of the days since the attic. It was Friday?

She was really glad to see Becky.

After a brief questioning by the local police and the medics, both women clung to each other as Smyth and Crystal's boyfriend, Matt Brown, were loaded into the helicopter for transfer to an inland hospital.

Matt, they learned, had a low tolerance for pain and confessed Crystal's plan on the ferry ride to Ocracoke Island. Smyth was right. Crystal figured with Smyth dead, the child would automatically be assumed his and a rightful Parker heir.

As soon as the medical team from the helicopter took over, they shot Brown full of pain medication which knocked him out almost immediately.

Smyth hung on to the last second before they loaded his stretcher onto the waiting helicopter. The bullet lodged in his thigh, cleanly missing an artery, but the closest medical facility to handle such an emergency was inland with no room on the chopper for Meg and Becky.

Meg hugged him and caressed his face with her fingertips. He smiled. "We're nearly through this, you know."

Meg only wished. They were partly through with it.

She smiled back, anyway. "I know.

We'll get through the rest."

Smyth grasped her hand, and then reached for Becky with the other one.

"Take care of her, Beck."

Becky nodded. "I will, you can bet on that, big brother."

Woozy, Smyth closed his eyes.

"We'll be at the hospital as soon as we can get there," Meg whispered.

He nodded. "I know."

Meg leaned forward and kissed him on the cheek. "I'll see you soon. I love you."

Smyth mustered a bit of a grin. "I love you, back," he whispered.

Then they whisked him away and the helicopter took off into the morning sky.

Chapter Twenty-Seven

The two-hour trip back to Nags Head did little to settle Meg's nerves. Becky tried idle chatter for a while, then gave up when Meg responded only with simple one-word answers. She was so worried about Smyth. About their future. After a while, they simply rode in silence. Meg stared out the passenger side window, not seeing.

She couldn't feel. It all happened too quickly with no time to think. The gunman. The shootings. The helicopter taking Smyth away.

She had to get to him and as quickly as possible. She hurt being away from him. It was physically painful. Like someone had severed a part of her soul.

Smyth had given her life again. Hope. And she needed him close. Her temporary escape had been worth risking everything to have those few precious days with him. Not to mention the freedom to fall in love.

But as soon as he recovered they needed to face facts. She couldn't go on running for the rest of her life. They had to do something. *Something.* They had to figure a way out of this nightmare.

No way was she ever going to give up Smyth. No way. She'd finally found love and happiness in her life. She'd do whatever she had to do to keep it. She wouldn't lose him.

A terror like she'd never known gripped her from the inside and refused to let go.

Vertical rows of steel suddenly flashed by outside Meg's window, startling her out of her thoughts. The sun glinted off the sparkling water. She straightened in her seat, rubbed her face with the heels of her palms, and looked at Becky. They were crossing the Herbert Bonner Bridge.

They would soon be in Nags Head.

Becky glanced sideways at her and smiled. "Back among the living?"

Meg half-heartedly grinned back. "Maybe."

Becky turned back to concentrate on her driving as they neared the center rise of the bridge. "There were a few moments back there when I thought I'd lost you."

Turning to view the ocean breaking in riffles between the islands, Meg replied, "Just thinking."

"You gonna be all right?"

Meg slowly dropped her chin. "Yeah. Sure. I just need to get to him."

Becky smiled and reached out to grasp Meg's hand on the seat.

"We'll be there soon."

After another moment or two of silence, they crossed the bridge, drove through Nags Head and into Kill Devil Hills. Becky slowed and turned into a local McDonald's.

"I hope you don't mind if we make a pit stop. I'm starved and I've gotta pee."

Meg shook her head. "That's fine. I could use a break myself."

Becky parked and they entered the restaurant. After a few minutes they picked up their orders and sat down near the windows to eat.

"I'm going to the little girl's room." Becky stood and Meg nodded and waited for her turn.

She unwrapped her sandwich, then took a big swallow of her cold drink followed by a sigh. For the first time in a while, she almost felt relaxed. Almost normal.

She took a bite of the sandwich, then nibbled on a French fry. Her gaze drifted out the window. Her breath froze in her lungs and she stopped chewing.

Two men walked across the parking lot. Familiar men. Looking very out of place. Her gaze shot to the black sedan with Illinois plates behind them.

Don't panic.

She reminded herself that she no longer looked anything like Megan Thomas, Bradford's wife. Her hair was short and black. She wore her bathing suit under a pair of shorts and Becky's spare shirt. She was tired, dirty and without makeup. She looked like a beach bum.

She heard the door open behind her and the two men conversing as they stepped toward the counter. She tensed, her ears buzzing.

Her gaze dropped to Becky's purse lying on the table. Without thought, she slowly reached for the purse, unzipped the side pocket and slipped the keys out. *Forgive me, Becky.* She prayed her friend would understand. Prayed Becky would figure out what had happened.

Somehow, some way, she would get word to her.

Later.

Slowly, Megan stood, bringing her drink with her and leaving Becky's purse on the table.

A pen and slip of paper jutted out. A note. Yes. Meg leaned over and jotted off a quick note to Becky. An apology as much as anything. Then she quickly walked to the front of the restaurant, staring at the back of the heads of the two men. She listened to them give their orders as she passed. Two Big Macs, fries, and Cokes. She slipped out of the restaurant and walked straight to Becky's car.

She got in and drove away.

Chapter Twenty-Eight

"He's dead."

Mack MacDowell drew back two fingers which seconds earlier searched for a pulse in Bradford Thomas' neck. It was difficult finding a spot not spattered with blood. He found no pulse. Knew he wouldn't.

The body was cold, bloated, bruised, and in the beginning stages of rigor mortis. It confirmed the conviction of the first officer on the scene. Thomas had been dead for hours. Now Mack only needed the medical examiner's confirmation to add time of death to the report.

Drawing a lengthy stare at the corpse, Mack frowned, wondering who had finally gotten to Thomas. There were half a dozen suspects, he imagined, none of whom would be brought in for questioning. Not now. Not after the D.A. had given the order to get Thomas at all costs.

Rudy's statement concerning Allen Crenshaw's death had put wheels into motion pronto.

But someone had beaten them to the punch and it ate at his craw wondering who. This one would be swept under the rug rather quickly, he knew. And all the better for the citizens of Chicago.

The streets would be a little safer for a while. Until someone else rose up the ranks.

Megan Thomas, though, was another matter. If only he could find her, tell her. If only she knew it was safe to come home. At least he hoped it was. If only he knew whether Thomas had called off his men. If only.

Mack flipped the bullet-riddled sheet back over the corpse and stalked away, running his gaze over the crime scene. He stripped the latex gloves off his hands and shoved them deep into his jacket pocket.

Not much to go on. The man had been asleep. No struggle, no prints, no evidence. Just a dead man with a hole in his head and several more in the trunk of his body.

Mack chuckled and ran a hand over his stubbled chin. Now he'd sleep forever, the bastard. Served him right, too. But he had to wonder who was lucky enough, or smart enough, to get in here without setting off alarms—to get to Bradford Thomas at his most vulnerable. It was almost as if Thomas knew the other person in the room. As if he trusted him—or her.

Mack paused, contemplating that thought as he continued to peruse the room. Blood stains arched against the back wall and soaked into the bed linens around the man. From the direction of the entry wounds and the spattering of blood on the far wall, he suspected the murderer stood to the left of the bed. Stepping across the room to assess the angle, Mack still kept a keen eye out for anything unusual, anything out of place.

"Mack, over here."

He turned to look at one of the crime experts going over the scene. His investigator picked up a bloodied pair of women's pants and a shirt from the back of the closet. He held them up, just pinching a bit of the fabric to inspect them, then bagged them as evidence.

Unusual. Professional murderers didn't leave damning evidence at the scene. This put a different light on the subject.

Even though he knew there was a good chance nothing would come of the investigation, he still felt the need to read a crime scene and develop from it what he could. It was his job. Even when he hated doing it. Even when the crime unit had already picked it clean.

Especially in cases like this. The mystery, the not knowing, peaked his curiosity.

Bustling in the door with a flourish, the M.E. greeted him briefly and turned his attention to the corpse and the attending officer. Mack toed the carpet beside the bed. The sun streaking in the window to his left caught a shimmering thread near his foot. Curious, Mack bent to flip it away with his forefinger, then at the last instant, leaned over and picked up the thin, golden strand, bringing it closer to his face.

A long, silky, blond hair.

Straightening, he glanced at the officer beside the bed and shoved his hand into his pocket.

"Find something, Detective?"

Mack pursed his lips, shook his head, and then took several determined steps toward the bedroom door. "Naw. Just a shadow." He waved off the man as he left the room. "Just a shadow."

When outside the door, he carefully placed the hair in a small paper bag he always kept in a side jacket pocket. Just in case.

****

"They're still out there somewhere, aren't they?"

Rudy Marshall stared at Mack MacDowell from across his kitchen snack bar. It had only been a week since she'd talked him into the scheme of faking her death to throw Bradford off track. One week since she'd moved into his apartment with an order to stay put. They'd acted quickly. Rudy didn't want to go into the witness protection program, but she'd convinced Mack MacDowell to make her dead. To do anything he had to do to convince Bradford Thomas that she was no longer alive. She did it for herself. And for Megan. She owed her that much.

And more.

Bradford's daily sexual demands and the threats he made on her life scared the hell out of her.

"Yeah," he returned.

She knew that fact ate a hole through him. Mack sloughed out of his leather jacket and flung it across the back of the sofa. He glanced up at her and Rudy dropped her gaze to the cutting board where she busied herself slicing carrots and potatoes for beef stew. Onions sat piled to her left, the sting of the aroma still in her eyes.

"So what's next?"

"We have to find them before they kill her." The deep voice still came from the center of the room. Rudy trembled at his words.

"Do you have any idea where to look?"

"Not yet. The house was clean. I have a feeling Thomas didn't keep anything of importance there."

"Obviously they've got some leads somewhere. Did you check the safe?" Rudy's eyes lifted at her words. Mack crossed the room and stood directly in front of her.

He reached out and snatched a piece of carrot from the cutting board, then popped it into his mouth. Chewing, he held Rudy's gaze.

"You didn't tell me about a safe."

Rudy was sure she had. Her chopping hand stilled against the counter. "Of course I did.

The safe where Megan found the money."

"Do we have a combination?"

Rudy nodded. "Yes."

"Where is it?" His stare intensified.

"In my purse."

"Is there anything else you're hiding from me?"

A slice of panic shot through her. Her fingers clenched the knife in her hand, but she never broke the connection between them. "No."

"You're sure about that."

"Positive."

Silence fell between them. Rudy awkwardly looked down, watching the knife slice into the remainder of the last potato.

"You have any idea who got to Thomas last night?"

Her gaze shot up at him. "Why do you think I would know anything?"

Mack leaned over the snack bar and peered into her face. He reached over and grasped a strand of her hair, letting it glide through his fingertips. Abruptly, he dropped his hand. Plucking another carrot off the cutting board and into his mouth, he chewed intently while watching her.

Suddenly, Rudy's mouth felt incredibly dry.

"You were on his payroll. You worked with him for seven years. You were his wife's best friend." Rudy felt the tension slide up her backbone. "And you were his lover."

Slapping the knife broadside against the counter, Rudy gasped and turned her back to him, crossing her arms over her chest.

"Truth hurts, doesn't it?"

"Yeah, it does," she admitted softly. "More than you know." Dammit! She didn't want to cry. Didn't want to admit to this man just how much it did hurt. But already she felt the sting.

"How could you do that to Megan?"

Rudy sighed and turned back to face him. "It happened before they were married, okay?

They were engaged, but...hell, it doesn't matter now. I was young and stupid."

"It happened more than that. In fact, I think it's been happening pretty regular."

Guilt burst up within Rudy. She'd done what she had to do to stay alive. To keep Bradford preoccupied. She had done it for Megan as well as herself. "I had no choice. He would have killed me! He was sucking me in, controlling me. I couldn't refuse."

She turned and stared at Mack, vowing she wouldn't shed the tears in her eyes. "He would have killed me."

Mack dropped his gaze to the counter. Rudy didn't think he believed her.

"Did you ever tell Megan?"

"No."

"You hated Bradford for marrying her though, didn't you?"

"I hated Bradford, but I couldn't hate Megan. I liked her a lot. We became close. But I could never tell her. Not even in the end."

"Do you hate Bradford now?"

Rudy chuckled. "Bradford is dead now."

"Do you still hate him?"

Rudy narrowed her gaze. "I'll hate Bradford Thomas with my last dying breath," she bit out.

"Did you hate Bradford Thomas enough to kill him?"

Rudy felt her eyes widen as alarm coursed up inside her.

"No," she rasped, shaking her head. "No, I didn't kill him." But she couldn't tell from the look on his face whether he believed her or not.

****

Rudy woke with a start. She frantically glanced around Mack's pitch black living room, startled out of her sleep by images just beyond her grasp. She'd taken up residence on his sofa-sleeper since she'd arrived, refusing the offer of his bed. He'd been kind enough to her, she didn't want him to give up his own comfort. Normally she slept soundly, but every time she closed her eyes tonight, she imagined Megan fighting off Bradford's men.

Then contradictorily, her dreams turned to Bradford. She saw him, lifeless and dead, with hard, cold eyes staring blankly up at the ceiling of his bedroom. Deep inside she felt relief at his death, but a part of her mourned him. She knew what an evil man he was, no good for any woman—a murderer, and more—but at times she remembered how he made her feel. Even if those feelings were wrong.

Then she thought of how he'd hurt her. How he'd hurt Megan. Hurt both of them.

Physically and mentally. And she remembered why she'd befriended Megan in the first place.

Because she'd felt sorry for her. Knew and felt her pain. Her imprisonment. Silently thankful it hadn't been her own.

It was why she'd gone to Mack and told him the whole story. This thing was bigger than she could handle. She would be forever indebted to him for taking her in.

Now, if only Megan would call.

Call? Damn!

Sitting up straighter in the bed, Rudy wracked her brain as her eyes widened in awareness. Why in the hell hadn't she thought of that before? The phone call. When was it?

What day? What had Mack said?

She had to ask him.

Fleeing from her bed, she slipped down the small hallway of Mack's apartment to his bedroom. The door partly ajar, she hesitated only momentarily then pushed it entirely open. A shaft of illumination from a street light beamed across his bed. He slept curled on his side, the white sheet on his bed tangled about his legs and lower body.

She saw the waistband of his boxer shorts dip just below his hairy naval. For an instant, Rudy wished for another reason to come to Mack in the middle of the night, but this night she had more important things to worry about than her own wayward thoughts. Besides, she was sure Mack thought her an idiot for getting caught up in the whole Bradford Thomas mess in the first place. She still wondered if he thought she'd killed Bradford.

If she could only help him find Megan. If they could get her out of this mess, then...

Rudy sat on the edge of the bed and shook his arm, dismissing the direction of her thoughts.

"Mack," she whispered. "Wake up. I just thought of something."

He groaned and turned over onto his back. His eyelids fluttered slightly, then it seemed as if he fell back into a deep sleep.

She shook him harder. "Mack!" Her voice rose. "Wake up!"

He jerked to a sitting position, his hands rubbing over his face. "What the hell?" He shook his head and opened his eyes wide as if to focus them on her. "What is it?"

"I just thought of something."

"In the middle of the night?"

"Yeah. It's important. About Megan. About the phone call."

"What phone call?"

His gaze riveted to her now, he seemed much more alert than a few seconds earlier.

Rudy scooted a little closer to him on the bed.

Glancing down at herself, she realized her short T-shirt and panties did little to cover her body. She consciously reached across and pulled the sheet over her thighs, revealing his. That wasn't any better. She glanced nervously at Mack.

"You told me someone called the day you were at my apartment. Someone asked for me. You told them I'd been murdered. You said the person acted strangely and hung up. I think that was Megan."

Mack stared at her. "Why do you think that was her?"

She shook her head. "I don't know. Intuition, maybe. I just think we need to check it out. Certainly we can pinpoint the day and pretty close to the time. Doesn't the phone company keep records?"

"They should."

"Can you get hold of them? And then there was the call to your office that same day. We know that was her."

He shook his head. "Moss took that call at the station, then he was called away on another homicide for the rest of the day. I didn't see him until the next morning. After he told me, I tried to trace the call, but he couldn't remember the time. A rookie had used his desk during the day trying to track a missing person and had received a dozen or more calls on that line. They were from all over the country. There was no way I could pin it down to one of them."

"But don't you see?" Rudy inched closer to him. "If we can pinpoint that other call, we might be able to compare the two lists and come up with the same city, or area, at least. I really suspect she's on the east coast, we know she called from Richmond, Virginia, about two weeks prior to that. Couldn't we give it a shot?"

He slapped the bed with his fist. "Okay, let's check it out." He sat up and reached for a pair of jeans. "If we're lucky, we can pretty much narrow it down."

Rudy held his gaze. "When you find out where the calls came from, are you going to go there?"

"Probably. It may be the only way to find her."

Rudy hesitated momentarily and bit her lip. "I'm going with you."

"No. You need to keep a low profile."

She wasn't going to be denied this. "Then I'll follow you. You can't stop me."

"The hell I can't." She watched his eyes grow narrow. "I don't need you hanging around."

"I know Megan. I can help you. I'm sure she's scared out of her wits and doesn't trust a soul. She's not going to trust you, either. Take me with you. You know she trusts me."

Mack held the connection between them for several seconds. "If she trusts you, then why didn't she tell you in the first place where she was going?"

"Dammit! She was scared. She had to do this alone. But I don't think that's the case now. She needs help. I can sense it."

Mack studied her face, then quickly reneged. "All right."

****

"Nags Head, North Carolina."

"The Outer Banks?"

"Yeah. Both calls. Different numbers, but same town. I think we've found her." Rudy shifted in her seat and stared back at Mack, half afraid to ask the next question.

"When do we leave?"

His gaze caught hers and held. She watched his eyes flick back and forth over her face for several seconds. "Fifteen minutes. Pack a bag."

"So soon?" Not that Rudy wasn't anxious to find Megan, but he seemed impatient, somehow.

"If you want to find her before she's dead. We brought in one of Bradford's goons today. The guy broke down under pressure. We have it definite. Two men were sent to the Outer Banks over a week ago with orders not to return until she was dead. They have no idea Bradford's dead, so they're still stalking her. If they haven't gotten to her already."

Rudy shivered and then rose from her seat on the couch. "I'll be ready in five."

Chapter Twenty-Nine

The island never felt so empty, so lonely, in all the years Smyth lived there. For the first time in an eternity, when he looked out over the ocean, he didn't feel peace. The only other time he'd even come close was when he'd lost his parents and his grandfather. But this time, this time it felt as if he'd lost his soul. As if Meg took it with her when she left.

There was no clue as to where she'd gone, what had happened to her. She'd left a scrambled note, yes, but there were no answers. Becky was frantic by the time she'd gotten to the hospital. When the nurses saw her frazzled state, they refused to let her see him until she'd calmed down.

He couldn't have done anything. Even if he could have left the hospital, he had no idea where to start looking. He kept telling Becky to be patient and wait, that Meg would call, that she'd tell them why she had left so abruptly.

But she hadn't called. She'd disappeared into thin air.

And now, three days later, he was back on his island hiding from his pain, praying she'd not gone back to face that bastard alone.

Praying that Bradford's men had not found her and taken her back against her will.

He'd tried the local authorities; they seemed reluctant to believe his story. When they'd checked it out with the Chicago police, they'd told him that a Megan Thomas had been reported kidnapped some weeks earlier and was believed to be dead now. They thought Smyth was just some loony character trying to capitalize on the reward money Bradford had offered for information. The local police looked at him like they would a crazy person. Smyth knew he wasn't going to get anywhere with them. Then he realized if the Chicago police thought Meg was dead, it would be better if he didn't rock the boat and make them think otherwise. She might be safer that way.

But it didn't help his pain, his wondering where she had gone—his biggest fear that she intended to go back and end this thing alone. That she intended to go back and confront her husband. He couldn't get their conversation out of his mind, the one they'd had in the kitchen when she'd told him that she didn't want him involved.

Had she intentionally left so she could handle things on her own?

God. He couldn't bear to think of that man's hands on her. Touching her. Bruising her. Violating her.

A grimace washed over his face as he felt the stab in his chest. He glanced away from the ocean to stare into the sand, his vision blurred. Dammit! It ate at his gut. Tore at his heart. He had to find her. He didn't have a choice in the matter. He had to do it. And he had to do it now.

****

After washing up the few dishes left days ago in the sink, Becky straightened the remainder of the kitchen, the bathroom, and Smyth's bedroom. She stripped his bed of sheets and pillowcases, then threw his comforter over the bare mattress. She didn't expect him back for quite some time and there was no need to leave the house in a mess. She felt quite certain that he'd stick around Portsmouth for a while. No reason for him to come back to a messy house, when he needed civilization again. She straightened the pillows on the sofa, then turned to let down the shades on the windows facing the ocean.

The door burst open with a loud crash. Startled, she stumbled backward, falling into a chair. Her voice failed her as two large men in suits lunged at her and pointed pistols at her head and heart.

Frantic, but paralyzed, she bit her lip to prevent herself from screaming. Her fingers dug into the arms of the upholstered chair to quell her shaking body. Every hair on her body stood alert. Sweat poured through her skin.

Neither man said a word. For the longest time, they

simply stared into her eyes, aiming their weapons at her, then abruptly, the one on the left lowered his gun slightly.

"She ain't her."

Becky wasn't sure she could trust her voice to her quivering vocal cords, but couldn't resist a snappy retort.

"Obviously, I ain't," she blurted out.

"All right, smarty pants, where's the Thomas broad?" the other one prompted, relaxing a bit. But he still didn't lower his pistol.

Becky eyed him in question. "Who...?"

Brusquely, the man on the right thrust his pistol closer to her temple. "Megan Thomas. Where is she?"

Allowing herself the sanity to close her eyes, if however brief, gave Becky a second to clear her head. Meg. They were after Meg.

"I don't know. She disappeared days ago."

"You're lying." She felt the pistol making an impression in the side of her skull now. She closed her eyes again. Then there was a click.

"Tell me," he ordered gruffly.

"No," a different voice interrupted from the doorway. "Tell me."

Becky snapped open her eyes at the strange voice. First, she saw the confused faces of her two assailants, then immediately afterward, noticed two more pistols buried in their flabby necks, cocking their heads sideways.

Two police officers stood behind them, firmly holding the guns. Her assailant still had his weapon pointed at her. "I'd think about it pretty hard," the man stepping inside the door ordered.

"If you pull that trigger, she'll die, but you're gonna go right after her. There's no way in hell either of you will get out of here alive if you pull that trigger, mister. If the girl dies, you die."

Becky held her breath, her lids grew heavy and half covered her eyes. Then the pressure released from her temple and the gun lowered. Within an instant, the two officers wrestled the gunmen to the floor. Becky exhaled, then tumbled into a chair. She sucked in another cleansing breath as they cuffed the men.

"Are you all right, ma'am?" She recognized one of the local police officers. The other man behind him, dressed in plain clothes, was a stranger.

"Yes. A little rattled, but I'm all right. I think."

The strange man turned to her. "Where is Megan Thomas?"

Becky stared at him for a moment. "I know a woman named Meg Thompson. That may be her."

"Where is she?"

"Who are you?" Becky wasn't sure she should divulge that information so readily.

"Detective Mack MacDowell, Chicago Police."

"How do I know that?"

Frowning, the man impatiently fished his wallet from his back pocket, flipped it open, and showed her his badge. Becky decided at that point she needed to trust someone. "She disappeared three days ago."

She watched Detective MacDowell briefly close his eyes, then glance back at the door.

Standing in the threshold was a woman who could have been Meg's sister. Her eyes held a worried expression. Several more officers entered the house and the scene erupted into a flurry of activity. Two police officers read her assailants their rights, then swiftly took them away.

Another pulled her to the side to take a statement. The woman and the Chicago detectives disappeared before she had a chance to ask them what the hell was going on.

****

The yellow police tape stretched across the front door of the house on Sycamore Street blew aimlessly in the breeze. Meg stood in the drive facing her house and stared at it. She wasn't prepared for a kink in her plan.

When she'd left the Outer Banks, she'd stopped in Elizabeth City to pick up her car and deposit Becky's in the garage at Smyth's grandfather's house. She was tempted to spend the night, thinking of a plan, but her fear and her desire to end this thing got the better of her.

Driving on throughout the day, she finally stopped for the night at a nondescript roadside motel in Virginia. The next day she drove straight through until she reached Chicago. Late into the night, she planned her strategy.

It was simple, really.

She would approach Bradford.

She would demand he give her the divorce. And if he refused, she'd pull out the pistol she'd bought in a pawnshop in West Virginia and be done with him. She was that desperate. She wanted out that bad. And even if she had to spend the rest of her life locked in solitary confinement, it would be better than dying the slow tortured death Bradford had promised her.

It would be better than looking over her shoulder for the rest of her life. And it would be better than risking Smyth's life with her own.

But it hadn't worked out that way.

What had happened here?

Cautiously, Meg approached the massive porch. Funny how at one time she'd loved this home, richly appointed and projecting the elegance and sophistication Bradford required. When she and Bradford were first married, she'd enjoyed the fineries of their lifestyle. But her life with Bradford was as false as the brick veneer of their home—it had nothing to do with the actual support of the home. And someday, it would come crumbling down around them, just as their marriage had. Now she'd rather have the simplicity of the beach house back in Nags Head. Or better yet, the one on Portsmouth.

Taking a breath, Meg dropped her scrutiny of the house and ducked under the yellow tape stretched from one column to another. Stepping across the porch, her pulse quickened as she considered the reason for the cordoned off home. Why had the police designated this as a protected area?

Immediately she thought of Cindy and bile rose to her throat. Nausea clutched at her stomach as she wondered if somehow, something happened to the girl. At the threshold, she turned and slid down the door at her back, her arms wrapped across her abdomen, and crouched on the porch. Oh my God! What had Bradford done with the girl? Had he killed her as well?

Meg dropped her head into her hands and began to tremble. She choked back the tears, vowing that this time she wouldn't cry. What had she done? Rudy was dead. And now? Had she caused something to happen to an innocent young woman as well?

Panicked emotion raced over her. What was she to do?

Glancing frantically from side to side, her heart pounded. Should she leave again? Should she continue running?

No!

She couldn't run anymore. She had to face whatever happened here. To know if she was the cause of that poor girl's demise. Shrieking tires on the pavement in front of her house startled her, bringing her quickly out of her frantic thoughts. Snapping her gaze toward the street, she watched a teenage kid, one she recognized as living down the street, peel out of a neighbor's driveway.

He'd scared the living daylights out of her.

So much so, she felt like running. Everything in her told her to run.

She took one step forward.

No. She wouldn't. She had to set things right. She had to find a way to make this nightmare end and get back to Smyth. There was nothing left for her to do. She had to go to the police.

****

Mack slid through the crowded outer office and tried to head undetected toward his own small office space. Another crazy Saturday night in downtown Chicago and he'd already had a helluva day trying to track Megan. They'd damned near combed the eastern seaboard and expanded the search for her vehicle with local cooperation, but they'd not had much luck. He feared the longer it took to find her, the slimmer her chances of making it out alive.

For Rudy's sake, and his own, he hoped they found her soon.

Living in close quarters with Rudy Marshall drove him to thoughts he'd best not entertain.

He passed a commotion in the hallway. It looked to him like a junkie coming off of a high with extreme paranoia setting in pretty damn quick. Three uniformed officers appeared to have things under control.

He headed down the hall, needing to finish up his paperwork and get home.

He quickly slipped into his office. Someone knocked as soon as he shut the door.

"It's open," he shouted as he shuffled through files on his desk. He glanced up as Moss stepped inside.

"Didn't know if you were making it back here tonight."

"Decided to drop in for a few minutes. Got to push the pencil a little."

"There's a woman outside waiting for you."

Mack raised a brow. "Now that's the story of my life, Moss. Right when there's a woman waiting for me, I've got a shit load full of paper work to do. You handle her."

"I already tried. She won't talk to anyone but you."

He huffed. "Must be my lucky night."

"Must be. She insists. She's been waiting for hours."

Resigned, Mack tossed a file down on his desk. "All right, where is she?"

Moss pointed down the hall to a small woman with short dark hair sitting on a wooden bench, not far from the junkie commotion. After a minute, she turned his way and looked down the hall.

"All right, Moss. I've got her."

Moss nodded and left. Mack walked toward the woman. An eerie feeling of awareness nagged at him as he drew closer.

"Ma'am, I'm Detective MacDowell. I understand you've been waiting to see me."

She stood and Mack registered something in the green eyes. She held out her hand. He took it, surprised at the strength in her delicate fingers. "Hello, Detective MacDowell. I'm Megan Thomas."

Mack stopped breathing for a second, then blew out a lengthy breath. "Mrs. Thomas, do you have any idea how happy I am to see you?"

Chapter Thirty

An hour later Meg sat on the couch in Mack's apartment with Rudy at her side and Mack sitting across from her in an armchair. As soon as he'd learned her identity, Mack whisked her out of the station and into his personal car. He needed time to think about the best approach to handling the situation, he told her, and their next steps to take. After recovering from the initial shock of learning that Rudy was alive and of Bradford being dead, she allowed Mack to drive her back to his apartment. For sixty minutes, they'd unraveled the mysteries of the past few weeks.

"So Bradford is really dead?" Meg whispered, searching Rudy's eyes for the truth.

"Yes." She nodded slowly to her friend.

For a moment, Meg held her gaze as the reality of her reply sank in.

"But I thought you were dead and you weren't. Why should I believe Bradford's dead?"

Rudy shot Mack an exasperated look.

"Bradford Thomas is dead, Megan," Mack interjected from across the room. "I can document everything. His body is still at the morgue. If you want to I.D. it, you can. But I assure you, he's dead. And it's not a pretty sight."

Bone melting relief washed over Meg as she sank deeper into the couch. It took a major effort to stifle her tears.

"No. I don't want to see him. I just want to be sure."

"It's true, Meg." Rudy reached over and clasped her hand. "You're safe...I'm sure. The two men we caught in Nags Head aren't going to bother you anymore. With Bradford gone, the organization is weakening. There are more important things for them to deal with at the moment.

They're too busy running for their own hides."

Meg stared at Rudy. "Nags Head? You were there?"

Mack nodded. "Found them at a house on the beach."

"Becky?" Terror gripped Meg's belly and she bolted upright. "Smyth?"

Rudy placed a calming hand over Meg's. "She's fine, Megan. Everything, everyone out there is fine."

Meg sat up straighter. "Rudy, we have to go to the police, they have to know what happened—"

"I've already done that, Megan. That was one of the major reasons the D.A. decided to focus on Bradford. My statement helped a great deal. It was also the reason I...we decided I should temporarily fake my death."

"But who killed him?"

Meg watched as Rudy slid her gaze to Mack. His stoic glance shot back. An extremely long pause filled with question settled over them. Then abruptly, he turned back.

"We're not sure yet. It could have been any number of people."

He turned to Rudy again.

Rudy broke the connection and slowly fixed her gaze on Meg's face. "Meg, we need to talk."

Now what? Meg sighed and glanced away. "Please don't tell me there's more. I'm not sure how much more I can take today."

"I know, you're exhausted. There's just one more thing. Even though Bradford is dead and Sam is going to be in jail for a mighty long time, we feel it might be a good idea for you to get away from Chicago. You still are not entirely safe."

Meg shook her head. This was all too confusing. Surely she would be safe with Bradford dead. "I thought—"

"Meg, do you know who that quarter of a million dollars belonged to that you took out of Bradford's safe?"

She shook her head. "I assumed it was Bradford's."

"It seems Bradford may have left some debts behind him. We're not really sure who that money belonged to."

Mack broke in. "Megan, I don't know if the money is a

problem or not, but we need to play this out with caution. You need to lay low. Bradford claimed you were kidnapped not long after you disappeared. After a while you were assumed dead. I don't think anyone but Bradford, and maybe Sam Lockbourne, knew what really happened. With Bradford dead and Sam behind bars, everyone else thinks you were kidnapped and are probably dead. It's been all over the papers. So, can you see how difficult it would be for you if you suddenly turned up alive? The media would have a field day, not to mention that if there were any lingering problems associated with Bradford, your life could be made a living hell for quite some time. He still has cronies out there. You'll be much safer, for the rest of your life probably, if you leave Chicago.

You might even consider changing your name."

"But where will I go? What will I do?" Meg questioned. Just when she'd hoped everything was working out, suddenly she found her world was upturned again. Her heart pounded.

"Is there a relative? A friend? Somewhere you could stay for a while until you figure out what direction you want to go in?" Mack asked.

"Maybe you and I could just take off to parts unknown," Rudy suggested. "We could handle it together, Meg. You and me." Rudy pressed her hand into Meg's.

Immediately, Meg's thoughts fell to the island. To Smyth. But somehow that seemed all wrong now. Too much turmoil still existed in her life. Too much upheaval. When she went back there, she wanted to be able to love Smyth unconditionally. To give to him what he deserved. To go to him whole and full of love, not riddled with doubt and question.

And right now, she didn't feel whole. Her life had disintegrated into a thousand pieces.

She wasn't even sure who she was anymore. She needed time for her past to fade into oblivion.

This thing was not done yet. And she wouldn't go back there, to him, until it was finished. She would not put

Smyth or Becky in danger anymore until she was thoroughly convinced all this was through.

She even thought about Smyth's grandfather's house in Elizabeth City. Reaching into her pocket, she fumbled for the key he'd given her. She'd never given it back and had kept it close for a long time, a reminder of all Smyth meant to her. But no, she couldn't go there either. It would be less safe for her to go back to where she'd first run.

Her thoughts turned to the small farmhouse in Indiana. Her own grandmother's home. It was empty and probably needed some TLC, but it was home. A refuge.

"There is my grandmother's house in Indiana."

"Good." Rudy glanced to Mack and he nodded.

"But what about the house here? Arrangements for the funeral. Shouldn't I stay and take care of all that?

"Put the house on the market," Rudy offered. "I can handle the details...or maybe I should have John Walters do it. I can funnel everything through him, since he's one of the few people who actually knows we're both still alive. Of course, we'll have to wait until the estate is settled, but if you give John power of attorney, we can handle it for you, even the funeral." Then, as if an afterthought, "Unless you want to do that."

Meg shook her head. "No. I just don't want it to be a burden to you or John."

Rudy stared into her eyes. "You're paying John and it's not a burden to me, Megan. Let me do this. I failed you so many times before. Let me make it up to you." Rudy's eyes held the gaze and Meg knew exactly what she meant. Meg had known all along that Rudy and Bradford had once had an affair. It just hadn't seemed worth losing a friendship over. Especially when her relationship with Bradford had taken a turn for the worse.

"All right. Handle it. Draw up the papers. I'll sign whatever you want."

Mack rose and joined Rudy. "Stay here for the night. You figure out what you need from the house and I'll see that you get it. Then we'll get you on your way first thing in the morning."

Reluctantly, Meg nodded. She was running again.

She turned to Rudy. "Can you come with me, Rudy?" she asked, impulsively. "Let John handle it all and we'll both go, together."

Rudy glanced from Meg to Mack and back again, then quickly shook her head. "Give me a few days to get things together, then I'll be up. I can't guarantee how long I'll stay, but...I tell you what, I'll bring you a puppy to keep you company. I know it won't be a proper substitute for my wonderful company, but it will sure help."

She grinned and Meg smiled. She knew that somehow, everything was going to eventually turn out all right.

A puppy. Bradford never allowed her to have a pet.

****

The old farmhouse loomed ahead in the Indiana countryside. Intense feelings of déjà vu washed over Meg and she had to force back the tears. There was a strange gnawing in the pit of her stomach.

She'd been extremely happy here in her youth. After her parents divorced, her grandmother took her in to raise. Her mother claimed she'd needed her space and headed for California, and her father was killed shortly afterward in a freakish car/train accident. Nearly two years later, her mother died of an aneurysm. Meg experienced the mood swings of adolescence, coupled with her sense of loss, but Grandma Rose took it all in stride. Meg had come to love her more deeply than she ever imagined.

Then she went to college. And soon after, Bradford made his entrance into her life.

Now she had come full circle back to Indiana's simple life, but this time, she didn't have Grandma Rose to help heal the pain. She had to do it all by herself.

The flat Indiana farmland that bordered the house sat barren. Years passed since crops were harvested from the fields. Even though Grandma Rose was a widow, she had seen to the farm, hiring help when needed, living off the land. But since her death, Meg allowed the land to lie fallow. She couldn't bear selling it, even though she had plenty of offers. And now, she was glad she hadn't.

She parked, got out of the car, and took in a deep breath. With her keys jangling from her fingers, she approached the back door. Hesitantly, she slid the old key into the lock; the door swung open smoothly with the practice of years past.

Meg stepped across the threshold into the old country kitchen. She'd called ahead to have the water turned on and the place cleaned up a bit. Gertie, the niece of Grandma Rose's neighbor, wasn't but a few years older than Meg. She'd kept an eye on the place for her the past few years.

Immediately, a sense of homecoming bombarded her weary body. She slumped against the doorframe. "I'm home," she whispered to no one but herself. Her eyes darted about the dusty, empty kitchen and then she smiled. Ghostly images of her grandmother bustling about the cinnamon-and-apple-essenced room, freshly scrubbed and brightly painted, came to her with a settling feeling of rightness.

"I'm back home, Grandma Rose."

****

With eyes gritty from lack of sleep, Smyth wove his way through the busy Chicago streets, keeping his eyes peeled for the street names he needed to find. It was early evening, and the stress of the drive from Nags Head, coupled with the anxiety of trying to find Meg and dealing with unaccustomed traffic, had given him a pounding headache.

He recognized the signs of a migraine, but desperately tried to ignore them. Horns blowing, wheels grinding into pavement, tires screeching as cars jockeyed for position made him nervous. It all only added to his pain. If he gave in to them—the pain, the nausea, the bright shooting lights behind his eyes—he might as well give up on it all. And he couldn't give up. He had to find Meg.

He hoped he wasn't too late.

Becky told him a Chicago detective had been looking

for Meg. He hoped the detective was trying to warn her, trying to get her to stay away from Bradford, but he couldn't be sure.

Perhaps it, too, was a trap. But Becky said the detective asked for Megan Thomas...not Thompson. At least now he had a name, or names, to go on. Bradford and/or Megan Thomas.

He'd driven night and day, hoping to track her. But when he'd arrived in Chicago, he hadn't a clue where to look first. The phone book gave him no indication. Finally, he'd tried the courthouse, searching property records. And then, bingo, he'd found the house on Sycamore Street, property owners, Bradford and Megan Thomas. After a quick trip to a neighborhood library, and a few quick searches on the Internet, he found what he was looking for. He set off to find Meg, hoping to hell and back he wasn't too late.

And if he came to a dead end there, he wasn't sure which turn he'd take next. If any.

Slowing his jeep, he spied the next street sign. If his calculations were correct, it should be Sycamore. His pulse racing, he quickly turned onto the street. Smyth held his breath as he spotted house number after house number, anticipation welling up inside him as the numbers drew closer to the one he sought.

Then, like a specter in the early dusk, the white brick house set deep in the lot towered before him.

His gaze immediately latched on to the For Sale sign posted at the curb. That's probably why he didn't see the two women standing on the porch until he'd pulled into the circular drive and stopped a few feet behind them. One woman was brunette and tall, the other of average size and blonde with her back to him.

Oh, God. Please.

He left the car idling as he crossed the asphalt toward them. He wasn't sure if he'd taken a breath since he spotted her. His chest felt tight, his head light. Long thin legs, shoulder length blonde hair. It had to be Meg.

The brunette caught his eye and he noticed she wore a red jacket with a familiar realtor's emblem embroidered on it. She held pamphlets and a clipboard.

Meg had decided to sell her house?

He said her name, barely more than a breath. Then he stepped closer to the woman with her back still turned. She conversed lightly with the realtor. He reached out to clasp her elbow.

"Meg?"

The woman turned and looked into his eyes, her expression questioning. He then remembered that Meg had cut and dyed her hair.

"I'm sorry." He spoke in a voice filled with despair and disappointment.

She looked at him, obviously puzzled. "Did you call me Meg?"

Smyth backed off. "No...Yes. I'm sorry. I...I thought you were someone I–"

Someone I love.

He turned to head back to the car. Dizziness and a ringing in his ears consumed him. She resembled Meg. That's all. It wasn't her.

He almost didn't register the faint touch on his shoulder just as he reached his car. He turned around and faced the same woman. She smiled, sort of.

"Your name," she began, "by any stretch of the imagination, wouldn't be Smyth Parker, would it?"

Chapter Thirty-One

"When are you going to forget this charade and get on with your life?"

"When my life is my own. Until then, I can't forget anything."

"Including Smyth?"

Meg rose from her kitchen table and went to the sink. She stared into its off-white porcelain depths, trying to ignore the anxious feelings Rudy stirred in her. She snapped her gaze back to her friend.

"I haven't forgotten Smyth, Rudy." *I can't. It's impossible.* "Nor have I forgotten that someone murdered Bradford. I just have some things to work out in my head."

She watched Rudy close her eyes. When she opened them, Meg knew what was coming next. "But Mack says–"

"I know what Mack says, Rudy. There's little danger now, but the thing is, I've lived with the fear for so long—"

"No, there's something else," Rudy interrupted. "It seems Cindy flew the coop about the same time Bradford was murdered. Her family says she's moved out of state. No one's heard from her. The Jag's gone. And you know, most of your things were gone when Mack went back for them."

"So they think...?"

"It's a possibility." Rudy studied Meg's face. "Look. I didn't tell you at first, but you know Cindy was living with Bradford. He could have gotten abusive with her. Maybe she was the one who finally had guts enough to stand up to him. Mack thinks they've located her and will probably call her in for questioning, but he also thinks she'll walk. Not enough evidence to link her to the crime scene."

Meg contemplated that notion. She felt a twinge of regret at having involved the girl, but she was an adult—and she hadn't followed Meg's instructions. Even with

Bradford dead, the reality didn't comfort her. She'd so often thought of killing him herself, hadn't she?

Could it be true? Was it finally over? Had Cindy taken Bradford's life and given Meg back hers?

Or had Bradford killed Cindy and buried her in the Jaguar somewhere? She didn't want to think about that. She hoped it was the other way around.

Meg shook her head. "I don't know if I'll ever really convince myself that it's all over.

And I can't tell you how guilty I feel involving—"

"Forget it, Meg. Cindy was a greedy young woman who made her own decisions. I tried to get her to leave. I went to the house and told her to leave. She wouldn't listen."

"But I just can't help but feel—"

"Put it to rest, Megan. You've got to go forward, now. Start over." She studied Meg's face. "What about Smyth? Can you start all over again with him?"

Meg turned away to stare out the window. It was hard to get the possibility that Cindy killed Bradford out of her head. If that were true, then...could she ever start over?

"Have you heard from him?"

Meg shook her head. "Heavens, no. He wouldn't even know where to look."

"What if he's searching for you? What if he wants to risk this, if he wants to find you?"

At the thought, a sliver of panic pierced Meg's heart. Would he search for her? "He couldn't. I never told him about this place."

"Why haven't you contacted him?"

Meg turned back to face Rudy. In exasperation, she quickly crossed the room and sat beside her. Grasping her coffee mug, Meg took a gulp of the lukewarm liquid, grimaced, then set it back on the table.

"He's probably living at Portsmouth. There are no phones there. No mail."

"You didn't answer my question."

Alarm coursed through Meg's body at the possibility of

allowing herself to think that she should have. "Rudy, I need some time, some calm to my life. I need Grandma Rose around me for a while to make me feel whole again."

Rudy rose. "And now you've had that. Look, I'm going to be blunt. You're a mess, Meg.

We've got to fix this. I know what it's like to be in love with someone and not be with them. It's hell. Get your life back. You deserve it."

Meg slowly stood, wrapped her arms about her friend and embraced her. Deep inside her gut, she knew Rudy was right. She knew what she needed. She needed Smyth. "And who are you in love with, my friend?"

Rudy pulled away and looked Meg in the face. Grinning, she dropped her gaze to the floor. "I think you know the answer to that one."

She did. It was Mack. Rudy couldn't stop talking about him the one night they shared together at Mack's apartment. They'd giggled like schoolgirls talking about the men in their lives. It was a welcome respite from all the pent-up turmoil they'd suffered weeks before.

Holding Rudy's gaze, Meg watched her eyes mist. She sighed, then reached out and grasped Meg's hand.

"What are you going to do with your life, Rudy?"

She shrugged. "I'm not going back to Chicago, that's for sure. I've decided to move on, maybe even find a new career."

Meg bit her lip. "Rudy, I'm so sorry. This has affected you as much as me."

"I'm fine, Meg. Don't worry about me. It's you I'm concerned about." Rudy whispered,

"Find your happiness. You'll never regret it."

Deep in her heart, Meg knew the truth, but could she go back now? She shook her head.

"I can't, Rudy. Not yet. I have to get past constantly looking over my shoulder, wondering if whoever killed Bradford will somehow find out I'm alive and come after me, too. I can't put Smyth in that danger. I won't. Even if I never see him for the rest of my life."

Rudy peered into Meg's eyes and waited a long time before replying. "Meg...Bradford's dead. Sam probably won't ever get out of prison. And they killed off almost anyone who had any connection with you or the supposed kidnapping. We even nabbed those two so-called bodyguards Bradford hired for you. You're perfectly safe. Smyth is perfectly safe."

"Rudy—"

She stood and grasped both of Meg's hands in hers and held them tightly. "Megan Thomas, I want you to listen to what I'm going to tell you and then I want you to forget every word I've said. For my sake, okay? Do you understand me?"

Meg was almost afraid not to agree with Rudy. The determined glint in her eyes showed her seriousness. "Rudy, what are you talking about?"

Rudy stepped closer to her. She spoke slowly, determinedly. "I killed Bradford. I did it."

Meg read pain, anguish, guilt, and satisfaction in Rudy's eyes. She breathed deeply and searched her friend's face. "Oh, God..." she gasped. "No."

"I did it for us, Meg. You and me. Everything I did was to set us free. Please believe me."

Megan sucked in a ragged breath. "Oh, Rudy," she whispered.

Rudy put a finger to Meg's lips. "Sh...it's okay. It's over and done with. I have no regrets.

Now, forget it."

At that moment Meg knew that she would never have another friend as loyal and as dear to her as Rudy would always be. She would take Rudy's secret to the grave—if it were, indeed, the truth. She had no idea whether Rudy really killed Bradford or if Cindy or someone else had.

Maybe Rudy just told her that to bring closure. She wasn't sure, but she loved her for doing it.

And she also knew that with those words, Rudy had set her free.

Free to go back. To the islands. To Smyth.

"Oh, and there's one more thing."

Meg searched her friend's face. "What?"

"I have a surprise for you."

"A surprise?" Confused, Meg sensed that Rudy wanted to drop the subject. Far as Meg was concerned, they'd never talk about it again.

"Yes." Rudy's face glowed. "It's out on the front porch."

Meg's shoulders dropped. "Rudy Marshall, if you got me that puppy you were talking about, you're going to have to take it back, particularly now that I've decided to return to Portsmouth. How can I travel with a puppy?" Rudy took her hand and led her through the living room of the farmhouse.

Rudy stopped by the front door, her eyes wide. "You're going back?"

Meg nodded, surprised at herself. "I think I just this minute decided."

Rudy grinned. "Oh, well...guess you'll just have to take this puppy with you. I assure you, he won't be a problem."

Rudy opened the front screen door and led Meg out onto the porch. She glanced first to her right, then left. Nothing.

"What did you do, leave him out here all by himself? Now he's gone and run off," she teased.

Smiling, Rudy shook her head and glanced behind Meg.

Meg saw movement out of the corner of her eye. A whimper came from behind her.

She turned around.

Her heart skipped a beat when she spotted Smyth standing at the end of the porch. Meg gasped. Every inch of his tall body seemed like coming home. His hair cut a bit shorter, dressed in jeans and a T-shirt, and his face held a tentative smile, but it was really him. She wanted nothing more at that moment than to bury herself in his chest. Her eyes immediately teared and a small sob exited her throat.

"Oh, my God," she whispered. "You're here.

And…what a puppy you are." She grinned.

Then her eyes drifted lower to the real puppy squirming in Smyth's arms and she couldn't help but laugh out loud.

"Yeah," Smyth whispered back, "and both of us puppies need some loving."

Meg flung herself into Smyth's arms, the beagle pup wriggling between them. The feel of Smyth's chest against hers and the warmth of his arms wrapped around her were the most precious things she'd ever felt. No way could she stop the tears. No way. Nothing, not one thing in her life mattered other than this—other than Smyth holding her so tight in his arms.

He threaded the fingers of one hand through her hair and then carefully tilted her face up to greet his. "I've found you," he whispered.

"Thank God," was all Meg could say before he kissed her like he'd never kissed her before.

****

The dark cocoon of warmth that surrounded Meg made her feel that she'd finally, for the first time in her life, found true happiness. With Smyth's arms wrapped around her, a leg thrown protectively over hers, he'd drawn her deep into the security of his sensual embrace. A wonderful aura enveloped them telling her everything was finally going to be all right. They were finally free to love.

And they made love deep into the night. The beagle's occasional whining from the box in the laundry room downstairs provided the only reason they'd risen from the bed since Rudy left them alone mid-afternoon. Thor, as Smyth named the puppy, reasoning that the little guy needed a big name, needed an occasional cuddling to calm his whining as well as intermittent trips outside to water the rose bushes. Although the pup managed little watering.

Meg breathed in deeply, her face against Smyth's chest, and relished the male scent his skin and hair and body emitted. The smell, a mixture of soap and perspiration, mingled with some of her perfume and his own unique scent. They'd showered earlier, together, and immediately made love again, leaving the sheets damp. She didn't care. She couldn't get enough of smelling, tasting, touching, and making love with him.

And Smyth was the same. They'd explored each other's bodies throughout the night, and now, sated for the time being, they slept, snuggled together like contented kittens with full bellies. Only they were full of each other.

Sometime later Meg rose and sat up in the bed. Smyth's arm reached out to snag her around the waist.

"Where are you going?" he groggily whispered.

"I'm thirsty," she replied, leaning back to whisper in his ear. "And Thor is crying again. I'll just be a minute."

She trailed her lips up his cheek and planted a soft kiss over his left eye. Smyth murmured, "Don't be long," then his arms fell slack around her in sleep.

Smiling, Meg gently laid his arms aside, then brushed back brown strands of hair from his face to watch him sleep. He was exhausted, she knew, having spent the past few days searching for her. It amazed her that he would do that. She'd never before known love to this depth.

How could she, after all these years, after all the pain, be so lucky to find Smyth? All she wanted, from this moment on, was to share his life. For them to grow old together and cuddle every night in their shared bed, with no worries to follow them.

For the very first time since she'd met him, she believed it could happen. The time had come to begin their lives anew. And she couldn't wait to get started.

Sighing, Meg rose from the bed and drew on a cotton gown she'd tossed on a chair beside the window. She wouldn't be long. She wanted something to drink and to cuddle with Thor for a minute or two—she suspected the pup missed his mommy—then hurry back to the warmth of Smyth's arms.

She crept silently down the dark staircase, turning on only a light above the sink in the kitchen once she'd arrived there. Thor quieted as soon as he saw the light. Meg peeked at him once, whispered that she'd be there in a minute and then went back into the kitchen.

She almost felt hungry more than thirsty. After opening the pantry door, she perused its contents, all the while humming a soft tune. Her gaze landed on a box filled with packets of gourmet coffees.

"Ah, ha!" she whispered as she pilfered through the packets. "Let's see, Deep Mocha Surprise." Her favorite. More chocolate than coffee. Not something she ordinarily treated herself to in the middle of the night, but this particular night she felt decadent and indulging.

What the heck! Life is good.

She removed the packet, then put the teakettle on the stove to heat the water. She turned back to the counter and emptied the contents of the wicked concoction into a mug. Still humming, she went to the laundry room.

"There's my little Thor," she whispered in a voice she usually reserved for infants.

Picking him up, she let him nuzzle her under the chin, his wet nose and tongue leaving slobber on her neck. "Are you missing your mommy, baby?"

Meg paced the kitchen, cooing and cuddling the pup while waiting for the water to boil.

Then she had an even more delicious thought. She opened the freezer compartment of her refrigerator. "Ummmm. Ice cream."

She yanked a carton of French Vanilla from the freezer, sat it and the pup on the counter, and then spooned out a generous scoop into another mug. Her favorite late night dessert, a scoop of vanilla ice cream with Deep Mocha Surprise poured over it. It was more milk shake than coffee.

Yum.

With ice cream carton in hand, Meg turned back toward the freezer.

The ice cream fell to the floor when a hand clamped over her mouth from behind and an arm grasped her around her waist. "Don't scream and don't move," a deep voice said.

At first she thought it must be Smyth playing a game with her. But no, he wouldn't do that. And as the voice registered and the hand on her mouth clamped tighter, she found herself being dragged and pushed into the shadows of the laundry room. This was no game. Panic like she'd never felt before gripped her from the inside out.

Then she noticed the little things. The heavy, almost labored breathing of the man holding her. The roughness of his callused hands. The moist heat of his breath on her neck. The stench of body odor that clung to his clothing.

Oh, God. Who? What? Where's Smyth?

He pushed her face first into the rough-paneled laundry room wall, the gritty texture bit into her cheek. His body crowded up against her from behind. A low chuckle started deep in his belly and quietly exited his mouth. The ominous sound sent shivers over her.

"How are you, Mrs. Thomas?" the voice behind questioned into her right ear.

Frantic, she tried to jerk away, to see his face, but she couldn't twist far enough around, his body pinned her too tightly against the wall of the dimly lit laundry room. Even trying to scream against his hand didn't work, it came out as a weak, muffled sob.

"Do you have any idea how I used to watch you? How I used to wonder how soft your skin was beneath those fancy dresses and suits you wore?" His voice, still menacingly low, tripped every nerve ending where his breath touched her. The voice. It sounded familiar, yet she couldn't find anything concrete she could grasp hold of. She wanted to ask him who he was, but his hand prevented her speech.

"No, you probably don't." His left hand snaked intimately beneath the side of her breast, firmly caressing up and down her side through the cotton gown. "I'm sure you have no idea who I am, do you?"

She remained still. How could she answer?

Closing her eyes, Meg tried to mentally check off likely

suspects in her head. No one came to mind. No one she could think of who would do such a thing to her. And what did he want? What was he after?

"You were always the Prima Dona, the boss's wife. So fine," he breathed into her ear.

"So fine. Like all his women. I can't tell you how many times I've dreamed of fucking you. How many times I've ached to fuck the boss's wife. I figured you deserved some variety, he'd surely had enough."

Immediately, he ground his pelvis into her from behind. Her cotton gown offered little resistance to his grinding. The feel of his thick arousal sickened her. Oh, God, what did he plan to do to her?

The boss's wife. Still her brain churned. Who was this man? If only she knew who she was dealing with, maybe she could persuade him to let her go. Maybe.

"I want to fuck you now. You know that, don't you?" he began again, almost in rhythm to his gyrations against her. "I've waited long enough." His left hand reached down to bunch her gown up around her waist. He smoothed that hand over her bare hip and Meg tried to squirm again and whimper against his hand, but it only served to arouse him further, for him to press into her harder and more firmly.

"Yes, I've waited long enough. I tried to find you even before your loving husband died.

Convenient, huh, that he should be dead. Works out good for you, doesn't it? Did you know he ordered me to take care of you? He even gave me permission to fuck you, my darling, before I killed you. So see, there's really nothing you can do about it. You were given to me, by your husband. Oh, but don't worry. I won't be rough. I know Thomas was rough on you, which was his style. I guarantee you I'll take things nice and slow and easy. I plan to fuck you for a long time."

Meg felt tears start to form in her eyes. There was nothing she could do. He was going to rape her, right here, with Smyth sleeping soundly in the bed above them. She had to do something. Had to get away.

He pushed his lips more intimately next to her face. "And fucking you isn't all I plan to do, my darling Megan. Oh, no, there are so many more pleasures I can give you with my tongue and my hands, not to mention all the rather unconventional places my dick can explore on your body. Oh, yes, my sweetheart, we are going to have a quite good time."

He paused and his labored breathing raked over her. "Of course I'll have to kill you later. That's why I'm going to get the most from you before I do."

Terror ripped up within her and Meg tried, once again, to squirm and kick away. Why was this happening now? Just when everything was fine? This lunatic not only meant to rape her, but kill her. Who was this he?

Suddenly, energy she didn't know she burst up with her. She gave it everything she had, thrusting her elbows backward and twisting in his arms. But he proved too strong. The only thing she accomplished was his hand slipping slightly down over her lips. If she waited, she might possibly be able to scream if she could twist and push one more time. And her scream might alert Smyth, but then, she would be putting him into danger as well.

He gripped her tighter and thrust her again into the wall. "I'm warning you, bitch. Don't do that again. Now that I've finally caught up with you, I don't plan to let you out of my sight. It took me days to find you. I've chased you from North Carolina to Chicago and now here to Indiana. If I hadn't lucked on Thomas' attorney leaving your house one day, I never would have located you here. She led me here, do you realize that? Your friend, Thomas' attorney and part-time whore. Oh, she has no idea she led me to you. I followed at a safe distance. I passed by once when she'd turned up this country lane. And I've been waiting, ever since she left this afternoon—man, it was hard waiting—but I wanted to catch you by surprise. Get you when you least expected it. I'll do the same with her later. I know where she is. I figure between the two of you, I'll finally get what I want."

What he wants?

Then it dawned on Meg. *He doesn't realize Smyth is here.*

"Let's go upstairs, Mrs. Thomas."

He stepped back and jerked her away from the wall. He doesn't have a weapon, Megan thought. Both of his hands were holding her. *He doesn't have a weapon!* Of course that didn't mean he didn't have one somewhere, just that he'd not produced it yet. Meg hesitated only a second, then as he pushed her, she faked a stumble forward and tried to drag him down with her, attempting to trip him up.

He lurched a bit and she twisted in his grasp. Something gurgled in the kitchen and he glanced away. His hand slipped off her mouth and she bit into his forefinger. Hard. He cursed and pushed her. The teakettle on the stove let out a loud hiss, then began to sing. The puppy howled. Meg screamed, propelled herself forward, grabbed the steaming kettle and swung it at the man, then ran out the laundry room door and into the night.

****

Smyth jerked awake. The puppy whining again. No, not the puppy. Pulling up to his side, he swiped at his eyes and ran a hand through his hair. Something else. Damn, he was so groggy.

Felt like jet-lag. The sound continued. What woke him?

Then it became more of a smell that caught his attention. A hot, steamy odor. His eyes shot open. There was a splat and a gurgle and a popping, hissing sound, followed by a high-pitched whistle and a loud thump.

It wasn't the pup.

He glanced to Meg's side of the bed.

"Meg?" Smyth called out again. No answer.

Then he heard her scream and the back door slam.

****

Meg bought herself only a few seconds time. He was behind her. Once she shot out the laundry room door, her brain had little time to assess her freedom before she had to contemplate the best way to safety. The car? No. The keys were in the house. The barn? She'd only back herself into a corner. The fields? Could she outrun him? Get to a neighbor's house? Damn, the nearest neighbor lived half a mile away.

No time for contemplation. She simply ran. The screen door closed with a splat. He was behind her.

Seconds later he barreled into her, throwing her to the ground, the tiny pebbles and sharp gravel of the driveway cutting into her knees, elbows, and cheeks. She fell forward with a whoosh, the force of his body knocking the breath out of her. Pain ripped across her chest.

She needed a moment to fill her lungs again, to take in several deep breaths. Clear away the dizziness.

He refused her that moment.

Flipping her over onto her back, he straddled her, sitting on her hips. His arms pinned hers to the cold ground at her shoulders. She finally got her first look. Vaguely familiar face.

Difficult to clearly discern in the moonlight. She met a man once, it could be him. Bradford said he worked in security.

"You goddamned bitch! I don't want to fuck around here! Now you've gone and got me all pissed off. Forget fucking you. Thomas said you weren't any good anyway. Cold as a goddamned fish, he said." Then he lowered his face closer. "But I'm still gonna kill you. Just as soon as you tell me where the money is."

Money? She didn't answer him immediately.

He gripped her face and leaned over her. Foamy saliva dripped from his mouth onto her cheek. "I said *where is the fucking money?*"

"I don't have any money," she bit back.

His anger increased. "Yes, you do. Thomas said you stole a few hundred grand from him. I want it! He goddamn owes me. He promised me a big payoff to see that you were put in your grave. I tried, man, how I tried. Even put two of my best men on it, but damn, you were an elusive bitch. Thomas was gonna be my meal ticket and then someone had to go and kill him. But since Thomas is dead, there's got to be a whole lot more where that money came from. I saw your house up for sale. There's a whole lot of property there that needs disposing of. Where's your Jaguar? What about the old man's Mercedes? I might consider holding off on killing you if you can get hold of a few hundred grand more."

He leaned closer and peered into her face. "I might even get in a better mood and fuck you yet. Might even think about keeping you around for a while." He looked up and glanced about him. "We're in the middle of the goddamned boonies. I figure no one round here is gonna hear if you scream day and night."

"There's no money," she told him quickly, pleading. "I don't have anything. There's nothing in Chicago, I swear. Just what I've got here, in the farmhouse. You can have it, all of it. It's over a hundred thousand. Let me up and I'll go get it."

Let me up and I can warn Smyth.

The intruder lapsed into a total frenzy. Shaking her and demanding money. Pawing at her gown. Meg fought him. Pushed his hands away as they groped. Screamed as he slapped her face one more time and called her a bitch. He lost all control. Shouting. Demanding. Meg cried, sure he would kill her anyway.

"Who are you?" she sobbed as she tried to fight his flailing hands. "Why are you doing this to me?"

He stared at her in disgust and stopped his assault. She welcomed the brief respite. "Who am I? You don't even know who I goddamned am? The name's Riker, Mrs. Thomas. Cyrus Riker. I worked for your husband for twelve years. Twelve long years. I did his dirty work and waited for the day that I would get even with the bastard. You've heard the story, haven't you?

Twelve years ago my wife worked for Thomas Industrials. In the secretarial pool. Blonde, green-eyed, just like you. Thomas took her, fucked with her mind and her body, and then killed her, the sonofabitch. Left her for fucking dead in the parking lot of one of his warehouses. She wanted out. She was coming back to me. She didn't want your bastard husband any more. Then he went and fucking killed her!"

Meg froze beneath the man as he stilled and stared into her face. She saw it in his eyes.

He didn't see her. He was seeing his wife.

Seconds later she registered the thunk as a shovel hit Riker square on the side of the head and he rolled off her in a dead heap.

Smyth tossed the shovel aside and bent to gather her in his arms. Amid sobs and frantic clutchings, she held onto the only concrete thing she could grasp at the moment. Smyth's voice, repeating breathlessly in her ear,

"It's over Meg. It's all over. It's finally over."

Epilogue

The twinge in Meg's back woke her. That and the two little knees poking into her breasts. She opened her eyes, knowing what she would see.

"Allison Parker," she whispered, "what are you doing in Mommy and Daddy's bed? Hmm?"

The three-year-old child tried to clamp her eyes shut tight, squinting until little laugh lines splayed out from her eyes and her lips turned up in a smile. Meg reached out and brushed brown ringlets away from her face and grinned at the child's innocence. Green eyes popped open.

"You woke me up, Mommy," she whined.

"You've been awake a long time, Munchkin," Meg whispered.

"I know. I was only playin' possum."

"Sh...let's let Daddy sleep for a while." Meg glanced to Smyth's back. She felt the twinge again.

"Daddy's awake." This declaration came from across the bed. Smyth rolled over and caught Allison in a bear hug, which brought screams and giggles from her.

"Don't, Daddy! Don't tickle me!"

Smyth stopped and peered into his daughter's eyes. "I wasn't tickling you."

"But you were gonna."

"I wasn't even thinking about it."

"Yes, you were."

"Well...maybe I was."

The tickling and laughter exploded. Meg laughed at Allison's bubbly giggles. She was such a happy child. Sitting up, Meg threw her legs over the edge of the bed. This time the twinge in her back raced across with lightning speed. She paused for a minute, then stood up and went to her closet.

"Smyth, did you check on the house?"

By now the tickling stopped and Allison sat straddling her Daddy's chest. She tickled him and Smyth faked his laughter.

"Becky called last night. They accepted our offer."

Meg twirled, then wished she hadn't. She reached out for the dresser. She had difficulty keeping her balance these days. "You didn't tell me."

"I was going to tell you this morning, you were asleep when I got in last night."

Meg nodded. She'd been awfully tired the night before. "How were things at the office?"

"Well, Art's slowing down quite a bit. I may have to start checking in more often than a few times a week. I think he's ready to retire."

"Are you okay with that?"

He nodded. Meg's hand went to her back, the twinge stronger this time. "I think I'm ready to go back in full time, Meg."

She knew this was coming. Little by little over the past three years, Smyth had become more involved in his grandfather's company, learning why it was so important to his grandfather.

Smyth, now a father himself, realized that what his grandfather willed to him allowed him the freedom and lifestyle he had today.

So many times he'd mentioned to Meg that he wanted to be able to do that for Allison and any other children they might have.

"I think that whatever you feel best is fine with me." She smiled and Smyth grinned back.

She changed into a loose jumper and slipped her feet into her canvas shoes.

"Where are you going, Mommy?" Allison jumped off Smyth's stomach and he groaned.

"To the hospital."

Smyth jerked upright in the bed. "What?"

"It's time."

He stood. "Now? It's too early!"

"Now."

"But we haven't closed on the house. The cottage is too small for five of us."

"Then the twins will have to move in here and we'll have to be cramped for a while. You know I told you they come early sometimes. We'll just have to wing it here then move to the bigger house down the beach when it's ready. It's going to need a bit of redecorating."

Smyth raced to his closet and started throwing on clothes. "How can you think of redecorating at a time like this?"

"You know how much I enjoy keeping the house nice for you and Allison."

"I know, but—" He side-stepped into a pair of green swimming trunks, and then added a pink golf shirt and his mesh beach shoes. Allison laughed. Smyth turned to his daughter.

"Allison honey, go call Aunt Becky. Tell her the twins are coming and to get here fast."

"'Kay, Daddy."

Allison hurried off as Meg watched. Allison knew Aunt Becky's number by heart. Becky spoiled her unmercifully. Smyth rushed to Meg's side.

"Are you okay?" His voice was quiet.

"I'm fine." She smiled up at him and Smyth drew her closer, then reached around to rub her lower back. "We might not be able to escape to Portsmouth this spring." They'd already discussed how difficult it might be with the twins. They only visited now and then, a retired couple had taken over the volunteer assignment right after Meg became pregnant with Allison.

"So we'll have to put it off for a while. We'll get back there. As long as we can get the house down the road here in Nags Head, I'll be happy."

"Do you still want to rent this one out?"

"Becky asked last night if she could have it. I told her she could. She wants to sell hers.

Later on I think she'll probably buy something else."

"Oh, that would be great."

Smyth drew back and looked into Meg's face. Another twinge snaked across her back.

He must have registered the grimace on her face. "It will be over soon, sweetheart."

Meg nodded and smiled. "Three kids, Smyth. Feel like running? This is going to be a lot of work."

He grinned back and leaned in to kiss her. "Not a chance, my love. My running days are over."

"Mine, too," she whispered, and kissed him back.

THE END

Dear Readers,

The ocean. The beach. The call of the surf and the tang of salt on my lips. What is more romantic than that? I'm not exactly sure why but the ocean plays a part in many of my books. *A Perfect Escape,* is no exception. In fact, I'm a bit partial to the Outer Banks of North Carolina, the setting of this book.

Smyth Parker is a volunteer caretaker of an uninhabited village on Portsmouth Island, a real uninhabited island which sits about five miles away from Ocracoke Island in the barrier islands. No one lives there except for the caretakers and the occasional National Parks employees.

People used to live there. In fact, the last inhabitants left in 1971. Imagine, living almost a lifetime on an island off the coast, no access except by boat, no running water, few amenities of life that we now think so commonplace. Your mail comes by boat and if you need supplies, you send the mailman back to the mainland with a list. Electricity? Likely not. Perhaps they had generators, I'm not exactly certain.

I learned of Portsmouth Island during one of my many visits to the Outer Banks. I long to schedule a trip over by boat to the isolated village. I just want to explore, soak up the history and the stories but alas, that day has not yet come. Someday. Yes. I will make that trek and I look forward to it.

The isolation and the wicked storms that pound the island became too much for residential living. Now, the island is part of the Cape Lookout National Seashore. While doing research for this book, I was able to discuss what living on the island is like with some of the volunteers who actually do live there. I wonder if that is something I might like to experience for myself. How strong a generator would it take to keep my laptop powered up?

So what other island books are in store for me in the future? That remains to be seen.

There are two characters in *A Perfect Escape*, however, who continue to niggle at me. I think they are trying to let me know that they might want a book of their own in the future.

What do you think? Do Rudy and Mack need their own stories told? Can you imagine the conflict between them? Did Rudy really kill Bradford and if so, could Mack, being an upstanding detective, ever forgive her for that?

I'd love to know if you think Rudy and Mack deserve their own book.

Feel free to email me at **maddie@maddiejames.net** and tell me what you think! I'd love to hear from you.

Maddie

ABOUT MADDIE JAMES

Maddie James is a prolific writer, a Food Network junkie, a wannabe gardener, and a closet hermit. She loves being at home (and working from home). Never one with time on her hands, she has dipped her toes into the publishing world in more than one facet of the industry, but her claim to fame is award-winning and bestselling romance novels that chase the happily-ever-after. Maddie is a member of Romance Writers of America (RWA) and its Published Author Network (PAN), and Novelists, Inc. Visit **www.maddiejames.com** to learn more about Maddie, and pen names.

~~~~~

I would love to connect with you! My next release will be announced on these social networks. Perhaps you'd like to connect, as well. Look for me on:

Facebook
Twitter
Goodreads
Google+

More contemporary romance by Maddie James
Falling For Grace
The Heartbreaker
Convincing Nora
Body Heat
Rawhide and Roses
Broken

You can find these books and more on my web site –
www.maddiejames.com

Thank you!

For purchasing this book from
Turquoise Morning Press.

We invite you to visit our Web site to learn more about our
quality Trade Paperback and Ebook selections.

As a gift to you for purchasing this book, please use
COUPON CODE Ebook15 during your visit to receive
15% off any digital title in our Turquoise Morning Press
Bookstore.

www.turquoisemorningpressbookstore.com

Turquoise Morning Press
Dip your toes into a good book!
www.turquoisemorningpress.com

CPSIA information can be obtained at www.ICGtesting.com
Printed in the USA
BVOW08s1807160214

345087BV00005B/264/P